THE DANCING FINN

The Dancing Finn

Ruth Jutila Chamberlin

NORTH STAR PRESS OF ST. CLOUD, INC.
St. Cloud, Minnesota

Cover art: Melody Martin

This is a work of fiction. Names, characters, places, and incidents—other than those recorded by historians and biographers—are the product of the author's imagination or are used fictionally. Any resemblance to any events or persons, living or dead, is purely coincidental.

Portions of this book that describe Minnesota and Finland have appeared, in nonfiction form, in the following publications: *Los Angeles Times, Atlanta Journal-Constitution, Hibbing Daily Tribune, Suomen Silta (Finland Bridge)*, "Epic Adventure: Crisis and the *Kalevala*" (Ph.D. dissertation, University Microfilms International).

First Edition, July 2006

Printed in the United States of America by
Versa Press, Inc., East Peoria, Illinois

Published by
North Star Press of St. Cloud, Inc.
P.O. Box 451
St. Cloud, Minnesota 56302
northstarpress.com

Prologue

The Silence ended on a holiday, Labor Day 1960, when one of my aunts called one of my uncles a phony—in front of everyone. He hadn't spoken to her for twenty-seven years, so naturally he ducked and tried to skip the whole deal. The rest of us had filled our plates and were squeezing in at the table, and now we sat down fast and waited to see what he would do. He hovered over his chair, deciding whether to sit, stand, talk, or not. *High drama.* For Halonens, at least.

And that was just the beginning. Old stories jumped up that day like accusers in a rowdy court, pointing out this person or that one, and pretty soon someone would be in tears or confessing something or whooping--very un-Halonen-like. As the day wore on, we all got the jitters. We had hated the Silence but had counted on it, mostly to save us from just this sort of thing! Yet there we were, forced to listen to this *clamor.* The racket of the truth being said, even in a whisper, banged on the eardrums and made me, for one, woozy. The past was a hidden thing, and dangerous, like faulty wiring. Usually when it spiked (and gave our static group a buzz!), we ignored it. But now the facts were getting out, and we were scared.

Here's where bullheadedness paid off. We did whatever it took. We grumped, giggled, yelled, cried, got scared and went away, came back and kept going, and by the time the moonlight won over the mist on the lake we had stomped the Silence to death!

Not that the habits gave up so easily—the instinct to hold back, the mistrust. The *metaphors*. For me, it was the metaphors. I had used them as shields against the Silence, but when the Silence fell away, they didn't. Twenty years later, here they are again! All over the place! They still rush in and tangle my feet, like so many Pekingese on leash, and I end up with accusers giggling and the moonlight stomping.

It's just that I don't need them anymore.

Contents

Part 1

Mining Town

One

Spinning with the Globe

W hen Aarnie told Rita his plan, she got breathy and hesitant, not her usual self at all (we were guessing, since we never did meet her), but he got on the train anyway and went to claim us. He stayed in Florida just long enough to round up our stuff and get us on the northbound train. The funeral was left to the people there. No one from Minnesota attended. This bashful man, who had no children of his own and no experience with anyone else's, got back on the train with two babies, diapers, rubber pants, baby powder, baby clothes, blankets, bottles, nipples, formula, and toys, an act that took courage in itself, to say nothing of the courage he would need when he got home.

Waiting at home were two nearly wordless Finns, my grandparents on the Halonen side. (Aarnie was an Olson.) They were silent for reasons no one talked about, my tiny, ornery Mummo, who did whatever she wanted, despite having one short leg and a built-up shoe, and my bald and bearded Grandpa, who went along with whatever she wanted. They had shown up in Mahoning when Aarnie was in Florida, and Rita had had no choice but to ask them in. Without consulting anyone, they had leased the Dakota farm to the hired man and come to help raise us, the daughters of a son they didn't claim. They had disowned our father in the early thirties, but when tragedy hit in 1940 and *someone* had to raise us, Mummo did her duty as she saw it, and Grandpa came along. She had either missed or dismissed the fact that Aarnie had a wife.

What Aarnie didn't find waiting at home was a wife. When Rita saw my grand-folks standing on the porch, bags in hand, she acted on an impulse she had been nursing for thirty days (the length of her marriage)—a cliché of desertion: she ran away with the Watkins man. She left a note for Aarnie on the drain board under a can of sink cleanser, and by the time he found it she was many states gone. Reading it, he learned what she had been up to. She admitted to philandering—providing evidence, she wrote, so that he could get an easy divorce—and gave a Kansas City address where papers could be sent. She ended: "Sorry, Aarnie. You're a good man and all, but I can't live with two old people! And I can't take in two orphans I don't even know! Besides, I'm not cut out for mining life."

Everyone agreed on that last part. She never *did* take to Mahoning. She was moony and standoffish; she never had the neighbor ladies over or borrowed sugar. The only person she was friendly with was the Watkins door-to-door man. Aarnie walked through the house with new eyes and saw the extent of her betrayal. Everywhere he looked, front room, bathroom, bed-rooms, closets, basement, he found Watkins products, not just the cleanser that pinned down her goodbye. (Rita's story was a secret, but we knew it any-way, and over time we added details, whispering bed-to-bed, building on snip-pets we had overheard. Mostly I added details, but Liisa would put in her two-cents worth from time to time. She wasn't much for words, but she needed sto-ries as much as I did.)

That's how we came to live in Mahoning with Aarnie, Mummo, and Grandpa. Mahoning Location was a mining town in northern Minnesota, a small village owned by the Hull Rust Mahoning Company—no stores, just houses and a roundhouse at the edge of a giant open pit. The mine itself was famous. It was the greatest mine on the Mesabi Iron Ore Range, which was the greatest iron ore mining system in North America. The big shots called

Mahoning "The Largest Open Pit in the World" and "The Man-Made Grand Canyon of the North." I had seen pictures of the Grand Canyon and the pit *did* look like it, a huge red-striped hole with islands left standing after the ore was stripped, and fingers of open mine breaching solid land, roads circling and winding downward. The neighbor kids said you could see twenty miles across. They were great ones for exaggerating, but the pit was big—three miles long, two miles wide, five hundred feet deep, according to the big shots. Tourists snapped pictures of the mine and bought souvenir tubes of ore, bright brave layers of red, orange, brown, shades of tan. Our teachers said Mahoning was "essential to the war effort" because it mined the iron ore needed for building tanks and planes. When we had air raid drills and had to hide in the dark, I felt smug and proud. The Nazis wanted what I had in my own backyard!

The location had dumps along two sides of it, long mounds that looked like normal hills but were really heaps of scrap ore overgrown with trees. Hidden in the woods on the farthest dump, the neighbor kids said, was a place where turkeys ran free and fears ran high. The turkeys ran after little kids' feet, especially feet in red sandals like mine, and pecked them until blood came. If you walked to the end of Turkey Dump you came to a lake as deep as the ocean. Sea dragons lived there. I knew the stories weren't true, but I humored the neighbor kids and never went near that dump.

As Liisa and I grew up, Uncle Aarnie was our protector. He didn't say much but he stood by, on guard, when Grandpa got steely-eyed or Mummo had a conniption. He was tall and spindly and had thin blond hair that let his scalp show red when he blushed. He blushed a lot; he was the shyest person we knew. He kept the scissors and knives sharp and everything else short, the lawn, his hair, his talk. When we had company, he lagged behind in the kitchen, peeking through the doorjamb, working up nerve to say hello to Finns he'd known all his life. When he finally came out, he would turtle his jaw back into his neck so no part of him stuck out too far. He was a hero of the bashful sort.

But Aarnie was a diehard Chevy man, and not even his great amount of shyness kept him from saying so to his public, his public being my Uncle Harald, who was a Ford man, plus whoever else came to the kitchen when they were arguing. Mummo gave them coffee and *pulla* sweet bread and left them to their feud, which heated up each August when Harald took his vacation. Harald claimed his 1946 Ford was better than a Chevy *any* day, in particular, better than either of Aarnie's Chevys, that *vomit-green* '39 roadster or that *bile-blue* '46 sedan. Harald grinned around the room when he said these words. He said his Ford was the finest car on the road, most reliable, made the best mileage, and so on. He snickered and called Aarnie's roadster a *mobster car*. He said it looked like a ladybug. He called Aarnie's newer Chevy a *pansy blue blob*. He said all kinds of mean things about Aarnie's Chevys. Aarnie's words were fewer and milder but no less ardent. Anyone who insulted his Chevys insulted *him*.

One day when Harald was getting louder than usual and Aarnie was getting purple in the face, I said, "Who'd like to go to Monkey Wards. You know, the wheelbarrow?" It was the right thing to say. Within the bounds of life on Planet Earth, Harald's favorite place to visit was Montgomery Ward. He faked reluctance but was first to volunteer, leaving the car debate for another time.

"Ya, well," Harald said. He ran a hanky over his head. "It's too blamed hot, but we might as well go."

Aarnie made his Adams apple bob up and down. He was a gratified man now that one party had removed himself from the fray. The misguided, stubborn-headed, mulish party, his expression said.

"She's a hot one, all right!" Harald pulled in so much air that he snored. It was only ten in the morning but already twice too hot, and Harald suffered in the heat. For as long as I had known him, he had been prematurely old and a little sick. He lost a leg in World War Two, and he had arthritis pretty much all over. He was my father's brother, Marcie's dad—a blond, sloping haystack of a man who had given in early to the pulls of the universe, out with electricity, down with gravity. His losing fight started on top, where an airy fluff of hair wafted and lifted of its own accord. From there on down, gravity took over, draping his brows like tieback curtains, drooping his eyelids, dragging at his cheeks and making a series of chins. Below the neck, Harald spread east, west, and south to his widest point, his waist, which he kept cinched in a genuine rawhide Dakota cowboy belt. The fact was, Harald had too much skin.

He sagged in all the ways a person can sag. He was gruff and stubborn, but he adored us kids, and we adored him back. When he talked to us, his eyes misted over and his face got busy. His eyebrows jumped, his jowls waved, his smile tipped up to meet his eyes as they dipped down. I figured we gave his extra skin something to do. He said, "Yessirree! Let's go have a looksee."

But he stayed at the table and lit another cigarette. A cloud of diverted challenge hung in the room. The screen door made a sound like *scrink* as it opened, like *scrat* as it closed, and Marcie came in holding a carrot by the root. When she saw how things were in the kitchen, she took on a mincey, nasal voice and recited a familiar ditty, waving the carrot greens. "Ah hawd to *lawf* . . . to see the *cawf* . . . run down the *pawth* . . . to take a *bawth* . . . in a minute 'n a-*hawf*!" It was our favorite spiel; she and I thought it was a scream (we were nine).

This too was the right thing to say. Aarnie flushed, and Harald said, "Ya! And *sveating*, too!" We all smiled in degrees of brashness and shyness. "Ya, and sveating, too" was the punch line to a Dumb Finn joke, the immigrant poking fun at his own poor English. Neighbor guy says to the Finn, "You must be working hard. I see that you're perspiring." Finn says, "Ya! And sveating, too!" None of us needed the whole joke. A few words did the trick.

Harald stubbed out his cigarette and got to his feet, cautiously, in honor of his arthritis, oofing a little. With one hand he made swipes at his hair, which bounced back as soon as his hand passed by. "Okey-dokey then! Let's get this road on the show."

"Abso-tively posi-lutely," I said. Marcie picked up the cups, and I went to the entry and creaked open the screen door. There was a thickness to the air, a laziness that seeped indoors with the hum of insects. We were in the worst of the dog days. I called, "Mummo? We're going to Hibbing. You need anything?" I bent the door outward but couldn't see her. Anyway, it was useless to ask. She'd say no. She kept the pantry stocked and her list up to date, and she didn't hold to shopping between Saturdays when Aarnie took her to the Co-op. Now she stepped out of the garage wearing barn boots and a paisley dress, an old felt hat of Grandpa's pulled low over her eyes. With an irascible flip of the hand, she said, "Go on then. Tell that Harald to slow down.

He's got *plenty*-time." Harald was known as a "sketchy" driver, too bent on talking to pay attention to driving. I had noticed that Mummo never got into his car if she could help it.

We took off in Harald's Ford, which had pedals adjusted for his wooden leg, the three of us lined up on the maroon plush seat. Harald put his window down and his elbow out; his other hand was free to act out stories. Before he could start in on his stories, which we'd heard too many times, Marcie sang, "My hat! it has! three cor!ners!" I joined in. "Three *cor*!ners *has*! my *hat*! And *had*! it *not*! three *cor*!ners, it *would*! not *be*! my *hat*!" We put in the hand and arm motions, further cramping the space in the car.

Next we sang, "John Jacob Jingleheimer Schmidt! That's my name, too! Whenever I go out, the people always shout, 'There goes John Jacob Jingleheimer Schmidt!'" We yelled more than sang, "Little Tom Tinker sat on a clinker and he began to cry, '*Maaa-aw! Maaa-aw!* What a poor boy am I!'" We stood up the best we could on the first syllable of each *Maaa-aw*. We did "Sweetly Sings the Donkey" as a two-way round, out-braying each other. We sang the Buster Brown Shoe song. In our night-basement, squeaky-door voices, we quoted, "What evil lurks in the hearts of men. . . ."

When we stopped to notice where we were, we were already on Third Avenue East, on the outskirts of Hibbing. Harald took advantage of the pause. "Say! Ever hear about the guy getting ready for bed?"

Marcie crossed her eyes at me. Of course we'd heard about that guy. But Harald told us anyway. He leaned on his Finnish accent and got all worked up and bugged out his eyes. "Dis kuy? Ees kettin ready for pet, see? Ee dakes off hees klasses and boods 'em in hees chagget bogget. Den ee hanks hees chagget on da toor-knop. Den ee dakes off hees hearing ait and boods it on da dayple. Den ee dakes out hees false teet and boods 'em in a klass. Den ee dakes out hees false eye and boods it in a teesh. Den ee dakes off hees wooten leck and boods it on da floor. Da kuy looks around and says, 'Heck! Ain't hartly nuttin left! Hartly bays to ko to pet!'"

We knew the joke by heart, but we gave him a chuckle anyway. I thought he was brave to joke about a fake leg when he had one, himself. Now that we were in Hibbing, he was cruising at the slowest drivable speed so that

8

we could people-watch. We all saw the man at the same time. He was nice-looking in his city clothes, walking toward us on the sidewalk, cradling a full grocery bag in each arm. But he had a problem: his trousers were slipping down. Since he couldn't fix them with his hands, which were occupied, he tried other means. In rapid succession he bent his knees out, took giant steps to the side, hitched at his belt with his elbows, and twitched his rear end. Nothing worked. Finally he stopped, and with a seriousness that spoke well of him, he hiked the bags higher and lowered himself to a half-squat, then took off in a modified duck-walk. We held in our laughter until he was out of earshot, and then we howled. Harald tee-heed, "*That* won't last long! Hope he doesn't live too far. Hope he has on nice underpants!"

Next came two women with identical hairdos. Long peroxided hair came straight up off their foreheads and made tall camel humps, leaving the women below either surprised or excited (it was hard to tell which), like Katzenjammer Kids in middle age. They held their heads very steady as they walked so as not to vibrate their hair. Marcie whispered, "Do you think they have the same . . ."

Harald and I whispered, " . . . hairdresser?"

"Or got caught in the same . . ."

" . . . wind tunnel?" We laughed and laughed.

The rest of the trip was routine. At Montgomery Ward we decided that the wheelbarrows cost too much, so we walked around the tractors and weighed hammers in the hand. At Woolworth's, we ate crisp-fried hamburgers and sweet grilled onions, and we twirled on the fountain stools until we saw specks. At the last, guilty minute, we bought candy orange slices for the people at home. Altogether a normal trip to town.

What marked it for all time was the new lore. After that trip, whenever a story was needed, Harald could say, giving away the punch line, "Hear about the ladies in the wind tunnel?" or "There was this guy walking like a duck . . ." These were punch lines that Marcie and I knew the lead-ups to. We had been *there*.

We had two layers to life in my family. One was visible to the bigger world, say, on a trip to Hibbing to see wheelbarrows, a kind of sturdiness we could lean on. The other was seldom seen outside our house, a mild terror conducted in private by Mummo. She ignored Liisa and me. She never touched us. She hardly ever spoke. To myself, I referred to her treatment of us as "the Silence," with a capital S. Of course we had the typical Finnish silences, over modesty, money, the birds and bees and so on, but at our house we had a *lot more*, and together they made up the one big Silence.

But the trouble was disguised. I knew I hated the Silence, but not how much. Or who else did. Or what it was doing to any of us.

We had to stay on our toes! The smaller silences were sneaky and could show up *anywhere*. When I was four, I found two in ten minutes, a record that would hold up for years. It's my earliest memory of any kind.

Mummo and Grandpa went visiting on Sunday afternoons, unannounced as was the custom, and they took us along. The Finns we visited were too old to have kids or toys of any kind, so Liisa and I were on our own. One Sunday, we were in the Makis's barn, petting the plow horse, when the daylight changed at the sliding door. A giant! Out of *nowhere*. We froze. His face didn't show against the sun, but his hair poked up like needles. One hand twitched in our direction. He moved from side to side in the doorway, choosing which of us to eat first. I was still deciding what to do (hide? or *poof!* disappear like magic?) and Liisa was saying we should *stay put*, when all of sudden he came at us, lopsided, making a rough noise in his throat and dragging a leg behind him! A *dead* leg.

We hopped to our feet in unison. We hightailed it out the side door, through the milk-house, past the pig pen, around the garden, across the yard, into the lean-to, and ended up, fidgeting and overheated, by the kitchen table where the grownups sat with coffee as calm as could be. A kerosene lamp that was cranked up too high was giving off a tight white brightness that blanked out their faces; the grownups were barely there.

"Who *is* 'at guy?" I said, hopping from foot to foot. "In the barn! He scared us!"

Liisa, who was six and had known about the Silence quite a while already, hissed into my hair, "Hush! . . . up!"

Gus Maki folded his arms and said, "Oh ya?" Even on a Sunday, Gus wore overalls and, even in the house, a billed cap. A medium-sized belly pooched out over his belt. No one else said a word. Liisa told me later that she passed the time by memorizing Gus's cap: "Argentina Mercantile." I liked the sound of the words. *Argentina Mercantile.*

"Who is he?" I asked again. Liisa tugged at the puff sleeve of my dress. I pushed her away. "How come he's *like* that?. . . *Huh?*"

Liisa whispered, "Be quiet!" and pinched my arm. The grownups kept their eyes on the oilcloth: teapots tipping in rag-tag rows, spots flaking through to the gray fluff. I was determined to wait them out. I put my fists on my hips and glued my oxfords to the floor. Stubby body, stubborn kid.

"*Well?*" I focused in turn on Mummo, Grandpa, Gus Maki, Helmi Maki. Each of them looked fleetingly at me with pity or patience (or *impatience*—who could tell?) and went back to staring at the oilcloth. Liisa made me an I-told-you-so face. No one said, "Don't worry. That's Seppo. He's okay," or "He's kind of slow but he won't hurt you." No one said anything. The grownups who were barely there gave us buttered *pulla* and motioned us outside.

A few minutes later Liisa was chasing me back inside, flapping her arms as I shouted at the grownups, "Why's 'at cow jumping on nat other cow, *huh?*" Again I waited in vain. Liisa stood stiff as a plank, blazing at me, her cheeks tensed in a way that said, *You know better than to ask.*

I *did* . . . already, at age *four!* It made me furious, even at that age, that no one would tell a kid *anything* about *anything.*

Then, when I was eight, our next-door neighbor lady left home for no good reason that I could see, and no one would talk about that, either. Eeva Rantala was a fretful person who seemed out of place in Mahoning, forever pining for Finland and for relatives there, pinning clothes to her clothesline in public mourning. One day, May-Louise and Billy came home from school, and their mother wasn't there. (Like my parents. Simply *not there.*)

Mummo wouldn't discuss Eeva. Neither would Liisa. May-Louise and Billy wouldn't, either, but I didn't think they knew anything, anyway. I tried to guess. Maybe Eeva died? Or May-Louise and Billy did something wrong, and their mother got mad and left home? Or she and Oskar had a fight? No one would say. Oskar hired a Finnish grandma to cook, clean, wash and iron, and life went on. When Eeva came home three months later, she was gaunt and gray, thinner than ever. Haunted-looking, I thought. No one referred to what had happened. No one explained why she had disappeared one day, and stayed away for three months, and come back looking like a ghost. Years later I learned that she had had a nervous breakdown. Why hadn't someone said so at the time?

The church had silences too, the main one being the language. Grownups spoke Finnish. Kids didn't. I knew the grownups meant well. By letting us be native English-speakers, they protected us from what *they* had suffered, the humiliation of practicing a new tongue, the foreign accent, the existence on the fringes of America. But I experienced another humiliation. By not knowing Finnish, I existed on the fringes of the *Finns*. I sang hymns in phonetic Finnish and heard sermons preached in Finnish, but I didn't know what I was singing or hearing. In the hymnbook, I found the name of Jesus, spelled the same in Finnish except that the J sounded like Y when you said it out loud. And I knew that *Jumala* meant God. That's all the Finnish I knew, except for Mummo's words, "*istua*" which meant "sit" and "*hiljaa*" which meant "be silent." So in church I sat and kept silent and understood not much.

The church was the Believers' Lutheran. We had lay ministers and held services in farmhouses. No card-playing, no drinking, no dancing, no instrumental music in church. Two other branches were even stricter. One, which included Finns we knew, allowed no hats or jewelry or short hair on women, no neckties on men, no movies for anyone. I had heard of a third branch that was stricter yet: no curtains and flowers in members' houses! I was glad we didn't belong to *those* branches. During most of the year we didn't meet for church on Sundays, but we made up for it at fall and spring services when we had a solid week of church. Finns drove to Minnesota from Michigan, the Dakotas, even California, stayed at members' homes, and gathered twice a day for services. Between services the grownups jammed the kitchen, eating, talking and laughing, the men smoking and dunking cardamom rolls in their coffee, the women getting up now and then to wash dishes. Babies got passed from lap to lap, toddlers made their way around the grownups' legs, and kids older than about three took cookies outside to find other kids their age. Teen-agers sat joking on the hoods of cars and sometimes played Sardines with us younger kids. More and more every year, I hoped to get squashed in a pitch-black silo, hiding nervously, flirtatiously, with certain of the older boys.

My favorite part of church was Uncle Harald, who happened to be the minister. (*Most* of the time he was. He took turns with two others from Michigan. For some strange reason, all of the ministers came from Michigan.) Services took place in the front room. Harald sat at a small table that had been set up with a white cloth, a pitcher of water and a glass, and Harald's own huge leather Finnish Bible. The congregation sat on benches laid with rag rugs made by the farmwife herself. When the time was right, an old man led off a hymn in a minor key, holding each note for the same extended time, each note sliding into the next as if reluctant to proceed. Then we all joined in.

After three hymns, Harald started preaching, hesitantly at first but gaining speed, like a locomotive in the mine, building up steam until he was going full-out, huffing and shouting and waving his hanky with a straight arm—*Runaway train! Get off the track!*—and doing his trick of saying a whole paragraph in a single breath, wheezing out the final words the way a bagpiper squeezes out the last few squeaks, winding up wispy and out of air but triumphant.

Thirty minutes into the sermon, Harald banged the table, *wham!* For a while he gave it a thump with every important word. Marcie and I watched the water pitcher with eagle eyes, thinking it might flip any minute and soak the Bible and Harald's pants. Harald's voice expanded in volume and conviction until he sobbed, then he hauled a hanky over his face and smiled a sad sweet smile, tipped his chin to his chest and peered up through the wool of his brows. He was a master with his audience. He stopped preaching at this point and simply chuckled, pinning us with his gaze and signaling people by twitching his brows. Old ladies slipped hankies from their three-quarter sleeves and daubed their eyes, got up and went across the aisle to embrace each other and weep and whisper. This was a mystery! *No one* hugged at our house, ever, but here even *Mummo* hugged the old ladies! Were they telling secrets, or comforting each other? I didn't know. Marcie didn't either, except she thought it had something to do with sin. It was very confusing.

But no matter how confused we got, we were not to ask questions. I tried once, the summer I was nine, after Sally Beth Jensen took me to Vacation Bible School in Hibbing. At her church, everyone was encouraged to pray and read the Bible, kids included, and I wondered why we weren't, at our church. I was a willful, selfish kid but secretly devout. Since about age five, I'd waited until Liisa fell asleep and then climbed out of bed, knelt, and prayed. I don't know where I got the idea, maybe a picture book. For sure, not from Mummo. She never spoke of such personal things as faith and prayer.

I decided to ask questions anyway. She was sitting at the kitchen table snapping green beans, and in the time it took me to pull up a chair she'd tweaked the tips off three six-inch beans and snapped each bean into one-inch chunks. I wished she would leave them whole. They were prettier that way. But Mummo's way was to *break* them! *Tame* them! Show them who was boss, and no-bones-*about*-it!

"Mummo, I was wondering," I began, then I saw that I'd folded my hands on the table as if acting out my question. I put them in my lap. "In the Finn church, how come we don't talk about praying?"

Her glasses magnified her eyes and her *rightness* and her *scorn*. She scorched me with one swift look. Having given me fair warning, she went back to twisting the heads off beans. *Chk! . . . Chk!* She was tiny but powerful.

"But if we believe in Jesus," I persisted, "shouldn't we at least talk to Him? And read the Bible?"

Mummo, who knew English perfectly well but seldom spoke it, said, "*Shhh!* Only *believe!*" Then she went back to work. I waited for her to say more.

She didn't. So much for questions. I wanted to scream, "Believe *what?* You always *do* this! *Talk to me!*"

Instead, I disengaged myself from the table and went outside. I would ride my bike. I would keep my head. Short of throwing pans or banging on the wall or banging on Mummo (none of which would get her to talk anyway), there was nothing else to do.

* * *

W<small>E HAD SILENCES OVER THE SIMPLEST THINGS</small>! Like names. Mummo never used our first names, not even to register us at school. I knew better than to ask why. (Grandpa didn't count. He never said anything, at least not to us. The few times I'd heard him speak, it was to Mummo, and in Finnish.) I had a theory about names, and I was telling it to Julianna, my newest friend in the location.

She and her family had moved to the boarding house three months earlier, her mother to cook and manage the place and her father to work in the mine. I envied her for her name: *Mary Julianna Marcella Rossini.* It sounded like music. She was the only Italian I knew. Mahoning kids were usually Swedes or Germans or Finns. Julianna had big brown eyes and bouncy brown hair, and a face shaped like a valentine. She had plenty of boys interested already, and she was only ten. We were riding our bikes down Engineers' Row, where the big shots lived with their wives and kids in big white houses across from the park. The miners lived with *their* wives and kids—or, in Aarnie's case, his sister's parents-in-law and his nieces—on the more crowded side of town, in smaller white houses exactly alike except for reversed floor plans in alternate houses. The big shots' houses were fine if you liked showing off. But I thought I had the best house in the location. It sat smack against the mine. Only a barbed wire fence separated our alley from the open pit and from a weed-clogged road that had once led down to it. My wheels were squawking, so I coasted a while to quiet them. "We never use our whole names," I said. "We go by our middle names. Here's what I think. Our first names are religious words, okay? And since we never talk about religion, I think our religious names weren't meant to be said out loud."

Julianna gave a truncated whinny. I gave her a surly look. What was funny about what I'd said? She said, "You gotta be kidding!"

"No, really." I felt bad because she had laughed, but I went ahead anyway, telling her my theory. "Anyway, kid, listen. Our middle names are Finnish. Liisa's whole name is Charity Liisa—Liisa spelled with two i's. Mine is—are you ready? *Mercy Katariina!*" I rolled the r-r-r in Katariina the best I could.

"Mercy? . . . Mercy? I like Kik better. Hold on, my barrette's slipping." Slowing down, Julianna veered, wobbled, and stopped at the curb. I pulled up beside her. While she undid her barrette, we stood with our legs bridging the low bellies of our girl-bikes. She caught a handful of hair, snapped it into the barrette, gave it a pat. "How come they call you Kik? Why not, um, Ka-ta . . . ? I can't say it."

"It's okay, neither can anyone else! Except Finns." I kicked at my axles and chain guard. Julianna rolled up her dungarees another fold, put her weight on her left pedal and pushed off with her right—once, twice, three times—and started off, wobbling again. I caught up with her. My kicks had worked: no more squawks.

Every day lately we had made this trip, the long way around to the roundhouse. The roundhouse was the heart of the location—repair shop, mine office, locomotive barn, anything having to do with the mine. Inside the roundhouse, a locomotive looked like a steel dragon with popped-out eyes and a pug nose, and cowcatcher chin whiskers that raked the tracks. It rumbled in the dark, eager to get going, and, when its turn came, it chuffed outdoors dragging a tail of empty rail cars, descended the pit in patient, slow circles, stopped at the appointed spot, and waited as a steam shovel loaded the rail cars with iron ore. Then it gave a rusty jerk that rattled its tailbones (*clank-clank-clank*) and started back up to the surface, complaining at every turn (*Chuh!. . .Chuh!*) and coughing soot (if it was a Monday, dusting the undies and bed sheets with crumbly black dots). We didn't know where the cars got unloaded, but the locomotives returned to the roundhouse to shuttle back and forth on webs of track—for *our* benefit, we figured, so we could hang on the fence and watch. That's where we were headed, the roundhouse.

"Our family doesn't believe in nicknames," I said, "but I think after my parents named me Katariina they found out how hard it was to say. For non-Finns. You know, the rolled r?"

"I *know*," Julianna said with feeling. "How do you say it again?"

"Kah-tah-*rrrree*-nah. So, anyway! Liisa was twenty months old when I was born, and she called me Kik in baby talk and it stuck. My parents must've thought a nickname was better than people getting their *tongues tangled*, trying to say Katariina! Or having a religious word like Mercy said in public so just anyone could hear it!" This time I did see the humor, or at least the weirdness, of this name thing, and I smiled ahead of Julianna.

16

"Everyone calls me Kik," I added, "except Mummo. She doesn't call me much of anything."

"Moo-moo? Is that your grandma?"

"*Moom*-moh. First syllable rhymes with 'room,' the second syllable, with 'oh.' Wanta stop?" We were near the bandstand at the picnic end of the park.

In her best Swedish brogue, Julianna singsonged, "Ya, sure, ya *betcha!* Ay bain t'ink Ay *do!*" We dismounted, kicked down the squared-U stands and lifted our bikes upward and backward onto the stands. Julianna sat on the steps of the bandstand. I sat on the grass. She said, "Whatever happened to your parents? If you don't mind me asking."

"They died when I was a baby. In a car crash. In Florida, where I was born."

Julianna lit up. "Florida? I always wanted to go there!"

I glared at her, hard as rocks. "Didn't you hear me? I said my parents *died.* I was just a *baby.* I never *knew* them." This wasn't like me, talking so boldly. It made me a little nauseated.

"Sor-*ry!*" Julianna said testily. "I didn't know what to say. I never knew anyone before who had her parents die."

"I didn't *have* them die, you know. They just died. They weren't thrilled about the idea, and neither was I." Usually I thought up smarty words an hour too late and never said them. Yet here I was, tossing them off, left and right. I had a headache and a stomachache, both.

"Hey, look!" she said. "You don't have to get all mad. I didn't mean anything."

I barked at her, "You don't know what it's like! Living with my grandmother? She never smiles! She never talks! I want to yell right in her face, just to get a rise out of her, '*Mercy! Charity!*' But nothing works."

Ticking my head to stem the dizziness, I let myself down onto my back. I took handfuls of lawn and squeezed my eyes shut: stripes of black snuck in from the side, red filled the middle, orange specks winked off and on, like fireflies. The earth picked me up and took me with it, a lulling, deliberate spin, a companionship of sorts.

"Kik? You okay?" Julianna's face was only inches away, crunched up and fearful.

"I'm fine. Why?" Lying there on my back, I took notice of the park. Daytime. Trees. The trees were a comfort. Leaves waving, urgently, one at a time. Like a bell choir, only silent. I thought I'd be their director: "Number Twenty-three, *go!* . . . Now, Forty!"

Julianna got up and swept grass snips from her knees. "Well, because you passed out, that's why. I almost called First Aid!"

"Where's my bike?"

"Over there. But your bike's not the problem. What *happened?*"

"Nothing." I smiled a little. I felt set apart. I'd gone away to a place where no one could find me. I hadn't planned to, but the result was nice. "How long was I out?"

"Couple minutes. Or a couple *seconds*, I don't know! Are you okay?"

"I got dizzy, is all." An idea flitted past and was gone, the seed of a revulsion. "What were we talking about?"

"*Names.*" Julianna said the word swiftly and righteously, as if defending herself. She seemed worried that I might blame her for my fainting, or whatever it was I'd done. "That's all. You were telling me about your name and your sister's name."

"Oh. Names."

After getting sick like this over puny things like names, I figured I wasn't normal. My family wasn't, either. Normal people could talk about names, couldn't they?

I had to guess what normal was. To me, being a Finn was normal. Being a Finn meant sturdiness as to character, modesty as to manner, loyalty to the Finnish church, and silence all around.

Two

Learning to Celebrate

Mrs. Granger reminded me of a robin, plump in the chest and cheerful. The first time I saw her, she was actually wearing robin clothes, a brown-speckled dress and a red vest. She was standing on a chair, pinning posters to the wall and chirping hello as her students filed in. When she was done, she hopped down and came past my desk, snagged my attention and chirruped to me, "Good morning! It's a lovely day, is it not?"

I gnawed at my lip, not knowing what to say. ("Yes, it is not" . . . ?) I finally shrugged and gave her a half-smile. Overjoyed with that response, she went to the blackboard and wrote four lines in teacher-cursive: "September 6, 1949. Mrs. Granger, Fourth Grade. Sandburg Elementary School. Hibbing, Minnesota." Mahoning kids attended kindergarten through third grade at the Mahoning School and from then on took the bus into Hibbing. The only other Mahoning kids my age, two boys, had been assigned to the other fourth grade. I didn't know a soul in Mrs. Granger's room.

For the first ninety minutes, we took reading and English tests. They seemed easy enough. Throughout the testing, a redhead named Jilly King, in the seat behind me, blew and panted, tapped her pencil and scraped her sandals on the floor. The desks were joined front to back, and when Jilly jimmied around, she put our whole row in a tremor.

Lining up for recess, Jilly got behind me and poked her face near mine. She had polka-dot freckles that I secretly envied. "Wasn't that awful?" she whispered.

I shrugged, not wanting to brag. It turned out Jilly liked recess a lot better than class work. As we waited our turns to jump double-Dutch, I asked her if she liked the *Little House* books. Jilly reared back as if asking *why*, when we were outside the classroom, would I be talking about *books*, of all things. Shaking her head no, she pointed to a row of roofs beyond the fence. "See those houses? I live there. By the school!" The proximity of her house to the school gave her a literal place of importance. "I have a cat who uses the toilet! We're gone all day, and he puts it in there. Really."

I didn't believe her about the cat, but I didn't say so. The girls who had been turning the rope quit, and they asked us to play Witch Hollow. I had never played that game, and I didn't know the rules, so I said no thanks. Jilly and I played One Two Three O'Leary with her golf ball until the bell rang.

When we got back to class, Mrs. Granger passed around reading books, new ones, straight from the bindery. I ruffled the pages of mine. They smelled stuffy and promising. This part of school I *liked* . . . . *Books!* The morning went by in a haze of words. Between assignments, I drew cartoons in my notebook.

The cafeteria was noisy and smelled of metallic tomato soup. I ate my roast beef on Finnish rye next to Jilly, who had potted meat on store-bought white. I had never tasted store-bought. I coveted Jilly's white bread and her baby sweet pickles.

After lunch we had a math test. I added, subtracted, multiplied, divided, then sat back in my chair, confident I'd get one hundred-percent correct. We checked each other's papers. When I got mine back, my head went dizzy. I'd missed four! I felt betrayed—by *myself,* in that each mistake was a simple one. I told myself to double-check next time.

The art teacher bustled in, a busy little woman named Mrs. Hughes, the type of teacher who believed in wearing hats to school. On this first day of school, to match a gray belted suit and chunky tie pumps, she wore a gray felt derby with a long turkey feather in the band. She had a fitful face but bore it bravely, as if life had let her down but she made the best of it. Before she could start her lesson, Jilly shot up her hand.

"Teacher! Kik here draws real nice pictures. You should see 'em!"

I crouched down in my seat. I didn't want attention drawn to my doodlings, and I figured Mrs. Hughes didn't, either. I was right. Being the boss was another thing she believed in. She sniffed. "*Well!* We don't need to bother with that. Today we shall draw *elves!*" Flourishing a brand new box of colored chalk (a limousine-length box that was hers alone), she chose an orange stick and raised it as if conducting a band. "You will watch me," she trilled, "and when I say, '*Go,*' you do what *I* do!" Whereupon she turned to the blackboard and whipped out a farm scene with hills and trees, making use of her orange, green, black, white, and brown chalk sticks. Then she put in the elves. They wore green suits and acorn-top caps and had unnaturally wide mouths that smiled at us—or *sneered* at us—from everywhere in the picture. They balanced on fence posts and peeked from the barn and hid in the branches of trees. The drawing eventually covered the whole board and the whole art period. We watched in dim fascination, learning art from Mrs. Hughes.

Near the end of the day, a nurse took us to the infirmary. She was slim and serious and was dressed in white—a slick white dress, a white paper-airplane hat, and white squishy shoes. We filed down the hall in lines, one for girls, one for boys. I registered the nature of the school: strict (the posted rules); clean (the polished floors); busy (the chalk dust in the air already, after only one day). The infirmary was lofty-ceilinged and smelled of rubbing alcohol. A row of high windows let in shafts of sun. The kids in our class stood and watched each other get weighed, a few boys nudging each other, scuffling, and turning laughs into coughs when the teacher looked their way. I stepped onto the scale. The nurse boosted the metal cylinder higher and higher, over too many notches. I stepped off, ashamed. I had never before felt overweight.

The nurse wasn't done with me yet. "I'm afraid you must stay home for a few days. It's ringworm." She indicated the mostly dried circles on my arms. I'd had a nasty case of ringworm in August—seventy-five circles, to be exact. But Mummo had treated it, and I had hoped it was gone forever. "Do you have cats at home?" the nurse asked me.

"One."

"One will do it. You can come back to school when the rings fade."
She gave me a note to take home plus a tin of vile-smelling brown salve.

Rejected. On the first day of fourth grade!

I ran off the school bus and into the house. It smelled of bread baking. Mummo stood a flat bread on its edge and cut off a crust, spread it with oleo and handed it to me. I took it with me to the garage where Grandpa sat at the workbench, fixing something small and metal, laid bare, in pieces. He said nothing. I said nothing. I climbed onto the push-pull swing and soared above his head for a long, long time.

* * *

September 6, 1949
Dear Marcie,

This was the first day of school and I had the lousiest day! I won't even go into it. I just wanted to say: <u>PHOOEY!!</u> I'll tell you about it when I see you. Mrs. Granger said our homework is to write a poem. I can't go back to school for a few days (ringworm!!) but I'll keep up with assignments. Most of the kids hate "pomes," but I'm OK. After supper I'll sit Indian-style on my bed and look at the wallpaper until the words come to me. Mrs. Granger wants four lines, lines A and C rhyming, lines B and D rhyming. Got any ideas? Until then, I'll blab on to you.

Here's what I wanted to say. I don't think you're the only one who's <u>adopted</u> in our family—well, I mean, you and Randall. I think I am, too!! I <u>must</u> be!! No one understands me except <u>you</u>, and you're not even a Finn! What I <u>don't</u> like is cooking and canning and crocheting, which is what Mummo and Liisa and your Mom <u>like</u> to do, and they're Finns. And Finns don't like to talk, either, or at least Mummo and Grandpa don't, and you and I <u>do</u>! So we must be sisters. What do you think? I got into the wrong family, ha ha! When we grow up, let's talk our husbands into living in the same town, okay? What town?

Love, Kik.

* * *

Looking back, I wonder where Liisa was and why I didn't talk to *her* about my bad day. Then I remember. We didn't talk much about *anything*. Besides, she probably had some committee work to do already, or a Girl Scout project. She was a joiner. I wasn't. She didn't mind following rules someone else made up and she didn't mind crowds. I liked making up my own rules and having one best friend at a time, not a bunch of medium friends. But I paid the price. If my current best friend was sick, I was left high and dry. I made it through the winter, but that spring I got smart and started a club.

Spring came early that year, as did my life changes—a new body happening, a flouncy strangeness as I ran. I ran a lot, aiming at the last of the ice puddles to make them squeak. I wore short sleeves even if I got goose bumps. The sun warmed deltas of alley mud and made them smooth, like plates of fudge, perfect for cat's-eyes, aggies, glassies. Since the neighbor boys were always around, and since they liked to play marbles, I played marbles. And mumblety-peg. The neighbor boys loved pocket knives, and they loved to brag. Sometimes I beat them at their own game. When my knife landed straight up in the mud—*thwang!*—exactly where I'd aimed it, *man oh man!* I yipped and jumped around and lorded it over those boys. Spring wasn't as good as summer, when I got to see Marcie and go to the lake, and check out books from the library bus, and read in the cold grass in our front yard, in the "ample maple-dappled shade" (I got poetic in the summer), but spring was a good time to start a club.

Mahoning was so small I couldn't always find friends my age, so the club members went from seven years old to eleven and came from all over the location. I thought of us like this: Julianna, the prettiest; Sally Beth, the pudgiest and cutest; Bitsy Stiger, the littlest; Carol Burgeson, the most developed (already wore a bra); myself, the deepest-thinking. The clubhouse was Aarnie's fishing shack. It had no windows and hardly any floor, just a hole and floor space for two folding chairs, so we perched anywhere we could, including on the grass that came up through the hole. In the mild seasons the shack sat in the alley, on vacation. In the winter, Aarnie hauled it out onto the lake behind the newer Chevy, chopped a hole in the ice, set the shack over it, and sat in the dark watching the light-blue square until a pike slid into view—the long silver body suddenly *there*; then he harpooned it, quick-as-a-wink, with a roped spear. Sometimes I went along. Liisa never did, not any more. She was a teen-ager that year, or almost, so she stayed home to comb her hair or whatever it was teen-agers did. If I went with Aarnie, I could either sit in the shack and not make noise or chase rabbits on the islands frozen in the lake. Usually I chose the rabbits. I pretended they would be my pets when I caught them.

Compared with ice-fishing and chasing rabbits, our club wasn't very exciting. After making a No Boys Allowed sign and eating bologna sand-wiches and voting on a name, Mahoning Adventure Club for Girls, we sat in the clubhouse, bored.

Lucky thing we had the mine. We didn't need to sit in the club house and be bored. We could go and watch the mine. It was like an ant farm, only *giant*, and with *sound*. Whistles tooted. Horns blasted. Dynamite blew up rocks. Giant machines milled around, changing the shape of reality. They looked miniature to us, they were so far down. Steam shovels swiveled and stuck out toothy bottom jaws, bowed to earth and scooped up a load of dirt (the overburden, near the surface, the iron ore, lower down; we knew this because we were mine kids), swung over to the rail cars and opened their jaws, swung back and did it again. Or we could play at the edge of the pit. Beyond the safety fence, a grassy slope invited us to roll down, which we did, somer-saulting or rolling like rolling pins or hurling ourselves curled up in car tires, rolling down the same hill we had slid down on cardboard when it had six feet of snow.

But, being kids, we still got bored. One Saturday when we were supremely bored, Sally Beth said, "I know! Let's do tubes." She meant Aarnie's inner tubes. Aarnie drove a Euclid dump truck down in the mine, a forty-ton rig with giant tires. When he stood beside his truck, the tires rose half again taller than he was, and Aarnie wasn't a short person. He brought home old Euclid inner tubes for us to play on. They were way too big to take swim-ming at Wolf Lake or Swan Lake or any other lake, too high to hold onto in the water, but they were great on solid ground. We found one in the garage (inflated, I was glad to see; filling it with the bike pump would have taken *hours*). We wrangled with it, stretching our arms around as much of it as we could reach, scooching it in little steps around the older Chevy and the work bench, and then plopping it on the grass. It made a *pling* when it landed. Lying flat like a doughnut, it was taller than most of us.

We had to struggle to get up onto it, but, once there, we bounced and giggled and shoved each other off. Every time, before playing King of the Mountain, we had a free-for-all—everyone trying to knock everyone else off, no holds barred. After a storm of shrieks and arms, Carol was the only one left standing on the tube.

She sassed, "Nyaa, nya-aa, *nyaa*-nyaa!"

"No fair using hands," Sally Beth said. Carol had knocked her off using her hands. (We made up new rules each time.)

Balancing on the tube, Carol brandished her backside. "I vote yes for bottoms."

"Bottoms are okay," I said.

Sally Beth trumpeted: "*Bot*-toms? That's where I win. Mine's bigger than all yours put together!" We scrambled back onto the tube, and Bitsy, the smallest and youngest, managed to get there first.

"It's not *that* big," I said. "But how about if you stand over there, not by me?"

"Very funny," Sally Beth said. "What about elbows?"

Julianna ruled, "No elbows. Shoulders are okay . . . Ready, set, go!"

We were bouncing in earnest when Harald and Inky and their kids drove up. This was a surprise! Usually we got to see them just in August for two weeks and then at fall and spring services. But here they were! In the *spring!*

Harald emerged from his Ford and called to me, "What-kind mischief you been up to, anaway? We thought we better come see." I ran over to say hi to Marcie. Harald went to the trunk of his car and lifted out a small motor scooter. He sat on the scooter's seat and revved the engine. "Gotta try this thing out."

Only after he'd taken it around the block three or four times, chuckling and bouncing his belly over the alley bumps, and circling behind the house again when we thought he was finally done with his turn, did he decide it was safe for us to ride.

More neighbor kids joined in, and so did Liisa and Randall, and all that afternoon we took turns, one kid riding the scooter, the rest chasing on foot. Harald stepped out of the house once in a while to hoot at us.

Five days later, when Marcie and her family left, the scooter stayed behind at our place. But riding it alone wasn't half as much fun, so the scooter took retirement in our garage.

How come Marcie had to live in *Michigan*, of all places?

* * *

We never knocked at each other's doors; we cupped our hands and called from the sidewalk, out by the street, the more syllables the better, as in "Ju-li-*a-a-a-a-an*-na!" It was a June Saturday and Julianna was calling, "*Kiiiiii-iii-iiiiik!*" She did a good job, I thought, dragging out that one stumpy syllable. From the front room window, I could see her and her brothers standing by their bikes. When they saw my signal, John Michael and Robbie pedaled off down the block, little imitators of their father in miner's clothes—denim jeans and flannel shirts, suspenders, work boots. Julianna had on her blue dress, a white pinafore and white choker beads. She looked a lot fancier than I did in my dungarees, but I wasn't about to change. Her new Toni made her hair stick out a little. Earlier that week, there had been a small crisis over the giving of this Toni. Robbie, who was only five and could be forgiven, had nearly ruined everything. He had found the bowl of neutralizer, the lotion that stopped the curling action and kept the hair from frizzing, and he washed his wagon with it. Mrs. Rossini didn't know it was gone until it was time to neutralize Julianna's hair. Since we didn't have stores in Mahoning, Mrs. Rossini had to call four neighbor ladies before she found an unused permanent kit. She used the neutralizer on Julianna's hair, and Robbie was giving up his candy money until he paid for the neighbor lady's Toni. Julianna's hair had turned out fine, I thought, just maybe a little enthusiastic.

"Can I go?" I asked Mummo. "And can I take an old pan and a spoon?" She sparingly gave permission. By the time I got outside, John Michael and Robbie had gathered a group of kids near their own ages, Sally

Beth from across the street, Mac and Toby Johnson, the twins from two houses down, and Mary Lou Hagenberger, the twins' cousin. Julianna and I were way too old for chivarees, but not old enough to stay home altogether. We used her brothers as an excuse. We said we had to take *them* to the chivaree, to let *them* have some fun. Sally Beth had a handlebar basket, so we put our spoons and pots in there, then rode to the far side of the location, five blocks away.

A dozen kids had gathered at the bride's house after the wedding. None of us knew the bride and groom, but they had been transformed from teen-agers into a fairy tale pair being photographed in her front yard, a chubby bride with a Miss America crown and her eager, skinny groom. They posed, cameras snapped, the newlyweds went up on the porch, and the rumpus began. We, the ragamuffins, banged our pots and pans and yelled. They, the royalty, threw candies at us. A fair exchange for a summer day, I figured.

The chivaree didn't last long. Julianna said, "Now what do we do?"

While I pondered the question, I unstuck a Bit-O-Honey from its wax paper fold and put it in my mouth. Julianna did the same. So did the others. Before the nougat was soft enough to chew and the nuts were floating free, the other kids had gone home. Only Julianna and her brothers and I were left there. I said, "How about we go look for that tunnel? The one Gerald found."

"Swell!" Julianna said. She liked using words from the 1930s and 1940s, and these days her favorites were "swell" and "'poon" (for spoon, kiss, neck), which in 1950 were old-fashioned things to say. "Come over my house first," she said. We rode to the boarding house where she dropped off her brothers and changed into pedal pushers, then continued through town and down the alley behind my house. We parked beside the barbed-wire fence that bordered the mine.

The fence was taller than we were, but it had footholds—handy spaces in the crisscross reinforcements—and was easy to climb. We had done it plenty-times. But as I held myself on the top wire, propped on stiffened arms, getting ready to swing a leg over, I lost my grip and fell. I hooked myself by the armpit on the puncture points of barbed wire. Hanging on the fence with my feet dangling, I passed out.

I woke up on the davenport in our front room. The room felt stuffy and safe. Julianna had run to my house when she couldn't get me down, and Aarnie had rescued me and carried me home.

There were times later on when home, or even the idea of home, could make me faint. But this time fainting had brought me home, and I was glad. Home right then was a sanctuary. This davenport, steady on the hard floor.

*　*　*

Summer lazed on, and we finally got to go to Swan Lake. In 1925, so the story went (another story we weren't meant to hear but just slipped out), Grandpa had bought two run-down cabins from a bankrupt owner. Before fixing them up, he had given them names: Ramshackle and Rickety. (The cabins were okay to talk about, but not the part where Grandpa gained from another man's woes.) "Ramshackle? Rickety?" I said to Marcie, "American sass, from a man who never talks!" It proved he had a way with words, *English* words, to boot! It was a mystery, and we loved mysteries.

Every August the two families spent two weeks together at Swan Lake. Harald and his family stayed at Rickety, the Mahoning bunch at Ramshackle, fifty feet away. Harald was always good for a joke, and Inky minded everyone's business. Inky's real name was Inga-Liisa, but she was Inky even to Mummo who was leery of shortcuts. (Somehow Inky and I got by with nicknames in a family that didn't believe in them.) Inky was a long-faced, no-nonsense ex-nurse who knew what to do in emergencies, a fifty-kilometer walker who for ten months of glory in 1932 had assistant-coached the United States Olympics walking team. She was taller than Harald by four or five inches, and bossy. I liked her very much. Both Marcie and Randall were adopted, and both were good-looking in un-Finnish ways (meaning they weren't towheads). In other ways, they were opposites. Marcie wasn't like anyone else I knew. She had a big straight nose and green eyes (whoever heard of green eyes?) and long, wild, curly hair that was a nut color with gold sparks in it. Marcie was like her hair—carefree. Randall was inward and surly. He read chemistry books for fun and took his pet skunk, Essence, wherever he went. To anyone who shrank from her, he'd say, "Don't worry, dummy, she's been de-smelled," and he'd run a finger down her stripe to prove it. Randall had a triangular face and bullet eyes. He didn't wear glasses, but he had a bare look to his eyes as though he *should*.

Marcie and I knew Swan Lake better than anyone. We recited the facts and made them a game. Smells: Mildewinnerrubeswildrosesdeadfishpine. Secrets: Where Nature Boy lives, how to get bloodsuckers off your toes. Puzzles: When Harald wears a two-piece woolen bathing suit, why doesn't he scratch? Before thunder explodes and breaks up the sky, why does the air turn vomit yellow? Why do noises *carry* so far at night, lovers fighting in a boat a mile away, sounding like next door? Rituals: Run bare-naked in the dark (just the girls) from the sauna to the lake. Put the Victrola on Slow and imitate the bass growl: "Reeeadd 'em and Weeeep." Show off in the water like little kids, yell, "Watch! Watch!" to Mummo and Inky, who sit knitting on the sand (and who in fact are watching, for our safety). Walk barefoot on blistered tar to the Weasel Creek Store, and mutter as you pass those snooty summer homes, *Stuck-up rich kids*.

It was Marcie's idea to get back at Bruly Tyser, the owner of the Weasel Creek Store. Bruly was a fussbudgety man who suspendered his pants to alarming heights and hated kids—the younger, the worse. He considered kids inferior to his inventory, too bad for him in that kids were the mainstay of his business. He had a watchdog named Ripper, an edgy bulldog with a drool, and if a baby so much as *aimed* his gooey fingers at a candy jar, reaching from his mother's arms, both the man and his dog would growl, and Bruly would say, "Uh-uh-*uh*! Don't touch! I'll get it!" For some reason, he pretended he didn't know Marcie and me. We were his steady customers; we'd been coming in for years! Yet, whenever we walked in, he'd say accusingly, "And what do *you* want?" What we wanted was his bubble gum—well, popsicles, too, and watermelon, sometimes—but mostly the bubble gum. Bruly's bubble gum was so fresh it still had powder on it! The pinky smell of it made our noses itch. Right in the store, he'd chop chunks off the bubble gum log, wrap them in squares of wax paper, twist the ends and hand them to us. Man, oh man, we loved that bubble gum! We figured he should pay us to advertise: One fat pillow fills the mouth! Makes summer into one long chew! If it weren't for the bubble gum, we wouldn't go near the place. We wouldn't give Bruly the satisfaction.

Harald was reading *The Cranston Call* on the screened porch when he overheard our scheme. "Now, you kids," he said, dropping the paper to his lap. "You gotta be fair. Sure, that guy don't know if he's on foot or horseback, but he's got his good points, too. Like ever'body else."

Marcie made her head bobble like a puppet head. "Oh, ya? Like what?"

Harald checked the upper line of screen for inspiration. "Well, lessee. For one thing, he keeps a nice clean place of business."

We coughed in scorn. Marcie said, "*Hngh!* He's scared we'll bring in germs."

"And that's not his only good point," Harald went on as if Marcie hadn't said a word. "He keeps *himself* clean and neat, too. You might say a little *too* neat?" He looked at us slantwise.

We tittered and hoo-hawed. Marcie crowed, "He uses so much Brilliantine, his hair doesn't *move!*"

I said, "He sparkles standing still!"

Harald feigned only offhand interest in our abuse of Bruly. "Now, you guys," he said reasonably. "At least he's clean. This neighbor guy in Deekota? He had so much dirt in his ears you could plant ruta-beggars in there, I'm not kiddin'! He was a *happy* kinda fella—*big* smile, alla time! He'd go *in* the sauna smiling and come *out* of the sauna smiling, and his ears were just as dirty when he came *out* as when he went *in!*" He snapped the paper and held it before him, pretending he didn't care if we liked his story or not. But he grinned anyway around the corner of his head, hoping.

Our plan involved Fred, a plate-sized turtle we'd found in a muddy creek. We took turns carrying him home in the crook of an elbow, Fred stroking the air in slow motion, scratching whatever his toenails could reach, our wrists or our blouses. He had a pointy overbite that gave him a wise and patient look. We planned to hide him in a paper sack and take him to the store, and then, when Bruly was busy with customers, we'd slide Fred into the showcase. Bruly collected rocks—boulders, really—and displayed them in a showcase on a layer of sand, along with seashells and jars of wrapped saltwater taffy, the theme being, according to his painted sign, "The Ocean Deep." Some of the boulders looked exactly like Fred. We figured that when one of them grew legs and a head and wanted *out*, Bruly would have a fit. Marcie and I would say, all innocent, "Why, Fred! How did you get in *there*?" And we'd take him home, laughing all the way.

We hadn't counted on Ripper's good nose. Ripper caught a whiff of Fred from a long way off, and, assuming the worst intentions against his master, he ran after us, spitting and whuffing, until we'd slammed ourselves safe inside of Marcie's cabin.

Fred went back to the creek that same afternoon, and we didn't go to the store for four whole days. In the meantime, we explored the woods behind our cabins. One day we traced a measly creek (not the one Fred lived in) uphill through stands of birch and pine, lost the creek, found it again, and went ahead when KEEP OUT signs told us we were trespassing. Abruptly, the terrain dropped, and below us was a lake we hadn't known existed. Through trees, we could make out slips of a big white house and outbuildings. We sized up the scene. No people or dogs, no cars. Probably a vacation place, probably no one here this week. We slid down the hill and crept to the house, alert to motion or sound. Soon we were hunkering on the wraparound porch, peeking through the window.

Right above our heads, a woman screamed. "*Get out!* And *stay* out!"

We leaped off the porch and ran for the woods, realizing only when we were flush on the ground that she had screamed at someone else, not at us. Hearts racing, we settled down to spy. The French doors burst open and two people tumbled out, both about thirty and drunk. She wore a downy blue dress with a frilly half-apron and high-heels, her hair in a Victory roll, bolstered behind the neck from ear to ear—an oddly dated style for a woman her age. He wore tan-colored trousers with a red tie and wide brown suspenders. They tripped over their feet, regained their footing. Nose to nose, they shouted at the same time. I couldn't pick out any particular words.

He pushed her away, yelling, "I'm *tired* of you, *that's* why! You and your *precious feelings*." "Precious" and "feelings" came out mushy, as if he lacked the gumption to speak in solid words. He flailed at the air and stumbled to the wall, pressed his back against it, slid down and sat with his knees up, nodding at the floor.

The woman came to our side of the house. We sank farther into the bushes. She shrieked, "*I hate you, I hate you!*" Drawing her apron to her face, she wept into it, untied it and threw it over the railing. She pulled the bolster from her hair and shook her hair loose. "You *beast*! I never want to see you again!"

When we last saw the two, he was lying on the porch, motionless, and she was sitting on the steps, tearing at her hair and rocking and moaning. As we snuck away, Marcie and I communicated without words. Her look said she was glad *this* didn't happen at her house. My sentiments exactly. I might have siren-loud silences at my house, I told myself, but at least I didn't have *this*.

Still, I knew how the woman felt. Sometimes I did that very thing, I moaned and rocked when I thought no one was looking.

*   *   *

After our two weeks at the lake, Marcie and her family—or "the Haralds," as Aarnie called them—stayed in Mahoning for four days before going back to Michigan. Marcie and I spent every possible minute together. Liisa showed no inclination to join us. The things that interested us didn't interest her. We liked mysteries, stupid jokes, and the idea of traveling the globe. Liisa liked baking and sewing and the idea of staying where she was for the rest of her life. Marcie and I woke up early, did the fewest chores we could get away with, and took off and rambled around the location. By the time we got back, Liisa would have a noon dinner fixed and a cake cooling. Everyone came to the table, and the food vanished. Liisa said that as long as we washed dishes she was glad to cook. Marcie and I had it *easy*. We'd grin behind our dishtowels, singing in falsetto like squirrels on helium, "Nice work if you can get it . . . !" We were selfish, lazy girls.

But Marcie was always egging me on, talking me into things I didn't want to do, like hiking two miles on a muggy, hot day, sliding down a dusty cliff, fighting off thistles and mud flies, all to see a dumb old Model T! That sounded like punishment. The car had been there as long as I could remember, in an abandoned field outside the location. The neighbor kids told two stories about it, both with the same theme: Death. In one story, a skinny old skinflint from Hibbing (no names were ever given) bought the Model T when it was new, and he liked it better than he ever liked his family. He bamboozled and cheated his way through life, and when he retired he said to his cronies, "This Tin Lizzy got me through the Depression. She kept me out of the rain and gave me a good ol' time! What'd the wife and brats ever do for me?" When he got sick unto death (that's the way the kids told it, "sick unto death"), he signed over his inheritance to his gardener, drove the Model T into a weedy field and bumped it along until it hung up on a rock. At that point, he put his head on the steering wheel and died. In the second story, a jilted seventeen-year-old boy, wanting to convince his girlfriend to take him back, pretended to strangle her. (Why he thought this would win her over, I had no idea.) By accident he killed her. He panicked. He weighted the body with concrete and sank it in Murphy Lake, a pit of putrid water four miles off the Hibbing-Mahoning Road. Then he drove his graduation gift, the classic Model T that he had wanted for years, into the same weedy field. . . . The endings were identical. The boy too put his head on the steering wheel and died, though it was never clear *how*. An old man could die of old age, but a boy?

"It should rest in peace," I said. "We should leave it alone."

"Chic-*ken*," Marcie said. She could never let things be. She actually wanted to see that dumb old hulk.

I complained, "It's too hot. We'd get all dirty."

"Party-pooper."

"And those sticker bushes! Let's get your dad to take us swimming."

"Yellow-belly, lily-liver!" She grinned. "Scaredy-cat! Wet blanket! Spoilsport!"

"Ya, well. We better at least wear long sleeves."

We set off after the noon meal on asphalt that smelled like rubber and was spongy underfoot. The sun hammered the tops of our heads. I was not being a good sport. It was *way* too hot for walking halfway to China!

"*Snakes*," I said. "I'll bet snakes live in the car. They're curled up, just waiting for us."

"There aren't any snakes," Marcie said. As if she knew. "But there's this murderer who escaped from prison and he sleeps in the car . . ."

"Ya! And he gets really mad when people wake him up. Let's go back."

She ignored me. We plodded ahead. A mirage fluttered at the skyline like a house on fire, then flattened like mercury. The soles of my feet burned through my shoes. The distance to the Model T seemed awfully long. Finally we came to the point of drop-off, dug in our heels and slid to the foot of the cliff, kicking up a fine dirt that followed in clouds and took a long time settling. We waded through waist-high thistles that pricked our hands and legs. Approaching the Model T head-on, we could see it leaning toward the passenger's side, front end higher than the rear, empty headlights focused on the sky. Every piece of glass was gone from the headlights, the side lanterns and windows. The windshield was merely a metal rectangle supported by triangle props. Seen as a whole, the car was a delicate, scooped-out convertible with narrow spike wheels, high fenders, and thin running boards.

I said, "It looks like a horse buggy, like in the movies," and then a light came on in my head. "Oh. 'Horseless carriage.'" The front end was a rectangular box with hinged covers that could fold up on either side to expose the engine. I found a hole for the crank but no crank. The cloth convertible top lay accordianed over the back seat, in tatters. The Model T was a mess, but even so it was noble.

Marcie went to the driver's side and whispered, "No one's here."

"You expected someone?" I whispered back. "Why're we whispering?"

"No reason." Precisely as she raised her foot to the running board, a crow cawed loudly from a tree nearby. Marcie flinched and made google eyes at me. She climbed into the driver's seat, which perched high and forward, like a refinement of the buckboard seat. I got in on the passenger's side. The seat was sticky with unimaginable substances. Marcie tried out the steering wheel on its long shaft, and I inspected the flat-faced dashboard and cramped knobs. We were absorbed and didn't realize we had company.

A shout came from the woods, a young male voice: "Who's there?" Three teen-aged boys carrying shotguns came around the trees. They looked criminal.

Marcie breathed at me, "Take it easy."

I whispered, "I *told* you we shouldn't've come!" I took another look at the boys. "I *know* them. The tall one's Tommy Sanders." I couldn't remember the names of the fat one and one with the pimples, but all three were bad news, I knew that much. They had quit school the year before and since then had practiced being mean, unemployed, and no-good. They had pretty much perfected those skills, from what I'd heard. I retrieved another name. "They call the fat one Tuba."

Tommy and Tuba came up to the car, but the third boy, who had poor posture and a poor idea of himself, hung back. Tuba came to my side and put one hand on the lantern, the other on the seat frame. "Wella wella wella, would you looky here!" he said in a voice too high and small for someone his size. He pushed back his cap in lewd courtesy. "If it ain't girlies. Litty bitty girlies!" A compromised sweetness came off his body, as if he'd rubbed strawberry jam on himself and not bathed until he had rubbed on more jam.

Tommy rested his hand on the steering wheel. "Hey, good-lookin'!" he said to Marcie. "Wanna have some fun?"

Marcie said coolly, "No, we don't. We were just getting ready to go home."

"Home?" Tuba squeaked. "Nope! We can't let you go home. Leastways, not yet." He feigned a snatch at Marcie, pulled back and tittered.

Tommy said, "You know, I think Tuba's right. You guys 're gonna stay right here." Tommy was pleasant enough to look at, with bright blue eyes and clear skin, a butch haircut that wouldn't stand up. Why did he act so obnoxious?

I said, "You're Tommy Sanders, aren't you?"

He bridled. "Do I know you?"

"I'm Kik Halonen. I know Carlene."

His face went tender. Tommy and his sister were allies in a family of enemies. More than once Carlene had come to school bruised, and more than once the sheriff had been called to their house. Carlene lived in another town now. I didn't know where. He concentrated on me and said slowly, "Yeah, now I 'member. You and her went skatin' once." The harshness was gone and the young boy showed through.

Then he got nasty again. "But you guys are *nuts*, you know that? Coming out here by yourselfs? Jus' *askin*' for trouble!" He nickered rudely and gave Tuba the go-ahead. Playing the ladies' man, Tuba squared his shoulders.

Images came to my mind, Carlene's house, a snow mountain in her yard, iced steps for climbing up, a curved chute for sliding down. Christmas lights in the window. Tommy playing in the snow with a collie. I said, "Didn't you have a collie?"

Tommy's face took on a pall. Without inflection he said, "He got ran over."

"That's too bad," I said. More images came, a dog running along a snow bank, chasing the school bus. The bus gets too close. The dog slides under the wheels, yelping and crying. *A screaming dog.*

How had I forgotten? I had been standing at the bus stop when it happened.

"Oh, Tommy! It was the school bus. I'm so sorry." His arms still barred Marcie, but his belligerence had dropped away. "Traveler," I said. "Wasn't that his name?"

"Yeh."

"Where did he come from? Wasn't he a stray?"

"Sister Belle found him over by Cranston."

"He was a pretty dog. I remember he had a soft coat. I'm sorry he died." Without planning to, I was following a tip a boy gave me in the second grade, Westley Johnson. He told me bullies backed off if you got them to talk about themselves. Westley was a quirky kid, but he had experience in the subject of bullies. His tip was working on Tommy. On me, too. I really did feel sorry for Tommy and his collie.

By now, any threat was nonexistent. Tommy was back to childhood, Tuba was moving into the field, and the boy with the bad complexion was in the same place, standing out in the weeds. Tommy said, "Take it easy," and he turned and walked away.

The sun stood watch, and not one creature made a peep. We sat there for a few minutes, just breathing, then we gathered our scattered senses and took them home.

The next day, same as with the Model T, Marcie poked fun at Turkey Dump. "There's nothing to be scared of up there!" This time she was right. We climbed Turkey Dump and walked its spine from end to end to see what we could see. Like the bear who went over the mountain, what we saw was the other side of the dump. Not one single turkey. The scariest thing about Turkey Dump was its isolation from all things living except for volunteer trees and crawly things.

As we headed back toward home on the path, Marcie said, "You know how Grandpa always looks mad? I think something happened a long time ago. Something awful. And that's why he has that look." She mimicked his palpable gloom. "Something made him that way. I wonder *what?*" She loved a riddle and would go to ridiculous lengths to make one up.

"He never learned to smile. They didn't teach that in Finland."

She made a dunce face. "I'm serious. He's a little kid, and he comes across . . . ?" She twiddled her fingers as she walked, thinking up awful things a kid might come across.

"A corpse."

"No! . . . A *carcass.* Moose . . . No, caribou. They have those in Finland. No, reindeer. A reindeer carcass . . ."

"He finds a dead deer and ever since he's been mad?" I rolled my eyes to heaven.

Marcie fanned away my words. "That's just the first part. Give me time."

"I know this much. He never smiles. We live in the same house, and I've never once seen him smile."

Marcie snapped her fingers. "See? That's what I mean! He's frozen."

"And he never talks, except to Mummo." Forging ahead of Marcie, I held back a birch branch. I released it too soon, and it whipped her face. "Sorry! You okay?"

She touched her cheek but found no blood. "I'm fine. But how did they fall in love? Can you see him kissing her? Or asking her to marry him? Hey! Maybe *she* asked *him*. Maybe she wanted to come to America and be a cowgirl!" Throwing her arms around to act out her song, she sang, "I want to be a cowboy's sweetheart! I want to learn to rope and to ride!" Switching tunes, she did her rendition of a yodel. "O yo-de-*lay* hee hoo! De yo-de-*lay* hee hoo! De yo-de-*lay* hee, yo-de-*lay* hee *hoo*!"

"You kill me," I said.

As we continued walking, Marcie said, "But really, what do you think she saw in him?" She answered her own question. "For one thing, he was handsome. Still is."

"Ya. He's got a nice face. And those eyebrows. And he has nice eyes, except they're always *watching*, trying to catch me doing something wrong." To the right of us were dumps fresher than this one, behind us, the mine and the location. The wind was stronger up here than it was on the flats.

Marcie churned past me comically, reversed directions and said in my face, "I have some news. We're moving."

"What do you mean? Where to?"

"*Cranston*!" She could hardly contain herself. Elation was leaking out all over.

I gasped. "Cranston? . . . *Our* Cranston?"

"Yes! *Your* Cranston! We'll be neighbors!" She took my hands and jigged me up and down. "Yo-de-*lay* hee *hoo*!"

I shook her off. "Sit down and tell me!" We sat cross-legged on the path. What was going on in my chest felt too rambunctious for the space inside there.

"My dad's selling the store," she said, "or trading, really, for a house in Cranston plus a motorboat and trailer. This guy wants to live in Hancock, and he talked to my dad a bunch of times. They made a deal. Dad's arthritis is worse, and this way he can retire."

"Why didn't you say so right away? *Today*, I mean?"

"We've had to keep it to ourselves for so long. We've known since March."

"*You!*"

"You can stay over at my house all the time . . ."

"And you can stay at mine! Man oh man, we're a couple lucky stiffs!"

I bent toward Marcie and a glittery future. *Marcie in the next town over!*

* * *

The biggest change after Marcie moved was that we got to spend Christmas together. That first year, we had a Christmas she would later call typical. I'm not sure about that. I'm vague about parts of the past. But I agreed that those were the good years, when the pain stayed mostly hidden.

Harald said he had a ghost story, as if ghost stories were normal at Christmas. He claimed this one had happened to *him*. (Why he liked ghost stories, I couldn't say. You might think a minister would steer clear of them.) We sat on the front room floor, and Harald sat in the stuffed chair. Glad to be on stage, he said, "Ever'body ready?" We nodded. The only light in the room was coming from the porch, streaking in behind us. Perfect for a spooky story. Even Harald's hair seemed flighty and ready to jump.

"It's goina be a true story," he told us.

"It's okay if it's not," Liisa said.

I elbowed her. "Don't interrupt!" I said, interrupting. With inflated good humor, Harald riffled his brows at us. "You all set then?" he asked. We said we were.

"Ya well! This happened in Nort' Deekota when I was twelve or something. I was in the barn, fixing a harness. Nobody was on the place. No one home. The folks were in town. The rest were someplace, I dunno. Anaway, I was the only one at home." He plumbed our eyes to see if we had caught the point that he had made so many times.

"You were home alone," Marcie said.

"That's right!" Gratified, he grinned and walked his buttocks forward in his chair. "So there I am, minding my own business, and I hear these sounds coming from the hayloft, right over my head! These hauling, *scraping* noises. And these *moans*." With no self-consciousness, and for our consideration, Harald moaned. "Aw-*oo*! . . . Aw-*oo*!"

I thought this was funny in a scary way, but no one cracked a smile. "Being a plucky lad," he said, "I went up the ladder and poked my head in the hayloft . . ."

We shouldn't have trusted him. We knew he liked to string us along, tell us some gruesome tale and keep us on pins and needles, only to stop it short with a joke. After describing the madman in the hayloft, a ghoulish man with hideous eyes and hawklike hands (Harald demonstrated by leaping at us) and hinting at the grisly fate the madman had in store for Harald the boy, Harald the man said, "He picked up a big metal hook and one of those . . . ? You know, one of those things you punch leather with." He mimed punching leather with a hand tool. "What's it called, an . . . ?"

"Awl!" we shouted, breathless.

"*All!* . . . That's right. That's all." We never should have trusted him.

The next day we got more snow, big furry fluffs that piled up fast and added to the two feet we had already had. The four of us kids went outside and threw snowballs, made snowmen and snow angels, and shoveled a path from the house to the garage. We stood and watched snow falling past our noses, a nearsighted flurry in 3D. We tasted the flakes, which were nothing on the tongue. When the wind got so strong it was hard to stand up, we went inside.

For two days a storm screeched, then calmed, then whipped up again. The third morning we woke to freezing rain and a buffeting wind, and a sky so compressed you could hardly see it. At noon, the porch thermometer registered forty-two below. A maple tree bent with ice tapped at the window as if begging to be let in.

Then the wind stopped, causing a vacuum of sound. Inky caught Marcie and me signing to each other that we should go outside. She warned us, "Don't go planning to go out there! Your nose will fall off and you won't even know it." We laughed. Inky said, "I'm not kidding. Your eyes will drip and freeze your eyes shut."

"We'll be *fine*," Marcie said. "Aarnie, you got any long johns I could use?"

Liisa and Randall didn't want to go out, so Marcie and I put their woolen clothes on top of ours, union suits, slacks, sweaters, socks, coats. We squared white dish towels at the forehead and tied them under our chins, then wrapped scarves around our heads until only our eyes and mouths were exposed. The grownups helped us pull on mittens, three pairs each, and tall rubber boots. We stumped to the back entry, but when we tried to open the door, we found a snowdrift blocking it. Forcing the door open, we pushed our bulks outside and entered a strange new landscape. Snow had frozen in swirls as tall as the house, and everything was coated with an inch of ice. Due to an accident of wind pattern, the path we had shoveled had only a foot of snow on it. We took arching steps down the path, having to crunch through the ice crust with each step. The process of breathing hurt the nose and throat.

Harald's voice sounded hollow in the cold air. "Hey, you guys!" he called. "I got a idea!" He was squeezing through the blocked door, Aarnie and Randall right behind him. Their breaths came out in rounded puffs, like speech balloons in comic books. The sight touched me to the point of quick tears.

I called back to them, "Hey you guys, *yourself.* It's *cold!* You sure you want to come out?" I said to Marcie, "Your mom wasn't kidding. My lashes are freezing shut."

Harald maneuvered the path in galoshes not quite buckled. "Holy Moly, it's cold," he wheezed. "How many shovels you got?" He was using his "Ain't we got fun" way of talking. He had many ways of talking, and I wondered why *this* one, *now.*

We filed to the garage and got out shovels, dust pans, trowels, any tools to dig with, and carried them to the biggest drift, a glaze of ice that aimed straight up for about seven or eight feet and then leveled off and joined the garage eaves. It would be an ideal snow house if we scooped it out.

We carved a door and started to empty the interior. Randall was unstoppable. He set a fast pace, saying to Marcie and me, "Better leave it to the men. Girls can't work as hard." Randall, making a joke? Marcie and I gave each other a slow wink and matched him, scoop for scoop. Aarnie was the tallest, so he specialized on the ceiling, chipping away peaceably, sputtering and spitting snow. Harald was shoveling at such a fast clip that Marcie got concerned. She told him he should take it easy, that we could do it.

"Naw!" he said. "I wanta show you guys somethin' when we're done."

We finished the snow house, which was big enough for all of us to stand in. A pale sun pressed through the ice that formed the ceiling and gave an illusion of warmth.

We started on Harald's next project. "We used to do this when I was a kid," he said. We rolled snowballs and shaped a tiny igloo about a foot tall, leaving a low opening on one side and gaps between the snowballs. When we were done, I went to the garage to get matches and a candle. Harald lit the candle and Marcie, who had the smallest hand, pushed it inside the igloo and secured it.

It was late afternoon, and the day had turned dark. We stepped back to admire our work. Points of light shining through the gaps made a filigree, and Harald looked pleased. Apparently this igloo linked him to the best of his childhood. "They say in Finland they made 'em in the woods. In Nort' Deekota, we put 'em in the field."

We liked ours just where it was. When we went indoors, we left the candle burning. From the kitchen we could see it glimmer, like a signal from the Fatherland.

Usually when the families got together Liisa kept to herself, but this time she teamed up with Marcie and me. We sang "Red River Valley" in thirds and "Bill Grogan's Goat" until everyone was sick of the song. We gave so many hints about gifts—"They're lacy and baby blue and you wear them under your dress"—that few surprises were left. We slept crosswise on two beds pushed together, shrieking into the night (*someone* could pinch with her toes). We listened to Buddy Bear on the radio. We were way too old for Buddy Bear, so we made fun of the theme song by yelling the words:

> Bo-bo-skee-deeten-dahten, wah-dahten-shoo!
> Wah-dahten-shoo!
> Wah-dahten-shoo!
> Bo-bo-skee-deeten-dahten, wah-dahten-shoo!
> I'm a deeten-dahten bo-bo Buddy Bear!

We made terrible fun of that show, took every chance to make fun of it. It came on every day, and we never missed an episode.

Finally, it was Christmas Eve. The men washed up and went to the table. Nothing much happened among the Finns until plenty of food had been done away with. For days, Inky and Mummo had had dish towels on their heads, scuffing around the kitchen, getting food ready, and like a clockwork figure Inky had appeared periodically at the swinging door, shooed a kid out, and disappeared again. Mummo and Inky had banned us kids from the kitchen, even Liisa this time, and smells poofing out of there had driven us wild. That night they served pineapple ham and scalloped potatoes, green beans with crisp-fried bacon, red-and-green-striped Jell-O with cream cheese balls, Ambrosia Jell-O, pickled carrot medallions, fresh white rolls, blueberry jam, mincemeat pie, pumpkin pie, whipped cream, ice cream. We ate in boisterous silence.

At some point beyond full, the men pushed away from the table and patted their belts. It was time for the gifts! We had already guessed what most of them were, but that didn't matter. We sat under the tinseled tree, sniffing evergreen: miniature candles tipped in their pinchers, singeing spruce—*Tssst!* We found ourselves in the red mirror balls, squashed, ugly baby-faces full of nose, and waited for Harald to play Santa and read off the names.

Hours later, after we had tried out the new games and played practical jokes on everyone and had a few played on us (Harald put plastic dog poop on the floor, causing us to shout, "*Ishka-bibble!*" when we stepped on it, and to step on it often), we ate more pie and fell into bed.

Marcie says Christmas was like that from then on. Maybe. Maybe not. But before she moved, Christmas was quiet, the five of us sitting around the house, none of us knowing how to celebrate. Marcie and her family made all the difference.

Three

Dance of the Bereaved

Grandpa's mind started failing that spring, sending him to search behind curtains for something lost, we never knew what. One mild May night he got up to use the bathroom but he left the house instead and landed at the roundhouse wearing long johns, his best hat, and no identification. Jerry Sullivan, the night guard, had quite a time figuring out who he was. But eventually he did, and he brought him home.

It was five-forty in the morning when they arrived. Aarnie was having coffee, Liisa and I were coming down to breakfast, and Mummo was starting to worry because she couldn't find Grandpa. At Jerry's knock, she opened the door and brought the men in. We gathered around to look at Grandpa, who seemed refreshed by his outing. Wearing a borrowed jacket over his long johns, he benignly stood his ground, not seeming to mind being the main attraction. Jerry Sullivan was a big man by any description—he towered over us and was equal to several of us in circumference—but he acted like a kid with a new toy. His new toy was Grandpa.

Patting Grandpa's back, Jerry said, "Yeah, we had us a good ol' time, di'n't we, Toivo?" To us he said, "Toivo here sat on the lunch table and made jokes. We had us a *lotta* laughs. You know, he's got pretty good English!"

With alarm I tried to picture Grandpa sitting on a table, having a good time and joking. And in English? . . . *Wait till Marcie hears this.* Jerry said, "One thing we noticed, right off. He sure does like his coffee! We musta had ten cups each, di'n't we, Toivo?" He beamed at Grandpa and was rewarded with a firm nod. "There's this fella lives around here, what's his name? Gorman? Lance Gorman. He comes in, sees we're tryna find out who Toivo is and he says, 'I know him. He lives on my block.' That's how we knew."

After a few more pats, Jerry entrusted Grandpa to the family. On a prompt from Jerry, Grandpa removed the jacket and gave it to him. He removed his hat and ran his hand over his bald head and down his beard, as though reminding himself he could grow hair at the bottom of his head if not at the top. We stood on the porch to see Jerry off. From the sidewalk he called, "Yeah, Toivo! We had us a good ol' time, di'n't we?"

Grandpa came indoors and reverted to his somber self. In Jerry's presence, he had seemed boyish and lighthearted. Was he in his second childhood? Reverting at times to how he used to be? Maybe Marcie was right. Maybe he *had* been a happy-go-lucky kid and something had changed him. We had no pictures of him as a child or as a young man. In the earliest photos he was forty and already stern. In later pictures he looked the same, the same deep eyes defying the camera, the same thicket brows. Only his hair and beard changed over time. As he lost hair from his head, he grew it out on his chin, until his head gave way to baldness, and his beard grew long and white. As Marcie and I had agreed, he was a handsome man.

But a person who made jokes? I couldn't see it.

Three months later he died. We had lived in the same house since I was four weeks old, but I had never really known him. The hot looks he shot at me when I was small and naughty were the only connections we had made.

The funeral would be held in Hibbing in a borrowed church. Three days beforehand, Harald and Inky and their kids came to stay at our place. So did Uncle Isaak from Alaska. His wife, Elsa, had to stay in Alaska with their daughter, Nell, who was the same age as Marcie and me. After years of trying for a second child, Elsa was expecting a baby, and her doctor didn't want her to travel. He feared for the baby's health. Inky told Liisa and me that Isaak looked a lot like our father, except that our father was shorter and not quite as broad across the back. That meant that our father, like Isaak, had ice-blue eyes and a sculpted face with the chisel marks still showing, and a dark cast to the beard even after shaving. Isaak and Harald were civil to one another but weren't anything alike. Isaak was mannerly and soft-spoken, an outdoors man who spent nights on a cot in Aarnie's room and days roaming the location. He came in to have coffee or dinner, and then went back outside. For Isaak, the stuff of life was in the open air.

In a moment of rare implied trust, Mummo asked Marcie, Randall, Liisa and me to sing at Grandpa's service. We said we would. On the morning of the funeral, Aarnie took us early to the church, a white rural chapel with a steep roof, a peaked steeple, and a cemetery up the hill, so that we could practice the hymn we had chosen, "Jesus, the Very Thought of Thee." During the funeral, we four would sit facing the congregation in pews meant for a choir, short rows set at an angle behind the preacher. I waved at the pews and said to Marcie, "These are for *regular* choirs. Finns don't *have* regular choirs. We don't have *any* choirs!" As if she didn't know. "But here we are," I said, "*ir*regular as they come!" I laughed alone, a stunted, angry laugh. I didn't want to sing. I wanted to walk out of there and keep walking. "Which pew would you like, young lady?" I asked Marcie, bowing, sweeping my hand this way and that. "This pee-yoo or that pee-yoo?"

"Take it easy," she said.

Liisa and Marcie, the sopranos, sat in front of Randall, the tenor, and me, the alto. As we practiced, women ferried food to the basement in preparation for the time, after the funeral, when people would pour downstairs for coffee and lunch. We could smell the separate foods as they passed by. Lasagna. Garlicky mashed potatoes. Smoked sturgeon. Pickled herring. Fish-head stew. Egg salad sandwiches. Watermelon rind pickles. Green olives. Black olives. Jell-O salads. Macaroni salad. Celery stuffed with pimento cream cheese. Cakes. Pies. Cookies. Cranberry whip. Raisin rice pudding. Prune pinwheels. Brownies. We salivated and swallowed as we sang.

The funeral proceeded like any other service. Flies batted at the window screens and the minister (a visiting minister, John Heiska) preached. People coughed. Babies climbed their mothers' laps. Old ladies pulled hankies from their sleeves. Same as any other service.

Out of the blue, I got the giggles. Violent, uncontrollable giggles. I couldn't stop them. They were like earthquakes. They started in my belly and stuttered outward to my elbows, which jabbed Randall in the ribs, rat-tat-tat. He scowled down at me, quite in control of himself. I grinned at him and snorted. I tried holding my breath, but noises kept seeping out: *Fuffle!* . . . *Gip!* My eyes watered. I wiped them and willed myself to relax. *Stop it!* I told myself. *You can stop.*

But I couldn't. Everything was funny. The crying babies, the flies. *The old ladies' hankies!* Marcie threw me a settle-down glance. I shrugged at her and giggled harder. My face ached from the rigors I was putting it through.

It was time to sing. We began. "Jesus, the very thought of thee/With sweetness fills the breast . . ."

Breast? . . . At *church?* I burped and chuckled, *Hup! Hup!* Fighting for air, I searched the walls for help. I decided to look at Grandpa in the casket. *That* should settle me down. But it made things worse. He still looked *mad!* That seemed hilarious to me, the funniest thing I'd ever seen. I tried to throttle my laughing, which then came out as "Mhhh-*ffppttt!*" and "*Hecchht!*" Then I thought that was funny. I was hopeless.

The others carried the singing load. Marcie switched over to alto.

> O hope of every contrite heart,
> O joy of all the meek!
> To those who fall, how kind thou art!
> How kind to those who seek!

We came to the last verse:

> Jesus, our only joy be thou,
> As thou our prize wilt be,
> In thee be all our glory now,
> Throughout eternity. Amen.

It was over. How could I crawl back? I had giggled at Grandpa's funeral! I had disrespected God, Mummo, Grandpa, everyone. I wanted to disappear.

But nothing happened. To the absolute credit of the Silence, no one said a word. No one gave me a scalding look. Everyone pretended that I had done nothing wrong.

Except for Marcie, who made fun of me by snorting at me, more than once. Leave it to Marcie.

* * *

When fall services came along, I got into *another* fix at church. Services were over for the day, but people still stood in a circle in the Koskinens' front room, singing, "Oh, Won't You Come with Me to My Father's House, Where There's Joy, Joy, Joy!" Every verse got louder and faster, and people were acting happy, even *clapping*. This was more excitement than I'd ever seen at church.

Without warning, Mummo slapped her hands together, then waved one arm high in the air and danced to the center of the circle. She twirled and twirled in a private kind of ecstasy, her face tilted to the ceiling, arms open wide. Strangely, she looked happy.

Mummo, *dancing*? And happy?

Intrigued, I watched her twirl. What was going on here? Dancing was *holy*. It was reserved for heaven. We would dance for joy when we got there. Until then, we weren't supposed to dance. So what was this?

Marcie had stayed home with the flu, so I couldn't ask her. Catching Liisa's attention, I asked her with my eyes. Her return look was noncommittal.

Mummo swept toward me and tugged at my arm. I was aghast. We didn't *touch* in our family! She pulled at me, wanting me to dance with her. I didn't like her clutching me like that. I shouted, "No!" Controlling myself, I said, "It's okay, really, but *no*," and I managed to pry her fingers off my arm. She moved down the line and got another grandmother to dance with her.

I was furious. I felt violated, *used*. Why embarrass a kid like that?

Then I felt guilty. Maybe I had been rude, shaking Mummo off? I had probably broken one of those rules no one told you about until it was too late.

Then I got mad again. Inside my head, I screamed: No one tells you *anything*! You have to *trip* over something before anyone admits it's *there*!

As the group broke up and shuffled toward the kitchen, I stopped Liisa in the hall. "Did you know about that? What *was* that?"

Using her height to advantage, she said, "A drink of the Holy Spirit. She was drunk with the Holy Spirit." As if that explained things.

"Who told you *that*?"

"Amos." She smiled at the sound of his name. Amos Aho, a purposeful young man, just might be the next lay minister. Liisa had a crush on him.

"*That's* why she was dancing? She was drunk with the Holy Spirit?"

Liisa spoke with long-suffering, the way a mother might speak to her wayward toddler. "It's a widow thing. Widows get happy like that sometimes. They dance because their husbands are in heaven."

"But that doesn't make sense! Why say 'drunk' when we don't even drink? And why would a widow dance? She should be *sad*!"

"Sad and happy, both. Mostly happy because her husband is with Jesus."

I mentally replayed Mummo's dancing, her grip on my arm, her drawing attention to me—her paying attention to me at all. Everything was out of character. Maybe she was drunk with the Holy Spirit?

I said to Liisa, "But I hated being grabbed like that! It felt . . ." I didn't know the word "coercive" or I would have used it. Mummo had never touched me for any reason, not that I could remember, anyway, and now, when she finally *did*, it was in this secret, public, insistent way that felt shameful.

"I saw it one other time, is all," Liisa said. "In Duluth. You weren't there."

"Why didn't you tell me? You should have warned me!"

"It doesn't always happen. You don't need to get so het up."

"But someone needs to explain these things *before* they happen!"

She wasn't paying attention. She was looking for someone, Amos, most likely.

I took stock of her and had a click of insight, or what I took as insight. I decided that Liisa wasn't just comfortable with the Silence; she cheered it on. It would be some years before I knew the truth about that, and about some other things besides.

* * *

Ironically, that same fall, someone else tried to get me to dance. It happened at the boarding house where Julianna lived. It was my habit that year, late in the fall and late in the afternoon, to ride over to see Harry Childers at the end of the Mahoning loop. Harry was a fifth-grader who had polio and had to stay in bed. He couldn't have visitors, but I could see him by fencing my hands at his window, and he could see me. After waving hi and good-bye to Harry, I coasted down Boarding House Hill, gaping at the boarding house and mouthing Harald's "Finglish" term for it—*poordin-haus*. The building was white and many-tiered, built into the hill in three stories. Verandas ran along two sides of it, and at sunset the windows glistened yellow-orange. I pictured parties going on in there all the time.

One Friday, Julianna invited me for supper, a prospect that pleased me no end. I got caught off guard by her mother's greeting—a kiss on the forehead. I couldn't remember being kissed by anyone, on the forehead or anywhere else. Mrs. Rossini was the perfect mother, I concluded. In the dining room, someone had put a white cloth on the table, plus candles and flowers, and Julianna and I folded and laid out marine-blue cloth napkins. I had guessed right about the parties. They did have them, and *this* was one.

"What are those for?" I asked, pointing to stemmed glasses at all the settings, including the children's. I thought I knew the answer, and the answer made me shake.

"Wine," Julianna said. "We all get some."

Those words! So matter-of-fact to her, so foreign to me. She could never guess how queasy they made me. She said, "My grandparents made wine in Italy—you know, from scratch? *Vino da tavola.* 'Wine for the table.' They grew the grapes and made the wine, and the kids always got to have a taste. We still do."

I wasn't ready for this! *No one* drank alcohol at our house. The only wine I knew anything about was Communion wine, and I wasn't ready for *that*, either. I didn't know what I should do when the time came.

We sat down. Pretty soon, Mrs. Rossini was standing beside my chair, holding a dark bottle in two hands and gentling it toward me. I said, "No, thanks," and she nodded agreeably and went on to the next person. So far, so good.

I had expected spaghetti or something else Italian, but Mrs. Rossini served roast beef, gravy, mashed potatoes, corn, and peas. At the table, in addition to Julianna and her family and me, sat five male boarders, single men who worked in the mine. The hired girl, Essie, was a tall, busty brunette. She refilled serving bowls as they emptied, and then she retreated to the kitchen. A boarder in his twenties ogled me across the table. He was handsome but overripe, already, at such a young age, pouchy and red-faced, stressed around the eyes. His smile was oily, and so was his hair, which curled in commas down onto his forehead. I ate my food primly, paying him no attention whatever.

After supper, Julianna and I cleared the dishes and carried them to the kitchen, rinsed them and soaked them for washing. A musical tweedle came from another part of the house: "Sunset Serenade" on a lovesick accordion. Mrs. Rossini said, "Okay, honeys, good job. Run along and have fun."

I decided that, yes, definitely, this was the perfect house to live in.

Off the long central hall, Julianna opened a set of double doors, and we stepped into a room that I found intimidating. I had impressions of cigar smoke, beer, shadows, a man dancing with Essie. Small lamps gave light to small areas and license for mischief in between. The room smelled like a cocktail lounge, or how I imagined one might smell.

"Let's play records," Julianna said. "Sunset Serenade" was still going strong.

The oily miner came up behind me and swept me into a dance step, chuckling into my ear. I struggled to get free. "*No*," I said. "I don't dance!"

He said, "Whatsa matter, you scared?" Smiling a downright evil smile, he held me at arm's length to look at me, then laughed and clamped himself onto me. I tried to push him away. We were stamping in one place, like wrestling standing up.

"It's against my religion!" I shouted, but he pulled me closer still. Something hard and intrusive pressed my belly. With a shove, I slipped free of his grasp, snapped up my cardigan and called to Julianna, "Tell your mom thanks!"

Julianna followed me out to the verandah I'd admired from the street. It held no attraction anymore. "I'm so sorry," she said. "Johnny gets that way sometimes. I forgot to tell you to watch out for him."

"It's okay. Thanks again." I ran down Julianna's steps and down the block, eager to get home where life was dull and as silent as the grave, but honorable.

Four

Such Is Life!

It was summer again, and Harald still wasn't speaking to Kaisa, but he let Inky arrange the trip. Kaisa had invited Marcie and me to Swan Lake for a week. Liisa was invited, too, but she couldn't go. She was getting three items ready for competition at the state fair, a raspberry jam that somehow left the berries whole, a quilt with a loon design, and a cake so chocolatey it could make the angels cry. I had to admit it. The girl was *good.*

It was typical of my family that I scarcely knew Kaisa even though she had been my mother's best friend. They were friends before they met their husbands, who were my father and his brother Esko. I didn't know much about any of them. I knew that the two couples were married in a double ceremony, that no wedding photos were taken, and that both couples settled in Lake Worth, Florida. That's all I knew. My father and Esko were Harald's brothers, but Harald never mentioned them. Neither did Mummo, and she was their mother! I never could understood my family.

I had met Kaisa and Esko, once, when I was eight. They came from Florida to see Mummo and Grandpa about some secret, and the four of them talked for an hour in the master bedroom. Kaisa had regal posture and a stocky build and came to Mahoning in a wool suit trimmed with fur. Esko was slim and a little bent-over. He had bushy brows and early-graying hair, and a cowlick that sent his hair up off the forehead, then down onto his face. I saw them for just a few minutes before the meeting and a few minutes after, but I could tell they made up their own rules.

One, they stayed in a hotel in Hibbing. Every other time we had company, Liisa and I slept downstairs on the rollaway, and the company slept in our room. Staying in a hotel was an un-Finnish thing to do.

Two, they didn't bring their kids. They left them in Florida. *Unthinkable.* Kaisa and Esko had identical twins, Naomi and Elise, five or six years older than I was. No one in Minnesota had met them.

Three, they didn't go to the Finnish church, even though fall services were going on that week. They didn't seem to notice Mummo's searing look when Kaisa said, too easily, "No, thanks," to Mummo's suggestion that they attend.

Kaisa and Esko were too *breezy* to be regular Finns! (Or at least Kaisa was. Esko was the mournful type). They seemed very much in love, and very rich, but, still, they were human. They had come all the way from Florida to see Mummo and Grandpa, but the meeting hadn't gone well. No one talked about it, but their faces gave them away.

They returned to Florida, and we didn't hear from them for years. Then, a week after Grandpa had a heart attack and died, Esko too had a heart attack and died. I tried to puzzle this out. Esko is estranged from the family, he doesn't attend his father's funeral, but a few days after his father dies, *he* dies, too! From grief, or regret? Kaisa moved back to Minneapolis, bought a boarding house and ran it as a weekend guesthouse. Recently she had also bought a vacation home on Swan Lake, two miles from our cabins. Marcie and I would be the first ones in the family to see it.

It turned out to be a bulky lodge made of big logs and sheets of glass. Kaisa let us off in front and told us how to find our room, and she went to park the car. We climbed a set of steps on the outside of the house and opened a door. We dropped our bags and gawked. I had never seen such a fancy room. We walked around on polished planks and an area rug that let our feet sink, taking it all in. Sunlight poured into the room from four tall windows swung open like doors. Sheer white curtains moved in the breeze. There were twin carved bedsteads, pouffy white coverlets, twin dressing tables with three-way mirrors, a closet as big as my Mahoning bedroom, a bathroom with double sinks and movie-star lights around the mirror, jugs of flowers. Sidling next to Marcie, I rammed her hip with mine. "Think we can make it work?"

She was handling bottles that Kaisa had left out for us, lotions and spray colognes. "Maybe." She grinned her gremlin grin. "A sacrifice, but we can do it."

"*Ya* but! A whole *week* with the Mystery Auntie?" I quaked in exaggeration.

"You think she kills company? Come for a visit and end up buried in the yard?"

I made big eyes. "You never know! Spider says to Fly, 'Come see me sometime,' nice as anything. Next thing Fly knows, he's *dead.*" I touched a satin pillow, and then I couldn't keep my hands off it. It felt cold and as smooth as . . . satin.

Bending to her reflection in her vanity mirror, Marcie smiled at me at an angle. "You can leave. I'm staying." She removed her curved side combs and took a nip of hair from one temple, twisted it, put a comb into it and raised it high toward the back of her head. She did the same on the other side, leaving the rest to surge around on its own.

I sat on a bed and bounced a couple of times. "I like Kaisa and all, but how come she gets people so upset? Like your dad?" Reviewing the question, I fixed it. "I guess your dad's the only one." I opened the night table drawer. Linen hanky, lavender sachet.

From inside the closet, Marcie said, "How should I know? My dad never talks about the Halonens. Mom, neither." Marcie came out with a white terry-cloth robe over her clothes, did a few fashion turns, then tossed off the robe and opened her top dresser drawer. "Empty," she said. "Enough space for my jools."

I got up to check myself in the full-length mirror and made a pickle face. All *wrong*! Pink and white were babyish! Standing there in my white sleeveless blouse and pink pedal pushers, I eyed Marcie. As usual, she looked fantastic. Her tangerine jumper made her face gleam. "Well," I sighed, "we'd better go. Is this outfit okay?"

"It's *fine*. You worry too much." She gave me a mock salute. "Ready if you are."

The inside steps led down to a stone and black-metal kitchen where Kaisa was cutting a lemon meringue pie. She smiled and asked if we had found what we needed. We said yes, the room was nice, everything was nice. A cup-sized Chihuahua sat at Kaisa's feet, virtually on her feet, lolling his eyes back in his head and looking mortified. What had upset him, a mistake he'd done in a corner? Strangers in his kitchen? Then I realized this was his normal look. I almost apologized to him. Kaisa had changed into a monk's robe of magenta cotton and done her hair in a convoluted twist and jabbed it with an ivory stick. With a pancake turner, she lifted a tall slice of pie and set it on a thick plate (a blue flower painted on this plate, a yellow flower on each of the other two). She said, "That's Pooka. He's not much for new people. Would you like coffee?"

Marcie and I flashed astonishment at each other. At our houses, no one under eighteen was offered coffee. We said *yes, please*. At Kaisa's suggestion, we went to see the rest of the ground floor. The kitchen opened to a wide dining room. The dining table was huge, the top made of glass an inch thick and rounded at the edges. The pedestal was a tree trunk three feet in diameter, set on its head. Roots reached out in all directions to hold up the glass. It gave me the heebie-jeebies, staring into glass and seeing roots! I thought it was like staring into the ocean and seeing octopus legs. (I was guessing, having never laid eyes on an ocean.)

At the turn of an L, the house spilled toward the lake, down two wide steps to a spread of whole-log walls and picture windows, foreign rugs, leather couches, and lambs' wool throws. A giant rock fireplace dominated the inner wall. A corridor led away to the interior—to Kaisa's room, I assumed. An open wooden staircase, the third set of steps I had seen so far, led to a balcony and to our guest room (and to two more bedrooms that Marcie and I had found, snooping on our way down). Paintings and sculptures filled the crannies created by the angled ceiling. I had trouble believing that a Finn could live like this—in this luxury, without apology!

As we sat down, Kaisa acted as bashful as I felt. Marcie and I stirred sugar and cream into our coffee to ease the sting of the grownup drink. Kaisa said, smiling at each of us, "Well then, what would you like to do this week?"

Marcie didn't know Kaisa any better than I did, but Marcie was never shy. She said airily, "Oh, we like to swim and hike . . ."

". . . and solve mysteries!" I blurted. My face flamed. I castigated myself: Why don't you keep your big mouth *shut*?

Kaisa gave me the briefest of nods. "And am I a mystery to be solved?"

Marcie walked right into it. Leave it to Marcie. "We wonder why my dad never talks to you." Inside my head I yelled, Marcie, you doofus! Why don't *you* keep *your* big mouth shut? I prodded my pie with my fork, jostling the meringue to make it slide off the filling. Drops of meringue-sweat sat in white valleys between brown mountaintops. I tasted the filling. More tart than sweet, the way I liked it. I tried the meringue. Sticky, like roasted marshmallow. It stuck to my fork. I skidded the tines through my teeth, trying to clean off the meringue without biting metal.

Kaisa said to Marcie, "I can't speak for your father. Have you asked him?"

"I've tried. He clams up."

"There'll come a time, later on," Kaisa said. "What are you? Twelve?"

"Going on thirteen," we said.

"That's too young. You wouldn't understand." Kaisa caressed her hair as if it might rise up and say too much if she didn't soothe it. "I'll tell you this much. I humiliated the family. I shamed them. So did Esko." To Marcie she said, "Your father thought we betrayed *him*, personally."

This got me to speculating as to what they'd done, but I didn't get far. Marcie pushed Kaisa more. "But if it has to do with you, why can't you tell us?"

Kaisa took a little pause. "Maybe when you're in high school, when you study world history. Maybe then we can talk."

World history? What in the Sam Hill was she talking about? Or *not* talking about?

Marcie bit the insides of her cheeks. "This family! Everything's so secret."

"You're right," Kaisa said. "We're a stubborn bunch. Still, it's a good family."

Once more, I tried to figure out Kaisa and Esko. They stay away for years, Kaisa claims they shamed the family, she doesn't let us meet her daughters, Harald never speaks to her. Yet she calls this a good family? I didn't get it.

Wanting to tackle at least *one* secret and also wanting to change the subject, I asked Kaisa, "How are the twins?"

A smile crinkled her face and made her different, motherly, not so distant. "They're fine, thanks. They're working in Ireland this summer. Their jobs turned out better than they first thought. They're waiting tables at a resort. College starts in October in Gainesville."

They were young for college. What were they, seventeen? I checked the walls and the sideboard, but could see no photos of the twins or of anyone else.

"That's why I came back, you know, to be close to the family," Kaisa said, going back to the same old topic. My diversion tactic hadn't worked.

Marcie asked, "But how can you be close to people who won't talk to you?"

"Sweetie, your father's the only one who won't talk to me."

I said to Kaisa, virtually shouting, "Why did you move away from Florida? You had sun there all the time! Here, we have thirty below!" Florida did seem glorious, and moving from Florida to Minnesota seemed backwards, but my real interest was in being pushy, in steering talk away from touchy subjects.

She was more gracious than I deserved. "Like I said, to be closer to the family."

A scary idea struck me. Since we already had Kaisa's ear, and since I'd already brought up Florida, maybe I could ask her about my parents! *They* lived in Florida. They *died* in Florida. Just thinking about them made my ears ring. They were beyond me, no matter how much I learned about them. Still, I wanted to know.

But she had finished talking. I'd missed my chance. She stood and said, "Supper is at six. You can do what you like until then." She explained where the beach towels were and told us to have a good time.

We got on our bathing suits and whiled away the required half-hour (after eating, before swimming) by inspecting the boathouse and the houseboat. Kaisa was the only person we knew who owned both. The boathouse was musty and damp and had water for a floor, a walkway around the periphery and equipment on hooks on the walls. In the center, a boat with a sleeping cabin gave away its shape under a marine tarp. It seemed like a captive, blindfolded and held by force in this dank hole.

By contrast, the houseboat was full of light. Moored at the dock, it rocked slightly after a motorboat sped by. We lowered ourselves to the deck and explored the tiny galley and tinier closets, the bunk beds, the table that made into a third bed, the blue canvas curtains on runners. We opened the cupboards and leered when we found the vodka.

"That sneaky Auntie Kaisa," Marcie said.

"She's not your everyday Finn, that's for sure!"

"You can say *that* again."

In the next few days, the talk never turned to the subject of my parents, and I couldn't find a way to work in my questions. So, the day before we were to leave, while Marcie read a book in our room, I went to find Kaisa. Not seeing her in the living room or in the kitchen, I went out through the terrace door, and there she was, in mechanic's overalls and rain boots, kneeling in a flower border. I asked her if she needed help.

She smiled hello, took off her gloves and picked a thread of hair from her eyes. "No, thanks. I like to dig. Why don't you get that pail and sit down."

I got the pail, turned it over, sat down. She put her gloves back on and assailed a bed of snapdragons. We didn't speak as she dug up a chink of weeds, whacked it with a trowel, set it on newspaper. After watching three such moves, I said, "Auntie Kaisa, I was wondering. Do I look anything like my mother?"

She hefted herself to her feet. Sloughing off her gloves, she read my face. "Mm, of course, you would wonder. What-say we go inside?" She put an arm around my waist and directed me toward the house. I wanted to turn and hug her and not let go.

Kaisa shed her boots at the kitchen door and went into the near bathroom, giving me time to get out the lemonade and fill two glasses. She emerged wearing slippers and a plaid robe, her hair redone. Taking a glass of lemonade with her, she led the way to the front room and settled on one of the matching couches. I took an easy chair.

She eyed me for an unnerving length of time. "You asked me if you look like your mother. A little, but more like your father. People must tell you that?"

"No one tells me anything." I felt sorry for myself, but I was trying not to snivel.

"Let's make up for some of that." Kaisa's eyes held a welcome that I wanted to dive into. "Your mother's hair was darker than yours, light brown. It had a natural wave, and she wore it in a bob. She was one of the first women in our crowd to cut her hair. It was risqué, you know, bobbed hair was. . . . Do you have pictures of her?"

"Two. One of her when she was little, and one of the two of them where they look like movie stars."

Kaisa leveled her face at mine, comparing me to my parents, I guessed. My parents were classy-looking, and by comparison I felt bland.

"Your mother *was* like you, come to think about it. She told me she was blonde when she was young, and her hair started turning when she was around your age. You remind me of her when you're thinking hard. Like *now*. She had a way of driving her thoughts into people. . . . So then. Pictures. Surely you must have others?"

I thought, *They're gone, no one cared!* I shook my head no.

"I'll be right back." She set aside her glass and pattered down the hall, and came back holding a hatbox in front of her, with importance, like a birthday cake with the candles going. "Pictures! Let's see what we have."

Pictures. I was hungry for them. Kaisa patted the couch beside her, and I went and sat there. She sorted snapshots until she found the one she wanted. My mother at about age twenty, posing beside a Buick sedan. Everything was high. High pompadour, high-shouldered dress, high-heeled pumps, a big flat gardenia pinned high on her lapel. She was fine-boned and her face was longer than mine, more like Liisa's.

"There," Kaisa said, handing me the picture. "That was taken just before she cut her hair. Isn't she pretty? All set for the dance!"

I looked askance at Kaisa. Didn't she know? I said, "Um. Did my mother belong to the Finn church?"

Something dawned behind her eyes, a glint from a distant time. "The dancing?"

"Yes."

"Ah." She took the chopstick from her bun and repositioned it, stuck it in again.

"Well, when Sofia . . . your mother . . . was growing up, her family went to the same church we all went to, the one you and your grandparents go to. She was baptized and confirmed but didn't often attend. When she moved out, she stopped going."

"Is that when you met her?"

"Yes, when we worked for families." Seeing my befuddlement, she said, "You knew, didn't you, that she worked for a family in Minneapolis? As a live-in?"

"I didn't know anything."

"She worked for a well-to-do Jewish family. Lovely people. Then she met some Finns who took her to Finn Hall, and that's where we met." Again she saw my vacant look. "The Brotherhood?" she said.

"No. But it's okay, go ahead."

"It was a social gathering spot for Finns. Your mother liked the stage plays and the suppers and speeches. We met, in fact, at a play. We hit it off and started going to Finn Hall dances. That's where we met Esko and Patrik. My, we had fun, the four of us! We were Temperance . . . *sometimes*." Kaisa chuckled with heavy meaning.

I felt pulled underwater. I had wanted information, and here it was. But were these people really my parents? These alcohol-drinkers? These partygoers? These *non-church, good-time, dance-hall* people?

"Excuse me!" I dashed to the bathroom and threw water on my face. I felt faint, and I was trying not to vomit. . . . Oh. And diarrhea! I made it to the toilet in time. As I washed my hands, I said to the mirror, See? You get sick over *nothing*. It's time you grew up. It's time for a new approach.

Back in the front room, when Kaisa asked me if I was okay, I practiced my new approach. "When I hear too much that's new, I get an upset stomach." My new approach was honesty.

"I'm sorry," she said. "Maybe I shouldn't have . . . ?"

"No! No, I'm glad you told me." A burst of freedom lifted me, almost physically. It went away quickly but left me gloating and toying with ideas. Ideas like growing up, making my own way, thinking my own thoughts—revolutionary ideas.

Kaisa said, "It strikes me, you *are* like your mother. She took everything in, like you do, sometimes too much for her own good. We told her she was too sensitive."

"Really?" I was nervous again. "Marcie says I'm too sensitive."

Her look was one of indulgence. "It was what gave Sofia the most problems. It was her blessing and her curse. She was a purist." I knew what the word meant, but in this case I wasn't sure if being a purist was good or bad.

Kaisa added, "She could get immobilized over details."

"That happens to me, too. Was she thin-skinned? I mean, did she get her feelings hurt all the time?"

"Yes. She did." Kaisa gave me a teaching look. "She was too literal. She got hurt too easily. She even got hurt on behalf of others. And when others didn't see things the same way she did, she couldn't understand. She never learned to tone down her judgment. If a friend or relative acted rude, instead of just noticing, she got *incensed*. She got upset about other people's problems, and they weren't really her responsibility."

This was hitting too close to home. "I know," I said. "Same with me."

"We kidded her. She was a good sport, she took it."

I too was being kidded, I was being given advice. But I hated advice! For a few seconds I couldn't think of anything to say. Finally I said, "Did she like books?"

"Books?" Kaisa appeared to run a series of pictures through her mind. "She liked ideas, but I don't recall a particular passion for books. Your father, now. *He* was the bookworm. We used to say he read the dictionary for fun."

My father, a bookworm! Like me. "Did he like puns?"

She raised her eyebrows. "Why, yes. I'd forgotten! We tormented him about that! Puns. An insult for such a bright man. How on earth did you know?"

I kicked off my flats and sat on my feet. "Just a guess. What else did he like?"

"You tickle me." She did seem tickled, or *crackled*. When she smiled, her normally elegant face buckled across its width. "You're intense the way they both were. Your mother's saving grace, her most charming trait, was her humor. She and your father loved to laugh. He was a funny man. And he was a poet, and a builder. He was good at about anything he tried."

"A poet? . . . He wrote poems?"

"No, not as far as I know. Some poets live their poetry."

I could hear Marcie coming downstairs. I had time for one more question. "What was *his* biggest problem?"

Kaisa didn't have to think about it. "He was stubborn. Most of the time he was a lamb, but dare to cross him, and you had a man who wouldn't talk to you but would sit there all day, not talking."

Bingo! I'd inherited traits from them both—oversensitivity from her, stubbornness from him, her color of hair and his love of words. And I was intense, like the two of them. I had learned all of this in one afternoon, and all it had cost me was a little nausea. I felt defined. Not invisible.

This time the freedom-gust did lift me, right up onto my feet. I told Marcie, "Sit down, sweetie pie. I'm serving!" and I sashayed into the kitchen to get the lemonade.

* * *

I found Liisa on her bed, embroidering under the clamp-lamp attached to her headboard. I sat on the vanity bench and said, for starters, "Guess what I found out? About . . . about our parents." I felt silly, not knowing how to refer to my own parents. I hadn't known them in person, so I'd never called them "Mom and Dad" to their faces, but "our mother and father" or "Sofia and Patrik" seemed too formal. They hadn't intended to die. They hadn't wished any awkwardnesses on us. But there were awkwardnesses, and, irrationally, I blamed them on my parents.

I waited for Liisa to look up. "I give," she said. She set aside the embroidery hoop. "What?"

"I found out they danced, and drank, and they didn't go to church!"

62

"I knew that."

"How? And how come I'm always the last one to know anything?"

Unruffled, Liisa said, "It was long time ago, back when I worked for Mrs. Hepponen. She told me about the Finn Hall dances and said our folks used to go."

"Didn't that bother you?"

Her eyes met mine, periwinkle purple, no concern showing. "No. Why?"

I changed my position on the bed, frustrated that we never got worked up over the same things. But, then, Liisa never got worked up over much of anything. I said, "Doesn't it get you mixed up, thinking about them? I mean, they're gone, we can't ever know them, they were so different from us . . ." I floated down a solitary river, going nowhere.

She said, "What bothers me is people thinking they *have* something on us, just because they knew our parents. Like that Mrs. Hepponen. She was gossipy."

"Liisa? . . . How come we never talk about our parents?"

"It's no use. Like you said, they're gone. We can't change a thing."

She picked up her embroidery, and that was the end of that talk. Even if she and I lived in the same house and slept in the same room, our lives didn't intersect much at all.

* * *

But we did have one thing in common, even if we hadn't yet admitted it—a screaming need to be hugged. I wanted to be held by a boy for *hours* and *hours*. Almost any boy would do. But twelve was too young to start dating. I needed to talk to Marcie. If anyone would understand, she would.

The first chance I got was the next Friday. I was staying overnight at her house, and we were belly-down on her bed, discussing schools and classes, hers and mine. I said, "Marcie? What do you think it's like to kiss a boy?"

She took hold of my face and kissed me on the mouth. A big smacker.

I yelled, "Ick!" and jumped up and hotfooted on the bed, dragging my pajama sleeve across my face. "What'd you do that for?" I batted at my lips and made spittoon sounds. "*Hawk! . . . Crrhht! . . . Pttew!*"

Marcie wasted her dimples on me. "It's no big thing. My mom kisses me all the time. My dad? *Never.* He's a Halonen, that's why."

She sat up to brush her hair. "Kiss-kiss!" she said, kissing the air, threatening to come after me again.

"You're crazy, you know that?" I took giant steps off the bed, took a Kleenex from a box on her desk and rubbed my mouth with it.

Marcie said, "*I'm* crazy? What about you? You're in this big hurry. Boys, boys, boys!" Now she was doing side bends in front of the long mirror.

"Well, *you* like boys." I felt like futzing at her. Whinging and ragging at her! I didn't want to be left alone in this. I sat on the bench and started to undo my braids.

"Ya but there's no hurry," she said. "We have all the time in the world."

I scoff-coughed. "'*All the time in the world.*' You sound like an old fogy."

She stuck out her tongue and waved it around. "You'll just have to wait for all those boys and their sloppy kisses. They like to get all *gooshy.*"

I said, "Ugh!" But, for form's sake, I finished my original thought. "But you said once that you wanted to start dating."

"Ya but I'm being the Voice of Reason." She was brushing her hair and also doing deep knee bends.

"*Ya* but, *ya* but! . . . Is that like rubbing your stomach and patting your head at the same time?"

"Hundred strokes, hundred bends. Might 's well do 'em at the same time."

When the braids were unwound, I was left with heavy zigzags. I combed them with my fingers, stood up and tossed my head from left to right and back again, enjoying the bigness of my hair. Then I stood stationary and rode out the dizziness. This kind of dizziness I *liked.* It was expected, self-induced. It was the unexpected kind I didn't like. I went to the vanity mirror and inspected my face for pimples. "Where do you want to go in the whole world?"

"New York. Paris. Wyoming. I want to see buffalo. The Wild West."

"You *are* the Wild West."

"Fun-ny."

I asked her if she planned to go to college. She said sure. I said my family couldn't afford it. Marcie had an answer for that. Marcie had an answer for everything. "You can pay your own way. You can work, borrow money, get scholarships and grants."

"How come you know so much?"

"I've been studying up." She drew a comb through her brush and rolled the dead hairs into a fuzz-ball. With a flourish she threw it into the wastebasket, calling, "Two points!" On the dresser top she lined up her matching brush and comb, gifts from her grandmother on the other side—tortoiseshell and porcelain, prettier than the brushes or combs at my house. Inky's family was high-tone. Inky was as plain as a ping-pong ball, but she was used to the nicer things. So was Marcie.

Marcie went to her closet and took out a big red towel. I got on the bed and curled into an S, flumped the pillow into shape, brought the bedspread over my back and tugged it into a cocoon. "Don't you worry about *anything*?"

Her laugh came from behind the towel. Bent in half, she had the towel pulled tightly behind her neck and was tugging the ends toward the floor. She swung upright and spiraled the towel at the forehead, tucking it into a turban that was a foot high and top-heavy. Raising her arms to shoulder height, she paraded for her audience of one, singing, "Chi-*qui*-ta Ba-*na*-na!" She managed to waggle her hips while keeping her head still. "Carmen Miranda! All I need is fruit. We're going to do facials." She slithered to the stairs and started down, balancing her head load. "Make a turban. I'll be back in a sec."

I got up and found a towel and wrapped it around my head. It wasn't as tight as Marcie's, but it would have to do. She returned with uncooked oatmeal in a cup. We added hot water and stirred, and in a minute we had oatmeal on our faces, a lumpy, revolting porridge, like school paste after a prank. We sat on the bench and studied ourselves in the mirror, the bumpy white masks, the dark circles where our eyes used to be. I made a ghoul's face. "Think the boys would like us now?"

"You and the *boys*. For*get* the boys!" Marcie picked up her school newspaper and fanned her face. "This has to dry, then it gets hard. You can't smile or it cracks."

"Oh, good. Then we'll *really* be cute." I touched my chin. "It feels goopy. Marcie? Don't you wonder about things? Like about praying and everything?"

"Nope! Neither should you."

"But what about people in the jungle? How do they get to heaven if they never hear about Jesus?" I picked at my face and got sticky crumbs on my fingers.

"My eyelashes weigh a pound each," Marcie said, not exactly on-topic. "Too much oatmeal. I've said it before, and I'll say it again. You worry too much . . . Hey, *I* know! We need a picture. I'll get my mom to take one. C'm 'ere!"

I scooted over on the bench. She globbed her cheek onto mine and we mugged for the mirror—dreary faces, happy faces, shock and fright. She laughed. "Cousin Kik and Cousin Marcie! Stuck together forever!"

That was Marcie. She whizzed along on the surface of life, never sinking to my depths or ever really falling for my moods.

* * *

We were in Inky's kitchen, and Inky was saying, "*Liisa's* now, they're high and light, no cave-ins in the middle." She meant Liisa's cakes. Behind her back, I mutely, facetiously, mouthed to Marcie, Cave-ins? Who cares? Inky said, "It's time someone taught you to bake. Emma doesn't have the patience."

Inky meant me. Someone should teach *me* to bake. Finnish women were bakers, and I was doomed to become one. If you were a Finnish girl, you grew up and married a Finn, and you kept baked goods handy at all times because company could drop by any moment. I *had* to learn to bake. Marcie and Liisa already knew how. Marcie had learned to bake with Inky, Liisa with the Girl Scouts. All I ever did in the kitchen was massage yellow dye into the oleo or wash dishes. If I hung around too long, Mummo scatted me out, probably to avoid my questions. I had a feeling she arranged her life to avoid my questions. At any rate, I knew nothing about fixing food, and I wasn't sure I wanted to.

But Inky had her mind made up. I would bake with her that very day. She was a champion baker. She made the Finnish standbys, *riisi pirraka* (Karelian rice cakes), *pulla* (cardamom sweetbread), *hiivaleipä* (Finnish loaf bread), *"flatti" leipä* (flat bread), but she also borrowed from other cultures. She made bakery-quality Lady Fingers, baklava, Napoleons, apple strudel, springerle, and almond spritz. She was an artist, no getting around it, and she was stooping to work with me, a novice. I decided to pay attention.

"We'll make a double batch," she said, "so each of us can have a good-sized hunk of dough." She handed out clean white dishtowels. We put them on our heads in a *huivi* style, clothes-pinned behind the neck. We tied on aprons. "Now go wash your hands," Inky told us. "Always wash up if you touch anything but food or equipment."

While we washed up, Inky went to the pantry and got out two stainless steel bowls measuring two feet in diameter, plus wooden spoons, yeast, flour, salt, butter, sugar. We put warm water and sugar in the steel bowls and stirred in the yeast, breathing the sporey fumes, on our way to being Finnish women.

I found out I was a messy baker—too carefree with the flour. My section of the floor was white, and so was I. Marcie didn't have a smudge on her. Neither did Inky.

"Kik?" Inky said. "How much do you know about your mother?"

That caught me off-guard. All of my life, people had avoided talking about my parents. Yet here, for the second time in two weeks, someone was talking about my mother! I looked at Marcie. She gave me a shallow nod. I said, "Not much."

Inky had a homely face to begin with—her teeth and eyes were too big, her chin hardly present at all—and when she screwed up her lips, the way she did just then, you might think she was disgusted. But on Inky it was a look of love. She said, "*She* did that, too, when she baked; she got it all over the place."

Too eagerly, I said, "She did? Did you know her?" Then I berated myself. *Of course* she knew her. Dumb question. Agreeing, Marcie spun her eyes at me.

Inky said expansively, "*Sure* I knew her! Oh, she was *something* all right, a real fashionable lady. She made me feel skittery sometimes, but that's okay. . . . Here, let me show you." With measured strokes, she pressed the heels of her hands on her round of dough, rotated it a quarter-turn, folded the far part toward her, pressed, rotated the ball, and repeated the process. Her dough was a silky, rounded mound.

I tried to do the same procedure—press, rotate, fold, press—but my lump stayed soggy and unincorporated. Tags of dry dough flapped around the lump as I kneaded, and my fingers stuck together. I stopped and rubbed my hands together fast, scattering scabs of flour. "How did she make you feel . . . skittery?"

Inky seemed unprepared to explain. She widened and constricted her eyes as if weighing the wisdom of saying more. Snatching a breath in the way of Finnish women, she pronounced two syllables of an inward sigh. "Yah!-*hah*! Oh, sometimes she seemed dreamy-like, like she was thinking so hard she was someplace else altogether."

"Was she nice?" Another dumb question! I didn't know how to say it: *Tell me everything about her.*

"She was the nicest lady ever was," Inky said. "She gave me a scarf one time that was made out of silk, a bluish color, but it had green in there too, real pretty. Her family came from St. Cloud. They had a Finnish language newspaper . . . at least I think they did?" She looked my way, but I wasn't any help. I didn't know anything about any newspaper. Besides, I felt kind of sick.

"Your Uncle Aarnie now, he's not much of a talker. I don't suppose he says much about their side?" I shook my head no. She said, "Such is life." This was one of Inky's favorite sayings. I thought it was ingenious in that it covered any contingency. Marcie plumped her loaves into pans and placed them on the warming shelf, laid a towel over them, and with a good-luck wave she fled, leaving me with Inky and the past.

My anxiety grew. I never knew how to act when I was alone with a grownup. Besides, Inky was playing with a taboo, talking so freely about my mother. I rubbed an itch on my forehead with the heel of my hand. Citing Inky's rule, I said, "I have to wash up." At the sink, I lied to myself: *I can take it, whatever it is, the whole works.* Nauseated and lightheaded, I went back to the table and kneaded some more.

Inky hardly missed a meter. "Aarnie saved her life once. Did you know that?"

"No."

"She and Aarnie were living on a farm. . . . That's funny . . ." Inky scowled. "I thought they grew up in a city. St. Cloud?" Again she looked to me for an answer. But I only shrugged. "Anyway, they were walking home from quite a ways away, and a blizzard came up, a regular whiteout. The snow was deep, and the wind was strong and cold, and Sofia wanted to stop and sleep in a snow bank. It looked so soft! She cried and begged Aarnie to let her stop and rest, she was so *sleepy* all of a sudden. But he wouldn't let her. He dragged her and pinched her until they got home. If he'd a let her stop, she would've *died.* He knew where the house was because their mother put a lamp in the window. He followed the light home. He saved your mother."

I had listened standing stock still. "Aarnie saved her," I said. I loved this story.

Inky drew her lips over her teeth for a moment. "It was *sisu,* that's what." Seeing the question on my face, she explained. "Guts. Backbone. It's what old-timer Finns say they have. They say they have *sisu* and can outlast anyone. Aarnie had *sisu,* and he saved your mother."

"*See*-soo," I said, practicing.

"Come to think of it, I did hear one more thing. Aarnie and your mother were the only children that lived, the rest died as babies. . . . Let's see, they must have lived on a farm 'cause this happened on a farm too. . . . *Anyway!* They walked to school from the farm and their mother would stand at the door and see them off. She was worried the *wolves* might get them. And one day they *did* see wolves—*two* of them! They were watching the kids from the top of the hill. But the kids kept right on walking to school."

"*Wolves,*" I said. "She was worried about wolves. My Grandmother Olson." I was testing the words "wolves" and "Grandmother Olson." Riches that I had.

"Well, getting back to your folks. Keep kneading, that's a girl. Of course, I knew more about your father, him being Harald's brother and all.

69

They used to be real close. Harald worshipped Patrik. Your father and your granddad, now, they didn't get along so good. Your father left the farm—you knew that? He sent money home, and he wrote letters. *Voi, voi!* Harald used to wait and wait for those letters."

She paused and did nothing for a while, possibly imitating Harald's waiting. Reviving, she said, "Harald told me Patrik was a real good letter-writer for a man. It broke his heart when Patrik never came back. He never got to see him after that."

Thumping my dough, I steamed under my breath: I *never* got to see him! That broke *my* heart, if anyone wants to know. I hardly dared to ask it. "Did Harald keep his letters?"

"No no no," Inky said carelessly, as if keeping them would have been the dumbest thing in the world. "They're *long* gone."

"Oh." I was desolate.

"Harald said Patrik shoulda been a teacher, he was that good with book learning. Take Harald now? He's more one to work with his hands . . . well, that, and preaching." Inky saw the way I was smashing my dough. "Here, let me," she offered.

She came around the table to help me. "Go easy. You don't want to kill the poor thing." I wished she would give me a hug, but she went back over to her side.

"We're almost done here," Inky said. She taught me how to cut my dough into loaf-sized chunks (a light sawing with a sharp knife), how to form a loaf (fold the chunk toward the outside, pinch seams along the bottom and ends), how to ease the loaves into buttered bread pans and set them to rise under clean white dishtowels.

But the best information she gave me was information about my parents. What Inky told me that day, plus what Kaisa had told me the week before, added up to what I knew about my parents when I was twelve.

Five

Trapped in the Sauna

I t was a Saturday night—in other words, sauna night—and Liisa and I and four Pesonen girls were in the Pesonens' sauna, up on the top benches where the fog was the hottest, because our own sauna was on the fritz. (Aarnie had built a sauna in the basement when he moved to Mahoning, and now he needed to fix it, something about plumbing.) Like most people in the second branch of the Finn church, the Pesonens had a big family, thirteen kids, and each one of the kids had a name starting with an S. At the moment, Susannah, Sanna, Starr, and Sylvia were with us in the sauna, four examples of the straw-haired sameness of the Pesonens, a hearty, broad-faced clan. Susannah was busy vaunting unsavory news. She was eleven and had a hankering for mischief.

"I'm telling you!" she told Liisa and me. "He was drunker 'n' a skunk! And *driving!* Lucky thing the cops didn't catch him! My folks got *real* mad. He almost got the belt. But like my dad says, boys will be boys. Sten has to clean stalls by himself! For a whole *month!*"

I couldn't picture Sten in this kind of trouble. The Pesonens' church had more prohibitions than ours did, and, in both, alcohol was high on the list.

71

"Where did he get the beer?" Liisa asked. "Not that I want any. I just wondered how he got his hands on it at sixteen."

Sanna tossed off her answer. "Oh, all the boys can get it." Sanna was eight and cagey for her age.

I said, "*Church* boys?"

Starr, who was Sten's twin, the milder half of the twinship, spoke up. "They get their kicks in high school, and the folks look the other way. For boys, they look the other way, not for girls. Boys get away with more. But then they come back and get married, and it's out of their systems."

I gave Starr a good long stare. Boys got special treatment, but it didn't seem to bother her. I said, "Doesn't it ever backfire? Say, a boy starts drinking and can't stop?"

Her eyes clouded over, as though the possibility had never occurred to her.

Sylvia said, "I know someone like that! Helmer Salonen." Like the two younger girls, Sylvia, who was fourteen, liked to pass on gossip, but she was softhearted about it. "He comes to church sometimes. He's pitiful, not ever really sober. He doesn't work but he gets a pension from the mine. Otherwise, I don't know what he'd live on. He'd have to be a beggar."

"His wife left him," Sylvia explained to Liisa and me. "No divorce, but a long separation, twenty-five years. . . . His wife's in Detroit with the kids."

There was a gap in the flow of talk. Liisa posed the obvious question. "But if they were separated all those years, and she lived in Detroit, how did they keep having kids?"

Maneuvering in difficult waters, Starr said, "He'd go up there every once in a while. They tried to fix the marriage. They had time to . . ."

". . . do the bed thing!" Sanna said, causing sniggers from Susannah and a riffle among the sisters. Starr shushed them.

Susannah reasserted herself as the queen of gossip. "I know someone who's married but seeing someone else on the side!"

"Let's not talk about that," said Sylvia. "Remember that cute guy at Karen's wedding? From Texas? He got a job in Chisholm, and he's moving up here!"

Suddenly I was a spectator, not a participant. I had to get out of there.

I emptied my bucket over myself and set it bottom-up on the bench, climbed down the risers and opened the door to the dressing room. It was forty degrees cooler in there. Wrapped in a towel, I wiped the steam from a tiny wall mirror and peered at my eyes. There was something I needed to think about, but I didn't know *what*.

I got dressed and went to the house. The lean-to was crammed with industrious boots and jackets of all sizes, ready for endless, messy, strong-back jobs in the field and barn. In the kitchen, aromas clashed, coffee versus the pine cleaner, everything scrubbed for sauna night, the same as for sauna night for eons backward and forever forward. I could hardly get out of there fast enough.

Outside, I slumped against the lean-to door, shutting the inside in. I gulped solitude. A dog barked on another farm. The yard was dark, no stars. My entire definition was inside this house—the group assumptions, the weight of tradition from two continents. Why, then, was I so glad to be *outside*?

*　*　*

January brought frigid, leaden days and a sky so low it pushed you down. Even so, I dawdled on my way home from school. I dared fate by walking on mountain ranges made by the snowplow, crusty peaks and dirty chunks of ice, trying not to plunge through. But of course I did plunge. As I pulled free, my knee socks stayed down around my ankles and my boots came up packed with snow. My thighs stung fire-hot with chapping, but I didn't care. I was glad to be alone. Liisa would get home first, and by the time I arrived she'd already be crocheting something or roasting a chunk of meat or cramming for a Girl Scout badge. I'd do my chores and schoolwork and eat supper, then skate on the backyard rink, again, *alone*. (The rink was Aarnie's doing. He had flooded the vegetable garden and let it flash-freeze, and then rigged a string of lights across it.) To me, skating was a form of romance, a teen-age fantasy. It turned out that romance and fantasy would make this January different from the rest.

Eight months earlier, Mummo's Wisconsin godchild, Margaret Aho, had met a Hibbing miner named Seppo Huovinen at spring services and had fallen in love. The marriage was to take place this January in Hibbing. Two days before the ceremony, Margaret brought the wedding party to our house for coffee. The groom's best man was a gray-eyed college man named Stuart— the dreamiest thing I'd ever laid eyes on. All he did was come in and stamp the snow from his boots, and *I was in love.* He was magnificent. He took over the house, seeming apologetic for the impact he was making. His camel over-coat was so roomy and broad-shouldered, I figured it was big enough for *me* inside there, too. Stooping to take off his boots, he winked at me and smiled. I went weak. I dropped into a stuffed chair, knocked *plumb* over by the promise of that smile.

For two days I was miserable and thrilled. I made up a love story. I pretended—no, I *believed*—that Stuart secretly loved me, that he'd choose the right time to tell others. I'd wait. He needed me to save him from the twitter-ing girls who would flock to him all his life. I memorized his every move. I never spoke to him. He never spoke to me.

I didn't know that Stuart was a forerunner of a new life, that he would go to the wedding with his fiancée and leave with no good-byes, or that in a few years I'd step out of my known existence and find, behind similar gray eyes and magic countenance, a tall handsome someone who would *stay.*

Six

Confirmed

The attic was as hot as a summer sauna, so we did our poses in our underwear. Mrs. Koski had set a mirror against the rafters for just that purpose, to satisfy the vanity in visiting girls. Marcie was twisting at the waist, Betty Grable style, one hand behind her head, the other on her hip, when she saw my arms and dropped her own. "You're not supposed to shave your *whole arms*," she groaned, "just *under* your arms."

"Oh." I stroked a forearm. "But they feel nice."

"They won't feel so nice when the whiskers come in!" Now she focused on my chest. "I don't believe it. You went and put makeup on your peel. . . . Didn't you?"

"Guess I should wash it off?"

"I guess *so*! I don't know what gets into you sometimes." Opening a dress box, she unfolded rafts of tissue paper and took out a fluff of white. She laid it on the bed, first slipping a hand beneath it and petting the bedspread as if vetting "chenille, pale-green" as a suitable backdrop. She tried prodding it into the shape of a girl, but the organza was so floaty it barely obeyed. When I got back she was still at it, picking at the ruffled cap sleeves, which didn't need much help. They sprang up like baby angel wings from the shoulders of the dress.

"You kill me," I said. "Marcie the tomboy wearing this froth? Just kidding. You'll look great. How come you know so much?" My underarms were spritzing cloves: Tussy Cream Deodorant melting in the heat. "Like what to wear, what to say?"

She made a one-syllable dismissive sound. "*Mhgh.* Just common sense."

"Not to *me*, it's not," I said. "You always do the right thing, I always mess up."

"You don't *always*, and I don't *always*. Nobody *always* does anything. I make plenty-mistakes. I just don't worry like you do."

"I know." I said this sadly, playing for sympathy. "I try too hard, and I *miss*, and then I go around feeling dumb and make more mistakes because I feel dumb . . ."

"So what? Re-*lax*, you're *fine*! Do we take our purses?" Marcie knew exactly what to do with her purse, but by asking me she was saying things were back to normal. My social gaffes were forgiven, my shaved arms forgotten. It was one of Marcie's best gifts, this impulse to save others from themselves, mostly me from me.

A whoosh of well-being came over me, and I wriggled for the fun of it. I went to the closet, edged my dress off its hanger and held it in front of me. "Marcie? Don't you ever feel different? I mean from Finns?"

"Why do you keep asking me that? You know it doesn't matter."

"But Finns are so proud," I persisted. "Proud of what?"

"How should I know? I'm not a Finn. Now hurry!"

I put on my dress and buttoned it down the front. It was white, too, naturally, but polished cotton and simple. I thought it suited me exactly. Lately I'd grown taller and slimmer, and my hips had sort of *settled*. (Marcie's had, too, I'd noticed. A sign of womanhood, I guessed.) New dimensions had shown up here and there, and the dress made the most of the ins and outs. But my face was still plump. I went to the mirror and made sunken cheeks. "You think he'll be there?" I asked.

Marcie laughed, a raucous chortle. "He'll be there. He wants to see me, doesn't he?" Her crinoline sat on the floor like an enormous upside-down white peony. Marcie stepped into it and fastened the waist snap. The crinoline stuck straight out, trembling slightly. She threw the dress over her head and her dimples disappeared. She thrashed her arms and her dimples reappeared. The crinoline was left quaking after all that action. Marcie turned pointedly away from me. I zipped her up.

"But, kid, listen," I went on. "What if he left with that other bunch?"

"He likes me. He'll be there." She reached behind her back and tied her sash into a bow. "Besides, he couldn't very well *not* show up, could he? His *father*?" She checked the bow in the mirror. "Now *hurry*."

I roused myself and started to braid my hair, watching Marcie at the same time. It was one of my favorite pastimes, watching Marcie. She didn't seem to mind. She didn't realize how different she was, how un-Finnish with that mannish face of hers. And that hair. Marcie flounced even if you ignored her hair, but her hair was *alive*, a reddish haze that moved in response to her moods, so powerful it made me swoon. Mine was thick and long too, but dishwater blonde, and straight. Starting at temple height, I tied off braids until I had braids springing up in a circle around my head. "How about if I go like this?" I said. "I'll go as a . . ."

"I know, I know, a switch board." She intoned the words as if bored to tears, but her face approximated amusement. I wove my braids into a crown and pinned them with hairpins. Then I took three daisies from a vase on the dresser, shook them dry, and jabbed them into a knob of hair over my left ear.

I aimed the ear at Marcie. "You like?"

"Nice. Here. Chew." She handed me a stick of gum, keeping one for herself. We undid the silver papers and folded the sticks into our mouths, chewed ten times, spit the wads into the wastebasket, and exhaled the scent of Beeman's into the room. She said, "No more icky breath."

"No more knocking people over dead. Man oh man, it's hot! What about skating? Don't we have to stay at the church, you know, after?" I dropped to my knees and put a hand under the bed and drew out a shoe box. Inside were my new white flats.

"Don't worry," she said. "Everyone takes pictures, and then we'll eat. We'll have time to change. Now come *on!*"

I slipped on the footies I had stored in the box, skimpy nylon shells that covered the toes and heels and let my feet slide nicely into the flats. Shoes on, I stood up. I held out one foot, rotating it. Marcie's shoes and mine were alike except for leather bows on the toes of mine.

I said, "I should've picked the plain ones. Mine are kind of old-lady."

Marcie hunched at me, eyes googled, her brows high. "They're *fine*. Now *hurry!*"

"Got your gloves?" I asked, waving mine. She waved hers. We'd chosen the same white cotton gloves with inside-out seams. On the hand, this type of glove hardly got started before it stopped—at the wrist joint, where a big fake pearl buttoned into a cloth loop. Marcie picked up her purse, a white box with a suitcase grip, and sent me out the door, then flattened herself against the door frame to let me back in. I'd forgotten my own box purse. The church was just next door, around a fence, up a driveway, but we had wasted time posing, and we were late. Pulling on our gloves, we ran.

Inside the church, people stood in groups or sat leaning over pews, catching up on visiting. I could see Mummo, Aarnie, Liisa, Inky. Harald would not be there. He was at home, recuperating from surgery. For years Marcie and I had assumed he would confirm us. In other words, he'd teach our class for two weeks and give us our first Communion. But four days before our class was to start, Harald went to the hospital in pain and stayed for an appendectomy. On short notice, Ray Tiskanen, a California minister we had never met, agreed to substitute. On Harald's insistence, Marcie and I had come to Minneapolis for confirmation school.

For two weeks we studied the English version of *Dr. Martin Luther's Small Catechism and K.G. Leinberg's Bible History.* Each student had a copy, a small tan book with a navy binding. I was curious: Did our church teach the same catechism as other Lutherans, even the ones who play organs in church? The publication page said the book had been translated from the Finnish edition of Olaus Swebelius, Archbishop of Uppsala, Sweden, published by the Rauha (Peace) Publishing Association in Calumet, Michigan, printed and bound by the Finnish Lutheran Book Concern in Hancock, Michigan. The answer was yes. This was a regular, standard Lutheran catechism.

Working from the book, we memorized the Ten Commandments, the Creed, the Lord's Prayer, and explanations for each. We read stories from the Old and New Testaments. We studied the Sacrament of Holy Baptism, the Sacrament of the Altar (or Communion, the Lord's Supper), Confession, and the Table of Duties for ministers, parents, wives, husbands, children.

Finally, answers to my questions! I even found a section for (of all things) *Family Prayers*. There were Family Prayers for morning, evening, before eating, after eating. They'd been in the Catechism all the while!

Bunched up at the altar, we exchanged pretend-scared faces, thirteen thirteen-year olds, girls in white dresses, boys in white shirts and dark slacks. Ray Tiskanen, old enough to be our father but confusingly handsome, motioned the class into position, two lines to his left, facing the audience. We would recite together what we had memorized. I worried that my mind would go blank when the time came.

As soon as we started, my worry went away. I felt liberated, but *cocooned*. Alone with God and well-contented.

We quoted the First Commandment: "I am the Lord thy God. Thou shalt have no other gods before Me."

Ray Tiskanen asked us, "What is meant by this?"

We answered, "We should fear, love and trust in God above all things."

We went through the other nine rules for a good life, from not taking the Lord's name in vain to not coveting what is our neighbor's. I was bowled over by the Ten Commandments, as if hearing them for the first time. I heard the iron-strength in them.

We recited the Creed, beginning with Article One: "I believe in God the Father almighty, Maker of heaven and earth."

Ray Tiskanen asked us, "What is meant by this?"

We answered, "I believe that God has made me and all other creatures, that He has given and still preserves to me my body and soul, eyes, ears, and all my members, my reason, and all my senses, and that He daily provides me with food and clothing, home and house, family, land, cattle and all that I need for this body and life, protects me and guards me, and keeps me from all evil. All of which He does without any merit or worthiness in me, but out of fatherly, divine goodness and mercy. For all of which I am duty bound to thank, praise, serve and obey Him. This is most certainly true."

We recited the other two articles and Ray Tiskanen asked us, after each article, "What is meant by this?" We gave the formal responses.

When we finished, we knelt at the altar to receive Communion. Ray Tiskanen stood before us and read, "Our Lord Jesus Christ, in the night in which He was betrayed, took bread, and when He had given thanks, He brake it and gave it to His disciples, saying, 'Take, eat; this is My body, which is given for you; this do, in remembrance of Me.'" He moved down the line, serving us nuggets of bread, having earlier told us we should eat them right then.

"After the same manner also He took the cup, and when He had given thanks, He gave it to His disciples saying, 'Drink ye all of it; This cup is the New Testament in My blood, which is shed for you, and for many, for the remission of sins. This do, as oft as ye drink it, in remembrance of Me.'" Again, he moved down the line. Each of us sipped wine from a common cup.

God's presence shone all around. Throughout Communion, I cried quietly, full of joy, reassured. *Confirmed.*

* * *

For the first time in our lives, Marcie and I planned to stay up all night. When supper was over, the newly confirmed and a dozen older kids got into cars and careened through Minneapolis, converging at the Cold Spot Ice Rink in a questionable part of town. We entered a jam-packed building, and in the din of a faulty loudspeaker, a grating pipe organ, and the accelerating juices of a few hundred teen-agers, we shouldered our way to the rental counter and shouted shoe sizes to a cheerless man who eventually, grudgingly, handed over our skates.

Marcie and I pulled on our figure skates, hooked them, tied them, then clumped down the wooden ramp and tiptoed onto the rink on our rickrack toe points. On ice we were a match for each other. We zipped in and out of the stream of skaters, loving it all, the *shoosh* of blades, the jouncy music, the ice chips in the face. We were passing the crowd around to the right when we almost hit a skater creeping along the edge. It was Marcie's heartthrob, Adam Tiskanen.

We circled back and came to a neat stop beside him, spraying frost. Recognizing us, he made a glum face and hung one arm over the balustrade to steady himself. He was definitely cute. He had a rugged, tanned face, dark brown eyes in sunken sockets, and ash blond hair that looked sun-bleached. He said, "You guys call this fun?"

Marcie was buoyant just from being close to him. "Guess you don't have much ice in Berkeley?" She grinned at him in a way that seemed intimate.

"What's there to *like* about this? It's *freezing* in here! And you can't hear yourself *think*." Adam was shouting above the racket. "And you have to wear these stupid . . . ?" He grimaced at his skates, which were about two sizes too big. His ankles flopped inward toward the ice. At the rental desk, men and boys were issued hockey skates, so Adam's skates had tall bulky blades with no jagged toes to help him stand straight.

Marcie said, "We'll help. Kik, you get the other side." I caught him under his left arm, Marcie took his right. He wasn't much taller than we were but was four years older and muscular, and we had trouble keeping him on his feet. We started off, Marcie and I taking long, strong strokes, more or less carrying Adam, Adam scrabbling at the ice with little pecks, muttering, "I hate this, come on, you guys, let's stop, my feet hurt, I *quit*!"

Marcie said, "You're doing fine. We'll do the loop once and then we'll stop."

We were as relieved as he was when we finished the loop. We tumbled him up the ramp and stood by as he undid his skates, put on his shoes, and got to his feet. "Ah, dry land," he said, smiling at Marcie. "That's enough skating for the rest of my life."

"I thought you were rather fetching out there," she said. Her eyes added: And wonderful, and handsome, and mine.

He gave her some thought. "I'll be over there with Hank and those guys, playing pinball. Come on over when you're done." His invitation politely included me, but it was intended for Marcie. Leave it to Marcie to find a guy this cute. I had seen his effect on people. Men took him seriously. Boys followed him around. Girls and women took double takes at him—even *Mummo*. She'd met him for the first time that day and had brightened at the sight of him, seemed ready to say something. The moment passed, and Mummo became Mummo again. But she had proven that Adam was an eyeful.

Marcie and I made a few more trips around the ice, but her heart wasn't in it. The more we skated, the better pinball sounded. After she left, the main lights went out, and rainbows swept the rink. The music slowed way down, and the announcer called out, "Pairs." A lanky, razor-burned boy who reeked of Old Spice asked me to skate. I said okay. We arranged ourselves side by side, he to my left, his right arm behind me, my right hand covering his at my waist, his left hand holding mine out in the atmosphere. Away we went, skating to "Let Me Call You Sweetheart." He was a good skater. We moved together in marvelous rhythm. *Dangerous* rhythm! So close to dancing! And so soon after confirmation! But I *loved* to dance—by myself in my room to music on the radio, or here with this boy to music on the pipe organ. We skated to "It Might as Well Be Spring" and "The Trolley Song." I was having a grand time. The Pairs mood was twinkly and dreamlike, full of maybes and what-ifs. Then, suddenly, the lights slammed back on. The organ picked up speed and made itself burp, skip, and exclaim, almost singing the words: "Yes, We Have No Bananas!" The announcer bawled, "*Ev'rybody* skate!" Little kids came hollering in from the sidelines, elbows flying, and the dreamy mood and the lanky boy evaporated in a raucous All-Skate.

It was after midnight when we got to Cork Lake. The Hevonens' cabin sat up from the shore on a lawn dotted with plum trees and fallen plums. Commencing with the business at hand, we ate pizza and hot dogs, had plum fights, swam and arm-wrestled, played ping-pong, badminton, football, sang, "There's a Hole at the Bottom of the Sea," and started over—pizza, swimming, and so on. We planned to keep at it until dawn.

I woke up on the front lawn in my bathing suit, lying on a big beach towel with a second towel draped over me. Beside me, a middle-aged man in black slacks and a white dressy shirt was doing sit-ups. He too had a towel under him. I bolted to my feet. My nose weighed five pounds, and my head felt mushy. The man was counting out loud. "Eighteen. Well, there you are! I thought you'd wake up soon. Nineteen."

I told him my name and asked him who he was. It seemed a sensible thing to ask.

"Twenty." He sat up and rested his arms on his knees, panting comfortably. "Jorma Levanen. I'm a chaperone."

"Oh. Hi. . . . Do you know what time it is?" The sky was a non-color, like putty. Did this guy's wife know where he was? By a lake in the middle of the night (if that's what time it was), doing sit-ups next to a sleeping teen-aged girl?

"Must be five?" Consulting his watch, he said, "Five-ten."

"In the morning?" My mind slogged along, checking off events, confirmation, the skating rink, pizza. . . . *Of course* it was morning.

Jorma got up, rotating his neck. "You fell asleep around three. Your friend came and checked on you. She's in the house."

In the front room, a bunch of drowsy kids had a game of Charades going. Marcie and Adam sat together on the couch. Waving to Marcie, I headed for the bathroom. As I passed an open door I caught sight of movement. A boy and a girl were jostling on a double bed, laughing and rustling under the covers. I reversed directions and marched back to Marcie. I sputtered in her ear, "There's a *couple* in that bed!"

"It's okay," she whispered. "It's Jim and Cora. They're just bundling."

I had that old sensation: everyone knew something I'd never heard of. "What's bundling?" Marcie got up and motioned me outside.

Once we got to the front yard, out of the others' hearing range, she said, "It's nothing to worry about. They keep their clothes on and nothing happens."

"You mean they don't have sexual intercourse." I wanted to remind her *I* knew a few things, too—well, things I had learned from *her*. I went ahead of her toward the lake, wishing I had brought a sweater. A fairy mist swirled on the surface of the lake. The air felt dense and wet, balanced between a warm night and a cold dawn. The sky seemed ready to burst with sun or rain, a rosy neutral that could mean either. We walked out on the dock, rocking it on purpose and making the water slosh.

"I think it's playing with fire," I said.

"It comes from the Old Country. From *your* old country, not mine."

How did she know *that*? Here again, I was the naïve one while Marcie knew it all. Trying to get back to more equal footing, I assumed a mask of worldliness and made up a big fake yawn. Marcie wasn't fooled. In fact, she was getting fussed. She said, "You want to hear this or not?"

"Go ahead."

"They used to bundle in Finland in the winter when it got too cold outside for courting. Engaged couples got to snuggle on a bed and stay out of trouble."

"Does the church know about it?"

Her look implied I was doing it again, worrying too much. "It doesn't have anything to do with the church."

"I still think it's still a dumb thing to do!"

Back to her normal self, Marcie grinned and taunted me. "Some day you could be the one in there, bundling with some boy, and *I'm* the one walking by . . ."

"Not on your life!"

"Wait and see." She smiled the way a troll might. That was Marcie, always getting in the last word.

* * *

A week after confirmation, we were picking tomatoes in my backyard, and out of nowhere Marcie said, "I'm going to marry Adam. He's the one. I can feel it in my bones."

"Well, good," I said, even though I didn't think she could pull it off. She was only thirteen and Adam was seventeen. A lot could happen in the next few years. "Um. Does he know you have these plans for him?"

"Nope. Not yet."

"It's true he couldn't keep his eyes off you."

"Older men *do* find me attractive." She showed me her profile. She was wearing Grandpa's gray church hat, and she did look good. "Adam is my dreamboat."

Holding up a fat tomato, I said, "The sun ripens tomatoes, right? So how come this one is green on top where the sun hits it and red on the bottom?"

Her consideration lasted, at most, two seconds. "I haven't got the vaguest idea."

"Me neither." I put the tomato in the basket, red side up. "You know what? I don't get nervous around Adam. Usually cute boys get me tongue-tied. Not Adam."

"Good, 'cause we'll live in Minneapolis and see you all the time."

"Great! . . . When will you tell *him*?"

"When the time's right." She took off the hat and held it between her knees while she snagged a band around her hair. When she put the hat on, her hair made a wedge of fluff behind her neck.

"He'll marry me." She said this with a know-it-all smirk. "You'll see."

Seven

Go Away and Stop Leaving Me Alone

T he carnival was coming to Marcie's town, and she wouldn't get to go. She was in Michigan with her cousins on the other side. But Liisa was going, with her friend Norma Peterson, who had a driver's license and the promise of her father's Nash for the whole day on Saturday. I heard Liisa talking to her on the phone. They planned to go to the carnival in the early afternoon, buy a roll of tickets, ride every ride twice, eat corn dogs for supper, see Buddy Manchester and the Prairie Rose Trio live on stage, watch the fireworks and stay until midnight when the gates closed.

It sounded wonderful! I wanted to go in the worst way. But I held back saying so. I figured Liisa *knew* I wanted to go. Good grief, she could tell just by *looking* at me! I thought *for sure*, she'd invite me.

But to help her out, I gave her little hints. "Sounds great. Wish I could go." She made no sign she got the hints. Still, I convinced myself she'd never leave me behind. As usual, I was at cross purposes with her. I shoved her out of my life on a regular basis, yet I wanted her to include me in hers—like now. My attitude said, in no uncertain terms, "Go away and stop leaving me alone!" No wonder she gave me the cold shoulder.

But that wasn't what I was thinking that Saturday. What I was thinking was: Liisa would take me along *for sure.*

The appointed hour came. Norma drove up. Liisa ran outside, got into the Nash and slammed the door shut. Norma pulled away. I raced upstairs and stayed in our room for an hour or more, later explaining my red eyes to Mummo and Aarnie with something about dust or feather pillows.

It was one-thirty when Liisa came home. I heard the toilet flush, heard her wash up, brush her teeth. When she got to our room, I got out of bed and accosted her, in whispers so I wouldn't wake the others. "How could you *do* that? Go off and *leave* me?" I was so mad I was stiff-armed.

She raised one shoulder an inch or less. "Norma asked *me.* I couldn't just turn around and ask someone else."

"I'm not just someone else! I'm your sister! You know, *sisters?* Supposed to *help* each other?" In the light of a half-moon, Liisa folded down her bed covers. Her natural poise mocked me.

Baiting her, I said, "I bet you didn't even *want* me along!"

I shouldn't have baited her, because I didn't like what she said next. She said, "I didn't think you'd want to be with the older kids." Her admission was a slap in the face. She had considered asking me but decided against it. Without talking to me.

Turning her back on me and on our disagreement, Liisa got into bed and rolled away to face the wall. I stood in the dark at a total loss, all possible retorts floating out of reach. In the week leading up to the carnival, we had operated as usual, not saying what we were thinking, not checking facts with each other. I had depended on fantasy, wishes, hints, Liisa, on her own reasoning. And, as usual, the result was an impasse.

* * *

My junior high was in the same complex as Liisa's high school, and we rode the same school bus, so I got to see firsthand the way boys were drawn to her. I couldn't blame them. She was a Nordic *looker,* a blue-eyed white-blonde taller than most of the boys, and rather than slouching as some tall girls did, she exaggerated her height by elongating her neck. In addition to being a knockout to look at, Liisa could bake, garden, sew, pitch a mean softball and name the constellations. You might say Liisa was the perfect girl.

Even so, even if she was a good cook, a good student, and so on, she could be *cold*. Like the day she killed my cat. Liisa had found him four years earlier in Johnny Johnson's hayloft, a black satin baby with a snowy bib, the only living kitten from a litter of four. He had never known human beings up close, but far from being timid he was thrilled to meet us. He nuzzled our necks and demanded attention in many voices—a "talking" cat, Maudie Johnson called him. The kittens were born in a hayrack on the ground floor. But one night a fox got to them and killed three. The mother cat moved her last kitten up to the loft, this black one, and Maudie said we were welcome to take him home. Mummo acquiesced. Since Liisa had found him, Mickey became her pet. But it turned out she didn't have time for a pet, and I got Mickey by default.

I got him just in time. I needed someone to talk to. I was only nine but confused already—about growing up, being a Finn, about lots of things. I had Marcie to talk to, but only in the summer (this was before she moved to Cranston). I had Mahoning friends, but they couldn't help with the Finn part (Marcie at least *lived* with Finns). I had Liisa, Mummo, Grandpa, and Aarnie, but they went out of their way not to talk. So I talked to Mickey. "Sometimes I get so mad! It just comes over me, I don't know why. I never tell anyone. How could I complain? I have a house and clothes and food. No one hits me like at Carlene's. So why should I be mad? It doesn't make sense!" Mickey didn't care if I made sense or not. He had a loud purr, and he listened well with his eyes closed.

He grew into a roving tom who would leave home for a week at a time and come back skinny, nonchalant, and hungry. He gorged on whatever food I could find for him, curled up on my bed and slept the sleep of innocents. That's mostly what he did with his life: sleep. Between forays into the cat world of Mahoning, Mickey found warm places, and he slept. He liked to sleep in cardboard boxes, and one became his casket.

One day during spring vacation, Mickey was sleeping in the alley, in a box left behind by little kids called home for lunch. Disaster struck in the form of Liisa at the wheel of the '39 Chevy. On weekdays the alley was a good place for cats to nap and for little kids to play. No cars used it from dawn to dusk;

the men were at work and few of the women drove. Liisa was an exception to the rule about women. She was learning to drive. Backing out of our garage, she misjudged her speed and got jangled, stamped on the wrong pedal, tore across the alley, ran over Mickey and crashed into the safety fence.

She found Mickey and came in to tell me.

I raced out to the alley, Liisa following. I didn't touch Mickey. He was obviously dead. I yelled at Liisa, "You *killed* him! How *could* you?"

"I didn't mean to."

"What did you think you were *doing*?"

"Trying not to hit the fence."

"Well, you *did* hit it! And you killed Mickey!"

Reasoning out her side of things, Liisa said, "He must have been sick. A healthy cat runs if he hears a car coming. I think he was dead before I hit him."

Nonsense. Mickey dead before she hit him! I kept giving her *what-for* and she kept giving me excuses: the pedal got stuck, the mirror was crooked, she didn't see Mickey. In all this talk, I didn't hear one word of apology.

She stopped talking. After a beat, I said, "Is that all you have to say?"

"What do you want me to say?"

I shook my head. I didn't understand her, not one bit! "Maybe 'I'm sorry' or 'Too bad about your cat'?"

She erased something from the air. "I told you, I didn't see him. Don't go getting all crazy." From her view, she had done her duty. She had told me what happened, had explained it was an accident. To her, that took care of it. As I said, she could be cold.

But I was cold, too. The whole time I was railing at Liisa, I never once thought of her safety. What if the fence hadn't caught the car? On the other side of the fence was the largest open pit in the world.

* * *

Mummo didn't approve of television, but she had relented and let Aarnie buy a set. Now she was a dedicated fan of a certain soap opera. (The TV sat on a table made by Aarnie from wood scraps, which sat on a rug made by the Lars Company from Mummo's sewing scraps. The frugality of using scraps balanced the extravagance of buying a TV.) At the moment, Mummo was sunk in her wing chair, absorbed in the woes of the Harrigans. Judging from what I'd seen in passing, I guessed the writers worked a list of problems into the characters' lives until they ran out of problems, and then they started over at the top of the list. A commercial broke in. Mummo put down the mending she'd been holding as a prop and took up a newspaper. She was silent for a bit. Then she clicked her tongue, a sharp sound of censure. "*Tscckk!*"

I was staying home from school with a chest cold, reading on the davenport. Since I was the only other person in the house I figured she was talking to me, if you counted clicking your tongue as talking. Reluctantly, I said, "What?"

"Shame *on*! Look!" She hoisted herself out of her chair and came to thrust the paper at me. She had folded it back to show the head-and-shoulders photo of a black man in a business suit. She rapped a finger in the region of his mouth.

"What? You don't like his mustache?"

She gasped and poked at the paper. "Looks *awful*! Colored men should never wear whiskers!"

Knowing I was breaking a rule, I decided to point out something obvious. "It's not really fair to say a whole *group* of people . . ."

Forgetting the soap opera, she limped furiously through the house and down the basement steps. Soon I heard a crashing sound—metal objects hitting concrete. I sighed. Again reluctantly, I shoved off my blanket, got into my slippers and went downstairs.

A canning box had fallen to the floor. Lids and rubber jar rings lay scattered at Mummo's feet. She was shoving jars of canned tomatoes to the back of a shelf. The jars clinked on impact, making me very nervous.

I said, "I'm sorry. I didn't mean to upset you."

"'*Sorry!*'" She spit the word. "What good is '*sorry*'?"

"Let's talk about it, at least," I suggested. But I knew it was hopeless

She cracked two empty jars against each other, and they shattered. "See?" she said. She held out her hands. They were not cut. I could hear her bitter, forceful breathing.

The scene was familiar. Mummo has a tantrum. She blames it on whoever is around, Aarnie, Liisa, me, or all of us. We tiptoe around, not wanting to upset her further, and eventually we go on as if nothing had happened.

Standing in the basement among the jar rings, I realized something else. Mummo was the only one at our house who got to show emotions. She gave herself permission. She showed her feelings in this sordid, acid way while the rest of us held ours in.

Still fiddling with jars, she threw punishing looks in my direction, enforcing the rules of the Silence. One: We were not to speak our opinions. Two: We were to feel guilt for having opinions different from Mummo's. Three: Mummo ran the show.

*   *   *

That same spring, I blundered into a lower-case silence that had nothing to do with *anything*, or not anything that I could see, anyway. It started with one of those innocent comments that blew up in my face. Liisa and I were setting the table for supper, and I was telling her about my homeroom party that day.

"We had cherry Kool-Aid with ice cubes made of ginger ale."

Mummo turned rigid at the sink. She stopped peeling potatoes and speared a look of steel right through me.

"What?" I asked her, knowing I was in danger just for asking. She took in two rapid, urgent breaths—*inward! inward!*—and went back to peeling potatoes.

I tried to guess. Was it the Kool-Aid? No. Mummo made it all the time. Ginger ale? No, she herself liked ginger ale. Ice cubes? . . . That was it! Ice cubes. We never made them! The refrigerator had its own dimpled metal ice trays, but they never got used. I saw them each time I put away the coffee cups, second shelf, far left, the zigzag dividers folded inside. We never took them down. We never mentioned them. That's the way the silences were, insolent but hiding in plain view, daring us to say we saw them.

Years later I learned what ice cubes meant to Mummo: *clinking drinks and fall-down drunks; steamy, seamy, illicit sex.* But on the day of the homeroom party, all I learned was that to Mummo ice cubes meant danger. I had no idea why.

* * *

For a couple of straight-laced Finnish girls, Liisa and I were good liars. She was fifteen and I was thirteen, and we had a partnership built on half-truths, a plan that drew us closer than being good ever had. We both had the same disease. We wanted to be held by boys. In order to get what we wanted, we lied.

My lies had to do with dancing and a basketball player named Rusty Mathis. Rusty had a fast car, and I was a fast girl. I was mad at Mummo, and I thought that by being bad I could get back at her. I was boy-crazy, ferociously so. I thought about boys all the time. I dreamed about them, pretended this boy or that boy was in love with me. Poor Rusty was being used. He was just a handy sample of the marvelous world of boys.

Most Friday nights, Julianna's father drove Julianna and me to school dances. I told Mummo I was visiting friends or going to ball games or to "class parties." Our junior high was one wing of Hibbing High School, an E-shaped complex of brick and Bedford stone that housed kindergarten through junior college, and the proximity of the schools made it possible for an eighth-grader like me to meet a junior like Rusty and for him to attend our dances without comment. For the first hour we slow-danced, obeying the chaperones' rule of no cheek-to-cheek dancing. Then, for the next two hours, we necked like crazy in his Studebaker. I was in a fever of lust, but I managed to stop myself and Rusty before we passed certain limits and managed to get back to the gym in time to meet Julianna's dad for the (guilty, giddy) ride home.

Liisa too was seeing boys on the sly. Mummo had forbidden Liisa to date until she was seventeen (little did Mummo know what I did in *my* spare time, at thirteen), so Liisa didn't tell the whole truth when she stayed in town on Fridays. She said she went to football games. What she didn't say was that she met her dates at the stadium, drove around, parked, and necked. From the sparse information I could get from Liisa, I gathered that she kissed a lot of boys—a *lot.*

The high school auditorium was a copy of the old Capital Theater in New York City. It had a forty-by-sixty-foot Broadway-type stage, box seats, a stage pipe organ, forty-five stage drops, and seating for 1,800 people. Hibbing High was a plum assignment for any student teacher, especially a teacher of drama and English. That fall, a student teacher let the privilege go to his head—Mr. Xavier Martin—a secret lecher who got caught in his lechery. People found Mr. Martin charming when they first met him. But he fell in their esteem from that point on, causing chaos as he went. (This last part we learned too late.) He was medium-height and fair-haired, built like a wrestler. His punched-in face and crinkled eyes endeared him to us girls. In the presence of adults, he was a model citizen. Alone with us girls, he made passes at us and insisted we call him Chip.

My friends and I liked to roller-skate after school, and we rode the city bus to the rink. More than once, Mr. Martin drove by the bus stop and offered us a ride. We would laugh artificially and accept, saying the bus took too long anyway and this way we'd have more time for skating. We ignored his "accidental" touches as we piled in. We should have reported him, but we were flattered by his flirting. We told no grownups about the rides to the rink, or the groping hands, or the rapid body presses in a crowded hall, or the smirk that smeared his face when he got that close.

Mostly he was attracted to Liisa, who accepted her beauty the way she accepted most facts, with a cool, unthinking calm. In a day of compact cheerleaders and pixie-poodle hair, Liisa made the most of her loftiness and her long, straight, naturally platinum hair. She rolled it up in socks at night, same as everyone else, but it went straight in the school halls and shimmered in curtains as she walked away, inspiring males, including Mr. Martin, to pursue her.

One day, in his pursuit of her, he got as far as our front door. After driving us home, he turned off the engine, got out of the car and followed us up the sidewalk. "I'd like to meet your family," he announced.

We didn't know what to say. We never had company except relatives or other Finns. Mummo had never actually said we couldn't have friends over, but we never did.

But a teacher? *Impossible.*

I scooted indoors to warn Mummo. She dried her hands on her apron as she went to the front door. She opened it to inspect the stranger, blocking entrance and giving the impression she was not to be trifled with. He was immune. Smiling so hard his eyes disappeared, he introduced himself as Chip Martin, insinuated a foot on the threshold, and launched into a chat during which he did all of the talking. No one invited him in, and when he left no one remarked on his gall.

A week later, on a Friday, Liisa agreed to meet Mr. Martin—or *Chip*, as he reminded her—at the stadium at half-time and go out for a bite to eat. Later she told me her instinct warned her, *Don't go.* But she ignored the warning.

She called home at ten-thirty and shouted in my ear, "*Come get me!*"

I asked her for directions and hung up. Without telling Mummo what the hurry was, I got Aarnie to drive me into Hibbing. We found the green stucco house on Seventh Avenue East. Aarnie parked at the curb but kept the motor going.

Liisa exploded out of the house and ran to the car, jumped into the back seat, yanked the door shut and pounded on the front seat, yelling, "*Go! . . . Go!*"

Aarnie eased into the street. Liisa sobbed and shouted, "He was *drunk*! I *hate* him! I told him he smelled like beer, and he laughed and said he hadn't had that much. Like a *stupe* I believed him! I got into his car. I can't believe it . . . *I got into his car.*"

Liisa choked and coughed, crying hard. I gave her a hanky. She blew her nose. "He said he had to drop something off at his mother's. *Sure* he did." She rested her forehead on the front seat, sat up and blew her nose again. "No one was home. I didn't believe him that his mother lived there. It was a creepy place, messy and hardly any lights on, and it smelled bad. He drank more beer, and I said I wanted to go home. He smiled with his eyes closed, the way he does? His face gets all red . . .

"He pushed me down on the davenport! He said, 'You know you want it' and some other ugly things. He held me down and put his mouth over mine." She dry-retched. "*Augh*! I *hate* him! I kept saying *STOP* and fighting, but he got madder and madder. He hit me in the face. I bit his arm and kept trying to get away. He reached under my skirt and pushed me down and hit me again. Then he tried to take his pants off and pin me down at the same time, and that's when I got away. I ran for the front door but almost didn't make it, he was chasing me! I made it across the street, and they said I could stay there. They let me call you." She huddled in the corner of the back seat, crying in gusts and pulling her cardigan around her.

Aarnie said, "Don't pay that guy no never-mind."

Startled to hear him speak, Liisa stopped crying. She rocked forward and backward, holding her belly and groaning in a monotone bass that sounded nothing like her real voice. Aarnie stayed occupied with driving. Aarnie, our silent hero. Our *mostly* silent hero. He always managed to say the right thing at the right time.

By the time we got home, Liisa was crying again. She stormed past Mummo into the dining room and flung off her coat, sat down hard on a straight chair and pulled off her boots, stood up and threw them across the room, one at a time, yelling, "How *dare* he!" with the first boot, which slapped the linoleum and slid under the buffet, "He was stinking drunk!" with the second, which hit the wall beneath the windows. She retrieved them and hurled them both at the same time. "How could I be so *stupid*!"

Now that danger was past, I felt like giggling. Liisa, of all people, having a fit! The boots were a nice touch, I thought. They made a nice *whap*. It turned out I was more surprised by Liisa's fit than Mummo was. Mummo, who wasn't supposed to know anything about any "he" Liisa was talking about, laced her fingers at her waist and made a pronouncement. "*No niin. You get him good.*"

Liisa listened. We all did. Whenever Mummo spoke, we listened. But "You get him good" was historic, a more pointed piece of advice than we'd ever heard from her.

"How?" Liisa asked her.

"Tell."

"Who?"

"The school."

So Liisa told Dr. Watterson, the high school principal, what had transpired at the house supposedly owned by Mr. Martin's mother and what had caused the bruises on her face and arms. As a result, Mr. Martin was placed on leave.

Dr. Watterson conducted an internal investigation. Eight girls besides Liisa, myself included, were brought to his office to report what we knew. For three days, clusters of girls clogged the hallways of Hibbing High, consumed with whispers as to the fate of Mr. Martin.

Then the tables were turned. Liisa was accused of wrongdoing.

She and I were called from class for a second time and taken to a room I had never seen. The high school and junior high principals, vice principals, girls' deans, counselors, and English and drama teachers sat around a large oval conference table, looking dour. Places had been saved at the table for Liisa and me. Dr. Watterson stayed on his feet beside a desk with a black telephone on it. He was a paunchy man who wore vests and a pencil mustache and seemed too tired to do his work. He was famous among students for his nervous tics, most of which involved pawing at his face and clothes.

He started out with me, asking me the same questions I had answered the first time. He accompanied himself with pats at his triple chin.

Did I know Mr. Martin?

Yes, slightly.

Had I accepted rides in his car?

Yes.

How often?

Twice.

Had he ever acted in an unseemly way toward me?

Yes. Twice. He touched my thigh.

Where was I when this happened?

In his car.

Had I ever been alone with him?

No.

Did I have anything else to add?

No. Nothing.

Dr. Watterson thanked me and turned to Liisa. Measuring his tie with thumb and forefinger, inchworming down its length, he asked her to describe her relationship with Mr. Martin. The room was a courtroom, and Liisa was on trial. I had never felt a stronger bond with her.

"There wasn't anything to it, really," she said, eyes roaming from person to person. Her voice was plaintive and thin. "He seemed polite. I rode in his car a few times with my friends or my sister. That's all . . . until that night."

She drove a look at Dr. Watterson, asking without words, *Do I have to say more?*

He grilled her the same way he had grilled me, except she had more to tell. At the end he took off his glasses and cleaned the inner corners of his eyes, again with thumb and forefinger. "We need to call your parents." He replaced his glasses and eased them into place with the bunched fingers of both hands.

"I live with my grandmother," Liisa said.

"Your grandmother then. Phone number?" He lifted the receiver.

"Meridian 46230." She shrank as he ratcheted the dial. He waited, whistling soundlessly and tickling his neck. The others sat without conversation or eye contact. I pictured possibilities at home, none of them good. Mummo hated the telephone. She might not answer. Or she might answer but hang up when she heard what the caller said. Or she might answer, listen, and say Liisa deserved whatever she got.

Mummo did answer. We heard Dr. Watterson explain who he was. Then he said, "Mrs. Halonen, I'm afraid we have a situation involving your granddaughter Liisa. The situation is this. Mr. Xavier Martin, a student teacher, has been doing his practicum here this term. There are reports that he has dated female students, and Liisa's name has been mentioned. As you must know, such dating is against school policy. There are severe remedies. What we need from you is any information you may have."

He quit talking and ran his pen cap along his tie clip, which looked like a fishing lure minus the hook. "Yes, fine," he said, "I appreciate that. Mrs. Halonen, are you acquainted with Mr. Martin?"

This time the pause lasted longer. Dr. Watterson unbuttoned and buttoned his vest and stroked his hair from the receding front to the trimmed nape. I wondered *what*, possibly, Mummo could be saying all this time. I tried to catch Liisa's eyes but couldn't. A loud bell rang. The halls filled with shouts and laughing, metal lockers clanging open and banging shut.

Finally Dr. Watterson said, "Thank you, Mrs. Halonen. It has been a pleasure talking with you. Good-bye." He replaced the receiver, giving no indication as to what had been said at such length by our grandmother who hardly ever talked and hated the phone.

When he next spoke to Liisa, he conveyed respect. "Your grandmother confirms what you have said, that Mr. Martin gave you and other students rides to the skating rink and, once, a ride home from a football game. . . . It was on this occasion that the, ah, incident occurred." (He obviously hated having to talk about this.) "Is that correct?"

"Yes."

"According to your grandmother, there was no actual dating." Disconcertingly, he turned mischievous. His nose and mouth looked ready for a sneeze. "She reports that she is personally acquainted with Mr. Martin, that he has visited her at her home. She referred to him as . . . 'Chip Martin' . . . and she called him a friend of the family."

A friend of the family? I didn't dare to look at Liisa. We both might laugh like maniacs. Everyone sat without moving.

Dr. Watterson visually checked in with his colleagues, and signals of assent went around the table. "You may return to class," he told us. "Thank you for your help."

We never saw Mr. Martin again. Liisa's name was cleared, due in large part to Mummo. In what must have been the longest speech she ever made in English, she had stood up to Dr. Watterson and cast the few facts that she knew (or had guessed) in a positive light. She had intuitively protected Liisa. And she had done it on the phone.

When we got home, I said to Mummo, haltingly, "That was a nice thing you did. You know . . . for Liisa."

She had been knitting in her wing chair. Now she put down her needles and yarn and stared at me until I got the message. I was not to mention this to her again.

I didn't.

Years later, looking back on that school meeting, I saw what was missing. None of the grownups spoke up for Liisa. None of them expressed concern for *her*, for her well-being. With shame, I realized *I* didn't, either. The whole bunch of us—the deans, the teachers, the principal and I—were too worried about our own necks to say a good word for Liisa. Just so *we* weren't held responsible for the scandal.

* * *

Liisa's boy-crazy days were over at age fifteen. After the Chip Martin fiasco, she stopped sneaking around. I did, too. Chip Martin cured me of my mad dash toward boys, doused me with ice water. I decided to wait to start actual dating. I also decided I wouldn't dance as long as I lived with Mummo. (But I hadn't told her I *was* dancing when I was, and I wasn't telling her now when I *wasn't*, so what difference could it possibly make?) When I made these changes, I had no real notion as to *why*. I couldn't reconcile the girl I had been at confirmation with the girl who, a few weeks later, started sneaking around with Rusty, or with the girl who'd recently reversed directions and stopped sneaking around. I wasn't proud of this reversal. It wasn't based on any sort of moral courage. I stopped sneaking around for one reason only: I was *scared* out of it.

A week had passed since the meeting at school, and Liisa and I still hadn't talked about it. I'd tried, but she had refused. One night as we studied in our room, she at the desk and I on my bed, I said, "How are you doing with the Chip thing? You okay?"

Remorse creased her face, but she went on reading.

I said, "It would be good if we could talk."

She let out a staccato sigh. "I'm okay."

"Aren't you mad at him?"

"Not really."

"You *should* be! . . . *I* am! . . . He's a *creep*! He makes my skin crawl!"

She agreed he was a creep, I could tell. "I've been thinking," I said. "Where do you think God was in all of that? Do you think He leaves us to our own problems? I mean, He knows everything and He's everywhere, so was He there in that house with you and Chip? Or in the car with me and Rusty?"

"I prayed," she said, "in that house. God helped me get away."

I digested this. Unthinkingly, I went on. "But what if Chip hadn't stopped? Even after you prayed? Where would God have been *then*?"

Her faced closed up. Too late I knew my mistake. I had just added the image of full rape, as much of it as I understood. "Liisa, I'm sorry! What a terrible thing to say."

"It's okay. . . . But that other part, about where God was? I think bad things happen to everybody, people who pray and people who don't. Everybody."

"Maybe so." I was playing with an idea, or fragments of an idea. "God is Love, right? And all-powerful. How about this? What if He uses all kinds of experiences to get through to us—you know, to show us He loves us? . . . What if He's right there in the experience, whatever it is, and maybe He changes it and maybe He doesn't, but either way He uses it to reach us? . . . What do you think?"

"Maybe."

"But, *Liisa*!" I jiggled around, absolutely in love with my idea. "It worked for us! God used the Chip thing and the Rusty thing—trouble we got *ourselves* into—to snap us out of it! . . . Well, me, anyway. I was *all over* Rusty. I mean, I was *cuckoo*, babe! I could've gotten myself in *big* trouble."

"Trouble? Like . . . *trouble*?"

"Ya."

"Me, too."

"But I thought you only *kissed* boys."

"I never went all the way, but I got close. Remember Danny Rich? We played around too much . . ." Her top teeth held her bottom lip to the count of about three. "I think I got a reputation . . . I think Chip knew I was *easy*."

"Liisa! You can't blame yourself! It was *his* fault. He tried to rape you!"

"He almost did."

A shiver spread across my shoulders and down my back. I said, "*Ick!* That ugly smile? His face all squished and red?"

"You used to think he was cute."

"I *know*! It makes me want to *upchuck*! . . . Man, that guy is a *jerk*!" Finally getting mad, she said, "He's a maggot."

* * *

As winter came and went, Liisa benefited from the Catholic concept of penance. Julianna had told me about penance, an idea foreign to Lutherans but fitting for Liisa after the Chip Martin deal. Not that she was at fault. She just needed to get back to her usual ways. She'd always been the perfect Girl Scout, had always done good deeds as a matter of course. But now she doubled her efforts. She baked cakes for shut-ins and washed people's cars, and read to old Mrs. Nelson who couldn't see well anymore. In April when she turned sixteen, she passed her driver's test and started driving to Hibbing on Sunday afternoons to tutor a girl named Sandy Marsh. She got Sandy's name from the Downtown Mission, where she was listed as destitute. (Mahoning had no destitute children. A miner's pay was not luxurious, as proven by the worn cars and bikes in the location, but it covered basic needs.) One Sunday in May, Liisa asked me to come along.

We were still in the garage, sitting in the newer Chevy with the motor off, when she gave me the ground rules. "Remember, don't go asking questions. And don't talk too much." She turned on the ignition and let the engine warm up.

I griped at her, "We haven't even left yet, and you're already lecturing me. What? You think I'll embarrass you?"

Cautiously, and repeatedly checking the mirrors, Liisa backed out of the garage. She made sure the alley was clear, then shifted into first gear and took off with hardly any jerk at all. Her driving had improved since she killed Mickey. "Well, you *do* get carried away," she said. "You get to talking and can't stop."

It was true. Sometimes I dived into conversation with my ears buzzing, not knowing where I was going or how to exit. The longer I gabbed about things that didn't matter, the harder it was to find a stopping point. By then people were eyeing the sky. But I wasn't used to straight-talk, either, like this from Liisa. Straight-talk made me edgy, fit to be tied. By habit, we kept our thoughts to ourselves; we never discussed anything long enough to know if we agreed or disagreed. The idea of We-don't-mention-that was familiar, at least. This kind of straight-talk gave me a stomachache.

Unhappily, I said, "I'll be quiet. I *have* met poor people before, you know." I wanted her to treat me as an equal, but it was useless. She'd always be two years older.

She said only, "Mmn," and stopped to let Julianna's cocker spaniel, Caramel, cross the street. He pranced along at his own pace, keeping his snout in the air as if he owned the place. His long gold coat rippled with every step.

I said, "Remember that poor family who lived in Hibbing?"

When the dog reached the other side, Liisa drove on with determination. She was the kind of driver who sat right close to the steering wheel. "The four little blonde girls? The stair-step girls?"

"Yes." I smiled. "They stood in line according to size! I wanted to adopt them."

Liisa kept her eyes on the road. "Me too. I wanted to take them home and feed them, give them baths, put clean dresses on them."

"That was *my* idea," I pouted. (Did she have to mooch in on everything?)

"We both had that idea," she said grandly. Liisa could be maddeningly mature sometimes. "They were sweet little girls."

Like a little girl myself, a jealous one, I boasted, "Mummo took me there *alone* one time. We took them stew and bread and a jelly roll." An odor memory drifted in, as fresh as the day it was stored. "The house smelled spoiled, like old fruit."

Liisa rarely remembered the same things I did. "I don't remember that. I just remember a family who needed help."

"I saw the mother's face! She was *humiliated.* Don't you worry about that? That the people you help will be humiliated by it?"

Her face took on a tenderness, and she looked like the Madonna. "The Madonna" was another concept I'd picked up from Julianna. "I just do what I can," Liisa said. She never had as many questions as I did about anything.

Every time I went to Hibbing I realized what a dinky place Mahoning was. We drove past warehouses, diners and car lots, small frame houses packed together, bigger houses with bigger yards and older trees, a business section, and on the far side of town we came to Lenton's Slew, named for an actual slough the size of two city blocks. As we passed the slough, we saw two boys skipping rocks across the backwaters. The buildings here were gerry-mandered affairs, divided into parts or boarded up, windows broken and patched with black tape. Four men sat, smoking, against a factory shed on a weedy slab of concrete. I guessed they worked in the factory and came here on Saturdays to relax. In a scrappy backyard, a young woman with clothespins in her mouth held a shirt by the tail, pinning another to the line. She caught me watching her and stared me down. I glanced away, scandalized: Did poor people do their wash on *Saturday?* An old woman in a dark dress and head scarf carried a coal basket across her yard. The people around here looked exhausted. It occurred to me that being poor must be hard work.

The apartment sat halfway back from the street, an afterthought on a narrow house on a narrow lot. Dandelions and not much else grew in the dirt yard. Liisa knocked. A slender brunette who looked forty-five but was proba-bly younger opened the door a crack. She raised her eyes no higher than Liisa's chin. She was sad-looking and weary, her dress faded and in need of a hem. She seemed as faded as her dress. Two toddlers hugged her knees. Liisa smiled. "Good morning, Mrs. Marsh. This is my sister, Kik." We said hello.

From inside the apartment came the screech of metal on metal. The woman turned away and called, "Milton, put that down! This minute!" Turning back to us, she again evaded our eyes.

Liisa said, "Is Sandy ready?"

Mrs. Marsh made a flaccid motion inviting us in. We stepped into a front room that smelled of Lux soap and mold. It was a beautiful spring day, but no fresh air came into the room. A teen-aged boy with a misshapen head came from the kitchen and shrieked. His face went into spasms, his hands flexed and contracted. He shrieked again. Mrs. Marsh went to him and put her hands on his shoulders. He resisted but allowed her to direct him to another room. The toddlers held her legs and went with her.

Returning with no children, Mrs. Marsh placed her palms flat on the backs of her hips. "The county is sent-ing someone out, like you said. They said maybe they could take Milton. They're starting some kind of school . . ." Her voice broke off. I flicked a look at Liisa. Liisa had arranged help for this boy Milton!

Mrs. Marsh folded her arms, reached one hand up and pinched a flag of neck skin and massaged it. "My husband, he don't like the idea. But he's gone so much, he don't know how *wearing* the boy can be." Again she settled her hands behind her hips. She sighed, the picture of a troubled mother desperate for an answer for her troubled child.

Liisa said, "Maybe the social worker could meet your husband? That might help."

Mrs. Marsh said listlessly, "Maybe. I'll get Sandy. You could take her to the park. She'd like that." She left us and went down the hall.

Sandy was seven and fine-featured, her skin so transparent that her veins showed blue. She had pretty brown eyes, but they were red-rimmed. Over a green striped dress she wore a pink wool cardigan that had shrunk in the wash and now rode above her waist. From what Liisa had told me, I knew that Sandy was the only daughter of Ann and Thomas Marsh. Mr. Marsh was a day laborer who kept hearing of a better job in another town. Having been moved too often, Sandy had never regularly attended school, and before Liisa's tutoring she hadn't known much about numbers or written words. Sandy gave Liisa a timid smile. Liisa introduced me to Sandy, and we left.

The park was a block away. Crossing the street, Liisa and I held hands with Sandy, and when we got to the grass we ran with her, swinging her between us. She laughed with pleasure but wrenched away as soon as she could, obviously not any more accustomed to friendly touch than Liisa and I were.

From the bottom of the jungle gym, Sandy aimed a happy look at us. We watched her climb to the top and get ready to hang by her knees.

She fell like a shot sparrow. She lay still on the packed earth, her head in a strange position. Liisa and I ran to her. The day went into nightmare mode. Time slowed to sludge. Sounds muted: shouts in a barrel. Liisa was screaming, or was *I*? "*Do* something! Get a *doctor!*"

The corner store had a phone behind the counter. The owner let me use it. Shaking and frightened, I called the operator. She connected me to Emergency. A woman took the information and said an ambulance was on its way.

I ran to the apartment. I told Mrs. Marsh what had happened. She opened her mouth and gaped toward the park. I said, "I'll stay with the children. You go." She hurried away.

More frightened than ever, I closed the door. The two small boys were playing with toy cars on the floor, and it came to me, inconsequentially, that one child was only slightly bigger than the other. The children didn't cry at being left with a stranger. Instead, they gave me solemn looks, as though they knew how serious this day was. Milton was nowhere in sight. I left him alone. I didn't want to upset him if I could help it.

Hours passed. I cleaned the kitchen, throwing out the leavings of yesterday's jelly sandwiches and bean soup. I fed the toddlers lunch and took them to the training potty. Returning with them from the bathroom, I saw Milton sitting on his bed, staring at the floor. He didn't look up. I sat at the table, trying to think and pray. Milton came out of his room, made a circuit of the apartment, took the peanut butter sandwich I had wrapped in wax paper and saved for him, and went back to his room. Later I looked in on him. He lay on his bed in a fetal position, a gray stuffed rabbit clutched to his chest. I gave the small boys crackers and milk. They went on playing.

I had expected it, but, still, the rapping startled me. Two policemen stood outside the door, midnight blue, their bigness swamping the porch. They introduced themselves. The younger one said, "Is this the residence of Thomas Marsh?"

"Yes, but he's not here. I'm Kik Halonen. Is it about Sandy? Is she okay?"

The older cop asked, "Are you a family member?"

"No. My sister tutors Sandy. Is Sandy okay?"

He checked his notes in a notebook. "I regret to inform you that Sandra Marsh died today at St. John's Hospital, at thirteen-thirty-four."

"Oh no." *Poor Sandy! Poor Mrs. Marsh.* The little boys, Milton.

I had another terrifying thought. Was Liisa responsible? I said, "My sister?"

Reading my mind, the older cop reassured me. "Your sister was not at fault, miss. It was an accidental fall. She is free to go."

I was relieved to hear it. But I had trouble getting the facts in line. "I can't leave. I can't leave the children. I have to stay until . . ." My mind felt weighted down, and everything I said seemed beside the point. Maybe death did that, made everything else seem beside the point.

I remembered the Chevy. "Our car's here. Could you bring Liisa here?"

"One of our officers will see to it," the younger man said. "Your sister won't be ready to drive. You might want to call a relative or neighbor to drive you home."

Did any of the neighbor ladies drive? I couldn't think. Aarnie was at the mine. No. It was Saturday. I said, "We'll work it out, thanks."

The policemen went away and I shut the door in a daze. I had to find out why the smaller of the two small boys was crying.

Liisa wouldn't talk about Sandy—not that day, not on other days when I tried to get her to talk. To me she seemed lifeless. She helped Mummo cook and she did her schoolwork, but that was it. She dropped out of Girl Scouts, she didn't plan on college, she didn't go out on dates. She did find comfort in the second branch of the Finnish church. Unlike ours, it held services every Sunday, and Liisa had started attending them with Starr Pesonen. This left me confused. She didn't have energy for much of anything, let alone a church stricter than ours. But she wouldn't talk about church any more than about Sandy.

Liisa had always been placid. Now she was more so, polite and steady. No disagreements between us. No rivalry. No sparks.

I could never have guessed how much I would miss the old Liisa.

Eight

It's a Great Life if You Don't Weaken

Say! You guys ever hear about the war?" Harald asked us. "Not the World War. The Winter War." He and Marcie were eating pie with us at our house. Randall never came over anymore, and Inky wasn't at the table, either. She was making applesauce for a sick neighbor, Mrs. Kangas—*our* sick neighbor, not Inky's. That's the kind of Red Cross person Inky was. In answer to Harald's question, Marcie said yes, Liisa and I said no. But it didn't matter. Harald was in the mood and would tell us anyway.

"Well," he began, giving the word a pulse of drama. "I was in it! In Finland!" I conveyed a question mark to Marcie, who was supposed to tell me things like this. She made a Howdy Doody face and mouthed Sorry.

Chuckling one "Heh," Harald leaned back to massage his stomach. "Ya well, I was skinny and full of vinegar and had both legs, so I went over to help those Finnis' kuys. It was in 1940, a coupla months there. Dead a winter!"

Edging forward, he changed his bearing. He leaned his forearms on the table and jammed his fists into his belly. "Here's the deal. The Russians were being *bullies*. They were scared of Hitler, so they kept pushing Finland

and talking big. They said they needed Finnish ports to protect Russia from Hitler! They wanted islands that belonged to Finland! . . . They were just gonna up and *take* 'em!"

His face was blotchy and seemed to expand as he talked. His health was always on the brink. I hoped he wouldn't pass out from getting too fired up. "Russia was so big to begin with, and they wanted more? Man oh man! They come up with some tom-fool excuse to fight Finland in 1939. They said the Finns attacked *them*! . . .Who'd believe that? Little, peaceful Finland? Attacking Russia?"

The insult was new to Harald even though the war was . . . how long ago? I did the arithmetic. Fourteen years. "Naw," he growled. "It was *them* the whole time! They kept *at* it and *at* it, and finally in November they pushed in just about the whole border of Finland on the Russian side. Six hundred miles! Whole *buncha* attacks at the same time. Twenty divisions, different spots . . ." His voice ran downhill, well past what he wanted to believe.

"The Finns now, they didn't think up this war. They didn't want to fight. And they had a *real* small army next to Russia's." He ran a hand under his chin and felt his jowls. "But they got ready anaway and fought like heck."

Harald gathered himself the way he did when he told a joke. "This next part is a good part. It so happened Finland had a real cold winter that year—coldest for a hunnert years! They had blizzards and ice, and those Finnis' kuys? They got *reindeer* from up in Lapland to pull their sleds like *dogs*! . . . Can you beat that?" He wheezed, laughing and coughing at the same time.

"They had those-kind *pieksu* boots, you know, with the toes curled up? And skis with leather straps. They put on white ski suits and skied *sneaky*-like in the snow. They knew the woods. They could sneak up on the Russians and bomb their camps! They sent 'em runnin', I'll tell ya! They'd show up, blast 'em with machine guns, and ski back in the woods. They knew the supply roads and they bombed 'em all to pieces!

"Those Finnis' kuys I was with? They even got the *cooks* to help! They'd run out in the road and put logs under the tanks, right under the tread. When the Russians got out to move the logs, they *shot* 'em!" He grinned at us. "Can you beat that?. . . *Cooks!*"

His manner changed again. With sadness, he said, "But Russia didn't take care of her men. When we took prisoners, they were prett' near starved. Sicker 'n' dogs. They had real thin coats on, and it was freezing out. They called us heroes just 'cause we fed 'em and kept 'em warm." Harald observed a moment of silence for the enemy.

"Well, some other countries, they helped Finland. Sweden, and Denmark, Norway, England, even Germany, there at the start. They gave guns and cannons and planes and like that. But not the U.S. At least, not much that got there on time. Ya, America was late." He seemed very sorry to have to say this.

"Anaway. Finland was way outnumbered. The war went on for four months. In that time, Russia had a quarter million killed. . . . Think how many they musta had, all told. Finland had maybe twenty-three thousand killed, something like that. The Finns were *brave*, I'll tell ya, and that's no lie.

"But Finland lost. They had to sign a peace treaty in March 1940."

He took in a steep breath and let it out in stages. "Russia took so much land. They took Karelia. It was a *big* piece of Finland. The whole eastern part, *gone*." Frowning away tears, he said, "And Viipuri, the second biggest city. And Petsamo, their one arctic port. And the biggest lake, Ladoga. Finland lost it all. And Russia was so big already. . ."

This single idea grieved him the most—the idea that Russia, so big to start with, had picked a fight with little Finland for yet more land. Even at this late date, Harald could not accept it. "You wanta know something? Those Russians had the nerve to say Finland *started* it! Not only that. They made the everyday Finns *pay* them, supposably to compensate for 'starting the war'! . . . *Humbug!* The Finns had to pinch and scrape to pay off that debt, for years and years! And they shouldn'ta had to pay it in the *first* place! I tell ya, it still makes me madder 'n' a hornet!"

Inky came in through the back door and heard the last of Harald's elegy. She said, "Hnghh! You telling them that? They don't want to hear it. Too much sadness." For some reason that I didn't understand at the time, she glanced at Mummo. Normally, after coffee, Mummo would have taken her knitting to the front room, but tonight she had stayed and listened to Harald. I tried to read her face. It was unreadable. Aarnie's was splotchy red and white.

"*No niin.*" Inky whacked at flecks on her apron. "I've got apple all over. It's a great life if you don't weaken! I'm goina take a shower. I won't be long." We knew for a fact that she wouldn't be long. She liked to say she took thirty-second showers to save time and hot water and soap. Marcie and I had timed her once. The water ran for twenty-nine seconds and stopped.

Marcie said, "Daddy? Did you have any relatives there? Like in the parts of Finland the Russians took?"

Harald marshaled his forces to keep up his demeanor, which seemed ready to dissolve into terror, or ruin, or some other state beyond his control. We saw him determine that whatever threatened him would not win. We wouldn't hear for some time what the threat was, or *who* it was. We would never hear it from Harald. Not directly.

His storytelling was over for the night. We disbanded as gracefully as we could, lifting off our chairs and leaving the room, no one speaking, no one touching anyone.

* * *

A few nights later Inky was at our house again, helping Mummo finish a quilt. The house was quiet. Inky and Mummo were upstairs sewing. Aarnie was reading the newspaper in the front room. Liisa and I were studying at the dining table. Abruptly, shockingly, a spate of angry Finnish broke the silence—Mummo's voice, loud enough to travel downstairs.

Liisa and I sat up, vigilant. Loudness was not a good sign.

Inky came down and said to Liisa and me, "Better come." We found Mummo on her back on her bedroom floor, gasping with her eyes shut, her mouth making an O with every rasp of air, which she took in hungrily. Her arms were spread wide, as if she welcomed this wracking of her body. We stood over her, not knowing what to do. She looked the same as ever—a little old lady in a house dress and cotton hose, one regular lace-up shoe and one orthopedic shoe, her bifocals oddly still in place. A model of decorum even now, except for this new shame of falling down.

"What's wrong?" I asked Inky, not wanting to know, not wanting to be there.

110

"She'll be fine in a minute." I wondered how she knew.

I made a paltry attempt to talk to Mummo. "Are you okay?" No answer. I said to Inky, "What do we do now?"

"Don't worry. It's happened before." That was news to me. But then, *that* had happened before, too, my hearing news late.

Liisa knelt and patted Mummo's shoulder. "Mummo? Can you hear me?"

I was offended! I was furious at Mummo for doing this, for doing this to us. I was convinced she knew exactly what she was doing, scaring us like this. I saw her fall-down as a tantrum, a way to make us feel bad, a ploy that said, "Either you do what I want or I'll die, and *then* you'll be sorry. But you have to guess what I want because I won't tell you."

Along with these mutinous thoughts came guilt: Mummo works too hard, I should help her more. But what kind of a fall-down *was* this, anyway? It seemed *wrong*. And *fake*. And what were Inky and Mummo arguing about? If I were to ask any of these questions, no one would answer. So I kept mum.

Mummo's breathing gradually returned to normal. When she opened her eyes, Inky helped her to sit up. I didn't offer my hand as that would have meant touching Mummo. Stiltedly, I asked her, "Do you feel better?"

She ignored me. She made sure her glasses were on straight, yanked her dress below her knees and held out a hand to Inky. This time Liisa and I reached out too. But she refused our help, peevishly, acting miffed at us for seeing her indisposed. Inky raised her to her feet and said, in effect releasing Liisa and me, "Everything is fine now."

We went downstairs. In accordance with the Silence, we said nothing about what had just happened. I hated that! I hated the fact that at our house, after an upset like this, we didn't talk or hug or make each other feel better. I groused to myself, *Here I am, at fourteen, still stuck in the Silence of my childhood—the strangling! belittling! accusing! Silence! It's not preparing me for the bigger world! It's crippling me!*

This litany is what I believed. I rehearsed it when I was alone. Sometimes the rage came on so strong my ribs felt crushed and sore.

* * *

111

Marcie in the meantime cruised along, altogether too happy. When-ever I had half a chance, I carped at her. "I was born into this family, yet I feel more out of place than you do, and you were adopted into it!" In fact, she didn't feel out of place at all. I felt like punching someone most of the time, and so when Marcie came over one day and started her nyah-nyah cutesy stuff, I was in no mood.

"He's going to be here!" She poked a letter at me, pulled it away. "It just so-o *hap*-pens," she sang, "that Berkeley's spring break is the same week as services!" She jigged around my room in saddle shoes, bobby socks, and a men's oversized white shirt hanging out over rolled-up jeans. Normal clothes. But of course on her they looked *Hollywood*. Leave it to Marcie.

"Read it!" she said, streaming the letter through the air. Still she didn't show it to me. "He flies to Minneapolis on Sunday, stays the night at Wally's, and on Monday they drive up. They'll be at the Hevonens' all week!" She did a back-flop onto my bed and tented the letter over her eyes, doing a few swim kicks.

I forced out two words. "That's great."

Marcie took the letter from her face. "I'll get to see him the *whole* week!"

"I'm glad."

She sat up so that she could see me. "What's wrong?"

Taking a chance, I said what I was feeling. "I'm happy for you, really. I'm a little jealous, that's all."

"Oh, *that*," she said offhandedly. "I'm not surprised. It's not the first time, you know. You're always jealous. Of me, of everyone."

My stomach lurched. I couldn't take in what she was saying. "What are you talking about? Like *who*?"

"Like Liisa." Marcie sounded haughty. "Every time she wins a prize, you're mean to her. You act like she's done something awful to *you*."

I croaked, "I *am not* mean to her!"

"Oh, yes you are. Everything has to be about you."

This was treachery. Marcie was talking like a stranger. She was usual-ly my mooring, a safe place. Now she was pulling herself away. I said, "What is this *about*?"

Marcie said, "You think you can hide it, but I see it. Everyone does."

Here was my recurring plight. Everyone knew something I'd never heard of, except this time the "something" everyone knew was that I was mean and jealous. Until now I had assumed, wrongly, and ignorantly, that I was a good sister to Liisa and a good friend to Marcie. Obviously I was not.

Short of breath, I said, "You talk to everyone? Like who, and what about? And what kind of a friend *is* that, anyway?"

Marcie jutted her chin at me. "Sometimes you make me so mad! I just never said so before. You get so balled up with your questions and your worries and your poor Kik act, you wear me out."

I sank onto the vanity bench and hung my head between my knees. I took in gulps of air, trying to keep from falling to the floor.

Even then, she didn't let up. "There you go again," she said scornfully, "hiding, just because someone challenges you. Grow up, Kik! No one's going to baby you out in the big world."

I couldn't get the right amount of air. The breaths I took were either too big or too small, either huge torn graspings or shallow puffs, anything to stay conscious. Later I would compare them to birthing breaths, the hard-work breaths of a mother in labor, as she shoves a newcomer onto the human stage, and the startled breaths of the baby, suddenly not in the same warm place, screaming in evidence of life.

What happened to me that day was a birth of another kind, the smart slap—and the shock—of waking to views beyond my own.

*   *   *

After a few glacial weeks, Marcie and I regained our friendship. She apologized for being harsh, but I said she was right. I was jealous and judgmental, I was afraid of new ideas. I set about trying to fix the part about new ideas. Clumsily at first, and reminding myself often, I forced myself to listen to others' views. I fought nausea and didn't run. I felt awkward doing this. I felt I was just going through the motions. But over time I learned that going through the motions was how growing up got done.

It was my season anyway to step out on my own. I had focused too much on Marcie and ignored my other friends, especially Julianna. So when Julianna asked me to share a baby-sitting job, I said fine. The newspaper ad called for two sitters for six children each Saturday for six hours, from nine in the morning to three in the afternoon.

Aarnie dropped us at a forbidding house three stories high and run-down. Toys lay wounded in the yard like losers in a local war. We tapped the lion's head knocker. The woman who answered was around forty, skinny, heavily made up and heavy-eyed—either sleepy or drugged—and was dressed for evening in a black sheath, black nylons, and black stiletto heels. Her hair had the dull density of black dye. Despite a forced gaiety of jewelry and red fingernails, she gave the impression of someone broken.

"Come on in," she said, not giving us her name or asking for ours, scattering words behind her as she teetered down an unlit hall. "We keep the place dark on purpose. We're light-sensitive." The house was truly dark. The day was overcast, and all the shades were drawn. No lights were on. My eyes took a while adjusting, as they would in a dark movie theater. Then I saw that the front room had no furniture. The dining room had a table and two chairs. In the kitchen, five children sat in a breakfast nook eating cereal and watching television. The screen flickered blue, cartoon dogs falling off cliffs, bounding back unharmed. In the poor light from the TV, I could make out twin girls about six years old and three boys ranging from about age two to eight. A baby slept in a bassinet.

"Hi," Julianna said, saying her name and mine. Several children looked up briefly and returned to their show. Tip-tapping down the hall came another woman, a carbon copy of the first, also wearing black clothes and four-inch heels, also looking injured. This one was in her mid-twenties. "Mother?" she said. "Did you get out the cash?" (Oh. The first woman was the *grandmother*.) To us, she said, "I'm Tessa Francher. When the contest man calls, take down the information."

Julianna said, "Um, the contest man?"

"On TV. You know, 'Spin and Win'? They're having that jingle contest. They're giving away a car, and we're feeling lucky. Tell 'em we'll be right

114

back. We can pick up the car Monday." She was dead serious. She expected to win.

The women picked up their purses and fur coats, fluttered fingers at the children and sailed down the hall, trailing a veil of oppressive perfume. As soon as they were gone, I wondered how to reach them in case of an emergency. I whispered to Julianna, "Do you know where they went?"

"No. I forgot to ask. I was preoccupied." She moved her eyes meaningfully around the gloom. I knew what she meant. Two half-open doors led off the kitchen, and behind them, I guessed, were the backyard, the basement, and raised-knife killers. Daring death, I scuttled to the doors and whammed them shut.

Julianna asked the children, "Do you know where your mother went?"

The oldest boy said, "The card room. They always lose."

A twin said, "That's where the furniture went. Gone with the wind!" She and her sister laughed without humor.

Julianna placed her lips in a line. "Uh, Kik, could I see for you a minute?" We went into the dining room and huddled on the two chairs.

"Isn't this against the law?" Julianna said. "I mean, gambling everything away? Making kids live like this?"

"What do we do, call the cops?"

She mulled this over. "Let's see how it goes. I wonder if they have beds, even."

We went back to the kitchen and Julianna snapped on the ceiling light. The children flinched, unused to light. The baby was awake. I felt an edge of her diaper; it was wet. I assumed the baby was a girl since the bassinet had pink ribbons, but who knew how many babies had slept in there?

I said, "Who can show me where the diapers are?"

A small boy dropped off the bench and led me upstairs to a bedroom done in red taffeta. The bed was a canopied four-poster, high off the floor. A cold wood stove stood in one corner. Tasseled shades covered the windows. The room smelled of cologne gone bad and clothes in need of cleaning, but on the bed was a pile of clean diapers, T-shirts, and towels. I thanked the boy for his help. Nodding sagely, he sauntered off.

When I finished folding the clothes, I picked up the diapers and went down the hall to check sleeping arrangements. I found two small rooms with blankets on the floor, no beds. In a room that stank of urine, lumps of boys' clothes lay on the floor, plus trucks and blocks. In the other room, girls' clothes lay in similar lumps along with a few dolls.

Dispirited, I went downstairs. Julianna was washing dishes. A twin who had been shaking a rattle at the baby went back to the nook. I changed the baby's diaper, wrapped her in a blanket, carried her to the refrigerator and took inventory. "Ketchup, chili sauce, a bottle of beer, four baby bottles filled with milk. What do we make for lunch?"

Julianna said, "Let's see what's over here." She opened the nearest cupboard. "Dishes. Cornstarch, spices." Another cupboard. "Better. Chef Boyardee, corn . . ."

In the next hours, we learned the children's names, played games with them, told them stories, watched them play outdoors. We gave them lunch and snacks. At supper time, because the women weren't home yet, we fed the children the last of the food. We bathed the youngest ones, checking for bruises and finding none. The older kids bathed on their own. We supervised tooth-brushing, put the baby in her bassinet and oversaw the older five climbing into their bedrolls. Throughout the day and evening, the children seemed emotionally flat. Counting in the baby-sitters, we made a sad little bunch.

Julianna and I sat in the kitchen nook and talked about our families, our fears, boys, religion, the future. We watched television, trying to stay awake. We phoned our families, saying the women were late, they should be home soon, any time now.

The women came home at four a.m. with food for the house and no apologies. We had agreed to stay for six hours. We had been there for *nineteen*. We accepted our pay and called Julianna's father and waited for him on the curb.

There was nothing to report to authorities. The children were fed, housed, and clothed, if badly. We felt sorry for them, but we couldn't upset our own homes for the vagaries of their mother and grandmother. We never baby-sat there again.

* * *

But the nineteen hours had done wonders for Julianna and me. In a rush of friendship, we decided to turn out for cheer squad. The cheer advisor, Miss Trimble, was doubling the size of cheerleader and song queen squads for all the major sports. New members would be rotated in, term by term, until the roster was full. We would try out for both song queen and cheerleader to have a better chance at one.

We asked Cora Munson, an athletic song queen with a bullfrog voice, to teach us the motions to the fight song:

> Hib-bing High School, hats off to thee!
> To your col-ors, true we shall al-ways bee-ee!
> Firm and strong, u-ni-ted are we!
> Rah! Rah! Rah-rah-rah!
> Rah! Rah! Rah-rah-rah!
> Hats off to Hib-bing Hi-i-igh!

Then we got Betty Jo Studeman, a cheerleader known for her tiny waist, to show us some cheers. She did "Give 'Em the Axe," giving a delicate cast to the vicious words:

> Give 'em the axe, give 'em the axe, give 'em the axe, where?
> Right in the neck, right in the neck, right in the neck, there!
> Right in the neck, the neck, the neck,
> Right in the neck, the neck, the neck,
> Right in the neck, right in the neck, right in the neck, there!

She followed up with "Riff Roff"—almost as brutal but not quite—and finished with a cartwheel:

> Riff Roff Ree!
> Kick 'em in the knee!
> Riff Roff Ree!
> Kick 'em in the other knee!

Finally, she did "V-I-C-T-O-R-Y," ending with the splits, legs flat-out:

Vict'ry! Vict'ry! That's our cry!
V-I-C-T-O-R-Y!
Vict'ry! Vict'ry! VICT'RY!

Julianna and I couldn't do cartwheels or the splits, and we needed to work on the cheers and the fight song, so we practiced behind the boarding house when the miners were at work. We didn't want an audience. Not yet, anyway.

On tryout day, we did the fight song and "Give 'Em the Axe," leaving out any splits or cartwheels. In a whirl of excitement, we were elected to the varsity football cheer squad. Being chosen was a thrill, and being fitted for the heavy wool H sweaters was another thrill.

But then came the hard work. The squad consisted of four boys and eight girls, and everyone was expected to have some special talent, back flips, or tumbling runs, or extra strength for the pyramid. Julianna and I had no special talents. Worse, every other girl could do cartwheels and the splits.

Two gyms stayed open after school for weight training, rope-climbing and so on. Julianna and I signed up for one end of B gym on Tuesdays and Thursdays. Our first day on this schedule, we stepped out of the girls' locker room in our fresh white everythings, T-shirts, shorts, socks, tennis shoes, into the rarified fumes of a high school gym after a long day. "Pee-*yew*," Julianna said. "It stinks in here. Like old socks."

I said, "That's probably what it is, old socks. Carol told me her brother didn't know he was supposed to wash his gym socks. He left them at school all year and kept wearing them, and by June they could stand up in the locker by themselves!"

Julianna sniggered a laugh and held her nose. "How cub boys sweat so buch?"

"It's their male prerogative. But then they shower and get dressed and come out looking scrumptious. I say they're worth it."

"Freddy is, stinky socks or no stinky socks." Freddy Markowsky was a senior and a sports hero. Julianna had a crush on him but had never met him.

We dragged out the springboard, the tumbling mat, and the vault. By turns we took off running, hit the springboard and did a handspring over the vault, spotting each other with a hand at the small of the back. After twenty minutes, we pushed the vault against the wall and left out the tumbling mat. I needed to practice my cartwheels.

"Watch and see what I'm doing wrong." I ran and skipped, arms in the air, went into the wheel off-balance and landed with a yelp on the rock-hard shoulder of the mat.

Julianna ran over to me. "What happened?"

"My tailbone. It hit the seam."

"Oo, ouch. Can you get up?"

I tried. "It hurts. Give me a second."

"Should I get someone?"

"No, it's okay. I'll be fine."

"I thought you *had* it there for a minute," she said. "But I guess you stepped off wrong. Try getting up." With Julianna's help, I got up and hobbled out of the gym.

The doctor said yes, I had injured my coccyx, and, yes, it would take time to heal, and, yes, tumbling could re-injure it.

That was the end of my cheerleading. An alternate was given my spot. Secretly I cheered. Now I would *never* have to do cartwheels or the splits.

*   *   *

In place of cheer squad, I had to take sewing, or at least that's how my schedule turned out. I went to the fabric section of Penneys and got flummoxed. I needed cottons, but there were so many! Row after row. Cotton bolts impaled on metal stands, sample-ends hanging to the floor. Damask. Shirting. Calico. Gingham. Summer weight. Polished. Plaids, checks, polka dots, stripes. I couldn't take it all in. I couldn't make the stripes stand still.

The back of my pattern read: "Fabrics: Cotton, raw silk, or silk broadcloth. Extra fabric needed to match plaids, stripes or one-way design, 2 5/8 yds. of 45 in. width, 2 yds. of 78 in. width." It didn't say what *kind* of cotton. Some were flimsy, some were starchy. How could anyone choose?

I meandered into the next aisle. Embroidery threads were terraced on a tall stand, a prism of colors, loops of thread in dainty paper rings. Very pretty. But embroidery was not for me. Too detailed! I wiggled my fingers, freeing them of the task of embroidering. I studied my hands. They were like Mummo's, square and short, probably able to "do" something. But what? Not embroidery, I'd already decided. That was Liisa's bailiwick, and she was welcome to it. Not knitting, either. Inky had taught Liisa and me to knit, and of course Liisa was a natural. The only thing I'd finished to the bitter end was a sweater fit for a chimp, not anyone with normal arms. Not sewing either. As soon as the class was over, I was retiring from sewing. Pinning patterns made my head ache, and bending over the Singer gave me neck cramps, and when I stepped on the pedal the thread snapped because the tension was wrong, and when I tried to fix it I twisted the knob too far, and the thread tangled in a clump under the pressure foot and stopped the Singer *cold*. Talk about *tension* and *pressure*. My sentiments exactly.

When I got to the yarns, I stalked along rebelliously, touching skeins and idly reading the names: Angora, Shetland, baby, crewel, eiswool, Isle of Skye, caddis.

Gaining interest, I took note of the textures—silky, raggy, ridged.

Now *this* was more like it!

I found a sales clerk and asked her if there was something besides knitting that I could do with the thicker yarns. Overweight and footsore, she moved her center of gravity from one nurse-shoe to the other. Amiably, she said, "Let's see now. I believe we had something. It's in the stockroom. Do you mind waiting?" She turned and hobbled down the aisle, leaving me feeling sorry I'd sent her on the errand.

But she came back gleeful and handed me a booklet. The woman in the cover photo wore a tunic woven in a rustic, knobbly pattern. Turning pages, I found more garments made of the same weave, hooded capes, shawls, coats, vests. Beautiful.

The sales clerk pointed to a name on the back. I read out loud, "Zoey Zakudy, weaving instructor." I noticed her address. "Hibbing? She lives *here*?"

The clerk was positively glowing. She knew she'd made a match. "That's her on the cover. She lives on a farm. She teaches but doesn't use this kind of yarn."

"What kind does she use?"

She gnawed at her lip. "Shetland? No, some other. She raises her own sheep and shears and cards the wool herself."

I thanked her and went to find Mummo and Liisa. They were in the kitchen section, fingering gadgets—gadgets I felt released from! I didn't need them. I would be a weaver! Not a super-duper Betty Crocker cooker who needed these gadgets. Not a seamstress. Not a knitter.

A *weaver.*

At home, I counted my baby-sitting money. I had enough to start lessons. I asked Mummo if I could do my Saturday chores on Friday after school. She agreed. I asked Aarnie if he would drive me to my lesson. He said he would. I called Zoey Zakudy and arranged my first session for the coming Saturday.

The week passed like molasses, but Saturday finally came. Aarnie drove me to Hibbing along with Mummo who would shop at the Co-op while I took my lesson. Zoey's house sat under a brood of maples, a tumbledown, sprawling house with hinged windows that made up the front walls and much of the low-pitched roof. Many of the windows were propped open. A frenetic kind of music drifted outdoors, taking me to castles and foreign meadows as I knocked. No one answered. Zoey's yard was a garden of weeds. A few flowers, left over from summer, were tired of keeping up appearances. Four daisies hung their heads and one stalk of hollyhock leaned on the fence. I saw no barn, no animals. I knocked again. The woman who came to the door had cropped brown hair and was shorter and stockier than I'd pictured her. She wore jeans, a khaki shirt, and tall suede boots. Her eyes, which were slightly crossed, flitted before coming to rest on my own. She laughed, "Hope you like Vivaldi! Ken puts it on, then he forgets and drives off. I couldn't hear you!" Her wind-chime earrings went *tink-tink* as we shook hands.

We stepped into a wide all-purpose room floored with rock slab, an expanse as tidy as the yard was untidy. Light filtered in through maple leaves that moved in designs on the floor. Zoey went to turn down the music, and I looked around. Her whole household except for bed and bath was in this one open space. The far end was furnished with couches and plants and an Oriental rug, only partially visible behind an ornamental screen. The near end was the kitchen-dining area. By a central wall stood two looms with weavings in progress, a Pilgrim's chair before each. Yarns sat on shelves in the middle of the floor, in baskets tilted away from the sun. Various weights of yarn in neutral colors. The colors of wheat, charcoal, sand, pewter, Palomino.

Enough shades to satisfy.

Zoey returned. I asked her if the yarns were from her sheep. "Yes," she smiled, "my Lincolns. Come, I'll show you." We went out the back door, along a path, through a gate and out into the pasture. Over a rise, there they were, about twenty large, broad-backed sheep with mounded coats of wool. Zoey went over to a dark-gray ram. "This is Cappy." The ram lifted his head and acknowledged Zoey. She rumpled his topknot. The ram went on grazing. "Sweet old thing. They're a peaceful breed. They're an old breed, from the eighteenth century. The wool has a luster I can't find anywhere else."

One sheep was a lighter color than the rest. "Is that a different breed?" I asked.

"They're all Lincoln Longhairs." Zoey spoke of her animals with affection. "That one's a White. We have Whites, Blacks, and Blues. The Blues go from nearly black to white-silver and gray." Her voice became conspiratorial. "If you want to, you can bleach the wool in the sun. It goes naturally to beautiful light browns, even a touch of *red*!"

"And you shear them yourself?"

"Sure!" She laughed again. "Ken and I. We get twenty pounds off the big ones."

I thought about lifting twenty pounds of anything, flour, or potatoes. Twenty pounds was a lot of wool. I said, "*Twenty pounds* off one sheep?"

"Not always, but sometimes. We wash it and dry it, and card and spin . . ."

It took me five minutes of sitting at a loom to know that I had found my art. I would do anything to be able to weave, baby-sit more, help Mummo more, give up my free time. Zoey suggested a plan. After four or five lessons, she said, I would be weaving on my own, and since I didn't own a loom I could keep coming here on Saturdays to use hers. She would show me how to set up a loom, start to finish, how to design patterns, change the warp and woof, troubleshoot, replace a broken bobbin or shuttle. Each week I could put a sum of money into a loom fund. When the fund held enough to buy materials, her husband would build me a loom.

I would have a loom of my own!

The only problem was telling the family. I knew the obstacles. A loom was too big. Too frivolous. Too specialized to one person's wishes. But I hoped against hope. Maybe we could put it in the dining room, or in the garage, or in the basement. Or I could sleep on the rollaway to make space in our room. Maybe Aarnie could convince Mummo, or Liisa would take my side. Maybe Mummo would say yes for once? I planned to tell them the next day after noon dinner.

During the meal, I blathered on and on about Zoey and Ken, about weaving and patterns and wool. Afterwards I insisted on doing dishes by myself. The others were rankly suspicious, but they let me do it. Aarnie read the newspaper. Mummo and Liisa got out coffee and dessert. I scrubbed away at the plates, mumbling without sound.

I couldn't wait. I brought my hands out of the suds and turned to them. "I want to buy a loom! for at home! Ken can build it and I can pay for it over time and Zoey will help me set it up!"

Watching for their reactions, I grabbed a towel and dried my hands. Liisa devoted energy to taking spoons from the drawer. Aarnie reddened. Mummo was the only one who looked at me, and she was not pleased.

Braced for resistance, I plowed ahead. "I know we can find room! And I'll work extra hard . . ."

The Silence made a whirring sound in the kitchen. My hopes were flagging, almost dead. "I know we'd have to change things around, but maybe . . .?"

Nothing.

That was how it worked. You could talk and talk, and if the others didn't approve of what you said they simply waited for you to stop talking. You could raise the roof, screech, cry, rant, whine, beg, it wouldn't matter.

I had known it all along. I would never have a loom.

The next Saturday, deflated, I told Zoey the news. She said, "That's okay. Keep coming here on Saturdays and weave all you want. Then, when you go to college, you can get a place big enough for a loom. How many years until college?"

"Two," I said without conviction. "*If* I go."

Zoey raised my chin with her fingertips. "Of course you'll go. And you can wait for your loom. Two years isn't forever. Let's make it two good years." She ran the knuckles of one hand down my cheek. "You're going to be one fine weaver."

It was Zoey who made the two years good ones. Twice a month, she drove me to Minneapolis in a dilapidated Packard that surprised me by making it back to Hibbing. She introduced me to her art school friends, to galleries and weavers' shows. She took me to coffee shops, concerts, plays, libraries, cathedrals, sports events. She nudged me toward the University of Minnesota and an art major. It was Zoey who opened the bigger world to me.

One fall day, when I was safely enrolled at the University of Minnesota and ensconced in Kaisa's house, Zoey drove up in Ken's farm truck. We lugged the loom upstairs three flights and down the hall and into my room, which was big enough, light enough, and private enough for a loom. Zoey set it up and left it there as a tangible lesson in patience.

Part 2

Pushing Away

Nine

The Pillow Storm

Marcie and Adam eloped two days after she graduated from Cranston High, four days after she turned eighteen. He drove from California to Las Vegas, Nevada. She flew from Minnesota. They were married by a judge. They honeymooned en route to Cranston where they packed Marcie's clothes, said good-bye to her family, and drove in a dash to Berkeley where Adam was finishing a Masters in math at the University of California.

All of this happened within a week. I hadn't had an inkling. No one had. Harald and Inky were left feeling dazed and ill-treated, but I was elated. By eloping, Marcie and Adam had leapfrogged over arguments against their marrying just then: "But you're still a teen-ager" and "It takes a year to plan a wedding" and "Your father won't want Kaisa helping." For Marcie and Adam, a wedding could have ruined the fun of getting married.

In her first letter as a wife, Marcie sounded like her old self. She made fun of her new name, Marcia Ann Halonen Tiskanen, saying she had more "nens" in her name than any Finn she knew. "Am I official? Now can I be a Finn?" Adam would get his degree by summer's end. Marcie called him a buzz saw. He'd done his B.A. in three years, now his M.A. in less than two. The only jobs he was applying for were in Minneapolis. His friends wondered out loud why he was getting an M.A., "just for teaching," but teaching was what he wanted to do. Her parents had warmed up, some, she said. They had turned Marcie's old bedroom into a den with a sofa bed. Which sounded fine to Marcie. She said she and Adam snuggled *wherever*—and no, she wouldn't tell me all about it. I'd have to learn about *that* for myself. She wanted to live in Minnesota and have Christmas the way it should be, complete with deep snow, igloo lanterns, stupid jokes, candles burning down the Christmas tree. She wanted to show Adam how Christmas "always was."

The two had a master calendar, and everything they planned came true. Adam got his M.A. in early August, flew to Minneapolis, found a job, and decided on a nice two-story rental house on a shady street. They moved at the end of the month. Marcie got a job at a camera shop and registered part time at the University of Minnesota. Adam taught math at Fendway Boarding, a stupendously endowed school for rich boys who left home at the age of twelve. He had replaced a teacher who had snapped major bones while water-skiing— or not actually water-skiing so much as colliding with a dock while on water-skis. The man's spirit had snapped as well, and he would not be returning to teaching. Late in the hiring season, Adam had been offered his job. That's the kind of sunshine that fell on Marcie and Adam.

I envied them their good luck, but I was pushing my own luck for all it was worth. College was a time of growth and change—that's what I'd heard, anyway. So, when I saw a certain posting on the student center wall, I developed a sudden yen to see Finland. The posting read: "Spend summer in historic Helsinki. Fellowship grant for two months. Intensive Finnish language and culture study. See your college registrar."

At the registrar's office, when I asked for an application, the clerk flapped her lashes at me. "My, but you're brave! Have you ever been overseas?" Her desk sign said her name was Shirley Murchison. She was young, about my age. Why would she think me brave? Then I noticed her hair. It was short, curled, molded into a cap, sprayed into submission, and tamped down for good measure. This Shirley liked her life stable and in one place.

"No, but I think it's time I went," I said. "When is the application due?"

"Me? I don't last very long away from home. I like my own bed."
Shirley fanned her cheeks with a brochure, as if the mere mention of travel
whipped up undue heat. She checked her books. "Four days from now, here
at the office. What will take the longest are the reference letters. They want
three. If you request them today and tell your people the due date, you should
be fine." I thanked her, and as I turned to leave she relaxed. She looked like
someone who'd had a close call but could stay home after all.

That afternoon I asked three professors for recommendations, and
retreated to my library carrel to read the application. It asked: "What are your
reasons for wanting to study in Finland? In what specific ways would the intensive study of the Finnish language and Finnish culture fit into your long-range
educational goals?"

I came up blank on all counts. I had no idea why I should go to
Finland. I doubted that I could learn the language. And I had no educational
goals, long-range or otherwise.

For three days straight, I worked on the application. I asked no one for
help, told no one what I was doing. If I won this grant, it would be on my own
steam. I read everything I could find on Finnish art, history, architecture, poetry,
folklore, current events. I took rough notes, planning to later fill in the gaps.

- Sweden owns Finland, 600 years (1300s to 1906).
- Finnish language is lost except among peasants, fisherman, farmers.
- Rise of Finnish nationalism, 1800s.
- College students collect folk runos from peasants. Elias Lönnrot,
  medical student, top collector. 1885, he publishes folk epic, the
  Kalevala.
- 1906—Russia takes Finland from Sweden. Finns resist "russification."
  Students revive Finnish language.
- Early 20th—Nationalism in art and music. Composer Jean Sibelius.
  Painter Akseli Gallen-Kallela. Architect Eero Saarinen.
- 1939—Soviet Union invades Finland (Harald's Winter War!).
  Finland loses war but wins world praise for bravery and for paying
  war debt to SU.

This was exciting! Finland rose out of the mist of history and became a real place. In a typing room, I hacked out a study plan. I would contrast expressions of *sisu* in the *Kalevala* with those in letters from Finnish immigrants in the United States, 1900 to 1930, to friends and relatives in Finland. I would have to learn to read Finnish, but that's what the grant offered, a way to learn the language. I would do research in Minneapolis, at the university's humanities library and the Immigration History Research Center, in Helsinki, at the University of Helsinki and the Finnish Literature Society, and, in Turku, at the Institute of Migration.

Late in the afternoon on the day the application was due, I slid the packet through the registrar's slot. Then I hid in my carrel. I had to work on my regular coursework.

When I looked up, the sky was black. I checked my watch. Eight-thirty. If I pressed my head to the window, I could see four floors down: curved footpath, gooseneck lamps and circles of light, trees being bandied by the wind. Two students walked by at double-pace, the thrust of their bodies telling how harsh the wind was. I put on my pea coat and packed away my books, elevatored down to the ground floor, and clunked open the exit bar on the night door, stepped out. The wind was spitting horizontally. I ran to the bus stop, glad to be going someplace warm.

Still in my pea coat, I sank into a stuffed chair. "Kaisa, what do you know about socialism and American Finns?"

She looked stricken. She put down her knitting and gazed at the yarn, at the fire, at her yarn again. To cover the strain, I stood and set down my book bag, pulled off my wraps, folded them, piled them on the arm of my chair, sat down and waited.

She gave me a sustained, inquiring look. "How did you happen to . . . ?"

"I've been reading Finnish history—about Red Finns and White Finns—for a grant I'm applying for. For a summer program in Finland."

I skidded to a halt. I hated being told news late, and yet here I was, telling Kaisa my news, late.

But she didn't react to the news of the grant. Something else had her in its vice. In a purposeful tone, she said, "You have hit upon our sins." She sighed and looked at me. "Are you up to it tonight? It has to do with your parents."

"I'm fine," I said, but my heart was doing skips. *My parents?*

Kaisa set aside her needles and their ribbon of first stitches and cooped the yarn ball in her hands, as she would nestle a kitten. "Where to start? . . . Maybe back when I met your mother. We were young and idealistic. It was the early thirties. The Depression had hit hard, and people had either lost their jobs or were afraid they would, and they were trying to find answers. Some Finns thought socialism was the answer, everyone sharing goods, no more rich or poor. Heaven on earth! They dreamed of utopian communities, perfect places to live. There was even a man named Halonen who started one in Canada. No relation . . .

"Well, some socialist Finns were active in the labor movement, and they supported better conditions in mines and factories. Not all Finns were union, mind you, and not all union people were socialists, but in public opinion there was a strict division. Red and White. Church Finns were called Good Finns, Temperance Finns, or White Finns. The union Finns were the Bad Finns."

Kaisa seemed embarrassed. "Union Finns were called Hall Finns, or Red Finns. Anyway, the union Finns held rallies at Finn Halls across the country, socialist meetings, mostly. Hibbing had a Finn Hall and was one of the most active branches. Hibbing was a center of socialism."

She snapped out of her somber mood to smile over this notion: Hibbing, *famous.*

"The speakers got people all stirred up. They were good speakers, and they talked about cooperation and fairness, putting people ahead of wealth, being honest, helping the less fortunate. It's ironic. . . . These are Bible themes, and the socialists didn't believe in God, most of them. . . . But they did good things. They set up food co-ops wherever Finns lived, Berkeley, New York . . ."

I broke in. "Is the Hibbing Co-op *socialist?* Does Mummo know?"

Something blinked on and off on Kaisa's face—spite, maybe, or shame—and left her looking bleached-out, unguarded. "At first maybe it was

131

socialist, but not now." She ignored my question about Mummo, I noticed. "The socialists were for racial fairness, help for the unemployed, better schools. The ideas sounded good, especially in such frightening times."

While she decided what to say next, I ran through what she'd already said. A lot of it dovetailed with my research. Red Finns, socialism, communism. The Soviets. The Winter War . . .

"Uncle Harald! That's why he's mad at you, isn't it? Because of socialism?"

She moved her features sufficiently to indicate yes. "And more. We'll get to that later. . . . At the beginning, your mother and I only went to plays at Finn Hall in Minneapolis, then we started staying for the speeches and rallies. Sofia wasn't political—she was a private sort of person—but she believed in equality and fair labor laws. I was a political person. I would've loved to be up on stage!"

For a moment, as she delved into memory, she looked optimistic and young. "Anyway. We met Esko and your father. They were earnest, talented, lovely young men. Mysterious, both of them. Esko was broody, Patrik was bright, and we fell for them in no time. We had such fun, the four of us! No matter where else we went, to the movies or supper, we ended up at Finn Hall. For ten years, socialist Finns had gone around the country and stirred up what people called 'Karelian fever.' They painted a sorry picture of the United States. They said rich Americans took home fat paychecks while poor Americans had no food. They described an ideal place with no unemployment, a new society built on socialist ideals, no rich industrialists telling you what to do. They said American Finns could be a part of the dream. It was Russian Karelia they meant, in the western Soviet Union, the part that was *Finland* before the Winter War. They needed loggers, fishermen, builders, anyone willing to work. People who went to Karelia would find conditions primitive, but if they worked hard they could build a new society."

Clear as day, it came to me: *I could have been born in Russia.* I said, "My parents went there, didn't they?"

A miniscule tic passed over her face. "Yes. We all did. We got married quickly, got our affairs in order and took the first train east. We didn't tell our families. We knew they would be angry. Russia was communist, the enemy of Finland."

Harald's grudge. I asked Kaisa, "When did they find out?"

"When we got back." She seemed pensive, apologetic. "My parents had died years before, and I have only one brother, and we were never close. So it was Harald's family who took it hard. . . .Well, in Karelia, conditions were terrible. We were prepared to rough it, but 'roughing it' doesn't even begin to describe it! The roads were like rock beds or mud ruts in the woods. Trains didn't run on time, when they ran at all. American Finns had sent so much money to Karelia—for trucks, schools, fishing ships—but there was no evidence that the money was being used right. We saw American trucks sitting in fields, falling apart. Our housing was in an old storage building. We had to put up blankets to make bedrooms. Esko and Patrik built houses, and Sofia and I worked in the construction office. We worked hard, but morale was bad, and we had language problems. Our spoken Finnish was different enough that Finns living in Karelia sometimes couldn't understand us.

"Which brings me to the Karelians. They didn't welcome us. We'd gone there to help them, willing, if it came to it, to give up our American citizenship! But the people didn't want us. We could see why. Foreigners got the best food and the best supplies. As bad as it was for us, it was worse for them. No fresh fruits or vegetables—and we were there in the summer! We kept comparing it to the States. In the States, even in the Great Depression, we had refrigerators and good streets, and fresh food any season. We were very discouraged. Very disillusioned.

"Then I got pregnant. I didn't want to have the baby there. . . . Well, bab-*ies*, but I didn't know I would have twins. I wanted to come back to the States. We all did. So we arranged to leave right away.

"But before we could leave, Esko got taken. He was arrested on a false charge!"

Kaisa glared at me as if asking, *Can you believe that?* Her sense of scandal over Esko's arrest, like Harald's over the Winter War, had not faded over time. She laid the heels of her hands on her eyes, brought her hands to her lap. "They took him away, no explanation. I was beside myself. *I didn't know where he was!* No one would tell me anything. Our ship would leave in twenty-four hours, and I had to decide. I talked with Sofia and Patrik and tried to think what Esko would say. I knew he would want me safe, the baby, too, so I did the most difficult thing I've ever done. I came home without him. Your parents came, too . . . It was like Esko had died."

Her mouth tried different positions before she spoke again. "A year later he sent me a wire. He was free. He was in Finland, on his way home. The twins were four months old when he got home. He said the prisons were like concentration camps. The Soviets talked about justice, but they were cruel to him. They accused him of sabotage, and of stealing money! They hit him and took him from place to place, and didn't get him a doctor when he was sick. Finally, a sympathetic Russian guard snuck him out, and he made a run for the Finnish border. From there, he came home."

Kaisa went down the hall to her bathroom. I inflated and deflated my cheeks, rolling a thought around in my head: My parents nearly gave up their American citizenship. For Russia, Finland's enemy.

When she returned, I collected my wraps. "Thanks, Kaisa. I'll say good night. We'll talk another time."

"Fine," she said. She looked ten years older.

* * *

It was a fledgling program at the University of Minnesota, Dr. Taggart told us. We, his Intro to Psych students, would meet weekly in small groups, to deal with personal issues. Each group would be led by a licensed therapist.

The plan appalled me! I didn't trust *anyone* with personal issues, and I didn't want anyone telling me what was wrong with me!

But attendance was required. In trepidation, I reported to an off-campus cottage at seven o'clock on a Wednesday evening. Timothy Suterman, Ph.D., was too young to be a therapist, but, already, as he opened the door, he was X-raying my brain. Therapists did that, I told myself, they could see right through you, see what you're hiding. I wondered: Did he consciously choose that therapist costume, the wrinkled chinos and loosened tie? What did he think—that I'd spill my guts? Tell him my *life story*, for Pete's sake?

His front room was small and welcoming—deep-cushioned chairs and twin davenports, a fire in the fireplace, photos on the mantel. But to me the place was alien. I didn't trust it. A normal family lived here. I didn't come from a normal family.

When all of the students had found places to sit, Tim, still standing, smiled at us individually. "Okay then, let's get started. I'm Tim, and I'm glad you're here. My wife and daughter are with my parents, so we won't be interrupted."

My insides contracted. Interrupted in *what?*

Sitting defensively, arms crossed, I checked out the other students. They looked as wary as I felt. Most of them had *their* arms crossed, too.

Tim said. "Everything we discuss here is confidential. You can feel free to say whatever you want. Nothing personal goes out of this room. Agreed?"

We agreed.

"I'll lead off each week. We'll help each other at different times. Who knows? I might have more problems than anyone." Again he smiled. I had to give him credit. He was trying his best.

"Joe," he said, "why don't you start off? Tell us your whole name and something about yourself." Tim brought over a dining chair and took a seat, closing the circle.

As students introduced themselves, I made up jingles to help me remember names. "Whoa! Look at Joe!" (Good-looking farm kid.) "Greg has gargantuan gopher glasses." (Thick glasses, ag major.) "Small Sarah sings." (Child's body, music major.) "Betty's even better in a boat!" (Nurse, canoes as a hobby.) "Mark barks." (Cocky, no major yet.) "Karin, why ar-en' you dancin'?" (*Kah*-rin, ballet dancer.) Superficial information. But it proved we were miles apart. We would never learn to trust each other.

Before my turn came, I warned myself: Name and major, that's all! No one needs to know anything.

I was the last one up. "I'm Kik Halonen. I'm from the Iron Ore Range. I'm an art major, and I weave Lincoln Longhair wool, rough-carded. Um, I never knew my parents."

Confounded, I closed my mouth. Where had *that* come from?

Tim said, "You might want to talk about that sometime. We'll give you a chance one of these nights, okay?" I nodded, but I had no intention of taking up his offer.

Mark dropped out after that night. By the fourth week, the remaining students had spent three sessions discussing personal issues. *Their* personal issues, not mine. I didn't want anyone discussing me.

That night, Tim made general comments about personality growth, then put a question to the group. "Do you see yourself as different from your parents or similar?"

My eyes brimmed over. Tim, who didn't miss a thing, said, "Kik?"

"I never knew my parents," I said for the second time to this group. The pain was as strong as if my parents had died that day.

Tim asked, "Are you ready to work on it?"

My heart was galloping, and my stomach threatened to empty itself on the rug, but I said yes.

"Good. Why don't you come over here." I went to stand by Tim in the center of the room. He asked the others to move the couches and chairs back to form a wider circle. They did so.

"Okay, Kik, don't use any words for now. Choose people and pose them into your family. Show them where to stand or sit, how to put their arms and so on. You can use me too if you need to."

Karin and Greg would be my parents. I dragged them to the most distant spot I could see, the vestibule, covered their mouths with their hands and turned their backs to the group. I stopped to think, then pushed them behind the coat tree and hid them with coats and jackets. Back in the circle, I chose Sarah as Mummo, Joe as Uncle Aarnie, Betty as Liisa. I placed Mummo standing astride, hands on hips. Facing her, I drew her chin up and pinched the air along her lip line. I put Liisa next to Mummo and arranged the side of Liisa closest to Mummo to mimic Mummo, her hand on her hip, and that side of her mouth stapled shut. I extended her other arm toward the class, her hand cupped as if asking for alms. The pose startled me. Before now, I'd never seen Liisa as needy. I had Aarnie stand behind Mummo and Liisa, his arms above them, angel-like.

I was finished. Tim asked me if this was my whole family. I said yes. He said, "Now I'd like you to put yourself in the picture."

Feeling ill-tempered, I gave him a dirty look. Why did he have to keep jabbing at me? I didn't know *where* I belonged! . . . I didn't belong *anywhere*.

But I immediately knew what to do. I was crying before I got to the floor. I lay on my face and stretched as hard as I could, my toes pointed at Mummo and my hands reaching for my parents.

After letting me cry a while, Tim said, "Now, Kik, put words to the tears."

I cried harder and tried to stretch farther. "I can't do it."

"Can't do what?"

"Pull the family together! I try and try. . ." I wanted to curl up and go to sleep. "Nothing works."

"You try, how?"

"I try to be good, but no one ever talks!"

Again, Tim let time go by as I cried. Then he said, "What do you need, Kik?"

"Someone to talk to me."

"Okay. Are you ready to get up?" I got to my feet and saw that the others were back in their seats. Tim passed me a box of Kleenex. I took a tissue, blew my nose, put the tissue in my jeans pocket. I took another one for reserve, wasting time.

Tim said, "You never knew your parents?"

"They died when I was a month old."

"And who is Sarah?"

"My grandmother."

"Your grandmother took care of you?"

"She *raised* me," I said tartly. "She didn't *take care* of me."

"Let's have you work with *her* then."

I had no objection. There was relief in mindlessly following directions. Tim asked Sarah to come to the center. "Kik, I'd like you to pose Sarah any way you'd like. Talk to your grandmother. Sarah, you can answer in whatever way seems best."

I put Sarah on her knees, although I didn't know why. (Mummo, asking for something?) I arranged her arms in an X on her chest and again stapled her lips shut. I stood back a few paces.

Tim said, "Now talk to her."

This activity seemed dry and directionless. Halfheartedly, I said to Sarah, "You never talk to me."

Mummo said, muffled by the staples, "Hmmpf."

"I want you to talk to me."

"*Hmmpf!*"

Right off the bat, I was blazing mad! Sarah was short and small-boned, like Mummo. She even looked like her with her mouth pursed like that. I was seeing Mummo here, hearing her. I yelled, "I hate this! You never talk! Now, *talk!*"

Working around her stapled lips, Mummo said, "I don't want to talk to you."

She had said it. Admitted she didn't want to talk to me. I shouted, "That's not fair! *Talk* to me!"

"No."

I bent down to her face. "I . . . want . . . you . . . to *talk* to me! *Look* at me!"

She swung away.

I screamed, "Aaaugh!" I stood up and shook myself. My arms felt pulled out of their joints, or not like mine at all, as if they belonged to some other person. I told Tim, "It's no use, it's always like this, she won't talk."

Tim handed me a bed pillow and asked Sarah if I could hit her with it. She said yes. He told me to hit Sarah if I wanted to but to keep talking to my grandmother.

I grabbed rabbit ears at one end of the pillow and got a tight grip. I didn't feel good about doing it, but I wound up and pounced at Mummo, stopping just short of whacking her. Regaining balance, I swung again and hit her, gingerly, on one shoulder.

"You don't care anything about me," I said. Reversing directions, I caught her in the other arm.

"Shame on you," Sarah said.

Mummo's words! . . . How did Sarah guess? I shouted, "You don't even know me! All these years! And you don't even *know* me!" I spun and hit her in the back of the neck.

She rallied from the blow. "You're a naughty girl," she said.

I yelled, "You kept me *prisoner!*" Taking a firmer hold, I swung and aimed at her head. But, again, she dodged. "You *smothered* me!"

"You're a bad girl."

"You kept me down!" I aimed once more for her head, but she flinched away. I tried again, but she moved again. I was enraged because she wouldn't stay still.

"Shame, shame!" she said.

"Stop it, *stop it!*" I was livid. I swung the pillow and plowed it into her hip. The impact threw me down onto one knee. I scrambled up, screaming, "I can never do enough for you! *Nothing is ever enough!*"

Mummo said, "You terrible girl."

"I am *not* terrible!" I brought the pillow down on the crown of her head.

She whispered terrible words: "You are not my child."

Crying in gusts, snot flying, I shouted, "That's right, I'm nobody's child! Not yours! Not my mother's! *Nobody's!* . . . I'm *no one!*"

The pillow hung from my hand, a dead duck. I wanted to quit. I dug out a tissue, used it, put it away. Tim said, "Don't give up. Stay in there."

I spun the pillow in a figure eight and banged Mummo on the shoulders again and again, screaming bang for bang: "*Give . . . me . . . my . . . parents!*"

"They went away."

"And you *kept* them away! You won't tell me *anything!*"

"I keep the secrets."

Tears were gushing; I was getting free! I lowered my face to Mummo's. "*Secrets!* All we *have* is secrets! I'm sick to *death* of secrets! I have secrets, too, and here's one. I never danced, just to please you, and it didn't matter! You didn't even *care.* You didn't even *know!*" I almost laughed. Talk about a pointless complaint! I could feel veins popping out on my temples.

139

"You keep this up," Mummo said, "and I'll get sick and die. Then you'll be sorry. It will be all your fault."

Mummo's favorite speech! Her unspoken, favorite speech.

I screamed, "*Aaugh!* Stop it!" I dropped the pillow and fell after it to my knees. Again I wanted to go to sleep, like my mother in the blizzard. "It's not my fault," I told Mummo. "I can't make your life right."

Out of the fog of regrets, I heard a certain truth. Mummo's life *wasn't* right. She was miserable, and her misery had nothing to do with me. I got to my feet and said, "Your life *isn't* right, is it?"

"When did *you* ever care?"

"Don't do that, don't." I was begging, dismayed at being caught in the same old trap. "Please talk to me." I reached to her and took her hand and raised her to her feet. A few seconds passed while Mummo straightened her clothes. She looked away, then at me, briefly, then at her hands. She said, "Maybe we could talk."

Now I cried for Mummo. It was *grief* that ran her life. What the grief was about, I had no idea, but I was crying her tears, moldy, soured, out-of-date, old-woman tears. Even as I cried, a small plan was evolving. I couldn't change how she treated me, but I could change how *I* treated *her.* Maybe forgive her, love her in spite of everything? I figured it was worth a try. We had been miserable long enough.

For starters, I gave Sarah a squeeze for being such a good little Mummo.

*   *   *

At the end of the term, Tim met with each of us separately. I gave him my observations of the Wednesday group: students learning to trust each other, at times succeeding, other times, not. Tim listened respectfully.

When I finished, he said, "You observe well. But where were you in the group?"

That got my fur up! I didn't want to discuss *me.* I asked him what he meant.

He said, "Are you aware that you see yourself on the outside, looking in?"

Tim was criticizing me. I *hated* criticism! Criticism stymied me, just stopped me in my tracks. How could I go on talking to him?

Risking barfing and passing out, I said, "Well, I did see my family in a new way."

"And how did you see yourself?"

Tears stung my eyes. "I'm afraid I'll end up like my grandmother."

"And that would be . . . ?"

"Frozen." I was crying again, shaking from the core. And here I'd been hoping I was all done crying.

"If you were frozen," Tim said, "what couldn't you do?"

"Love anyone."

"You never felt loved? Or accepted?" I shook my head no. "And when you were little and didn't feel loved, how did you see yourself?"

"Plain," I said. "Not lovable."

"And angry, and confused? As if you might be to blame?"

"Yes." I took a quick look at him, astonished that he knew.

"It was not your fault." Then he said it again.

In response, I gulped for air—for once, in a healthy way. There was more to that meeting and to others I had with Tim, but the common, saving element was that someone was hearing me out, giving me all the time I needed to say what I needed to say. Based on what I told him, Tim believed the near-faints that plagued Liisa, Mummo, and me were caused by anxiety. "It's a type of panic," he explained. "It used to be called hysteria, or a case of the nerves, or the vapors."

"Does it run in families?"

"We don't know if it's genetic, but members of one family often react the same way to problems. How we handle problems is partly learned, and in your family you might have learned ways that don't serve you well. But you can change. You can take note of situations that cause you anxiety—and then, when you're ready, place yourself in these very situations and practice new responses. Talking helps, too. Talk to a friend, or your sister. I could write you a prescription, but I think you can improve on your own."

I felt better already. My problem had a name. *Anxiety.* Just knowing what to call it took away some of its power.

* * *

But, perversely, during the next few months, I kept adding anxieties, like those surrounding Peggy. Peggy was a beatnik, one of a fluid cadre of students who enjoyed sex and drugs wherever they found them and in fact made opportunities for the same by living together in groups. We met in Life Drawing and fell into an easy friendship, studiously sketching nude male models and going out for coffee afterwards. The conventional name Peggy didn't fit her. She wore feathers and beads in her hair (an unshackled whirl of orange) and came to class in dresses meant for Medieval ladies, velvet creations with important sleeves and laced-up bodices. Peggy was a walking judgment of the female costume of the day, the tailored blouse and prim straight skirt of the prim straight college girl. It was Peggy's sense of freedom that attracted me.

I wasn't doing too well with my own freedom. University life was amorphous and left me rudderless—everyone on a separate schedule, no one knowing where anyone else was, for hours on end. I didn't have the wisdom to set limits. I skipped over any inborn sense I might have had and instead entertained any notion that came along. Freed from Mummo's strictures, and living with Kaisa, who demanded little, I opened my mind to anything that might teach me a thing or two, Ouija boards, Tarot cards, I Ching, Up Table, trances, séances. I was convinced that if I found the right combination I wouldn't be anxious any more. Tim had helped me to see my anxiety. Now I wanted to get rid of it.

So, when Peggy asked me to go with her to Brunhilda's house, I didn't put up much of a fight. "She's an old soul," Peggy said. "She has the gift of second sight. She can tell you things about yourself, maybe even about your parents."

It was the part about my parents that snagged me. I said okay, I'd have lunch at Peggy's house and then go see Brunhilda. Brunhilda was a medium, a seer. In Peggy's world, such people were the norm. In mine—before college,

142

at least—they were *taboo*. But if Brunhilda could tell me about my parents, I'd gladly spring ten dollars and see what she had to say.

In its heyday in 1900, Peggy's Victorian house likely spilled over with children, girls in pantaloons having tea with their dolls, boys in sailor suits rolling hoops on the lawn. In 1960, it spilled over with undergrads in ragged clothes, with their incense, cannabis, and other trappings of the fringy. We made our way through a dim front room and into a dimmer dining room. I nearly tripped over a man lying flat on his back on the floor, naked, his arms spread artfully to the side. Meditating, I guessed. Peggy led me around him to the kitchen. A girl with long black hair was chopping carrots on a butcher's block.

Chop! . . . chop! There was danger here.

The girl looked at me with eyes that were empty, like a statue's. Peggy said, "This is Narissa. Narissa, Kik."

I said hello. Narissa did not. Peggy went to the refrigerator. "Yogurt?"

"Sure," I said, but I had no appetite. I wanted to leave. Now.

Narissa adjusted the position of the knife and held it as for chopping ice, with the blade aimed at the floor. She snarled at me, "I could kill you, you know! I could do it!"

I was stranded on the wrong side of the kitchen. The doors that led to escape—the doors to the backyard and the dining room—were on the other side, beyond Narissa.

Peggy was gliding toward Narissa without seeming to move, saying appeasingly, "Narissa, honey, it's okay. Everything's fine."

Narissa bunched herself, ready to spring at me. She seethed, "You think I'm kidding? I could do it! Right *now*."

I was afraid to make any big moves, or any moves at all. Two feet from Narissa, Peggy stopped. She said, "It's okay, Narissa, you can put it down, no one's going to hurt you, we're going now."

Narissa ground her teeth and threw the knife to the floor. She clapped her hands over her ears. "*Ow!* It *hurts!*" She looked daggers at me. To Peggy, in a tone of explaining herself, she said, "It's Tony. He can still get through. He tells me things through the radio."

In one seamless action, Peggy and I got out of the kitchen and around the supine man, out the door, down the steps and into Peggy's VW. Peggy started the engine. I put on my sunglasses. Behind their cover, I side-scoped the front door. Narissa hadn't followed us. So far. But the way Peggy had parked the VW, backwards in the driveway with the car's nose to the street, I was on Narissa's side if she ran out waving the knife.

We made it out into traffic without incident. "She skips her meds and gets that way," Peggy said, "and then she takes some other junk. I guess you could say she takes the wrong drugs for what ails her."

"Has she ever hurt you?"

"No. She knows me. She only gets that way around people she doesn't know. She'll feel lousy later on and be sorry for something, but she won't know what."

"Can't she get help?"

Peggy's mouth pulled down at the corners. "You mean the loony bin? They give her so much stuff in there, she comes out like a zombie . . . *Blotto*. Then she comes back here and pretty soon she's back to this."

"Her family . . . ?"

"They kicked her out. They're in New York."

How could Peggy be so accepting? What would I do if I had a friend like Narissa? I didn't have an answer.

The planter on Brunhilda's porch was a toilet bowl blooming with orange and yellow marigolds. The door opened and there she was—a short, sweet-faced woman of four hundred pounds in a passion-flowered muumuu. She was maybe fifty years old. As she stepped onto the porch to offer her hand, she moved like a dancer. Her feet were child-sized, and she wore pink satin ballerina slippers. Tossing her white side-ponytails, she smiled, singled me out and cooed, "My teacher told me about you! He said to be on the look-out for you, that you are very powerful!"

I'm thinking: *What a bunch of baloney. Peggy set this up.*

Brunhilda took my hand in hers and quivered. "Oooh! I can feel it!" She pulled me indoors. With Peggy at our heels, we wove our way through an indoor herb garden (the former front room), parted a curtain of beads and stepped into Brunhilda's office (the former dining room). A desk faced us, and two chairs sat in front, also facing us.

"What do we do first?" I asked, sounding nervous. I *was* nervous.

Brunhilda said, "Take off your clothes. I do my readings in the steam bath. The towels are there." She pointed at a stack of large thin towels on the corner of the desk. She left the room, and I glared at Peggy. She hadn't said a *thing* about any steam bath! I doubted she'd even *met* Brunhilda before today. Peggy pretended not to see me glaring and doubting. She seemed even more reticent to disrobe than I did, if that were possible. We got our clothes off and tied towels around ourselves. Then we yoo-hooed through the beads to say we were ready.

When Brunhilda came in, she said to me, "I'll take you first." Peggy gave me a smudgy smile. (*Definitely* a setup.) The steam room was nothing like a sauna. The steam was contained in a steel cylinder laid horizontally on six legs. Brunhilda raised the lid the way she would open a casket, revealing a bed of slatted wood in place of satin pillows. She indicated a chair by the wall. "Put your towel there." I put my towel there.

"Get in on your back," she instructed. "Your head goes here." She indicated the neck-sized semicircle in the bottom half of the tank. Once I was inside, the top half of the hole would come down, leaving my body in the tank and my head out. As I climbed in, I felt like a lady in a magic act. The question was: would my head stay on my body?

Brunhilda closed the tank and sat on a chair near the top of my head, out of my line of sight, and massaged my temples, working her way around to the back of my neck. "Thank you, oh yes," she said, talking to someone else, not to me. "I can see that. Oh, yes. My spirit teacher says you have tears locked up." (Now she was talking to me.) "And you are very brave. You have a mother at home, or . . . ?"

"Grandmother," I murmured. I was drowsy from the heat and the massage.

"She is serious-minded. You are sad when you think of her."

How did she know *that*? I was galvanized inside my steel tank. What had I gotten myself into? *Literally* gotten myself into.

She said, "I see someone sitting and rocking. A man. . . . How is it now? Oh, yes, I see. There is a man—a friend, or a neighbor? He is an angel, and he watches over you."

Uncle Aarnie?

"You have had many past lives, and this one is a test. . . . What's that?" She again listened to a voice I couldn't hear. "My teacher says you were once a Buddhist monk, very devoted. And another time, a nurse in England. A Florence Nightingale nurse."

Brunhilda spoke words I couldn't understand. Then she said, "Before that, you were a man. A follower of the Carpenter. . . . Yes! My teacher says you were a barefoot follower of the Carpenter."

The Carpenter? . . . That woke me up!

In a flash I saw it. This was a fake *religion*! All this muttering about past lives and spirit teachers? There was only one Spirit Teacher I felt safe with, the *Holy* Spirit! I knew my Catechism, after all! Spirits *existed*, sure, but not all of them were *good*. The evil one, the leader of the whisperers (I refused to honor him with a name), might get some pieces right, like the part about Aarnie, but he missed out on the bigger truth.

But, man oh man! The evil one knew just how to hook me! He'd had his spirit-toady whisper hints to Brunhilda, who passed them on to me and stroked my ego, and fed me tidbits to keep me listening, until, at the right moment, and because I believed in Jesus (in a lukewarm way, something I needed to remedy), she throws in the bits about the Carpenter and myself as a barefoot follower!

Talk about *sneaky*! and *blasphemous*! How *gullible* of *me*, to climb into this steam can! I said, "Excuse me, I'd like to get out."

When it came right down to it, Brunhilda did me a favor. She shocked me back to my senses. Or partway back, at least. I would do more stupid things before I was done with her world, but she shocked me sufficiently, anyway, to get me out of that tank.

* * *

The fellowship!

I read the details. Monthly stipend. Housing allowance. Grants for travel to and from Finland. Grants for travel within Finland.

Wow!

I looked around the student center for someone to tell. Bending to the little service window, I said to the student aide, "I got it! The *fellowship!*"

The tall Inuit in the flocked blue sweater was a person I'd never met, but he gamely arranged his face to wish me well. As he stooped to the window, his breath came out as peppermint.

But before he could speak, I saw the clock. I reached in and patted his sleeve. "Gotta run!" I was late for class, but I'd won the grant!

The next weekend I went home, and Mummo collapsed again. It was something I said that made her collapse. I said, "I won a grant to go to Finland next summer." She got visibly upset and crumpled to the kitchen floor, gasping and fighting for air. I recalled something from the earlier collapse. She had been upset *then*, too—though at Inky, not at me. It happened that Inky was at our house this time as well.

When Mummo came around and caught her breath, Inky helped her up to her feet. Mummo arranged her clothes and looked up. When she caught sight of me, her sternness fell away. She regarded me with affection, a virtual flood of loving looks.

"Silvi," she said fondly, surprised to find Silvi in the room. Whoever Silvi was.

"Silvi's in Finland," Inky told Mummo. To me, Inky said, "Silvi is her sister." (How did Inky know *that?*) As soon as Mummo saw Aarnie, she seemed to remember where she was, and her face closed up again. She chafed her face with her apron, picked up the potato peeler and got back to work.

I felt slammed, rejected. Cheated of her affection. She had given me loving looks when she thought I was someone else, but not when I was back to being myself.

When Aarnie went out to the garage, I followed him. I sat on a stool and watched him sand a tabletop. He ran the sander in the direction of the grain, the length of the table, four or five times each way, switched it off and tested the table surface with his hand.

"It happened one other time that I know of," I said, "a few years back. Has she fallen any other times lately?"

"No-o." He pulled the plug from the socket and wound the cord around the sander, and set the sander, exactingly, on a shelf. He took a rag from a hook and wiped sanding dust from the table.

"But is she forgetting things? Like when she called me Silvi?"

Admission showed in his face. He blushed, not wanting to say.

"What? Tell me."

"One time she thought she was in Finland." He was going way beyond himself to say this much.

"Only that once?" His eyes answered: More. I asked, "How often?"

"Two, t'ree times." He gave me a laden look and rotated the rag in his hands.

Late in getting the message, I said, "We'd better get her to a doctor. What do you think?" He nodded okay before I finished talking.

The realization brought me up short. He was afraid she would die. She was no relative of his, and she was obstreperous, impossible to put up with, but in his own way he was devoted to her. He had shared his house with her for twenty years and would be lost without her. His loyalty put me to shame.

The doctor gave Mummo a prescription for anxiety. "In addition," the doctor told Liisa and me, "your grandmother has senile dementia, early symptoms. Her memory will fail over time." He suggested hiring a woman to help with housework and to keep an eye on Mummo's medicine.

Mummo refused to hire help or to take medicine. But again I felt better just knowing what we were dealing with. *And* we had a crack in the silence.

Ten

Jeff

I was studying off-campus in the Full Moon Café when a male voice said, "Do you know the *Kalevala*?" I had to twist in my chair to see who had spoken. He was at the table behind me, the rangy, good-looking guy who audited English Poets. What was his name? Terrence?. . . No. *Torrence.*

"Oh, hi. You're Torrence, right?"

"Jeff." He stood up, swung his chair over to my table and sat on it the wrong way, his extra-long arms flung over the back. He had burnt-umber hair that sprung up in sprigs, an incongruous top for his classic Mediterranean face. His eyelashes were so black and sooty they looked made up for the stage. "I don't use Torrence. Sounds like a flash flood. I could hardly wait for college. I'd sign up as Geoffrey and no one would know! But then I got here and forgot and wrote the whole thing down." His smile was off-kilter and beguiling.

I smiled back. "I'm Kik. What *about* the *Kalevala*? Are you a Finn?"

He laughed. "Irish-Italian. Torrence Geoffrey Marconi. No relation to the inventor. I heard your name, Halonen, a Finnish name. So I wondered if you knew the Kalevala."

"I know it's the Finnish epic . . ."

He didn't wait to hear what I knew about the *Kalevala*, which wouldn't have taken long. Making his chair hop toward me, he said, "It's a folklore treasure. A gem of Finnish nationalism! Do you know Sibelius' Second?"

For a non-Finn, he was mighty well-versed on things Finnish. "Nope," I said, hoping he would stop this grilling. I was batting zero. "How'd you get interested?"

He got to his feet and spanned his chair—he was taller than anyone I knew, including Inky—and fished around in a pocket of his suntans. He pulled out a palm-sized medallion and handed it to me. It held the raised image of an old woman stirring a pot over a fire. "Know what this is?" He stepped out of the bridge and spun his chair, sat on it the normal way, slid his elbows to the center of the table and bent over them, grinning up at me. This guy was a show all by himself.

"Nope," I said again. He took the medallion and examined it, his head level with my shoulder. I could smell lime shampoo. At close range, his hair looked silky. I had an urge to fluff it.

"It's a *Kalevala* medal. From Runo 20, 'The Making of Barley Ale.'" Animatedly, he told me that a college friend of his, a Florida Finn, had given him the medal and introduced him to the *Kalevala*. He spoke with a convert's zeal. I told him about my Finland grant, he became more animated, and we lost track of time.

So it happened, in this inauspicious way, that I found my tall handsome someone who would stay. It took a while for the truth to sink in, but, yes, that first day in the Full Moon Café, I did check. They were gray.

* * *

It was mid-February when Jeff and I met, and every Friday night from then on we had dinner with Marcie and Adam—meals by Adam, desserts by Marcie, music by Dave Brubeck. The two men became friends the day they met, Jeff the philosopher, gangly, optimistic, a person who caused levity with his loose limbs, and Adam the math whiz, medium-sized and firmly-packed, a realist with an eye for the absurd. One was the man of my dreams. The other was the brother I had always wanted.

"It's not safe, from what I hear," Marcie said one Friday night. "You could get stuck in there and never come back. I mean, not ever."

Jeff chuffed, "Huh-huh," from the back of his throat, his form of mild laughter. "Stuck in where?"

"Say you think you're six," she said. "What if you couldn't come back?"

Directing a scowl at his wife, Adam said, "It's a waste of time even thinking about it. Why trust anyone to *do* that to you?"

Marcie puckered up and sent him a fat kiss through the air. "I didn't say I would. I was the one who said it wasn't safe, remember?"

I said, "There's this guy in my history class, and he says he can do it to anyone in ten minutes. He says the problem is that some people get caught without meaning to. One time he was hypnotizing this girl, and this really susceptible guy was sitting behind her, and pretty soon he falls asleep, not the girl!"

Jeff said, "He got hypnotized by mistake?"

I giggled. "Ya! He's just watching . . . and *z-z-z-zt*! He's *out*."

Jeff laughed. So did Marcie. Adam did not. He was irate. Adam's sense of rightness ran in a straight line and allowed no detours, certainly not for amateur hypnosis. He was the conscience of the group. If we wandered too far away from the prudent, Adam brought us back. Jeff never said much about Adam's judgments, but I'd noticed he usually agreed with them. Marcie was . . . well, she was Marcie. Not much ruffled her.

None of them knew it yet, but *I* had wandered away from the prudent, very far away. And I was still lost. I dreaded what the three would say when they found out.

"Why mess with it?" Adam said.

Leaning his way, Marcie air-drilled his ear with her finger. "You're cute when you get mad! Anyone ever tell you that?"

"I'm not mad." He pulled away, half-frowning, half-smiling, annoyed that we weren't taking him seriously. "But there are better things to do with your mind than turn it over to some misfit."

Jeff said, "Speaking of misfits, Warshall keeps asking us over. We should go. His house is from the turn of the century. His mom does some kind of publishing there."

"That guy's weird!" I said. "He wears a tie to class. And he's sneaky! He goes around staring at you with this Chessy Cat smile, like he's *got* something on you."

Jeff said, "He doesn't have many friends."

I decided to side with Jeff. "What the heck. Let's go see the weird guy's house."

Adam turned sly. "Here's the deal. We'll go next week on Saturday. But first we'll have supper at Sonny's place and have *poi* and meet his wife. They have the roundest baby you ever saw. *Then* we'll go see the weird guy's house. Sonny's from Hawaii, and he's homesick for *poi*. He says he misses *poi* more than he misses the beach."

"What's *poi*?" I asked.

"Taro root. You cook it. You pound it into a paste. You let it ferment. You eat it."

Marcie and I gagged. She said, "Yum." Adam smirked like a small boy teasing girls with worms.

Warshall's house gave me the creeps. It was pretty enough, a wide-bodied, four-storied, grandmotherly house with gingerbread eaves and lace at the windows, but as we came up the sidewalk someone touched a curtain on the top floor. A prisoner in the attic? An insane aunt? Warshall's mother, Mrs. Warshall (Warshall was the only person I knew who went by his last name), opened the door to welcome us. She was thin and imposing in a ruby gown and ankle-strap high-heels, her hennaed hair frenzied into a furze ball. She had painted her lips and eyelids purple and tweaked them up at the corners in a failed attempt at perkiness. Offering us an icy hand, she simpered slightly in response to each name.

"Adam," she said, meeting the last of us. "Do come in."

We stood in a large foyer of shut doors and a high arching ceiling. Warshall now appeared, head down, grinning like a satisfied hyena, a pear-shaped guy with a sun-lamp-tanned face. He wore a white long-sleeved dress shirt, and instead of chinos and loafers, which Adam and Jeff wore, as did most college men, Warshall wore pressed gray wool slacks and wing tip shoes. From behind his back, he brought out two bouquets of red roses and handed one to Marcie, one to me. I stammered thanks. I was suspicious. How could a college student afford *roses*? How did he earn his money, anyway, gangsterism, or gunrunning? Gambling? Earlier in the week, after Jeff had told him we'd come for a visit, Warshall had gone away for an hour and come back to give Jeff a leather briefcase. "For friendship," Warshall insisted. The gift made Jeff uneasy, and he tried to refuse it. Warshall wouldn't take it back. Jeff had told me that, after this evening, he planned to let Warshall down gently from this fictional and too-fond friendship.

While his mother hosted his guests, Warshall surveyed the group, surreptitiously licking his lips as if hungry for our reactions. Mrs. Warshall drew our notice to the marble floor slabs from Georgia, the wall tiles from China, the wallpaper restoration that had taken two years so far, but what intrigued me most was the desiccated old man who materialized behind a slit-open door, aimed a malevolent eye at me, drew back and silently closed the door.

Following Mrs. Warshall, we looked into two parlors, a dining room, a billiard room, a butler's pantry—all richly appointed but *dead*. She said, "We don't have many guests. The house is special." Zeroing in on Jeff, she sparkled a smile at him. "I have a notion that *you* are, too," she told him, primping at her hair. "I believe we're ready to go down." She set off down the hallway, keeping to the left of a staircase that led up, turning a sharp right and heading down a staircase positioned beneath the other one.

"Be careful," she warned. "It's dark. The light on the steps is broken."

We felt our way down to a landing, veered right, took a few more steps down, veered right again, went down several more steps, and found ourselves in a square, chilly, room-sized access hall. The lighting made our skin chartreuse. On the wall hung a series of posters of angry, blood-red mythical beasts, all claws and teeth and bulging eyes. Eager to see something real, I said, "You do publishing of some kind?"

"Here." Mrs. Warshall went to a door, opened it, snapped on a light. The low wattage revealed three gray metal desks piled with slim booklets. Picking up a booklet, she read the title to us, *The Inner Guide*, and the names of sample chapters, "Three Ways to Discover Your Past Lives" and "The One True Prophetic Way." She gleamed at us with carnivorous greed.

In distress, I pictured Brunhilda and her steam can, the séances and trances I'd taken part in. My involvement in the occult was still a secret from Jeff, Marcie, and Adam. Desperate to get Mrs. Warshall off these subjects, I asked her, "Where do you do the actual printing?"

"Over there," she said, both pointing at and disregarding another door. She shut the office door and asked us to make a circle. Since we were already standing in a loose circle, she took a place at Jeff's right, physically lifted his right arm until it was parallel to the floor, and then arranged his hand to curve down. Taking two steps away, like counting off for gym, she raised her left arm and curved that hand up toward Jeff's, without touching it. She glowered at Marcie and me, expecting us to follow suit.

Fighting off giggles, we put down our roses and obliged her. Mrs. Warshall arranged her right hand down toward Marcie's upturned left hand. I stood between Marcie and Jeff and curved my hands in the appointed way. Our circle was pretty small, no Adam, no Warshall. (Where *was* Warshall?)

Adam was on his way up the stairs. He said, "Good night, Mrs. Warshall!" To us, he said gloomily, "I'll be in the car." His eyes asked Marcie if she was coming. She made dimples and gave him a small nod, indicating that she'd be there soon. Jeff signaled to me that we should indulge Mrs. W. just a jiffy longer, and then get the heck out of there.

"Do you feel it?" she said. "The *electricity*? I'll teach you a song!" Raising her chin and, like a lark inspired by dawn, she sang, "O halo of night, come visit us . . ."

Jeff withdrew his arms and faked a look at his watch, saying rather loudly, "You know, we really must be going!" He scooped up the roses and shepherded Marcie and me toward the steps. "Thank you for the tour. We can find our way out."

"Here!" Mrs. Warshall cried. Heels ticking across the floor, she ran ahead of us. She whipped open the last door by the steps and reached in to click on lights. Reflexively, we looked in. Against the far wall stood a large square throne and a six-foot phallic stone. In the center, facing the throne, stood a speaker's podium. Statues cavorted around the perimeter of the room, their postures suggestive of an orgy. Black and white photos lined the walls, unclothed people in unseemly poses.

We were sneaking backwards, getting out of there, when Mrs. Warshall warbled, "We rent out this sanctuary—to societies of enlightenment! You can join the ancients!" Indicating the podium, she said, "You stand there and confess allegiance to the high priest! You gain admission! Learn the rites!"

We made a hasty exit up the stairs and out the front door, saying good night to Warshall, who had reappeared, sniggering and tittering on the porch, and to his mother, who had tapped up the steps behind us and was calling, wanting us to come back and see more wonders inside the house.

Warshall's house was good for laughs, the four of us getting away, *fast*, in Adam's car, shouting and laughing, recounting this wacky detail and that one. But in real life the otherworldly held no laughs for me. The occult was supposed to have freed me. But it had done the opposite. It had imprisoned me. Images woke me at night—writhing, obsessive images, erotic and binding. Each time it happened, I was left shaken. I couldn't get back to sleep.

That spring I was two separate people—one, a good student falling in love, chastely, with Jeff, the other, a driven, amoral "seeker" who kept up the séances and, without reason, repeatedly got doped up on too much wine and went to bed with Peggy's male house mates, any of them, all of them. What I did at Peggy's house I did in rage, driven by an impulse that seemed beyond me. I didn't want to do what I did, but I did it. I lied to everyone. I felt torn apart.

None of my friends except Peggy and no one in my family knew anything about this other life.

Eleven

Turnarounds

To my surprise, during spring services that year, Kaisa went back to the Finnish church. I went with Aarnie on Friday night to the Koskinens' to pick up Mummo, and there was Kaisa, having coffee with the church ladies as if she'd never been away! I stared at her, hardly believing what I was seeing. I had seen her in Minneapolis that same morning, two hundred miles away. She had known I was going home for the weekend, but hadn't offered me a ride. She hadn't said a word about this!

I felt betrayed. My rebellious Aunt Kaisa, the one relative I'd depended on to do the unexpected, had gone back to the old ways. Of her own free choice.

But then, standing at the Koskinens' kitchen door, I realized that Kaisa was being true to form, after all; she was doing the unexpected.

The next day, in Minneapolis, she told me it was time for her to mend fences. We were back on neutral turf, in her big white house with the curtains blowing—until now my place of refuge and rebellion. She said, "I couldn't do it halfway, once I decided. Which, by the way, was after you left for the train. I called Emma and found out where services were. I needed the whole package. Emma, the church, Harald preaching."

"What did he do when he saw you?"

"Almost died." She smiled with asserted courage. "You know Harald. He never acts uncertain. But he did when he saw me at church."

"What did he say?"

Her bravery fell away. "Nothing. I said hello, but he turned away. But I didn't go there to make him feel bad. I did it to be back in the fold."

I understood. I had my own yearning to be back in the fold. I fought a welling surge to tell Kaisa everything. The trances. The men. *Everything.*

But at the end of a subsonic fight, and in stubborn proof that I would resist help to the point of self-destruction, I said nothing.

Eventually, however, the need to *tell* won out. One rainy Sunday night, wet and disheveled from having walked at random for hours, I slipped into a small Episcopal church. A dozen men and women stood laughing and talking in the entry hall. When I asked to see the priest, a jovial gray-haired man stepped forward and said he was Father Caplan. He wore sandals and cotton socks, and a full-length, button-down black robe.

I said, "I need to confess."

He said, "Of course. Come in! We're about to start Evening Prayer."

That wasn't what I had in mind. But I went with the group into a side chapel. On my knees, in chorus with the others, I read aloud from the *Book of Common Prayer.* The light of God filled the place. I was safe. As we said the words of that day's Psalms, I wept. After the service, the people gathered around me in a group hug, again laughing. By happenstance, I had hit upon the monthly meeting of charismatic (pentecostal) Episcopal priests and their wives, a group who believed in healing, inside and out. I agreed to meet Father Caplan at the church, two days later, to make a formal confession.

In my room at Kaisa's house, following Father Caplan's instructions, I wrote out a list of my sins, every wrong that I could recall doing in early childhood, elementary school, junior high, high school, college, right up to the minute.

I reported to the church at ten in the morning. Father Caplan brought me in and led me down a short hall, opened the door to a prayer room and stepped back. I went weak with remorse and joy. The room was the *flip-oppo-*

site of Mrs. Warshall's sacrilegious throne room! This one was gracious and inviting: bookshelves and soft rugs, a bay window, sun and plants, a prayer stand with a red velvet cushion for the knees. A single straight chair faced the window.

Father Caplan sat in the chair, his back to me. I knelt on the cushion and read aloud from a card he had handed to me, the introductory lines of the penitent. Then in tears I read off my list of sins.

When I was done, Father Caplan assured me of God's forgiveness, using another set of prescribed lines. He suggested that I read Psalm 126 at home. Before dismissing me, he said, "And pray for me, a sinner."

I could have confessed in the Finnish church. It did have a form of confession, one based on the priesthood of all believers: a lay person confessing to another lay person, or to a minister, or to God alone. But this formal rite was what I needed just then. It placed my confession in time and space. I figured that, from this point on, if my past ever haunted me, I could think back to this *particular* time, this *particular* space.

* * *

After dinner the next Friday night, while we were still at the table, I told Jeff and Marcie and Adam about the other life I'd led, the men, the trances, the whole works. I ended by saying, "I hate for you to hear this! But I had to come clean. I promise it's over. For *good.*" I was anguished and out of breath, and out of courage.

They had listened, disbelieving. Marcie shook her head in small irritated jerks. Adam looked peeved. Jeff seemed ready to say something, but then he didn't. Too late, I realized I should have told this to Jeff *first*, in private, before blatting it to the group. For months I had blocked him out, had pretended, at times, that he didn't exist. I had risked losing him. In fact, I now thought fearfully, *I might have done just that.*

I said, "Jeff, I'm so sorry." He avoided my eyes. His face was strained and drawn.

Adam lurched out of his chair and paced behind the table. "That is so stupid! How could you be so *dumb?* . . . You led a double life!"

"That's what it was," I said, "double. I was torn in two. And it *was* stupid."

Marcie clucked her tongue. "You never *did* have brakes. You go any which way!"

"Do I, still?"

She was grim. "Not so much any more, but it sure got you in a mess this time!"

Adam sat down, but he didn't let up. He lectured me at length, railing at me for my lack of respect, for myself, the family, for the three of them.

I apologized again. Marcie was angry that I hadn't trusted *her*, I hadn't said a word of this to her, all those months. I told her, "I was terrified."

"If you were so terrified, then why'd you *do* it? Why couldn't you snap out of it? Didn't that psychology class help, or Christianity?"

"I guess I was in a trance myself! Nothing seemed connected to anything else. I didn't know the rules of the bigger world, and the only rules I knew were Mummo's. So I tried everything . . ."

"There you go! Blaming someone else. As if Mummo made you do it."

"I know. . . But when I judge myself and everyone else by Mummo's rules, we all *fail*, and then if I throw out her rules I don't know *what* rules to use."

Marcie said, "You *do* know right from wrong."

"You're right. I do." I picked at a torn fingernail.

Jeff cleared his throat, but it didn't work. His voice sounded rusty as he said, "Well, it's in the past now." He wasn't quite himself yet. His eyes were unavailable, blocked by something as strong as steel mesh.

"Marcie's right," I said. "I did know it was wrong. But when new ideas were making the rounds, I had trouble judging good or bad. I tried to be open-minded. I told myself that 'new' didn't necessarily mean 'bad.' I sometimes didn't even like the new idea, but I thought I should try it anyway. But then I went overboard. And even if I don't try new ideas, I feel disloyal to Mummo for even thinking about them . . ."

"See?" Marcie said. "You think through *her* filter. Not yours."

159

"I know, it's automatic! I'm trying to stop."

Adam said, "That business about trying everything? It's not just dumb, it's dangerous. You're lucky you're not addicted to drugs. You're not, are you?"

"No. It's one thing I didn't try."

"What I don't get," Marcie said heatedly, "is that you did all this non-sense after you met Jeff."

I sent Jeff another mute apology. "I know. I don't think for myself. I worry I'll walk out of here and *still* not choose the right things."

"Including me?" Jeff said softly, granting me a small reconciling smile. His voice was back, his eyes too, almost.

Grateful for any levity, however small, I told him, "*You*, I choose. If you'll have me." We exchanged a tentative glance. My head felt stuffed with scoldings and cold, raw intentions. I said, "But Marcie's right. I don't have good brakes. Or good fences."

Adam moaned. "Metaphor overload."

"Kik, you exaggerate," Jeff said. "You're not that wishy-washy."

"But I drive myself nuts! Say I make a rule, like I don't want to hear dirty jokes. When people start in on them, I don't know what to say! Anything I think of saying is too Goody-Two-Shoes."

Adam said, "Don't say anything. Just walk away."

"That would be uncomfortable."

"The first time anyone does anything new, it's uncomfortable."

"Oh." This was a maxim I'd never heard. "But I feel uncomfortable a lot. I feel guilty, whether or not I have anything to feel guilty about."

"That's just Finnishness," Marcie said.

This made me a little mad. How come she'd let me flounder, then, all those years? I said, "You always told me you didn't know *what* Finns think."

"Ya well, I figured it out. Finns are supposed to be humble and brave and pinch pennies. And feel guilty if you don't do it right."

Adam said, "'Finns don't buy what they don't need.' 'Finns go-without.'"

"That's the 1930s," Jeff said, "the Depression. We all grew up with it. We feel guilty if we don't save money like our parents." He clamped his hands behind his head and audibly popped vertebrae. "Our generation *runs* on guilt."

Adam said, "It's worse for Finns. We're better at guilt than the rest of you."

"Especially if you grew up with Mummo," I said. Hearing the yammer in my words, I tacked on a disclaimer. "But I'm not blaming her . . . !"

"Glad to hear it," said Marcie.

After a pause during which we looked at the flatware, Jeff said, "Okay, Kik, we forgive you. But you can't be such a loner. You need to stay close to us. We're going to hold you to it."

Marcie said. "Right. Don't go wandering off by yourself."

"Okay," I said, feeling fenced-in in a good sense. "Thanks."

"And you need to get serious about the faith," Adam said. "You were so far out there, it's *no wonder* you got screwed up."

Marcie put on a fake surprise. "Isn't this the same man who argues with everyone about God and evil?"

In a tone that said he'd spent his ire, Adam directed his news at Jeff and me. "I figure *I* need to get serious about the faith too, since we're starting a family."

A baby! A baby wasn't part of the master plan, not yet. But a baby was due in July, and Marcie and Adam had already worked out a budget based on one income alone; she would quit her job when the baby came. She was grateful for snobby old Fendway, she said. It paid a living wage and had good medical insurance. She wasn't fond of faculty teas, she told us, but she'd put up with them for the sake of the benefits.

I said, "I need to be here when the baby's born! I won't go to Finland."

"You *have* to go. I'll be mad if you don't."

Marcie had been placid so far about the baby, but now she blasted forth. "But I'm not ready for this! Me, a *mother*? . . . Colic? and braces? and college?" She laid the back of her wrist on her forehead, like a vaudeville damsel who can't pay the rent, and wailed, "What've I gotten myself into?"

Twelve

Castles in the Air

Mummo had a rule against sitting on the edges of beds, so I sat down on the sewing bench. We were in her bedroom, and she was ironing linens. "I've been wondering," I said. "What was Ellis Island like when you and Grandpa came through?"

A mild accusation crossed her face. I knew what it meant. It meant I had never shown an interest in her life *before*, so why *now*? She finished ironing a pillowcase, folded it into thirds the long way, into quarters the short way, and added it to a pile on the dresser. When she turned to me, her glasses were a little steamed up.

"Young people don't want to hear," she said.

"I do! I'm sorry I didn't ask you sooner."

She made an irascible gesture and unplugged the iron. "Better take those," she said. I put the pillowcases in the hall closet, and we went downstairs.

After setting out coffee and *pulla*, we sat facing each other at the kitchen table. Not unusual for two people about to have coffee, but unusual for us. So intimate! Until recently, if I'd found myself in such a predicament, I'd have bounded to my feet and done something else—*anything* to avoid being alone with her. But I'd been practicing my new plan, zapping her with an affection big enough to cover her prickles. It was working pretty well. It still felt artificial, but less so as time went on.

Certain items stayed on the kitchen table, always, ready for anything, the blue-and-white lake scene sugar bowl from Finland, the Black Hills toothpick holder, the square glass ashtray with the saw-tooth lip for balancing a cigarette, the Popeye pepper shaker and Olive Oyl salt shaker. Mummo aligned them and said, "Ellis Island?"

I said yes.

Her features pulled inward around her peaky nose. "He came first," she said. "He worked in the Chisholm mine. Then we came."

She came to a halt, and I hoped she wasn't *done* already. But she started up again. Finland had too many hard years, she said, bad crops, too many rocks, no rain, then too much rain, while America had good weather and rich farm land. Grandpa came to the States to work in the mines. When he saved enough money, he bought steamship tickets for Mummo and my father, who was three years old at the time of sailing. My father got sick on the ship, she told me. "Prett' near died."

Of what? I wondered, but I didn't interrupt. This was a big occasion, Mummo talking.

"*No niin* . . . We saw the Statue, then that Ellis Island place. It was short. You know, *short*." She held her hand barely above the table. "Couldn't hardly see it. Then we saw flags and . . . eh? Like a . . . ?" Her hands showed round shapes and high places, possibly towers.

"Like a castle?" I guessed.

"Ya. Like a castle." She described transferring from the ship to the Ellis Island ferry, approaching the island, arriving, seeing crowds on the dock. Her forehead furrowed. "I thought Toivo would be there . . ." The sentence frittered away as she stood on the ferry deck with her child in her arms, straining to see her husband.

"Well," she sighed, "no Toivo. We got off. People were selling foods, there was lots of noise. No one talked Finn. They said go to a big room. It had big windows." Her hands again showed me what her words could not, in this case, tall vaulted windows. "One guy, he did this." She held out her palm, traffic-cop-style. "He got a guy who talked Finn." Her relief was evident sixty years beyond her need. "He helped me with the trunks. We waited in the big room. They had these ropes." With one hand she made the motion of a snake. "So many people!"

She told me that a doctor stood at the top of the steps watching people walk up, judging whether they were healthy enough to be USA citizens. She pantomimed the medical checks, imitating the eye test by hooking a finger as if to pull up her eyelid. Wincing, she said, "*Voi, voi, voi!*"

I winced too, and changed the subject. "Was my father still sick?"

"Mm?" Mummo was lost in thought. "No," she said, returning to the present. "I had to hold him in the big room, he wanted to get down and play and run. I pushed the boxes with my feet . . ." Under the table, her feet shoved imagined burdens, one shove, and another. "We went outside and Toivo was there."

I didn't say what I was thinking: Why wasn't he there earlier? Why didn't he help you through Ellis Island? Did you love him?

Mummo was finished talking. But we had made good progress. I had asked her about Ellis Island, and she had answered. We had actually talked.

"Thank you, Mummo. For telling me."

"Ya, well," she said in despair.

Thirteen

At Least We Don't Have *Those*

A call from Mahoning meant only one thing. Bad news. "It's Liisa," Aarnie said without preliminary. "She fell down, couldn't hardly breathe." I pictured Liisa on the floor, Mummo on the floor, myself on a chair with my head between my knees. The women in our family seemed to have trouble staying upright.

"Is she okay?" I asked him.

"She's laying down," he said.

"Has she seen a doctor?"

"Emma said no doctors."

Aarnie would not have called unless he wanted me to come home. This was Thursday. No classes till Monday. "I can make today's train. Can you pick me up?"

On the drive between Hibbing and Mahoning, I wheedled out of Aarnie the fact that before Liisa fell she had been talking about college. That, anyway, was good news. In my opinion, she was wasting her life. She should be in college, two years ahead of me. Instead she was a file clerk, going nowhere. Our high school dean had urged her to apply for college grants, and she had done that and won two academic scholarships. But she had let them lapse when Mummo made it known she was needed at home.

My arrival caused embarrassment in the Mahoning kitchen. Everyone knew the reason I was there, but no one alluded to it. Mummo was cutting onions at the sink and, beyond glancing up to acknowledge my presence, she didn't change her position. Liisa said, "Hi," and kept setting the table. Aarnie stood by the back door with his hands in his pockets. It dawned on me that he'd taken time off work. Dear Aarnie.

Ignoring the rules, I went to Liisa and gave her an unpracticed hug, a clumsy grab that clunked our cheekbones together. That too embarrassed the group—not the clunk, which of course wasn't audible, but the hug itself. A community intake of air sapped my courage. I backed off and hugged my own arms.

"What happened?" I asked Liisa.

"I'm fine. I got dizzy, is all."

"Were you nauseated? Did you faint? Has it happened before?" I peppered her with questions without looking at Mummo or Aarnie; I knew Mummo's face would be frigid and Aarnie's would be red. Aarnie let himself out the back door.

"Not really," Liisa said carefully, letting me know it *had* happened before. "Is everything okay in Minneapolis? Auntie Kaisa?"

"Forget Minneapolis, we're talking about *you*. I think I'll do some more checking."

Her fear was momentary. "Kik, *don't*. I'll be fine. What do you mean, some more checking?"

"Can we talk upstairs?" This too was a breach of rules. We never admitted that anyone discussed anything in private.

"Okay, we won't eat for another hour," Liisa said, and she went ahead of me up to our old bedroom. Like Liisa's life, the room was stuck in the past—pompoms and high school photos crowding the mirror. She closed the door. Appearing anxious, uncertain what this meeting was about, she sat down on the vanity bench. I settled on the foot of my bed and got right to the point.

"I think you and I might have the same problem . . ."

She sat up straighter. With a stiff mouth, she said, "Like what?"

"You know that group I was in? That counseling group? The leader thought you and I might have some . . . emotional problems."

Liisa got up and skyscrapered over me, cupping her elbows with white-knuckled hands. "I don't have any so-called 'emotional problems.'"

"I'll just talk about *my* problems, okay? Sit down. Please?" She sat down but crossed her arms and legs as if guarding her soft parts.

"Whenever I hear or see something new, I get dizzy," I began. "It doesn't have to be big. The littlest things can make me sick! Like if my friends are playing cards. You know how it is? You get cold, then hot, your head is a bomb about to go off, and your stomach jumps around. You wish you could vomit and get it over with?"

She understood. Her face was giving her away.

I said, "I hate that! . . . You know those two times when Mummo collapsed? Both times, it happened when she was *upset.* Same with me! Every time, just before I get sick, I'm upset about something. I'm feeling scared, or trapped, or mad."

"Me, too," Liisa said. "I get a headache, and lately this fainting thing."

We chanced a look at each other. "In other words," I said, "if we get upset, and if we think we can't change whatever is upsetting us, we get sick. How dumb is that?"

"*Really* dumb," she said. Somehow this struck us both funny. It felt good to laugh with Liisa. I had wasted much too much time competing with her, watching her every move and keeping score.

I had a brainstorm, and I tried it out on Liisa. "When we were kids, we couldn't talk to Mummo, right? Her ideas were the only ones allowed. If we had a different idea from hers, we got the silent treatment. . . . All true?"

"True."

I said excitedly, "How about this? We never got to *practice disagreeing!* I don't know how to disagree without getting sick. If a friend disagrees with me, I think it's the end, the friendship must be over! . . . I'm 'either-or.' Either my friend agrees with me or she's not my friend. Either we agree with Mummo . . ."

". . . or we're dead," Liisa said.

"Yah! Dead!" I bonked myself on the forehead. "We *did* grow up in the same house, after all."

Liisa said, "If someone gets mad, I think, Please don't be mad at me, I'll do anything, just don't be mad . . ."

". . . because if you get mad, I'll dissolve! I'll melt, I'll lie down and die," I said.

"Which sounds a lot like falling on the floor, choking."

"Or hanging over a sink, trying to breathe."

We sat in our spots, commenting to ourselves: "Hmmh," and "That's it." I said, "The guy who ran the group, Tim? He thinks we can stop it."

"How?"

"Practice."

"That's *it?* Practice? That's all he said?"

I repeated what Tim had told me about anxiety, including the suggestion that Liisa and I try new responses to everyday problems. We thought about this for a while, trying to come up with new responses, thinking so hard I thought I heard grinding sounds.

Liisa said, "I can't think of any."

"Me, neither!" I said, suddenly not caring if I could or not. "You know what I used to call it when Mummo wouldn't talk? I called it the Silence, with a capital S."

"I called it 'Shame *on!*'"

"Ya." I grinned at Liisa, remembering. "It was 'Shame *on!*' and then snap on the head." I did a finger-snap on the bed pillow, propelling the middle finger off the thumb. "Hoo, that stung! . . . You know what? That was the only way she ever touched us."

Liisa lowered her voice, reminding me that Mummo was downstairs, almost within hearing range. "I called her the Ice Finn. She always seemed mad. She still does."

My stomach felt unsettled. "Liisa? Are you ever scared you'll end up like her?"

"All the time."

"Same here. I had this dream once where she calls you from the top of the stairs to bring up the newspaper. You go, but it takes you a long time. I can hear footsteps, Clump! . . . Clump! But there's too long a time in between. I go to see what's wrong, and I see you're getting smaller and smaller. You're about as tall as one stair step! You can hardly get your feet up the steps, but you're trying hard. It still scares me."

Liisa had listened with a galled recognition. "That's me trying to do things her way. I never could."

We both had tears starting. I felt newly orphaned. "Ah, Liisa! We were poor little girls. No mother or father, no one to baby us. Didn't you ache for someone to *hold* you?"

"Yes . . . but I think Mummo was scared of us. I remember when she fed you a bottle, she held you out here . . ." Liisa curved her arms in front of her as if holding a wide package. We frowned at the picture she had drawn.

I said, "I remember one time when we were little, we were over at the Pesonens', and one of the college girls took me on her lap. It felt so good! Kerplunk, right *there*. I was so comfortable I didn't want to leave."

"That's why I was crazy for boys," Liisa said. "I liked their arms around me."

"Me, too." I mentally tapped my fingers, timid about trusting her but needing to try. "Here lately, I really got messed up though." I told her about Brunhilda, Peggy, the men, the church confession.

Very gently, without judgment, she said, "I knew something was wrong. I'm glad it's over." The peace in the room was palpable.

We sat for a while without talking. Taking a different direction, I asked her, "Do you ever have trouble knowing the right thing to say? Like when you meet someone important or you have to make small talk? *I* do! Either I say too much or I say the wrong thing. Here's a fer-instance. You know me and books. Everything I know about etiquette came from old novels, and that can *backfire*. This girl in my Lit class, Daphne, went to her grandfather's funeral, and when she got back I said what I thought I was *supposed* to say. I said, 'Please accept my condolences on the occasion of your sorrow.' She screwed up her face and said, '*Huh?*' And I had to stand there and *explain!*"

Liisa giggled. I hadn't heard her giggle since we were kids, and not often enough then. She said, "I've done things like that."

"You? You're always in-control. When *I'm* nervous, I'm a regular flibberty-jibbet. You're the opposite, you're quiet. That's better than jabbering like a jay bird! I want the jabbering and the dizziness to *stop*." But jabbering more, I said, "Speaking of dizziness, I was looking it up in a book on Chinese medicine and—nothing against Chinese medicine or anything—the titles were a riot in English. The index didn't list 'dizziness' or 'anxiety' or 'depression,' but it did list . . ." I reached for my purse, found a note and read from it. "'Convulsions from liver fire and phlegm' and 'Reckless marauding of hot blood.'" I gave Liisa a side-glance. "At least we don't have *those*."

She reared back. "'Reckless marauding of hot blood'? That sounds like *me* with *What's*-'is-name!" Our laughter had a ragged edge to it, but it went back years and brought us pretty much up to date.

When it was time to go downstairs, we didn't hug, but we did risk a straight-on smile. Which for us was a big advance.

* * *

Liisa had found her man, or at least that's what he said. She introduced me to him the day of our hot-blood talk. His name was Bill Renfro. He was a fifth-grade teacher in Hibbing, a tall, brainy, kindhearted man with striking blue eyes and a black crewcut, a non-Finn who attended the other Finnish church. I thought he was perfect for her. After just a few dates, he had asked her to marry him. She hadn't made up her mind.

As she drove me to the train depot, I said, "Well? Do you love him?"

"Sure. But I've been thinking about college."

"Great!" I could hardly sit still, this was such good news. "You can take classes and get engaged, too! You can get married and work part time, go to college part time, find an apartment cheap. You love someone, you marry him, and then whatever happens, you work out together . . ."

"You're doing it again."

"Bossy?"

"M-hm."

"Sorry. I should mind my own beeswax. But if I were you, I'd snap him up *fast*."

"Busybody," she said.

170

* * *

On my next trip home, Mummo said she had something for me. She hobbled ahead of me upstairs and into her bedroom, went to her highboy and opened the middle drawer. She ran a hand under folds of sewing fabric and brought out a lightweight tan envelope—a strange size, about five inches by eight inches. I caught sight of foreign stamps and foreign handwriting. She pulled a map and a booklet from the envelope, no letter. I wondered what had happened to the letter and who had written it.

"We went to Finland," she said, unfolding the map on the bed. It was yellow and frayed. Finland was bigger on it than on other maps I'd seen.

I said, "This was made before the Winter War!" Someone had outlined the old and new borders with a black crayon, showing a crescent bulge of eastern Finland that was no longer Finland. Grievous marks. Lake Ladoga, which the Soviets took from Finland, looked extremely large, more like a sea than a lake. Without Lake Ladoga Finland looked like Minnesota, shot through with scattered small lakes. Blobs of blue swept down the map of Finland in a southeastern slide, left behind, I guessed, by melting glaciers.

"And this," Mummo said, handing me the booklet. It was a tourist guide to Helsinki, dated Summer 1927 and written in English.

"How long did you stay?" I asked her, but she was already halfway to the door. I called thanks and turned to study the map. I walked around it, torqued it, peered at it from all sides. Seen on the skew, the new Finland was a dancing lady, twirling away from the viewer, one arm on the way up, her skirts twisting and swirling at her feet. I decided that the lady was Mummo, making up for lost time.

I treasured these gifts from her. I would take them with me to Finland. They might help me to find what I was looking for.

* * *

But so much had changed since I had applied for the grant. Now the trip seemed frivolous. How could I leave Jeff? Or Marcie, having her baby in July? Or Mummo, who suddenly seemed fragile?

171

Everyone said *Go.* Still, I had to force myself to pack.

Seeing me off, Jeff was his irresistible self. He trapped a flying strand of my hair and tucked it into a braid, and held my face in his hands for a long time, just smiling. He said, "Have fun. Don't worry about a thing." He kissed me and sent me off with one of those private Jeff-looks that always jangled me.

I had to force myself to get on that plane.

Part 3

The Old Country

Fourteen

Was That *to* the Taxi or *From?*

T he forest held on tenaciously, almost to the runway. I had guessed, wrongly, that we would approach Helsinki from the Baltic Sea, but we skimmed a nubby green for miles and miles and landed in a clearing. So this was Finland! Finland was a *forest*, or a big part of it was. I had heard the Finnish adage, "Finns are forest folks who only recently came in from the woods." If so, I thought as we taxied in, they didn't have to come far.

After I passed customs, I made my way through a moderate crowd toward a placard that read, "Katariina Halonen, Finnish Language Institute," held by a short, white-blond young man. He gave me a bashful smile and said he was Jorma Heikkinen from the Institute. He handed me a nosegay in U.S.A. colors—red rosebuds, white baby's-breath, blue bachelor's buttons. We found my luggage, he making polite remarks, I making polite replies. After directing me to the shuttle bus and bidding me a pleasant stay, he left.

I took a rear window seat and watched passengers get on the bus. Many of them looked familiar! An old woman had Mummo's pinched nose and tetchy mouth. A blonde teen-ager had Liisa's fashion-model cheeks, and one man, like Harald, had more flesh than absolutely necessary. Even Aarnie was there in a man who hid himself not by folding inward but by arching away. Catching my eye as they came down the aisle, these Finns didn't nod or smile the way Americans might. Instead, they stared. They filed silently into the bus, waited silently for the aisles to clear, silently took their seats. What was it about the Finns and silence?

As the bus rumbled on, I stared at the Finns in return—harmlessly, in that I was staring at the backs of heads. The hair shades ran the gamut of the ash blondes, with one or two grays thrown in, and a few brunettes. I looked out the window: only airport buildings and fields. I was hungry for answers. To what? To some undefined puzzle I'd come all the way to Finland to solve.

We arrived in Helsinki, and I soaked up the sights. The city seemed contradictory. It was modern but also ancient. Simple but elegant. Unadorned apartment buildings had their own parks and playgrounds. Dark office blocks had flower stalls at the ground level. As with people on the bus, Helsinki seemed familiar. I felt like calling to Finns in the street, "Hello, people! I'm *ho*-ome!" But I wouldn't know how to say it in their language.

That first night, the only night I'd be spending in a hotel, I bathed and put on a nightgown, sat in bed and ate a supper of airline rolls, cheese, and chocolate. The room was high and narrow, most of the width taken by the camp-sized bed I sat on. At the far end, a crank window faced a red brick wall. I got up and looked down. The only thing visible was a clean concrete alley. Back in bed, I snapped on the radio knob built into the wall. An accordion played a polka. A man made droll remarks in Finnish. I turned it off.

Finland's clock ran eight hours later than Minnesota's. It was time to sleep. But my mind wouldn't relax. Pictures flipped past me like cartoons in a comic book. Ruffle the pages, watch the corners. See the Roadrunner run! *The Roadrunner.* I took refuge in the image. The Roadrunner was *American*—arrogant, irreverent, staying a step ahead. I picked up my novel and tried to read. I couldn't concentrate. I put the light off and tried to sleep. It was no use. My mind was keeping my body awake.

I was ecstatic. I was in Finland! *My ancestral land.*

* * *

The girl smiled hello, shyly, and continued to write in her notebook. Her writing was left-handed and seemed backwards and upside down, but was exquisite—curves and dips like ocean waves, dots like the starry sky. The girl herself was exquisite. She had rich brown skin, big black eyes, and long black hair left loose. She wore a blue floor-length skirt with a white silk shirt and high-heeled sandals. I introduced myself.

Again smiling, she said, "I am Layla. From Algiers."

Was that a city or a country? I didn't know. To cover my ignorance, I said, "Have you studied Finnish before?"

"No. Have you . . . ?"

"No. I'm a Finn, but I don't speak the language." I could hear how silly that sounded. Layla averted her eyes as if the impossibility of my words shamed us both. I hurried to say, "What I mean is, I grew up in the States with my grandparents and they spoke Finnish, but I didn't learn it." That didn't sound right, either. So I said, "Have you been in Finland long?"

I was glad the teacher intervened. From the front of the room, she called, "Good morning, students!" All other talk ceased. She looked about forty and had dark blonde hair and a friendly face. She exuded good will. "My name is Elena Pelka. Welcome to Finland!" She asked us to introduce ourselves, and so we did. Five men and seven women, from India, Japan, Italy, Denmark, Poland, Algeria, the United States. I was the only American.

In British-accented English, Elena said, "I hope you enjoy learning Finnish. It is a very old language, different from other Nordic languages, and part of the Finno-Ugric group that includes Lapp, Hungarian, and several languages near the Ural Mountains in the Soviet Union."

I listened with all of my corpuscles, vowing I would learn this language or die trying. *There's* an Americanism, I thought, "die trying." Americans do exaggerate.

"Finnish is spelled phonetically," Elena was saying. "Each letter is pronounced, with the main stress on the first syllable. Thus, *kauppa*, or shop, is said 'kah-oo-pa' rather than 'kah-pa' and *sauna* is 'sah-oo-na' rather than 'sah-na.' Finnish is an agglutinative language, that is, it builds its meanings from distinct parts. Because of its phonetic spelling and agglutination, Finnish is a rather easy language to learn. You may have heard otherwise."

She smiled playfully at two young men, who hesitantly returned her smile. I assumed they had already tried to learn Finnish and hadn't done too well.

"We will meet every day for three hours, starting at nine hundred hours, or nine o'clock, with a fifteen-minute intermission. You will take no examinations. Each day in class, you will practice speaking Finnish. Do not be sorry to make mistakes! Mistakes are a part of learning. Afternoons you may use for study and sightseeing. Some tours have been arranged. You may join the tours or make your own plans. Questions?"

There were no questions, so she handed out the instruction books. I opened mine to a drawing of a man saying to a friend, "*Illoinen hyvää!*" Translation, "Jolly good!" I checked the publishing data. Sure enough, London.

With more animation than I'd expected from a Finn, Elena acted out stories, stepped into the hall, came back as various characters, made jokes, helped us pronounce Finnish words. The sounds of the language were comfortable to my ears; I'd heard them all my life. Now I would learn to *speak* those sounds!

The short words and sentences seemed simple. I read the exercise list for the first lesson. "*Se on kauppa*" meant "It is a shop." Aha! I could memorize nouns, put them after "*Se on*" and make actual sentences—"It is a car (*Se on auto*)" and "It is a house (*Se on talo*)" and "It is a street (*Se on katu*)." I'd be speaking Finnish!

But of course I couldn't keep simply pointing out cars and houses. I had to learn this language. In the back of the book, I found the burgeoning forms a Finnish word could take. *Kauppa* grew into *kaupallinen* (commercial), *kaupankäynti* (trade, business), *kauppakoju* (stall), *kauppaoikeus* (commercial law), *kauppasulku* (embargo, blockade), *kauppatavara* (merchandise), *kauppias* (merchant), *kaupunginosa* (district), *kaupungintalo* (town hall), *kaupunki* (urban) and so on.

How did anyone say such long words, or memorize them, or sort out verbs and prepositions to go with them? I'd lulled myself into thinking this would be easy. Not exactly. At the end of the first day, I had a doozy of a headache. Other students were learning faster than I was. Either I had become immune to Finnish as a child and it would never sink in, or I had a language deficit. Whatever the cause, I was hardheaded when it came to learning Finnish.

That first day after class, Layla and I went out for lunch. She led the way across the wide brick plaza below our building into a district of narrow, attractively twisted streets and noon traffic, office buildings and coffee shops. I was shocked to see a baby asleep in a buggy outside a restaurant, the parents nowhere in sight. Finns were known for their honesty, but this was crazy! Finns trusted strangers not to steal their babies?

The bakery/cafeteria smelled heavenly, a busy, handsome place of mirrored surfaces, indoor trees, and a clientele of students, shoppers, and business people. One old woman in a tailored hat and suit sat stationary above her food, apparently savoring the high point of her day. At a display case of ready-to-eat foods, Layla pointed to an open-face rye sandwich of Lappi cheese and pimento. I chose a beef pasty. We moved our trays to the coffee bar. Layla said, "For you? I do not drink it." I placed a white pottery cup and saucer on my tray and poured a cup of very dark coffee. I gave the cashier too much Finnish cash, trusting her to give back the right change. We found a window table, and I embarked on my first experience in the completely satisfying Finnish lunch.

Layla asked me, "Do you have brothers and sisters?"

"One sister, two years older. And you?"

"I have many," she said with affection. "Four sisters, five brothers."

"That *is* a lot! You must miss them."

"Yes. We came to Finland three months now. My husband is a student, in architecture. Ahmed." From her purse she took the photo of a baby. Smiling broadly, she thrust it at me. The baby, who appeared to be three or four months old, had been propped like a doll in the corner of a sofa. She was a tiny replica of her mother.

"She's adorable," I said. "What is her name?"

"Jamilah." After giving the picture a lingering look, she put it away.

"How did you happen to come to Finland?"

179

"My father knew a man from Finland when I was a girl. Mr. Hansson. He came to my country. He is a nice man."

"Did he speak your language?" My actual, secret question was, What *is* your language?

"No, we did not speak Finnish, and he did not speak Arabic, but he used French and English. And Swedish. He was a Swedish-speaking Finn."

Out of my knowledge zone again, I said, "How do you like living in Finland?"

Layla spoke with caution. "Finnish people are nice people . . ." Her face asked permission to say more. "But I do not understand something. You are Finnish. Maybe you understand . . . I do not understand the silence."

Silence? I had a good idea what she meant, but I asked her to tell me more.

"Finnish people do not talk, but they look at me," she said. "They look and *look*."

"They look at me that way too," I said.

Her large eyes grew larger. "At *you*?"

"Yes. They stare. In America we think it's not polite to stare."

"What is 'stare'?"

"Look very hard at someone." I gawped at her. She got the idea. I said, "But people in Finland stare all the time, so staring must be okay here. I don't think they mean to be rude."

Already embarrassed at what she was about to say, Layla said, "Finns are the same, all Finns. All white skin, no black hair. They do not look at *me*."

"Do you feel invisible? Like you weren't even there?"

Understanding washed over her. "Yes! They look at me but do not see me. They see my skin and my hair. Not *me*."

"I'm so sorry if people don't see you."

She repeated, "I do not understand the silence."

I sighed. "I don't, either. *I* had silence too at home, with my grand-parents. I wanted to talk about everything, but we never talked. I felt different from everyone, like you do in Finland. I grew up missing my parents. They died when I was a baby." Here I was, telling my deepest truths to someone I'd known for four hours.

Her eyes welled with tears. She said, "I am sorry for *you*."

This beautiful young woman from a culture I knew nothing about, someone I had known for four hours, understood.

* * *

Language study proceeded slowly. Layla and I quizzed each other over lunch, breaking into laughter as we garbled sentences. *"James tulle postioimistoon. Hänellä on mukana pari postikorttia ja kirje"* meant "James comes to the post office. He has with him a couple of postcards and a letter." I found such gobs of letters impossible to say. My tongue balked. I could memorize vocabulary words for a given day, but I couldn't string the words together. When I had to compose sentences, I got cases confused, and I mangled Finnish grammar. In Finnish, a preposition came after a noun and changed the meaning of the noun. If Elena asked me to say, in Finnish, "Tom goes *from* the hotel *to* the station *by* taxi," I might say, "Tom goes *to* the hotel *by* the station *from* the taxi." The chances of being wrong were endless and could get Tom in a heap of trouble.

Ten days into the course, a Chicago historian named Deborah Stern joined us. She was a language genius. On her own, before coming to Finland, she had mastered a semester of Finnish in two weeks. She could hold conversations in Finnish. After her first day in class, I invited her out for coffee.

At the restaurant, I, the Finnish-American, placed my order in English, "Coffee, please," while Deborah, the Jewish-American, placed hers in beautiful, lilting Finnish, *"Vanilja jäätelö ja iso kuppi kahvia, kiitos!"*

I knew what she'd said: "Vanilla ice cream and a large cup of coffee, thank you!" But I couldn't have invented the sentence myself.

I was a bonehead in my own people's language.

* * *

Throughout Helsinki, tram tracks fanned out and took one wherever one wanted to go—museums, the zoo, an amusement park, even a castle. One day I boarded a jam-packed tram at city center, aiming for a flea market at the other side of town. The tram took off with a promising whir. I was standing in the aisle, hanging on and feeling free, when the tram stopped and two female tram guards got on. In navy blue suits and military shoes, they stormed the aisle like Gestapo agents, acting out a rule I had heard about but had temporarily forgotten: *Produce a ticket stub or get off at the next stop.* The tram started up again. One guard pushed her chest against me, indicating that I should find my stub and be fast about it. I rummaged through my handbag. No stub. I got to my knees, dumped the bag and sifted the contents. No stub. The lady was making dire sounds. Other riders were watching me as if I were the only show in town. Shaking, I opened my billfold and thumbed through the slots. In the last possible slot, I found it. The stub! I showed it to the guard, and she stalked off without comment.

The tram rocketed on. I sat back against the wall like Raggedy Ann on holiday, my legs in the aisle and my smile in place, my rag-doll mind saying, Welcome to Finland! Welcome to Finland!

* * *

I loved Helsinki. It was a great place not just for tram travel but for walking. Starting below our classroom and armed with a map, I could walk to parks, libraries, book stores, bakeries that sold crusty Finnish breads, theaters that showed American films. I went back to certain places again and again just for the twang on the senses. At the cathedral-like post office, I listened: wooden clogs on marble, *clip-clop*, then, a hush; the ceiling soaked up noise. At the waterfront, I sniffed the sea air and watched fishermen selling fish right off their boats. Seagulls dive-bombed, crying and screaming, trying to steal fish. At the train station, the screaming whistles made me miss Mahoning, but they also made me yearn to climb aboard and go as far as the train would go—Mongolia! Siberia! the outer limits of the world!

Then there was Stockmann. In the States I avoided department stores—too much pressure to buy things I didn't need—but Stockmann was different. Stockmann boasted fine Finnish design in everything it sold, practical items in clear, strong colors—clothing, shoes, sports gear, office and home fur-nishings, kitchenware, stationery, notions, toys. Stockmann had everything, a beauty salon, international books and newspapers, swanky take-home meals, imported foods. Outside in a kiosk, a fast-handed vendor wrapped flowers in record time. He whipped florist's paper into a capped cone, covering the blos-soms as well as the stems, looped the string into a carrying handle, and sent the Finnish businessman home with a briefcase in one hand and a flower cone in the other. Stockmann was the ultimate in department stores.

One day when Layla and I went shopping, Stockmann was busier than usual, noisier. On the main floor a crowd had gathered around a man who was shouting. The shouting alone caused us to walk in that direction. In Finland you didn't hear much shouting, and here was a man shouting in the middle of Stockmann, and in Swedish. I laughed when I saw what he was selling: *veg-etable slicers*. Sweaty and winded, the man was slicing potatoes into a bowl, amazingly fast. Slices flew out of the slicer, but too many missed the bowl and scooted off the table, and they were slopping up the floor. The man's fingers were slimy with potato juice. When his glasses slid down his nose, he nicked them back up with his knuckles and kept selling his wares, smiling in apology.

I said to Layla, "We have the same thing in the States, some guy sell-ing vegetable slicers! On the way home, my uncle would make fun of him. He'd say, 'Yessir, folks! This slicer does *everything*! It *slices*! It *chops*! Why, it'll even toast your *noogies*!'"

Layla frowned politely, not getting the joke. I said, "It's okay. I never understood it either." She went off toward children's clothes and I took the stairs one flight up to home furnishings. I needed dishtowels, nothing more, but I got sidetracked by Finnish inventiveness. I stopped to look at kitchen rugs that looked like cotton but were plastic, easy to wipe clean, and sauna floor mats made of chunks of car tires wired together, and long-handled dustpans with hinged covers in red, blue, or apple green. I kept thinking that Liisa would love this place. I picked up a blue hinged dustpan. Very conve-nient, no bending. I had one like it in my Helsinki dorm room. Why didn't we have these dustpans in the States? . . . Well, we *did*, but only in hotel lob-bies.

Standing there, holding the dustpan, I compared Finns and Americans. Finns were famous for honesty and hard work, Americans for independence and friendliness. Finns were homogeneous. Americans were assorted. Finns had one set of laws for the whole country. America had different laws from state to state, with exceptions to every law. I mentally reran a Finnish law that had recently stranded me: *If a holiday falls on a Friday, that day becomes a Sunday.* Need cash? Too bad! The banks are closed. Need milk? Too bad, stores are closed, too. When I complained to Elena, she smiled and gleefully repeated, "If a holiday falls on a Friday . . ." Like most Finns I'd met, she assumed that the Finnish way was the right way, the one logical, sensible way to do anything.

I felt *half-and-half.* In the States, I felt Finnish. In Finland, I felt American. My genes resonated to the Finnishness of Finland, but I craved things *American.* American music, American slang, American *nonsense.* I longed for stores to stay open on Fridays.

I bought eight blue-and-white-checked dishtowels, four for Mummo, four for my dorm room, and set off to find the candles and fancy paper napkins. I needed to stock up on hostess gifts; Finns had a nice habit that we students had adopted, taking a small gift to any home visited. I cautiously passed the glassware aisles. Here, of all places, I didn't want to break anything. Here were international prize-winning designs, glasses made to look like bubbly ice, bowls like wings in flight. *Ethereal.* I kept my hands to myself until I was well out of reach.

I wanted to find out if Stockmann gave away cardboard boxes. I needed a file box for research notes. When I saw a woman kneeling before a cupboard, stocking goods, her head virtually inside the shelf, I bent toward her and said, "Um . . ."

Without removing her head, she said, "No English! No American!"

How did she know I was an American? Was it the "um"? What did Finns say instead of "um"?

* * *

184

In contrast to the typical Finnish café, this campus cafeteria lacked beauty altogether. It was gloomy and utilitarian and had high khaki walls. It seemed camouflaged, prepared for war. But there, more than anywhere else, I felt the protected foreignness of Finland. Lining up behind students who dressed all in black, I bought yogurt and dark coffee, took a corner table, and plunged into books I had only skimmed for the grant application. This day's reading had to do with the *Kalevala*.

Remembering Jeff's question, "Do you know the *Kalevala*?" and missing him mightily, I opened a biography of Elias Lönnrot, compiler of the *Kalevala*, and was transported to the early 1800s when Finnish college students saved Finnish folklore from extinction. During centuries of foreign reign, remnants of Finnish culture had rested with the peasants, in the hinterlands, in folk poems and rune songs, and Lönnrot was the all-out winner in recording them before they disappeared. As a Swedish-speaking Finn, he first had to brush up on his Finnish, and then he made thirteen trips, chiefly to the eastern lake country, in areas later lost to Russia. He met farmers who lived so far apart they couldn't see each other's chimney smoke and liked it that way. They sang folk runos for him, and he recorded them in logbooks. One photo showed his handwriting, spiky and slanted sharply forward. Another showed the man himself, a snub-nosed, merry-faced doctor-in-training.

Lönnrot described an event he felt privileged to witness, a song fest held in a remote cottage. It was a contest of endurance, memory, and creativity. Jostled by watchers on all sides, two champion singers straddled a wooden bench, face-to-face, clasping right hands as though shaking hands, holding cups of ale in their left hands. Accompanied by the *kantele*, the Finnish lap harp, and enduring jeers from the audience, the two took turns singing runos, or folk verses, inventing them on the spot if need be, in the galloping "Kalevala" style (a meter borrowed by Henry Wadsworth Longfellow for his poem, "Hiawatha"), singing until one singer either fell over drunk or ran out of verses. These runos would later be added to the epic Lönnrot would name the *Kalevala*, and would later inspire stories by J.R.R. Tolkein.

Next I tackled the *Kalevala* itself. I wasn't fond of myths in general, but I got caught up in the *Kalevala*'s tales of greed, rivalry, love, war, told in a mix of fantasy and history, Christianity and paganism. Some stories were bloody, some were funny. The characters had human traits and reminded me of people I knew. Louhi, the mistress of Pohjola (northern Finland), was a little like Mummo. One Louhi story starts out with Lemminkäinen, a Don Juan who can woo the ladies but can't sing. He sings anyway. A crane sitting on a stump, counting his toe bones, hears the awful singing over six villages and seven seas. He screeches and flies off in a flap. His screeching wakes Louhi, who then discovers that the Sampo, the magic mill of plenty, is gone. *Stolen!* (It's Väinämöinen, the wily old singer, who's stolen it.) She becomes a giant bird and gathers her warriors under her wings. She sets off in hot pursuit. Like Louhi, Mummo seemed bigger than life when she got mad, a power to contend with.

Väinämöinen was like Harald, blustery and vain. When Ilmarinen, the innocent blacksmith, refuses to go to war in northern Finland, Väinämöinen *tricks* him into going. He sends him to the top of the tallest tree to retrieve the moon from its branches, then he *blows* him north. This was like Harald and his Ford-bragging, and poor innocent Aarnie.

I came across another Harald story, but I didn't recognize it as such. The birth of a sacred Child sends Väinämöinen into an epic slump. He knows the Child will replace him as leader of the people, but he hates to give up his power. Eventually, he admits his time is up, and, mustering his sullied majesty, he sails away a hero. Deposed, but still a hero.

We hadn't come to that chapter yet in real life.

* * *

Elena had asked me to stay after class, so I waited by her desk. When everyone else had gone, she said, "Timo and I want to invite you to dinner this evening. We will celebrate his students' high marks in Russian."

I recoiled. "*Russian?*"

She laughed, "Yes, but it's okay. It is Soviet *politics* we do not like. We like the language and the people. And the food. Tonight we will go to a true Russian restaurant."

"Will all of his students be there?"

"Oh, no! This is to celebrate the *teacher*. He did not know if his students would make good marks, and they did. So we will treat you to dinner." Smiling, she answered my silent question, *Why me?* "I have told him about the American Finn who asks so many questions! Shall we meet you at your flat? At nineteen hundred, seven o'clock? I have your address."

Aromas met us on the street and drew us in, heady, winey, complicated smells, as if sauces only dreamed of by chefs around the world had been invented here and were simmering backstage. Music came from deep inside the restaurant, an instrumental plinking that pulled at the emotions. We followed our host, weaving among tables and hearing the talk of many nations. The decor was decadent and overblown. Red plush love seats, curlycue chairs, purple tapestries, starburst chandeliers. Every table was set with black-banded china on a starched white cloth, a napkin tower on each plate, flowers, a small pink-shaded table lamp, and a *samovar*. Dining alcoves draped in velvet lined two walls, one step up from the main floor. The host delivered us to ours. A tiny mirror on the wall reflected lamps on other walls plus the color red.

As we sat down, the musician ambled toward us. He was towheaded and young, maybe in his late teens. His shirt was cream-colored, cleric-collared, side-buttoned, and billow-sleeved. The instrument he played was like a triangular mandolin painted with tiny flowers. The tune was familiar and seductive, extremely sad.

As he walked away, I asked Elena about the instrument. "It's a *balalaika*. The song is a traditional Russian love song."

"It works for me," I said, pining for Jeff.

Timo perked up. "Well, Kik! Do you enjoy Finland?" He was a small man with a twinkly face. Lines radiated in all directions from eyes the color of a spring lake. He seemed to find his world amusing.

"I love it," I said. "My father was born in Finland."

"Oh, yes? In what city?"

Before attempting the city's name, I prepared my tongue. Whenever a Finnish R came at the front of a word, I had to back up and take a running start, roll up my tongue like a carpet and let it fly. Burring the R, I said, "*R-R-R-R-Rantasalmi!*"

Delighted, Elena said, "Rantasalmi? Timo was a child there! He took holidays there with his uncle and aunt." Timo's smile lit up our corner. "They have died by now," she added, "but we have friends in Rantasalmi. I wonder if they know your people."

"I don't know if any still live there," I said, regretting my poor knowledge.

Timo said, "We will find out." Acting the part of the professor that he was, he took pen and notebook from an inside pocket of his suit coat.

I said, "They would be Halonens or Saaris."

"Halonen is a common name, Saari as well. But we will try. Your grandfather's name?"

"Toivo Halonen. My father was Patrik Halonen. My grandmother's maiden name was Saari. Emma Saari. She has a sister in Finland, named Silvi." I prattled on, strewing flecks of information and not knowing when to quit.

Timo wrote down the names. "Date of birth for your grandfather?"

"I don't know." I wished I had asked Mummo more questions.

"Your father's date of birth?"

"I don't know that, either."

"It's okay! We can start with the names."

Elena asked me about my grandmother. I explained that she and Grandpa used to live in North Dakota, that my grandparents and my uncle raised my sister and me on the Iron Ore Range, that Grandpa had died ten years back. Again, I didn't know how much to say or when to stop. But by happy chance I stopped on time, as Timo was bursting.

"The Iron Ore Range!" he exclaimed. "I have relatives there, in Chisholm."

Odd! A *Minnesota mining town* mentioned in a *Russian* restaurant in *Helsinki*. Suffering a clinch of homesickness, I smiled and said, "Finns live in bunches in the States. If you find one Finn, you find *lots*. But I don't know anyone from Chisholm. Well, wait. The Hibbing Makis have a brother there. They come to church sometimes."

"Is that the Laestadian church?" Timo asked. He gave me his sunburst smile.

"I don't know that word."

Once again the teacher, he said, "The Laestadians are pietist Lutherans. In the nineteenth century, a man named Lars Laestadius protested the formality of the state church of Sweden. Of course, you know Sweden owned Finland at the time. Laestadius believed in a lay pastorate, no rituals or liturgy. No pianos or organs in church."

"It must be the same, then! Ours is the Finnish Believers' Lutheran. It's strict. No alcohol, no dancing. Two other branches are even stricter. They think fancy things are prideful. Is it the same here?"

Timo and Elena nodded tolerantly. "Much the same," she said. "The families have twelve or thirteen children. They don't believe in birth control." (*Oh.* So *that's* why the Pesonens have so many kids.)

For the next two hours, food arrived at a leisurely pace, engaging the taste buds by a system of delay. Bear paté (bear!). Herring marinated in Madeira. Tartare of cold smoked reindeer (reindeer!). Fried wild duck with rowanberry sauce. Cloudberry soup (warm), seasoned with Swedish punch. Sherbet, cheeses. Every bite melted in the mouth. This was a Russian brilliance I had never imagined!

Still, even if the food was divine, how could Finns patronize this place, only twenty years after the Winter War? The question came to me a few times during the meal, but I didn't let it ruin my appetite.

The conversation turned to travel and places of interest in Finland and never returned to my Rantasalmi relatives, if any existed. But Timo had said he would try to find them, and I had a feeling that if they could be found he would find them.

* * *

Midsummer 1960

Dear Jeff,

I'll write this in pieces as the night goes on. I think of you all the time! I wonder what you'd say about this or that, I hear you laughing, Huh-huh. I want you walking next to me, always! But I'm making the most of the time and I know you are, too. I can hardly wait. Meanwhile, here's a running account of the night.

Midsummer is a big deal here. It happens on the longest day of the year. Elena invited her students to her farm for an all-night party. She and Timo are celebrating with neighbors. Counting all the beds in the neighborhood, she said there would be a bunk for everyone when morning came.

The cuckoo here isn't a clock. It's the real bird in the forest. Folklore says it brings good luck. It's 8:17 p.m., and the cuckoo has just now called 18 times (this bird keeps strange hours). There will be a bonfire later on the lake shore—which will add more light to the lightest night of the year. But first, sauna.

The sauna is down by the lake, and I asked to be able to bathe alone. Usually groups of women go in together, but I'm not feeling that communal. I cover the window with a towel so people on the shore can't see me but I can see them. Most have already bathed. Earlier I saw some men run out of the sauna, run into the lake and run back to the sauna. This I saw from a respectful distance. People are dressed in parkas (a light rain), talking and standing around what will later be the bonfire. Now it's a giant teepee, a 50-foot pile of branches held in place by timbers leaned against it. A tractor-trailer dumps its load of scrap wood and rumbles off to get another load. I take my time. I'm home. Or part of me is home, steaming in a sauna by a Finnish lake. I feed birch to the fire and throw water on the rocks, and I steam. A Finn becoming a Finn all over again. Thus baptized at 120 degrees F., fever hot, I feed the fire for the next person, dress and climb the hill.

Elena and her mother and aunts are in the kitchen. Someone says, "Cognac?" I sip some. It burns the throat but glows afterward. We finish in time for more guests, coffee, cakes, the bonfire.

The sun never really goes down at this time of year. Normally the night would be bright right now (almost midnight)—actually sunny—but now we have a white sky and drizzle. Neighbors gather as the night goes on. They stand on shore, eating, drinking, talking, or wait in boats. (Is it time yet?) A teen-aged boy cousin of Elena's shakes benzene on the woodpile, ignites it and whoosh, nearly sets himself on fire. But he's safe. Fire rips at the wood, flames and smoke go straight up. I asked Elena why they have bonfires on the brightest night of the year. She told me the story. Long ago, evil spirits came down at Midsummer, attracted by the sunny night, and people built fires to scare them away. When the church adopted the holiday, it renamed it Juhannuskokko or St. John's Fire. There's the mixing again of folklore and Christianity.

190

Later: We can see bonfires around the lake at other farms. Our fire whips at the ashes, and flakes fall like confetti on the children's hair— princes and princesses of Midsummer. Islands reflect in the bay, the water is still. A Chinese exchange student plays a game with kids on the shore, counting in Finnish: "Yksi, kaksi, kolme." Men light up cigars. A tipsy college man chases a toddler in circles, the child giggles. We roast the sausages—makkara—giant hot dogs threaded seven or eight at a time to an antler-type tree branch. Burnt, with the skin bursting. Eat 'em with brown mustard. Mm-mm, good.

That's it! Midsummer in Finland. When morning comes, we head for bed via the woods, *reeling* with the fragrance of lily of the valley, the best-smelling flower ever. It grows in the shade of the forest. The unspoken-for maidens among us pick seven kinds of wildflowers to sleep on, so their future sweethearts will visit their dreams. I already have a sweetheart.

Did I say how much I miss you?

Love, Kik.

* * *

The invitation gave me tingles. The docent at the Finnish Literature Society had asked me if I'd like to see a *Kalevala* logbook, written by Lönnrot. (Yes, thank you! I *would*.) I'd spent several afternoons reading at the Finnish Literature Society, a skinny palace of a library and the storied meeting spot for Lönnrot and fellow folklorists of the nineteenth century. Finnish folklore study was highly regarded internationally, and this library housed many of the reasons why, including ownership of the *Kalevala* logbooks.

The docent put on white gloves, went to a glass-paned bookcase and withdrew a tall narrow hard-backed journal, opened it and held it toward me. There was Lönnrot's spiky handwriting! I scanned the page clumsily, still not speedy at reading Finnish. But I recognized the story from the English version, "Väinämöinen's Wooing of the Maiden Aino." In a wayside cottage a century and a half earlier, Lönnrot recorded the tragedy of Aino. Aino is like Liisa, beautiful, sought-after and, unless she wants to be caught, *uncatchable*. Rather than marrying the old rune-singer as she is expected to do, Aino walks into the sea and drowns. Aino's mother weeps bitterly. Her tears turn to rivers. The rivers form rapids. Islands rise in the rapids. Three birch trees grow on every island, and in every tree sit three golden cuckoos. The first golden cuckoo sings to Aino, the second, to her rejected suitor, the third, to Aino's mother. The third golden cuckoo sings, "Gladness, gladness!"—a strange message for a mother who has lost a child. The cuckoo sings this song for the mother's life-time.

Like Aino's mother, Mummo was sad. Maybe she too had suffered a loss and never recovered. The third golden cuckoo sang what I wished for Mummo: *gladness*. She resisted things happy or free, but I wished she could be both—happy and free.

I thanked the docent, who bowed to me with her gloves on. I went down the exit steps, pushed open the tall double doors and stepped back into modern Finland.

*   *   *

Elena hosted sightseeing trips two afternoons a week, and one day she started below our classroom. Most buildings on the plaza were mustard yellow brick, sober-faced and many-windowed. *Russian*-looking. "This of course is the Senate Square," Elena said. "You see the Cathedral there." She pointed to the massive, tall building, majestic and broad. "The Senate Square represents much in Finnish history. Helsinki began as a market town in 1550 near the Helsinge Rapids. Twenty years later, the plague killed many residents and then the city burned to the ground! At the time Finland was owned by Sweden, and Swedish officials ordered the city of Helsinki be moved to this site. Again, it had fires! Then the plague! Then an invasion by Russia . . ."

Her composure slipped. Mention of Russia did this to Finns, I had noticed. "In 1808," she continued, "Russia occupied Helsinki and in 1809 it made Finland a Grand Duchy of Russia, and named Helsinki the capital. What we see here was begun during that period. The Senate Square buildings were designed by Ehrenstrom and Engel, in the neoclassic style, completed in phases between 1818 and 1852. The statue there," she said, pointing, "is Alexander II. Erected in 1894, the work of Runeberg and Takanen."

Elena paused until two students stopped talking. She smiled at them and said, "The Finns wanted independence. Finns are a proud people. We have always wanted to be free. Finally, in 1917, Finland fought a war with Russia, and we won our independence. A most joyful victory! Every December 6, our Independence Day, we celebrate our victory. People carry torches and walk in the streets, and we stop right here. Remember, it is dark in December—we have almost no sun in winter—and it is very cold, often windy. Torches are held high in the dark, and the wind whips the flames. Officials make speeches into the microphones, here on the steps. A men's chorus sings songs of Finland. The wind in the loudspeaker makes sounds come and go in the microphone. People still weep on Independence Day, our freedom is so precious to us."

With a start, I returned to the present. The Senate Square was warm and sunny. Not freezing cold and dark and windy. I glanced at the statue. The Russian ruler stood in the very spot where, every year, Finns celebrated their freedom from Russian rule.

Elena identified other structures on the plaza, the Government Palace, city administration branches, University of Helsinki buildings including the main library, and the Sederholm House, the oldest stone building in Helsinki, designed in rococo style. "Roe-cocoa," I wrote. I'd look it up later.

Over the weeks, Elena showed us a Finland we might not have found on our own. That first day, she took us to Hvitträsk, the former studio-residence of three architects who lived there with their families, all at the same time, Eliel Saarinen, Armas Lindgren, and Herman Geselius. It was a charming complex of Karelian-style buildings and sunny living spaces, decorations on door posts, and, famously, rumors of dalliances with unmatched spouses, courtyard trysts under the spying moon.

The same three men designed the National Museum, this time featuring the national Romantic style. I gravitated to the Lapp costumes in the basement. Sturdy T-shaped dresses with blue and yellow piping as decoration. Red and blue felt caps edged in many rows of woven trim. Fantastic, curled-toed reindeer hide boots, so tall and vast that they covered the thighs.

We went to the forest retreat owned by composer Jean Sibelius and named for his wife, Aino, a homey house furnished with plump sofas and chairs. "Sibelius needed complete silence when he worked," Elena said. "When he was composing, he sent his children outside to play in the woods." Silence surrounded the house even now. Sibelius' white wool suit hung on his bedroom door, pressed and ready for his next sea voyage.

Tarvaspää, the castle home of Akseli Gallen-Kallela, was planned by the artist himself, a maze of crannies and step-down rooms, carved doors, artwork on every surface, the flights and whimsy of an original mind. Outside, beneath the trees, sat a sauna house blackened inside and out from wood smoke.

At the National History Museum, my favorite display was a stuffed two-headed calf. He stood in his window, looking around in the broadest sense. I knocked on the glass: *You awake in there?*

In the Helsky handicrafts shop, artists sat at looms, weaving signature fabrics. Samples of their work hung on stanchions and on the walls. One woman was weaving a fluffy cotton *poppana* or "popcorn" fabric, designed with red, orange, and pink stripes, with points of powder blue. *Poppana* was exceptionally hard-wearing, she told me. With her permission, I touched the fabric she was weaving. It felt like chenille, tufted, soft, and sumptuous. I didn't want to leave that shop.

One Thursday, Elena ended class early and took us on a lunch tour of an icebreaker ferry. Finnish ferries were floating hotels with steel prows, called icebreakers because in the winter, when the Gulf of Bothnia froze solid, they kept the water lanes open between Finland and Sweden. During the summer, the ferry lines invited the public aboard for a guided tour and a complimentary buffet lunch. We first were shown the observation decks, staterooms, game rooms, movie halls, and gift shops, moving up and down levels on wide carpeted stairs lit with pin-lights. Then we lined up for lunch. Elena had chosen a Thursday because every Thursday in Finland is Pea Soup Day. We had an ambitious pea soup that stayed where you put it, delicious bread, and a fluffy cranberry whip. To ferry company executives, the tours meant ticket sales for the overnight Stockholm trip. To us students, they meant a stolen hour of glamour and free food.

Among the places that Elena showed us, my favorite was Seurasaari, or Folk Island, a reconstruction of historic farms and villages. Buildings had been hauled to the island or built there as copies and arranged as an enclave in the forest, notch-log cabins like those built by Swede-Finns in the 1600s in Jamestown, Virginia, a small frame church, a really big house that could board thirty people, a summer sleep-house with a second floor that overhung the porch. We gaped at a Paul Bunyan-sized rowboat carved from one log. It was so deep I wondered how anyone could climb into it, and so long that the nether parts vanished in the gloom of the moorage house. It was strong enough, Elena said, to take the pastor to his island congregation in almost any weather (and big enough, I figured, to take the congregation to the pastor if need be).

Next to a tiny log cabin, Elena said, "This building is hundreds of years old. It has just one room and a loft." She motioned us inside.

The interior was dark. One small window was the only source of light. The walls were black with soot. On the far side a work counter ran along the wall. A wood stove, sink, and table and chairs completed the kitchen area. On the near side, two box beds had been built into the wall and draped with homespun. Poles set across the rafters were threaded with flat rye bread rounds, baked with a hole in the center, exactly like the hardtack we bought at the Co-op.

My research came alive in this house. Some Finnish woman (who maybe looked like Mummo) had lived out her life in this tiny place. She had raised her family, cooked, baked, salted and preserved meat, woven fabrics, sewn clothes, made lye soap, boiled laundry, dried clothes outside in good weather, indoors in bad, buried ice in the winter to cool food in the summer. Every spring she scrubbed soot from the ceiling and walls. Before all celebrations—Name Days, weddings, state holidays and, after Christianity came, in the 1200s, also baptisms, confirmations, holy days—she fixed food for months in advance, since her guests might stay for weeks. All in this tiny house!

As a result of Elena's tours, I saw Mummo and Grandpa in a different light, as carriers of great cultural wealth. Why hadn't they told us about Finland? Didn't they miss the forests and the people, the way of life? The beauty and art? The bravery? Why sacrifice *Finland* for the hardship of starting over?

For the first time, I missed my grandparents. I wished I could talk to them. I mourned the rigidity of their closed lips, whatever the reasons. With Grandpa, it was too late. But I still had time to talk to Mummo.

* * *

JULY 5, 1960. MICHAEL HARALD HALONEN BORN TODAY
stop HANDSOME STRONG stop FULL HEAD DARK HAIR stop
PARENTS PROUD RELIEVED stop LOVE ADAM.

* * *

July 6, 1960 (Received July 16, 1960)
Dear Kik,

If I could have sent up fireworks to tell you, I would have! Michael is
the sweetest smelling thing! I put my face to his chest—it smells like <u>flax</u>.
Kik, babies are great! I don't know what I <u>thought</u> about before Michael.
Adam is jealous, me being so wild about the baby, but I try to give the new
daddy as many kisses as the baby gets.

My mom was here when the baby came. Oh, that reminds me, if anyone tells you childbirth is a breeze, don't believe it. It's not called travail
for nothing. But the other part is true, too. It's worth it when the baby is
safe and sound. Mom's been a trooper. She'll stay and help until I'm back
on my feet. I'll be in the hospital a few days. I insisted on nursing him (the
staff encourages bottles) and I'm glad I did. I get to see him more often
that way. He's growing fast. Come home soon, Auntie Kik!

Love, Marcie

* * *

July 8, 1960 (Received July 18, 1960)
Dear Kik,

Michael is changing even while we watch him! He's fantastic. His eyes
are something special. He looks at us, so <u>hard</u>, and gets his arms and legs
going like he can hardly stand not talking. Adam about pops his buttons!
He takes piles of pictures. I'll send you some when they're developed.
No, I won't, they might cross in the mail.

Hurry home.

Love, Marcie.

* * *

JULY 8, 1960. SOMETHING WRONG WITH BABY THOUGH FIXABLE stop PRAY STAY DON'T WORRY stop ALL SEND LOVE JEFF TOO stop ADAM.

* * *

JULY 8, 1960. WILL COME HOME NOW IF YOU WANT stop PLEASE WIRE IF SO stop PRAYING EXTRA HARD stop LOVE KIK.

* * *

JULY 9, 1960. THANKS BUT STAY stop MICHAEL IMPROVING stop BILIRUBIN stop MARCIE FINE INKY HERE TO HELP stop LOVE FROM ALL stop ADAM.

* * *

I asked Elena if she knew what bilirubin was. "It's a substance new-borns have," she said. "Why?"

"My cousin's baby is having a problem, something to do with biliru-bin."

"The baby passes bilirubin out of the body with other waste, and sometimes it collects and doesn't pass. My sister is a nurse." Elena said this in a confident, nurse-like way. "What does your cousin say?"

"They say he's better and that I should stay here and finish my work. But I keep wondering if I should go home."

She gave me an evaluative once-over. "You have . . . how much longer in Finland?"

"A week of research when class is over."

"Why don't you write to your cousin, a good long letter. Then use your time here. You will not be coming to Finland again soon—and maybe you can find your relatives in Rantasalmi. That would please your cousin." With a nurse's healing touch, she rubbed my shoulders as she spoke. Nursing talent must run in her family, I thought.

I did as she suggested. I wrote to Marcie, and Jeff, and Kaisa, the family in Mahoning. Then I gauged my time toward finishing Finland well.

* * *

In the dream I kissed a baby's hands, one hand, and then the other, saying each time, "Baby hands!" The baby gurgled and offered me his fingers. He played with my face. His palms pushed at my lips and felt bunchy and warm. I woke with baby hands active on my mouth and with a new ache for the unknown, a counterpoint to the ache for my parents. This ache was for Michael, who was unknown to me at that point, but *alive*.

* * *

Timo had scoured church records and phone books and found a Silvi Saari in Rantasalmi. He had called her. She was Mummo's sister. He said it was lucky she used her maiden name, or he might not have found her. He had arranged for me to meet her and in fact to stay overnight with her.

I had all kinds of resistances! The poor lady was probably a hundred years old, and senile, or bedridden. She wouldn't know any English. My spoken Finnish was *primitive*. I could hardly get past Hello. How could we fill up two whole days?

But, to please Timo, I said okay.

After emotional goodbyes to Layla, Elena, and Timo, I gathered my bags and boarded the bus. I was scheduled to do three days of research in Turku, write and mail my final report, then go to Rantasalmi to meet Mummo's sister.

Instead, I wanted to go home. I wanted to see Marcie and the baby, Liisa, Aarnie, Mummo. And *Jeff*. He would be in Canada until the end of September, but I wanted to be on the same *continent* with him, at least.

Doing research and writing my report and meeting Mummo's sister were the last things I wanted to do.

Fifteen

Finding Gold

Innish cows trotted the same as American cows, flopping along looking bored, and flipping their legs out to the side like girls running girly on purpose. The farms in Finland were like toy farms. Yellow house, green barn. Red house, blue barn. No junked tractors, no peeling paint. How did Finns manage it? Such universal neatness?

Having rolled west for the needed number of hours, the bus ran out of farmland and came to Turku, the next big city after Helsinki clockwise on the map. Turku sat on Finland's spongy southern tip where a spatter of islands split the Baltic Sea in two, into the Gulf of Bothnia which headed north between Sweden and Finland, and the Gulf of Finland which went west toward Russia. From the bus window, Turku seemed made up of stone castles, handsome plank buildings, spreading trees, and a river that coursed through town. Street markets and flower stands gave the air of a perpetual fair.

I got off at a park and walked uphill past businesses and churches, and downhill to a neighborhood of cottages and front-yard flower gardens. On a quaint side street, I found my rental, a Lilliputian house behind a short white fence. A ruddy young woman greeted me cheerfully, picked up her rucksack and hurried off on holiday. I stood in the arch between kitchen and front room. From there I could see everything, and everything was miniature—tile fireplace, bedroom, bath, even the flowers in the back yard. *Enchanting.* I put on the teakettle and forgot my urgency to get home.

The next morning I packed a sack lunch (a stocked refrigerator came with the rental rate) and walked the three blocks to the Institute of Migration. The archivist, who resembled Kaisa but had freckles and lighter hair, came around her desk to shake hands. "I am Sinikka Levanen. We received your letter, and we are happy you are here. The director is in another town today, but he asked me to greet you."

Going ahead of me through connected rooms, she gave an overview of the library: the photo displays and card catalogs, the old and new books, the collection of oral history tapes. When we completed the circuit, she left me at a table near the card files.

Soon I found *gold.* The institute had everything I needed, letters from the United States to Finland, journals, post cards, academic studies, books, magazines, news clippings, Ellis Island documents, emigration figures. Most of it was written in Finnish, but I could falter through. Armed with a Finnish word guide, and translating roughly, I could get the gist of any Finnish text. The first letter I picked up was written by a teen-aged live-in maid working for a wealthy family in Michigan. Her heart had been broken, she wrote, by the son of the household, who had wooed her and led her on but dropped her for a girl "of his own class." In a worn leather account book, a Minnesota miner practiced his new tongue: "Room, 2 dollers. Wiski, 1 doller." This was an unscrupulous treat, reading private papers a half-century old.

In records of Ellis Island, called the Isle of Tears by more than one writer, I found photos of Finns as they entered the United States. They had posed soberly for the camera, men in watchmen's caps, women in scarves tied under the chin, whole families in folk costume. I tried to imagine their fright as they entered Ellis Island and answered questions in English, giving memorized answers to memorized questions. "Name? Occupation? Country of origin? Any relatives living in the States? Who paid for your passage here? Is anyone meeting you? Can you read and write? How much money do you have?

Show it to me now." Some applicants had to answer further questions. When necessary, translators helped inspectors to weed out disallowed people. I noticed that when Mummo and Grandpa passed through Ellis Island, in the first years of the new century, the law restricted polygamists, prostitutes, epileptics, insane persons, beggars, and anarchists. All applicants had to undergo "the sixty-second medical exam," including the test Mummo had described, the lifting of the eyelid with a buttonhook to screen for glaucoma. Doctors chalked symbols on the chests of people with medical conditions—E for eye disease, H for heart ailment, Pg for pregnancy, X for mental retardation, a circled X for insanity. Chalk-marked people had to step aside. Some people were forced to return to the countries they had just fled.

I came across an astounding fact. For years at Ellis Island, Finns were not listed as Finns! During the busiest years—1892 to 1926—most Finns were counted as *Russians*. What an insult to Finnish pride! But apparently no sacrifice was too high, not even the shame of being called Russians. The goal was admittance to the United States, and the gate to the United States was Ellis Island. Whatever Ellis Island required them to do, the immigrants seemed willing to do.

On a whim, I looked up "Emma Saari Halonen" and "Toivo Halonen" in the card file. I expected to find nothing. And that's what I found under Mummo's name.

But I did find something under Grandpa's name.

Stunned, I noted the reference number. When I looked up the holding, what I found was a diary he wrote on the trip that he and Mummo took to Finland in 1927.

Sixteen

The Diary

Finland Trip 1927

By Toivo Halonen

Tr. from Finnish by Eeva Saarinen, Institute of Migration, Turku, Finland. June 1953

June 1. Harald drove us from home to Bismarck. It rained as we left. From Bismarck we went by train to Minneapolis; $27.46 for two people was the fare.

June 2. Arrived in Minneapolis at 7:15 a.m. It was cloudy, slightly rainy and the trees were lovely in fresh green leaves. We bought tickets at the depot, $90.22 including transfer for the trunk and luggage. The insurance was $5.75 and we got a sleeper ticket for $12.75.

June 3. The weather was nice when we left at 7:45 for Chicago by Great Western Railway.

June 4. Arrived at 8:00 at the Great Western Depot. We left at 10:00 on the Baltimore-Ohio Railway to Jersey City via Washington, D.C.

June 5. Arriving at 8:00 we were in Washington for 30 minutes. En route to there, first was level scenery then hilly and not so nice farmland. We got to Jersey City at 2:30 and the bus ferried us over the Hudson River and then to Harald Square Hotel where we stayed overnight.

June 6. At 10 we left for the pier by cab (which cost $1.00) and immediately onto the ship. The ship did not leave until 1:30. Nice weather in the afternoon but at night the fog caused the air to get real cold.

June 7. Cold air continued. There was a strong NE wind. On board was good housekeeping and satisfying food. We had several meals of fish, well prepared that one could enjoy eating. Also several kinds of meats were served with meals.

June 8. Cold continued.

June 11. It got clearer in afternoon with stronger wind that continued through the night.

June 12. The wind lessened in the afternoon.

June 13. Clear at first, in afternoon clouds and some rain.

June 14. Clear. East wind against us as we sailed eastward, which caused the ship to sway.

June 15. Clear, afternoon clouded and in evening it got foggy.

June 16. Arrived in Goteberg [sic] at 9:00. We were taken by streetcar around town to see beautiful parks and nice buildings and then a large estate and villa where we were served the midday meal. The population of the city is larger than Helsinki and the whole town is quite clean. No one understood English except the ship personnel, though this is a port city. At 10:00 the ship left from the port and we continued to Helsinki by way of the so-called Large Belt.

June 20. It was clear for the ship to arrive in Helsinki. At 5:30 we began to see the town and islands, and by 7:00 we arrived. A pilot ship arrived and the customs personnel who examined the ship about 2 km. out of the South Port. Singing and music greeted the travelers and the orchestra on the ship responded by playing a hymn and Pastor Mäkinen from New York thanked the welcoming committee with a few words. There were special crowds because yesterday a royal delegation from Norway had arrived to visit Helsinki. No room in the hotels.

In the afternoon we got to Professor Aarnio's hospitable home where Mrs. Aarnio delightfully welcomed us. Now we have spent a 24 hr. period basking in the warm hospitality—just out of the sauna. The heating unit was of more modern continued heating type but the water heater is of a unique design, a large kettle with a wood-burning space below, sort of a Paul Bunyan cup with warming unit below. [Pages missing. E.S.]

June 22. We went to [name obscured by author. E.S.] The farm has large buildings constructed by a relative nearly 150 years ago. The old house had eleven rooms within, and the workers' living quarters and chambers were in separate buildings. There was a large grove surrounding the main house so you could not see the house from the west or southern side. Some trees were nearly three feet in diameter and the fir trees at least eighty feet high. After a battle at Parkumäki, another relative, an Army Officer, was hanged as a spy on one of these trees.

The estate comprises of 550 hectares of land on which space for eight cottages on a strip are now separated into plots, according to new laws, so that left 350 hectares for the home place where there is still a good growing forest and good farming area.

June 23. In the morning, we looked at the fields of grain and farming operations, and the weather was beautiful. They were making ready the Juhannuskokko arrangements. In the evening we felt our gathering and conversations with the family eternalized us with them.

Then they hurried to the kokko doings where Juho was the master of ceremonies. The neighborhood young people lit the fire, as it had to burn a while, and we older people stayed and rested so that we could be able to go in the morning to church.

But we overslept and we had to hurry to the boat which would take us to the village, and then, because there was no other way, we ordered an automobile to pick us up. They seemed slow in coming so we started walking towards the direction to go and didn't get very far when a car arrived. Not the one we ordered, but we stopped it because there were only two men in it, and got a ride to the place where the car we ordered was to arrive. And then when we met that car, the driver turned the car around, though in a tight place. It cost 5 marks. Someone else paid for it before I had time to ask the price! We changed quickly to the car that we ordered which then was driven fast, in spite of our cautions to slow down, that we thought we would not arrive at the church alive! Although the road was narrow and curvy and hilly, and it was about 10 km. to the church, fortunately and safely, we arrived at church just in time for the beginning of the service, not as some former churchman, to the ending!

Rector Lepisto was questioning some young people for confirmation. He had that part of the program, and then he did the confirmation ritual one by one. So they became members of the church according to the old custom. Then Rector Lepisto preached about Zakaria's revelation in a Quaker fashion. There was enough instruction and information for young and old people, and setting himself up as a master, so that even a stranger could hear that he must be a heaven-sent spiritual balloon! The mechanically-produced hymns are now prevalent in Finland as elsewhere in the world. But I forget myself and start on another subject, whereas as a visitor I must return to the task at hand.

When we returned by boat, again I was not quite quick enough to pay for the ride. Slackness may appear an advantage but self-esteem suffers when some other one pays! One learns in time, though one doesn't get wise! The Ahonen boys came by steamboat to get us, and that evening we went to Kurikkas'. I recognized Kurikka from his former appearance though he has aged even as we. His hearing was failing and he had a problem breathing so he could talk very little and walked very slowly. We . . . [Page missing. E.S.] [Date uncertain. E.S.] . . . ship to Teemassaari to Hog's Jaw Pier, where Matti Salonen directed us to their home in Rantasalmi where we lodged overnight. Here was also our other former home.

After breakfast we walked to my birthplace, which now is owned by Virta. There I took my first steps in this world and spent my childhood. There also the "Serpent of Sin" stung the heel to poison one completely and the longer it lasted the worse it got. Then appeared the desire of fulfillment of passion. During confirmation days I began to think about the state of blessedness of the soul, and how one could avoid the fulfillment of desire and its consequences but I didn't find the strength and the worse it got. I knew how to differentiate between good and bad even better perhaps than some others, for I had been raised in the light of the Word as well as anyone else who had been taught. But I lacked the strength to live properly so when the first trials arose, I could not deny myself, even as many others have not denied themselves. I was overcome by sin and transgressions and had died away from God. My journey in sin started there at this place, and if it . . . [Words obscured by author. E.S.]

We went to the old storehouse to look for our initials that my two brothers and I had chiseled in the broad granite rock alongside that building when we were young boys, and I soon found them even though they were covered by moss and lichen. My initials were the farthest from the wall. The initials of the two persons above mine were made by hands that had long ago numbed and stiffened in death. When the third one's hands will stiffen is unknown, but surely this is the last time I would gaze with tearful eyes upon my boyhood scenes.

From the storehouse I went to the familiar sliding rock where I have worn out many seats of pants sliding down, even as my father had before me, on that sloping granite formation. So as I looked around me there awakened vividly many childhood memories which had been long forgotten. But now they returned like yesterday. Perhaps it is best that good and bad vanish in memory. Of that place and life I would have much to write but I will leave that now to the bygone past, once more to return to memory-land, for I feel these eyes will never again view these sights in this life, no matter how wonderful they might be.

Then I proceeded to meet and talk with the present owner who was with his workers in the field, storing hay on poles to dry and cure. Though I was a complete stranger to him, after introductions, when he realized who I was, we made acquaintance quickly. It was already lunchtime so we went toward the yard for continued discussion and joined the other people in the party who had stayed with the mistress of the place. Then all of us went to look at the fields which had been expanded.

The names of all the meadows and bays around Tiemas Lake were unforgettably impressed during my childhood onto my mind. I made no mistakes in naming any of these places when we were looking at them. At the beach we also looked at our old swimming places and the rocky shore. After viewing them briefly, we returned again to the house which was so familiar to me. [Pages missing. E.S.]

June 28. It seems like there have not been six dry days during this month, when it hasn't rained at least a little. The vegetation is beautiful all around. There will be berries, an abundance of berries, since flowers abound everywhere. In fens the shrubs are full of blooms that will materialize when the Lord sends warmth to ripen the fruit. Then we hope to pick berries as we did when we were little raggedy, baggedy boys long, long ago.

There's that old quirk again; I forget reality and begin reminiscing in poetic vein. The Creator's creation in splendor reigns in sparkling new dress again, more beautiful than royalty attains. With the morning sun's warmth the dew drops go, the flowers wilt away and so the petals slowly fall and fruit abundantly is borne, each kind surpassing another, strawberries sweet near lingonberries that will glow crimson when they ripen later, so plentifully tucked around the crannied logs. The wilderness clasps all this abundance within its arms, unplowed, unplanted, untended. Even in the wildest craggy places, berries grow, for boys to gather and enjoy! There will be tasty berries for cottage pudding, berries the finest roasts enhancing.

Perhaps it's best to cease this poetic rhapsodizing of the Lord Creator's deeds, and hope that my reveries and evanescent dreams come true in proper time, that I not err and air castles build. Truly to all who would listen, I'd leave these my feeble observations as my memorial to fellow wayfarers when I am gone to that eternal mysterious dwelling realm of the departed.

July 4. Sunday morning (yesterday) the wife and I slept till a little after 10 and hurried to attend church at 11, arriving with 5 min. to spare. The church is certainly of immense dimensions, having a seating capacity of 2,500 people. The pews in our sitting area were spaced for 14 people each. It rained Sunday, so there weren't very many in attendance. In the afternoon we visited several places that had ancestral relationship, and also attended a name day event for Eila Korpela at the house, a cousin of some degree.

July 5. Today we were to Savonlinna, where the wife and I lived for some period, a town of considerable size and ancient. I will describe it for those who have not seen it. It was built around and because of the fort that St. Olaf established before Columbus discovered America, in the fifteenth century. The fortress structure still stands in its original location poised on an outcrop of granite rock, built so sides of the fort extend to water's edge, and completely surrounded by water from the Saimaan waterway. A rapid current goes under the pontoon bridge on which one crosses to the fort. The town is built on a series of relatively small rock formation islands and connected together by bridges. The extent of the Saimaan waterway is hard to realize except with the aid of a large map. In the summer tourist season one could enter a ferry-type boat near Helsinki and zigzag up past a close point near here, and on NW up to a point close to Oulu, between 400 and 500 miles, with living quarters aboard, covering about a week of time.

We went to a market to make some food purchases, etc. We dined at a classy eat-house-casino where Finnish marks vanish like magic but the food was good and plentiful. Moose crossing signs are seen often.

July 7. We have been served capitally with interesting variety, such as piirakka and blood cake, etc. The roadsides are so very green and the trees thick with foliage since they have had an abundance of rain, to the dismay of farmers. [Pages missing. E.S.]

July 9. Today we dined at a nice eat-house (smorgasbord style) with plenty of good wholesome food.

July 10. To our intense regret, the lady of the house, Mrs. Kuusisto (Sr.) suffered a heart attack in the following early morning and was taken by ambulance to a local hospital and placed in intensive care for at least a couple of days. Her response to treatment was encouraging and she was hopeful she could return home before our departure, which we naturally were trying to hasten so our presence wouldn't burden our host household too severely. One married son lived in upstairs quarters in the senior Kuusisto house and the son's wife had been hospitalized for some couple of weeks but had returned home prior to our arrival with specific instructions to remain in bed to restore health, but with the household upset created by the senior lady's hospitalization she couldn't remain at rest and thus was at least directing her sister in meal preparation and household management. So the following day she was hospitalized again and the men were left in complete command. Verily, we are beginning to feel our presence is a jinx to these good people.

In spite of their medical misfortunes these people, both father and son, volunteered to drive us around the countryside to call on relatives. All seemed to universally share the feeling we should allow them more time since this was our first visit back to Finland (and the last to spend with many of these aged relatives).

Neither of the ladies were allowed to return home from hospital before our departure although the senior lady was to return later in the day of our departure. The junior K. drove us to Kuopio to reach the train at 7:10 a.m. We left at 5:40 and arrived in time for securing fare permit cards on any Finland railway for 12 months, our baggage checked. Three cheers for our chauffeur and his trusty service!

We did some visiting with a man named Kangas. He had spent several years in the USA and had learned the language fairly well. He was of a talkative sort and inquired into our birthplaces, so it developed, after hearing us say we lived in North Dakota, that he'd spent a night in some lonely prairie farm place in North Dakota, and after some thought, he said it was some Pelkonen. I asked if it was Walter Pelkonen he stayed with and he said yes. It thus developed it was the nearest neighbor of the Mattson family and further Pelkonen had by that time moved onto the Mattson place, so it was indeed our next neighbor farm. Imagine the surprises that can be in store even at such a distance from home.

Sun. we visited an ancient church near Kemi built sometime in the 16th century, of granite rock with walls 3 or 4 ft. thick, still in very serviceable condition, in fact the receptionist who came by a buzzer in the entry, and who was also the narrator, said weekly services were held here. In the entry was posted a sign requesting visitors to remove headgear as YOU ARE ENTERING A HOLY SANCTUARY! Among other things, the entry contained a stockade with 10 holes for 5 men (providing they each have two feet) where unworthy men could be locked in so that righteous ones could spit on the guilty. Inside was a punishment bench for erring females. The narrator went into considerable detail about the early history of the church, the strife resulting from the Lutheran reformation of a Catholic-dominated leadership. A young minister in the 16th century spearheaded reform in this church and braved bold accusations of advancing false doctrine. This minister vowed his doctrine was correct according to Bible interpretation. Well, he died in his forties over 200 years ago, a young man, and his body very obviously still contains both flesh and skin, even on the fingers and toes, lying in a glass-covered casket of oak, which was said to be the fourth casket the corpse occupied, because of decay of the wood. The narrator said there are several dozen burials beneath the floor. The body lay a couple feet below floor level, quite clearly visible, in the nude. Some vandals had desecrated the remains by slashing the stomach open and breaking one hand off. One offender had to be carried away from the scene, immobilized and blind. His condition was restored within a year and he later returned to admit his guilt, seeking in some way to make restitution. The other vandal, the one who broke off an arm, lost the same limb shortly afterwards. Gruesome, but repeated as heard.

We went over the border to Sweden to Haaparanta, where the customs officers just give an OK gesture to go on. People go back and forth to chase bargains. Checking clerks speak either language with equal ease. [Pages missing. E.S.]

[Date and locale uncertain. E.S.] . . . had coffee, we went to the beach. This was a broad sandy expanse where thousands of people could easily sunbathe. There also were hundreds of dressing huts, and hundreds of bathers lounged around like little children in the hot sand, wearing nothing but the scantiest of swimsuits, even the women. Also many men wore nothing on their upper body, and mixed groups of men and women lolled about minus covering except on their bottoms. The women as well as the men were baking their thighs in the warm sun. This unusual sight was shocking, seeing such behavior openly in public for the first time in our lives, but eventually one gets accustomed to anything.

July 15. Sunday. We went to church and the cemetery where during our American absence many friends and relatives had been laid to rest, awaiting the great day of resurrection when the trumpet sounds and all from Adam to the present come together, some blessed by the Father, some self-condemned. We rode in Heikkinen's horse carriage to another Heikkinen brother's place. There we were served again most graciously.

As it was Sunday, we rested in accordance with God's law. At 2 p.m. there was a Sunday School test and a Bible study at Hannulas' cottage, and there we had a chance to hear Luukanen's Bible interpretation. He was the best of the present local ministers, though not born again, which made him an even more dangerous, self-righteous preacher since the people praised him so!

There was an air show where eight aircraft arrived, one a double-decker. But all of them were seaplanes that land only on water because in Finland there are very few places where terrain is suitable for runways for liftoff and landing airplanes. These seaplanes are more convenient. It appears that air traffic has developed in Finland as in other parts of the world, also advancement has come about in all kinds of athletics. There were thousands of people to view this air show, which was a benefit for the air service, but there were surely quite a number of people who did not pay. Also for the athletic events later on in the evening, there was an admission charge of 10 marks per person. In Finland they now use pennies hardly at all, only marks.

July 16. We were again at the beach to tan our bodies in the warm sunshine. The wife burned both front and back of her neck, so that she had to get medication for it.

July 17. By ship we went to Paukar Bay to visit Aunt Ilkka. Although she is over 80 years old, she is yet a very pert, spry grandmother, and believes her sins are forgiven in the name and blood of Jesus, utterly depending on His grace. We had a chance to go to a home-type (religious) meeting for the first time since being in Finland. There had gathered over twenty believers to whom God had given a new birth, according to His will, into hope in Jesus' resurrection from the dead, and who belonged to the living faith and who were spiritually humble and trusting entirely that their sins were forgiven by grace.

At 3:00, we said our eternal farewells to the Hannula family and invited them to come to visit us, but they declined, saying it was impossible for them to do so.

We mutually forgave errors and weaknesses as asked, for the sake of Jesus' grace and sacrifice. They accompanied us to the canal and there we said our good-byes. We believe we will never see them again in this lifetime, so we left them in God's care and grace. He is their strong and gracious support. As the ship bore us away we again were overcome by grief at parting from these dear friends and relatives.

July 19. In Turku two days past we saw the wife's sister Silvi, who is staying the summer with a sick friend. She welcomed us gladly and hoped we could stay longer, but this evening we had to part because the ship was leaving for Stockholm, and there was no time to linger. She took us to the pier, and at 8:00 p.m., the ship left the port.

July 21. We were in Stockholm at 9 a.m. They took us by auto to the railway station, through the town and over many bridges. It is a large city with much traffic as cities have, and otherwise a beautiful and clean town. The depot is a large, roomy building. A little before 2 p.m., the train left to take us across Sweden to Goteberg [sic]. The first part we traveled through mountains with many tunnels and though it was a long ride it made good time, just as rapid as any in America, although electric-powered and for that reason very clean. The journey lasted six and a half hours, even though the distance was 350 km. Middle Sweden is excellent farm area, level and well-cultivated although the shorelines on both sides were rocky and hilly, especially the east side. At Goteberg [sic] we were taken to the ship's hotel for supper. We were given a coffee break on the train in the dining car and then were taken to the ship to sleep.

July 22. In the morning we had breakfast on the ship, and then the women were taken to the doctor for medical examination. Our luggage had to be labeled and marked first and then would be loaded on the ship, but then to find one's luggage and trunks was something else. There were 3,000 or 4,000 trunks so that one didn't know where one would find one's own until they loaded the marked ones on the ship. Then as the quantity lessened, I finally found our trunks and got the needed numbered labels and slips so that in New York I could claim them by number. Many travelers had three or four trunks, which increased the quantity, of course. Those trunks were wedged very tightly in loading and unloading, and the workmen in the hold walked over them all or pushed them around so much that the bottom ones surely cannot last many trips. [Page missing. E.S.]

Seventeen

Rethinking

Tllere was no hint of sundown—the sky would stay white all night—but a stir at the front desk gave warning of closing time. I returned the diary to its spot and packed my bag, said good night to Sinikka, and walked to the cottage in a fog, my head full of Grandpa's words. And one photographic image.

Before the diary came to rest at the institute, someone, maybe Grandpa himself, had slipped a snapshot between two pages, a memento of the air show he mentioned in the diary. Thirty or forty people stood on a beach, looking up at the sky. The snapshot showed a stretch of sea, a small wooded island, and a seaplane moored on the water. The seaplane had a large swastika painted on its side. I knew from research that the swastika was a traditional Finnish good-luck sign and the mark of the Finnish Air Force. It had nothing to do with the Nazi symbol. Still, in 1960, the sight was unnerving. Grandpa, like most of the men, had come to the beach in a suit, tie, and a formal hat. One young man wore only swim trunks, staring up, holding a towel around his neck. Two women dared to appear in public in bathing suits, which resembled flapper middies with low waists and skirts that hung to mid-thigh. The rest were in street clothes, either dropped-waist chemises that stopped at the knee or more traditional dresses that skimmed the ankles. Mummo of course was in the second group. Tipping her parasol so that she could see the sky, she squinted into the sun. She looked *happy*, happier than I'd ever seen her look, except the day she danced, after Grandpa's funeral. She seemed thrilled, expectant. Her face reflected the freedom of flight. How had that face turned to stone?

No clues in the photo. And none in Grandpa's diary.

But the diary gave plenty of clues about Grandpa! I'd been right about his love for words. He was poetic, he used figures of speech, he told anecdotes, he poked fun at himself. Marcie had been right, too; he *was* different when he was young. The diary proved he was emotional, funny, judgmental, righteous—and remorseful. He was fifty-one when he wrote the diary, not young, but ashamed, still, of his boyhood sex drive. I felt a kinship with him. Like him, I was prudish, I judged others but fell short of my own standards, I loved metaphor and was intrigued by human foibles. A lot like Grandpa! But the whole time he lived at our house, he never let us see these traits.

I decided to get permission to copy the diary, certain that when others in the family read it, they too would feel, as I did, that they had never really known him.

Now I had another ache. I had to rethink assumptions I had nourished all my life. What I had read in Grandpa's eyes as judgment might not have been that at all. It might have been a *pleading*.

Eighteen

Mummo's Sister

Timo had predicted this would happen. He said the closer I came to Rantasalmi, as Western Finns got off and Eastern Finns got on, the louder the bus would become. It was *true*. Finns, joking in public? Timo had called Eastern Finns the Italians of Finland. He had said they were emotional, they talked with their hands, they loved music, poetry, word games, puzzles. Listening to the babel on the bus, I figured I'd found my people. Someone would meet me in Rantasalmi, Timo had said, but he hadn't said who.

As I stepped off the bus, a female voice called, "Katariina! This way!" I headed toward a woman whose clothes (aviator jumpsuit and ankle boots) cast the day as an expedition and whose hair (brown, blunt-cut at the jaw) flapped in the manner of beagle ears as she rushed to greet me. The epitome of welcome, she shouted, "Hullo! I am Silvi!" She gave me a muscular handshake.

Mummo's sister?

"My car is over there," she said, grabbing my bags and taking off for the parking lot. I tripped behind her, having trouble keeping up. She came to a stop beside a squatty yellow sedan. She laughed, "Terrible car! Russian-made! Cheap! But it runs okay." She put me and my bags inside the car, me in front, my bags in back, slamming the doors hard (they did sound kind of tinny). The car was still rick-ticking, back-talking, and cranking up to speed when she threw it into reverse and screeched out of her parking spot, standing in turn on the brakes and gas pedal. We zipped through the lot, engaging other cars in serial near misses, and rushed into traffic on the main road. I held my breath, hoping we wouldn't die.

I didn't know what to say, so I said nothing. I glanced at the woman as she drove, trying to match this Silvi with the one I'd imagined. She was taller than Mummo and less rigid, by far. Her hair was . . . ? *Frisky.* Mummo's was right-eously bunned. They didn't seem at all like sisters, so I was surprised when I narrowed in on Silvi's nose. It was an exact copy of Mummo's little beak.

But *Mummo's sister?*

"So you are Katariina!" she shouted above the rattle of the engine. "Emma wrote me all about you."

"Kik. You can call me Kik. She never said anything about you."

Her chuckle was throaty, as hoarse as hay bales. "Oh, yah! She's a tricky one, that one. When she wants to keep a thing hushed up, she does it better than anyone."

"Why would she keep *you* hushed up?"

Silvi was speeding down the road and looking at me at the same time, making me very nervous. I found myself watching the road in her stead, ready to yell if we were about to crash. "Who knows?" she said. "To have her own life, could be. She and Toivo had their troubles, you know. Can't you stay longer than two days?"

"No, but thanks. Your English is excellent. Where did you learn it?"

"I have two English clubs. One American, one British. We speak only English. But I learned it back in the forties when I flew planes."

"You flew planes?"

"Yah!" She chuckled again. "I was a lady flyer. But I gave it up when I turned seventy."

"Seventy? . . . You can't be seventy!"

"Oh, yes. Seventy-four!" Her laugh was a perfect Ha-ha-ha.

I rode along beside Mummo's pilot sister in a tinny Russian car, casting about for reality. This was a lot to absorb.

216

* * *

In the tradition of Finnish summer sleep-houses, the second floor overhung the porch. The house was a product of chisel, broadax, and saw—no nails, only wooden pegs. Squared logs had been notched and dovetailed to extend six inches beyond the corners of the building. Silvi climbed the steps, gesturing to me to stay on the ground. She had changed into a corduroy dress, and its moss color blended in with the logs. Using the porch as a speaker's stand, she said, "I was here with Emma. I was with her whenever she allowed it. She was my idol! When she went to America, I missed her very much. And after Julius died, my husband, I missed her all the more. We had no children, so I flew my plane to Sweden, France. Sometimes I went by commercial plane and train."

"Did you ever go to the States?"

She gave a clipped answer, "No." I had hit a sore nerve, but she did not elaborate. She asked me to come up onto the porch. I went up, and for a second we stood facing the door as if *it* would tell the story, not Silvi. She said, "I will tell you about Midsummer 1892. I was seven, Emma was seventeen. We came here to work. The door was swollen from the rain. Emma put down the blankets and lifted her skirt."

Silvi whisked her skirt into her arms, exposing pink flowered tights. "Emma did things like that, lifted her skirts, she shocked people. Ladies were supposed to keep their skirts below the ankle." Getting waylaid in the past, Silvi murmured, "I wonder why we wore such long skirts? In all that mud." As for me, I wondered why a woman Silvi's age would choose that chopped-off haircut. But on her it looked right.

"Well," she said. "No one was there but me, and I didn't care! Emma pulled on the door . . ." Silvi put her right foot on the frame at waist height and gripped the handle with both hands. She gave it a tug, and the door gave way with the creaking of damp wood. She whipped her skirt down. "Emma picked up the bedding from a bench we had here, and we went inside. She kept saying, 'Oh, I hope they're late!'"

Similar to houses on the folk island, Silvi's sleep-house had a single room, built-in beds, table, chairs. With one finger Silvi tested the table for dust. "We were behind time. We had had rain most of May and June, the start of a cold summer, what we call a 'green winter.' That put us behind, and we were typical Finns. We took pride in being thrifty, even with time. So when it rained, we worked indoors. We cleaned the house and got the near-beer going and washed the bedding. The blankets were slow to dry. We had to hang them around the stove in the house. Finally we were ready to make the beds. But company was due any second! Emma complained that the boys didn't help enough. We had two brothers, Erkki and Arvo. They later died in the Civil War. She wanted to trade chores with them. She said *she* would hook up the horses and drive the wagon to the forest, *she* would get wood. *She* would build a bonfire tall as a mountain. *She* would light the fire and *make the white sky roar.* She talked like that, *big*, like an American."

I tried without success to picture Mummo here, in her teens and talking big. I pressed a bed with one hand. It was hard and unyielding. The bed curtain was buttery soft, an off-white linen woven in a geometric pattern. Homespun. The same fabric covered the duvets.

Homespun! "Did my grandmother spin and weave?" I asked Silvi.

"Emma? Sure . . . We all did."

Mummo was a weaver! Why hadn't she said so?

"I'm a weaver, too," I sulked.

Silvi said, "Oh, ya?" She didn't think weaving was anything to write home about. "So anyway, we hurried." Silvi went to a bed and pretended to make it up. "Then we went upstairs. Go! See!" She made shooing motions toward a ladder nailed flat to the wall. I climbed up and stuck my head into the loft, which smelled of wet sawdust. Muted daylight came in through glass panes in the roof's triangle. Mattresses and blankets were piled against the walls. No one had slept there for a long time. When I came down, Silvi said, "Everything was clean. We had scrubbed the day before." She mimed spreading a cloth on the table. "We put a new candle here." Just as in her story, the room was clean and a candlestick sat on the table on an ironed linen square, and the candle was new.

"Now, the sauna."

We hiked uphill on a dirt road, and as we passed a forest a cuckoo sang three double calls: "*Cu*-cu! . . . *Cu*-cu! . . . *Cu*-cu!" The song was charming, lower in tone and richer than the call of a cuckoo clock, and mournful, like the coo of a dove. I kneaded a knot in my throat. The cuckoo's call made me both happy and sad. I felt restless but also riveted to the spot. I wanted to hear the call again! My mind went to the *Kalevala* and the imperative of the third golden cuckoo: gladness, in spite of everything. Was that even *possible*?

Silvi said, "That day too, as we walked by, we heard a cuckoo." Maybe the cuckoo I heard was related to cuckoos Mummo heard! She used this same path, after all. She passed this same forest. The idea of Mummo on this path gave me the chills.

"Emma was so happy. She loved everything. The cuckoo, the lake. The way the wind skipped on the water. . . . She loved Karl."

Silvi turned to me, waiting for the obvious question.

I asked her, "Who was Karl?"

"Our cousin." Silvi spoke the words with pride, a storyteller's vice. "She told me their secret and made me promise not to tell." Again she waited for the question.

"What secret?"

"They were in love and wanted to get married."

"Not Grandpa?"

"This was before Toivo . . . Emma and Karl grew up together. They were the same age, they looked alike, they finished each other's thoughts. They were the best of friends. Then they fell in love. It was a strong new pull, she told me, like a magnet. She dreamed about him day and night. She couldn't imagine life without him."

"What happened?"

But Silvi was telling the story her way. She resumed walking and I followed. We went downhill past a field where horses grazed, and a lake surrounded us on three sides. We rounded a wooded bend and came to the sauna, a small red building at water's edge. It had its own dock—convenient for those after-sauna jumps, I figured. As we went up onto the porch, Silvi said, "It was the same in 1892." We entered the dressing room, where she waved at wooden pegs on the wall and rag rugs on the floor. "Except, then, the sauna was red-hot. Father had started the fire early and we were bringing clean towels. Emma went into the steam room." Silvi opened the door to the next room. "Emma filled a ladle and threw water on the rocks and steam came up in a cloud. She put her face in it and said, 'Oh, Karl!' and laughed."

Mummo, laughing?

The story would continue elsewhere, it seemed. Silvi took me back to the main house, up to the second floor bedroom she and Mummo had shared as girls. A china doll sat on the mantel, dressed in ecru lace and frozen in time. A vain historical coyness kept her eyes flirty and her arms reaching out, her fingers twirked according to fashion, the red-apple cheeks blushing to eternity. "We got back to the house, and Emma ran upstairs and washed—we had a jug of water and a bowl here—and put on her new dress. She had made it herself, for Karl to see. She braided her hair and put braids around her head." Silvi took a look at my hair. "Like yours."

I said, "Like mine? I thought I invented it! Mummo never said a word!" I felt oddly let down. Mummo had never acknowledged *one thing* we had in common, but according to Silvi we had at least two, weaving cloth and wearing our hair in a crown.

"She wears it in a bun now," I added crossly.

Silvi's expression warmed. "You are like her. More than just the braids."

"How?"

But she would not be drawn in. "Like her, that's all . . . Emma got herself ready. The new dress made her bumps, eh, her shape, more bumpy, but it was ladylike, high at the neck. Emma didn't want to upset people, not with everything at stake. The skirt fell to the floor and hid her corrective shoe. She wasn't shy about her short leg, but she felt better when it didn't show. We had lily of the valley in a vase. She sniffed them and said she would die without Karl. She put some flowers in her braids." I could see myself in the mirror on confirmation day, daisies in my braids.

"Emma took a big breath and smiled. She was ready. Mother was already calling, saying company had arrived. Viena, Karl's mother, the sister of our father, had placed herself at the bottom of the stairs. She was a proud person. She liked to wear big skirts and big hats. Appearances *mattered* to her. She said, 'Why, Emma dear, you look lovely!' Emma came down, not looking at Karl. But she was aware of him, his shoulders, his arms. She told me everything later. He teased her and tried to make her laugh, almost automatically drawing her to him. But she held back. She greeted each relative, giving only a little look at Karl. Their chance would come later. It was early yet. It was Midsummer, after all! The bonfire party would go on until dawn. At some time during the night, she planned to get Karl off by herself."

We descended the stairs as Mummo had done. "But something was wrong with Father," Silvi said. "Normally he was easy to be with, he played jokes with us. He said we were his strong-headed daughters. But recently he had been cool to Emma. She tried to explain it away. Spring had been hard, she told herself. Rain ruined the barley. Father's horse broke a leg and had to be shot. He was discouraged, that was all! Midsummer would lift his spirits. But as she walked by Father, she caught his eye. There it was again, that harsh look! She was worried that he knew about Karl.

"Father said, 'Emma, could I speak with you, please?'

"She started shaking! Right into her thoughts about Father had come his voice! She went into the parlor with him. I couldn't go in, but later she told me about it."

Silvi showed me the parlor, a staid room furnished with a grand piano and scarlet rugs, upright velvet chairs along the walls. "In here was Reverend Hirvonen. He had a potato face and a funny way of walking. We liked to joke about him behind his back, but he was a nice man. He had two churches in the lake country and was our family minister. He had confirmed the boys and Emma—I was too young yet—but he had never before come to our house. Only an emergency would bring him here.

"Father told Emma, 'Sit down, please.' Her mouth went dry. She sat on the piano stool. The space closed in around her. Reverend Hirvonen said, 'It has been brought to my awareness that you and Karl Lindstrom are in grave danger. It is wrong to marry one's cousin. The church cannot approve. I must forbid you to see him again.'

"The room blinked off and on, she told me later. She said to Father, 'It can't be! I want to see Karl! Bring him here so we can talk to you.' Father said no, that Karl was being sent away. He had been taken home to pack his clothes. He would be taken away immediately. Father said it was better this way.

221

"Emma stood up and shouted at Father. She said it wasn't fair, he couldn't *do* this, they hadn't done anything wrong! Father said he believed her. He wanted to keep it that way. She was shaking so badly her teeth made actual noise.

"She asked Father where they were taking Karl. He would not say. She asked him if Mother knew of this. He said yes. Emma knew that Mother would never approve this plan. Emma said so to Father. His eyes told her she was right; Mother knew but did not approve. But this was a small, bad-tasting victory in a big, bitter defeat for Emma.

"Father and the minister left the room. Emma was alone. Somehow she had to make it through the night without Karl. She had to make it through her life without Karl."

I blustered, "She should have run away with him!"

Silvi nodded. "She wanted to. But no one would tell her where he was."

"Well!" I said indignantly, "Karl should have refused to go! Or waited until your father was away and come after her." Following this line of thought, I switched from Karl's side to Grandpa's side. "Karl was a coward."

"Possibly," Silvi said. "In any case, they never saw each other again."

* * *

The next building she showed me was two hundred years old, a long, one-story cottage painted an apricot color. We entered the kitchen, a convivial cave barely big enough for a tile fireplace in one corner and a small table in the opposing corner, a cook stove and a sink, and proceeded through the house. The dining room exploded with light. Sun rays hit the mirror above the sideboard and bounced off the white tablecloth, making a beam so bright I thought it would ignite the rocking chair, a high-seated, tall-legged rig that looked ready to rocket to the moon. We passed the parlor, a dark, unbending place, and two embroidered bedrooms, and a master bedroom of pale green dignity. Completing a circle, we came to a study behind the kitchen. It was outfitted with an oak desk and a captain's chair, leather-bound books, a glass-paned cupboard, and pictures of my family.

One was a duplicate of one that we had at home, a studio photograph, posed and unnatural, Grandpa in Amish whiskers, Mummo without glasses. Dressed in black, they sat with fortitude in wooden chairs on (what I assumed to be) horsehair cushions. I stooped and peered at pictures on the lower shelves. In a second studio photo, Mummo and Grandpa sat with two boys about eight and four years old. The boys—my father and Isaak, I presumed—had square faces and sunken but lively eyes. Their double-breasted coats and knee pants were black or dark navy, and so were their socks and shoes. The next picture was a snapshot, three boys standing by a barn. My father looked about twelve, Isaak, eight or so. The toddler must have been Esko. On each boy, wide suspenders held trousers on a body not quite big enough for the trousers. Next, another studio photo. (*Amazing*, I thought. Mummo had actually put up with all this posing!) Mummo wore glasses and faced the world from an upholstered chair, Grandpa and four boys standing around her. No one touched anyone else. My father was full of himself, a handsome teen-ager with hair parted in the center and swept back. Isaak was pouty, not wanting to pose. The two younger boys wore shoes that turned up at the toes. At first glance, the young Esko and Harald bore no resemblance to their adult selves. But, the longer I looked, the more I saw the men in the boys, and also Liisa's cheekbones on Esko, and my jaw line on my father.

This was eerie, bending to a shelf in Finland and having my family look back at me. In fact, it was making me dizzy. The past was beckoning, but I couldn't get there. I straightened up and asked Silvi, "How did you . . . ?"

"Emma sent them." She opened a drawer, removed a photo album, laid it on the desk and opened it. On thick black pages, corner stickers held pictures of us in Mahoning, not many, as Mummo hadn't had many to send, but copies of the ones we had at home. Grandpa picking raspberries. Baby Liisa in a buggy in bonnet and sun dress, scowling at the camera. Liisa and I at eight and six, posing by the older Chevy. Liisa and I at twelve and ten, by the camellia bush.

"Did Mummo say anything about . . . ?"

"Oh, I know everything!"

This made me mad. Why would Mummo write to Silvi, so far away, and never talk to us, so close by?

"This house is a museum, really," Silvi said, closing the door that led to the kitchen. On the back of the door hung a dun-colored army uniform, her final display on this walkabout. "It belonged to a man who was hanged."

"The spy? The one in Grandpa's diary?"

Looking girlish and mysterious, like Nancy Drew herself, Silvi cackled. "I put the diary there."

Silvi put the diary in the Institute! She seemed to have had a hand in everything. She said, "Emma sent the diary to me when Toivo died. She hoped Finnish students would think twice about leaving Finland if they read it."

"Was she sorry she went to America?"

"Let's just say she had strong feelings. I have some things to tell you."

"Have you read the diary? It doesn't sound like Grandpa."

Silvi's eyes had a piercing quality. She had that much in common with her sister. "He had two sides," she said. "That's part of what I have to say."

But whatever it was that she planned to say, she wasn't going to say it just then. Her attention was focused outdoors in the trees. I stroked the uniform, which was made of wool so prickly it almost cut through skin. "Why did she have this?"

Silvi made her way back to the house and to my question. "It was sentimental. Emma thought he was wrongly put to death, that he wasn't a spy at all. He was accused of being a traitor in the Civil War, but all he did was steal a Red uniform. It was hard to tell who was who in those days, White Finns, Red Finns. People suspected each other. The uniforms were the same except for different color bands on the sleeves." I checked the uniform on the door. No bands of any color on the sleeves.

"Just because he owned this uniform, and because of some things he said, he was called a friend of the Russians, and he was hanged. Emma thought he was innocent. That's the way she was. She made up her mind, and that was that."

I recalled *plenty*-times when Mummo had made up her mind and that was that.

Silvi said, "It was maybe ten years ago when I wrote to Emma and said the man's things would be auctioned. She wanted the uniform, so I got it. The man was our relative, did I say that? Our parents left the two houses to us. So I keep the uniform here."

Some puzzle pieces fell into place. "Grandpa mentioned this house in his diary, didn't he? Workers' quarters? . . . in the trees?" She nodded. "And when he said the house belonged to a relative, he meant Mummo's relative, not his?"

Silvi did a version of the Finnish sigh, "Yuh!-huh!" She actually pronounced two syllables with the two inward breaths. "The man was hanged there." She nodded outdoors at a gnarled, solitary, very old tree. I shivered. The man was hanged right here.

"Emma was already in the States when Father died—Mother had died years before—and she wanted me to have the bigger house. She said she would pay to keep this one in good repair. She had the money Father gave them. I haven't told you about that yet. Toivo never did take money from Father. He wanted to support Emma by himself. She invested her money in Finland, and I used the earnings to keep this house up. It's in her will. You and your sister will get this house when she dies."

My nausea had found me in Finland. I said, "I don't feel so well!" I hurried to the kitchen, dropped into a chair and put my head between my knees. Silvi brought me a glass of water. I sat up and took a drink.

"I get dizzy when I get shocking news," I said, jigging my head to clear the fuzz. "I almost faint. Mummo does that, too, sometimes."

"*No niin.*" Silvi did another double sigh, a skill unique to Finnish women. "Emma held too much inside. I'll tell you more. But, first, coffee."

*   *   *

She changed into a frilly white sun dress and served coffee in a surprising place, her entryway. Ten broad steps led up from double front doors to the first floor. On either side of the steps, level with the first floor, was a railing-edged platform that held tropical trees. A picnic table and benches sat on one platform. Mullioned windows let in the sun and made the entry into a greenhouse. As we sat down to rich dark coffee and rum cake, large green plants looked over our shoulders.

225

"I must tell you about your grandfather," Silvi said. "Six months after Karl was sent away, Emma and Toivo attended the same christening. He had recently moved from Tampere to Savonlinna, but he had spent his boyhood in Rantasalmi, near here. So Emma already knew him. He was handsome and clever, a locksmith and gunsmith. When my father saw Emma being civil to Toivo, not harsh the way she was to other men, he made them an offer. He would give Emma her inheritance immediately if they would get married. They agreed, but with Toivo's proviso that Emma use the money as she wished. Toivo knew about Karl, and Emma knew of Toivo's trouble with alcohol and women. They wanted to forget the past and make a new life. They got married and lived in Savonlinna. It took Emma seven years and many miscarriages before she became a mother. That was Patrik."

My father.

"He was a sweet child. Very precious to Emma. When he was a baby, he took sick with a bad fever. . . . This is where the story starts. Emma told me every detail. She said it was important I know everything. I will tell it to you the same.

"She was worried when the fever would not break. She rocked him and washed him with warm water, but the fever stayed. He hardly slept for two days and nights. Emma refused to have him bled as her neighbor Helga suggested. Emma thought that bleeding was witchcraft, not medicine. Toivo let her decide. It was one good thing about him, she said. He let her run the household her own way.

"Finally Patrik slept. Emma put him in his bed and smiled at his chin. It was like Toivo's, except tiny. She put her hand on his forehead. He was no longer hot. She rubbed the small of her back and went to make coffee.

"Then she remembered Toivo's new idea. He wanted to go to America! To Emma, America meant adventure. As a girl she had loved adventure, but lately there was a lack of it. She loved little Patrik. She loved baking and cooking and keeping house. And she loved Toivo in her own way. Still, she wanted more. The idea of America made her heart race. She wanted to go. But she couldn't understand Toivo's hurry. Leave a good business and start again in a strange country? He didn't speak English, and he didn't want to learn. She knew his pride would stand in the way of speaking a new language. She could not understand his hurry to leave Finland.

"While she was making coffee, Toivo called hello from the door. He hung his hat and coat, took off his shoes and came to the kitchen in his socks, a handsome man of twenty-seven. Emma smiled and said, 'You're home early.' He said he had good news. He would leave in two weeks. He had the papers. He would go to America first, work and save money, then Emma and Patrik would join him. Emma was excited, listening to him, but still confused by his eagerness to leave home.

"Two days later, Emma found something she wished she hadn't found. She was preparing to steam Toivo's best coat. She emptied the pockets and found a letter in an inside pocket. It had a woman's handwriting."

Silvi reached behind her and brought out a rubber-banded bunch of letters. Sorting through them, she found the one she wanted. "Emma didn't want to have this around her, but she wanted me to keep it. For history, I suppose. I will translate."

She read, "'My dearest Toivo, This letter is being sent via Tuomas and brings with it my fondest greetings. I must tell you that you are going to be a father. In four months' time, I will give birth to your child. I am sorry I did not tell you before now, but you must not worry. I will find good people to adopt the baby. Then I shall leave Finland. I am going to Australia to live. You will always be in my heart, but, please, let this letter be good-bye. Your wife and your boy need you. I remain, Your Aili.'"

Silvi said, "Emma thought she would faint."

I thought I would, too. Another woman had Grandpa's child? . . . What was the phrase in his diary? Something about "the desire to fulfill passion"?

Silvi continued. "The day was black for Emma. Finally Toivo came home. She didn't need to say anything. He saw her shaking and looking at him in a certain way. He said, 'You found the letter.' So easily he said it! As if she could absorb this and go on!

"Emma said, 'Is *this* the reason for America?' He admitted it was so. He said Aili was an old friend, that when he visited Tampere he went to a lake party, and she was there. She had been drinking. So had he. She flirted, and, after taking sauna with the other women, she sat on a chair on the dock— naked, in front of the men! Toivo went with her into the summer house. There wasn't much to their affair, he said, only that weekend. But, yes, she did get pregnant."

Another puzzle piece. "Did people use ice cubes back then?" I asked Silvi. "In alcoholic drinks?"

"I don't think so. Why?"

"Mummo never uses ice cubes, and she got mad once when I mentioned them. I think they remind her of drinking and this . . . this affair. I think she got the idea, from TV or somewhere, that ice cubes go with alcohol . . . Poor Mummo!"

Silvi went to her desk, wrote something on a card and handed it to me. "These are the people who adopted the baby. Americans. It was a private adoption."

I read the note. "George and Melba Sakari." The names rang no bells. I put the card in my purse.

"*No niin.* Toivo told Emma Finland was too small, that everyone would know everything. He said he needed a new place where no one knew anything. Emma said, 'You! How about *me?* How do *I* get over this?' He said he didn't know what to say; he said he was very sorry. He had a face that showed whatever he was feeling, and now it showed shame. For a minute, Emma thought there was hope. Then she remembered, and she started shaking again.

"For the second time in her life, she was hearing news she thought would kill her. First, Karl. Now, this. But she had to go on and make the best of things, if only for little Patrik. What she really wanted to do, she told me, was to go to sleep and never wake up."

I thought, I *know,* Mummo. I know the feeling.

After coffee we moved into the parlor, tracked by Silvi's cat, a hefty white muff who waited until I was seated and then pounced on me. He footstepped around my lap before dropping heavily, like a sack of potatoes, onto my skirt. He rolled into a ball and fell asleep smiling and purring. Silvi said,

"Toivo went to America first and Emma went later with Patrik." She was talking distractedly, fingering letters. She opened one.

"Here. She burned my letters, she told me. She didn't want people in her business. But I kept hers. This one she wrote in . . ." She looked up the date. "May 1921."

Silvi glanced up at me. "This one is difficult," she said. I raked the cat backwards, grasping his fur, taking comfort in it before whatever was coming, came.

Translating, Silvi read, "'Sister, this may be my last letter for a while. We have had a terrible time. You must know everything from the beginning. It will help me to tell it. It started on the prairie. I was walking for pleasure. It was windy and the prairie roses were out. They are a soft pink, and they grow close to the ground. You can't see them unless the wind blows or you stand on top of them. I felt free, like a girl. Patrik and Isaak were gone. Patrik was in town on a job. Isaak is living in Fargo. He and Toivo argued last week and Isaak left home. I don't know if he will ever come back. Toivo was in the barn. Harald and Esko were at school. Baby Matilda was with my neighbor Mary Hanson at the house.'"

I said, "Baby Matilda? They had a *girl*?"

Silvi sighed. "I wasn't sure if you knew. She was a year and a half." She read more. 'I had reason to be glad. The house was peaceful. Toivo was staying sober, and he and Patrik had stopped arguing. I feared for so long that Toivo would start drinking again and hurt the children. But now my fears seemed groundless.'"

Injecting something not in the letter, Silvi said, "There was one bad time before Matilda was born. Toivo got to drinking and he went crazy. He chased Emma and the little boys into the root cellar—with a shotgun. He threatened to kill them! Emma bolted the door shut. Toivo banged on it and shot the gun in the air. A neighbor man happened to drive up. They lived a long way out. People hardly ever came by. Emma thought it was God Himself Who sent that neighbor man to help. The neighbor man rescued them and they were safe. But that's how it was with Toivo. Alcohol made him crazy."

She read on: "'From the top of the hill I could see the schoolhouse. Miss Hollowell does the best she can, teaching kindergarten through eighth grade, but the children speak Finnish. She isn't Finnish, and she has a hard time getting them to speak English. Harald says the kids make jokes in Finnish and get Miss Hollowell nervous. Talking about Finnish and English brings me to Toivo again. Silvi, he still doesn't like to speak English. Don't be impatient with me. I am writing and writing to avoid telling you what I must tell. I knew already in Finland that his pride would stand in his way. When English must be used, say, at the bank when he takes out a feed loan, he has Patrik or me go with him to speak for him. In other ways, before now at least, when he wasn't drinking, America had improved him. He was a better husband and father. I know he still feels he was my second choice, and Silvi, I *do* still think of Karl. But I tried to be a good wife. You hear me speak now in the past tense. When I got back to the house, I took Matilda from Mary and swung her in a circle. My little angel.'"

Silvi again editorialized. "Matilda was a chubby baby, blonder than the boys. She was born when Emma was forty-five. After so many miscarriages—another two after the boys were born—Matilda was her miracle baby.'"

Finding her place in the letter, Silvi read, "'The baby played one of her hiding games. She hid my eyes with her hands and laughed when I took her hands off, then she patted my face and sucked in her cheeks to give me a kiss. I gave her a blizzard of kisses and put her down with her toys in the play-fence. I sat down to have coffee with Mary. She said she was sorry to tell me, but she thought Toivo was hiding bottles. The day turned cold. Mary said he had come in carrying a bottle. When he saw her, he put it in his pocket and went back out. He must have thought I had the baby with me, because he was surprised to see anyone in the house. Mary had walked over, and so no cars but ours were in the yard, and no horses. Mary left. The boys came home and dropped their lunch buckets on the pantry counter and came to the table. I gave them buttered bread. I must tell the smallest details.'"

Silvi too wanted to tell details. "Emma said once that if she had to choose one word to describe each boy, she would say Harald was the joker, Esko was the thinker, Isaak, the woodsman. But when it came to Patrik, she wondered if she knew him at all. He was book-smart, but hard to reach. She decided his word was . . . in English? Mystic. That was your father, some kind of mystic."

I took the words and held them to me. Book-smart. Hard to reach. A mystic.

"'Harald took a bite of buttered bread and teased Esko, saying Esko had a girlfriend, Minna Korpela. Esko got mad and told him to stop lying. Harald laughed with his mouth full. Harald is generous and mean by turns, whereas Esko is quiet and thinks too deeply about everything. You hear me going on and on, trying not to tell the next part. I told the boys to play in the woodshed and to take Matilda with them. They could take their bread, but they should go now. Harald asked me—was I making them a surprise? I said, yes, now go. Oh Silvi, how can I say it? While I looked for Toivo in the barn, he went around the back by the birches, into the woodshed, and he went berserk. He shouted at the boys and swung an axe at a wood pile to scare them. But he hit Matilda. He didn't see her hiding there. Playing her game. She was gone that fast. Silvi, how can I live?'"

I ran to the bathroom and vomited. These were the pictures in Mummo's mind. And in Harald's. A sunny day, a woodshed, the father crazy-drunk. He shouts and swings an axe. Hits the baby. Two boys watch, mouths open for screaming, no sounds escape.

Grandpa killed his baby girl.

An unspeakable crime. Literally. No one spoke of it. But it had controlled us just the same. The people who survived that day were maimed by it. They had brought the shame to our generation. We didn't know the story but we knew the damage, the fire of frozen rage, the rumblings and steamings, the eruptions barely averted. The habit of holding-in.

"Toivo didn't go to prison due to a legal error," Silvi told me when I returned. "The case was dismissed. Toivo was never the same. He never drank again. He went back to church, but he stopped talking. Patrik left home. He told Emma he couldn't stand the ice in the house. Isaak went to Alaska to work and never came back.

"Emma wanted to die. But the small boys needed her. They kept her going, she said. She never did get over losing Karl, or Toivo having a baby with that woman. Or Matilda. Matilda's name was not to be mentioned."

Silvi glared at me. "I waited a long time for someone to come from America. Emma won't live much longer. Someone in the family had to know."

Part 4

Home Again

Nineteen

Broken Constellation

Mummo died while I was flying home. Liisa met my plane with the news. "I found her on the front room floor," she said. "Aarnie was over at Harald's, and I had to call the ambulance and wait. It was *hard* waiting like that, with Mummo on the floor. I knew it was too late. She wasn't breathing."

"Oh, Liisa. I'm so sorry! I wish I had been here."

"Me too." She seemed worked up, even angry.

I said, "I can't believe this! . . . Had she been sick?"

"No."

"Good." I moved my head up and down. "That's good." In dismay I added, "You know what I mean. I'm glad she didn't suffer."

We were being carried in a current of humans toward Baggage Claim and Ground Transportation, not finding much to say, mostly platitudes and sighs. This was awful. Mummo, *dead.* I wanted to run home and be a child again. I would take my chances with an ice-cold living Mummo, who would resist me like a plastic shield and bounce me back onto my own resources, leaving me where I had started, motherless. No, that wasn't it. I wanted to make things right! She wasn't supposed to die yet. I wanted to say I was very sad about Matilda. I wanted to *hug* her, at least once.

The P.A. system asked Mr. Brice McCaffery to please pick up a white courtesy telephone, Miss Iris Kittering to meet her party at the United Airlines counter in the main terminal. We threaded through a glut of people going the opposite way. A boy about ten years old, chasing another boy, caromed off my hip and kept running.

Liisa said, "It doesn't seem real. Aarnie was a big help. I called the ambulance, then I called Aarnie. He came home, then Inky and Harald came. We got the funeral home to come and get her." She seemed to need to say the same things over and over. "It was hard, waiting, with Mummo on the floor."

I didn't want to hear it! I wanted to pick up a white courtesy phone and try for better news. I said, "What do we do now?"

"Like what?"

"Like who stays in the house, what about a will, who arranges the funeral?" I had no idea what a person should say at a time like this.

"The funeral is Thursday. I don't know about any will. I don't know about the house. It's too soon." She made these statements without any rancor. "When does Jeff get back?"

"Not till classes start."

The baggage carousel was going around empty, squeaking and jerking as if it might break down, the fitted plates fanning to accommodate corners and folding for the straight-away. People stood staring at the plastic strips hanging over the chute that would deliver their bags. Two duffels thunked down onto the belt. One landed askew and had to go around on its nose. Luggage stuttered onto the carousel, a navy suitcase, a black bag, a ski box tied with rope. People either snatched at the pieces or continued watching.

Liisa said, "The phone was off the hook. You know how she hated the phone? It was off the hook."

* * *

At the Mahoning house, Michael was doing push-ups on a baby blanket on the front room floor. Marcie was on all fours before him, saying, "Atta boy!" Drooling and smiling, he bobbled on his arms before dropping to the blanket. He burrowed his nose in it, still smiling. She lifted him and snuggled her face into his belly, and a shower of baby giggles came from Michael. When he raised his head, I saw how vivid his features were.

"Marcie," I breathed, "he's beautiful."

"*Shoo* he is!" Marcie held Michael at arm's length to grin at him. Both baby and mother chuckled. "He's jus' the bes'es', cutes' thing ever was!"

What was wrong with Marcie? In a few short weeks she'd turned into a baby-talking foof. Proving my case in living color, she said, "Is zis the poo-fect baby or not?"

Not sure how to enter the conversation, I said, "Is he okay now? No problems?"

"Nope! Good as new." She got down on her back and floated Michael on her tummy, rocking him from side to side. Swaddled in his blanket, he was enjoying the ride.

I said, "I talked to my Finnish teacher about bilirubin. She said they put the baby under a special light, a bili-light. Did they do that for Michael?"

"Yup." Marcie curled upward to kiss the top of Michael's head. "And he's all bett-o now! Aren't you, you cutie-pie? Let's go find those *boodies!*"

That was the end of that topic. Marcie made it to her feet in one graceful move, her son a natural part of her. At the window he nestled into her neck, interested a great deal in her and not much in the birds.

About then, when I was feeling a tad left out, she brought me in. "Michael honey, you need to get to know your Auntie Kik here. She'll ask you questions till the cows come home. She's driven me nuts for years. You have my permission to ask her all the questions you want. *You* grow up and drive *her* nuts! Got any questions now?" She put her ear to his mouth and made Oh and No faces in my direction.

I smiled. Turning serious, I said, "How are you doing about Mummo?"

"It's best that she went fast."

A typical Marcie answer. Short and to the point. But that was the end of that topic, too. I didn't how to talk to her anymore.

* * *

Liisa, Aarnie, and I were sitting at the kitchen table, eating Liisa's beef casserole. "I heard some really sad things in Finland," I said. "Did you know

Mummo fell in love with her cousin? But couldn't marry him? And Grandpa had a drinking problem? And he had a child by another woman and that's why they came to America?"

Somewhere near the start of this blurt, Liisa and Aarnie had stopped eating, their forks in midair. I should have shut up right then, or now, but I floundered ahead. "And Mummo had a baby girl, and Grandpa killed her by mistake?"

I had done it again, said too much too fast. Besides, none of this was table talk. "I'm sorry. I . . ."

Aarnie's face had colored, a rashy burn that crept to his hairline. I could tell that he had known some or all of this beforehand. Figuring that since I'd jumped in at the deep end I might as well swim on, I said to him, "You knew about Matilda, didn't you?"

"Ya." He didn't like to admit it.

"Who told you?"

"Inky."

Finally giving in, Liisa asked me to tell her what I had heard in Finland. The hot dish grew cold as I summarized Silvi's stories.

At the conclusion, Liisa said, "There were rumors like that in the Pesonens' church. About Grandpa when he was young."

"The Pesonens' church? How'd they get into it?"

"I overheard an old lady say it was lucky Harald wasn't like his father. I asked her what she meant. She said, '*Voi, voi!* The drink and the ladies!' Then she acted like I had done something wrong. So I left it alone."

"When was that?"

"I don't know. A year ago."

"And you didn't tell me!"

"That would be passing on gossip."

"Is that what I was doing, passing on gossip?" I asked, genuinely wanting to know. "I thought I was passing on information. It was too much to carry by myself."

"It's okay," Liisa said. "But you could've waited till we were done eating."

She was right. My timing was rotten. Ever since coming home, I'd felt aimless and unreal, out of place. I missed the old group—Mummo-Aarnie-Liisa-Kik. At least it was familiar. Without Mummo, the family had no shape, no assignments that defined us.

So, the next day, I started trying out Mummo's old jobs to see if something fit. When I thought no one was looking, I'd slip a role like Attic Cleaner or Curmudgeon over my head like a costume and take a few steps in character, only to bump into Liisa doing the very same thing. This brought piffs of anger from both of us followed by terse, tense efforts at getting back to normal.

I felt displaced. And I wasn't the only one. I saw the same thing happening to Aarnie and Liisa, Harald, Inky, everyone. As scratchy a person as Mummo was, she had been our hub, the sun we had circled to keep life going. Relatives drifted by looking lost, trying to find a new hub or a new constellation altogether. To myself I groused, What *is* this? Our solar system breaks down and it's up to the *planets* to think up a new one?

No one talked about this part of grieving, this loss of place and definition. As usual, no one talked much about anything.

* * *

We stood on opposite sides of the dining table, waving a tablecloth to make it billow, lowering it, flattening air pockets with our hands, working at a good pace to get ready for company. Harald and Inky and some Duluth people were coming for coffee in two hours. "Just think," I said. "Mummo did all this without complaining."

Liisa gave me a certain look.

I said, "*I* know, *you* did a lot. I was the sluggard."

Illustrating my point, Liisa made one more swipe across the cloth. She went to the buffet and pulled both knobs of the shallow top drawer, stepping back as it squeaked open. I hadn't noticed the squeak before, but now I could see Mummo, so much shorter than Liisa, putzing with silver plate in the purple velveteen tray. Liisa brought the spoons to the table and laid them out, virtuously, in a herringbone.

"My mental calendar's out of whack," I said. "I skipped summer here, and I can't get caught up. I think I'm stuck somewhere back in June!" I laughed a short *bip*. "Oh, well. I guess I'm ten months ahead for next year!"

Liisa gave me another of her looks.

"Joke, Liisa. Leettle joke."

"How can you joke? Mummo's dead."

"I'm sad, too, you know," I said, feeling feisty. "But life goes on."

"*You?* . . . Running off all summer? No wonder you lost track of time."

I was incensed. "You call that running off? It was a fellowship! Besides, how could I know she would die? I couldn't have kept her from dying!"

"But how can you make jokes? You could show some respect."

"Like you?. . . I should make my sadness into a *show?*"

Taken aback, Liisa met my eyes. Hers were stripped and defenseless.

"Liisa, I'm sorry. Your sadness isn't a show. This is Mummo's time."

"What would *you* know about it?"

Slowly it sunk in. She was trying to tell me something. "What am I missing?" I asked her.

"I was *here*."

"And I wasn't."

"And you weren't."

"If I had been here, then what?"

"I wouldn't have been so scared," she said.

* * *

Early that evening, Inky called and said she had something for Liisa and me. "Harald's over at Matt's, and Marcie and them are over at Jacobsons'. They won't be back for, oh, couple hours." Without asking, I guessed she wanted to show us the boxes. Mummo had marked four cardboard boxes with Inky's name, and we had given them to her the day before. I checked with Liisa. She said fine. We had nothing else to do. The house was clean because we had cleaned it for company. After coffee, Aarnie had driven the Duluth people to Chisholm. He would be staying there to eat. Liisa and I had eaten sandwiches for supper, so we didn't even have dishes to wash. We had felt our way through the past two days, doing what had to be done, not knowing what came next but finding out by doing it. The funeral was the day after next. For now, we existed in a bubble. Normal life had receded, and a lull had taken its place. The only thing expected of us was dealing with Mummo's death. I told Inky we'd be there in twenty minutes.

As she set out coffee and cookies, I said, "So, you looked at the boxes?"

"I didn't have time until today. Such is life! There's some old pictures in there and address books, calendars, papers you girls did at school." This last reference brought a stab of emotion. Mummo saved our schoolwork?

Inky said, "But that's not what I called about. Some lawyer guy from Hibbing called. A Mr. Hebert. He said the executor—that's me—needed to come see him."

"A lawyer?" I asked her. "Are you sure? We've never had a lawyer."

"Sure I'm sure! I went to see him. Had Harald take me. He gave me this for the two of you." Ceremoniously, she handed Liisa a ten-by-twelve-inch manila envelope held shut with a prong fastener. "I don't know what it is," Inky said. She had obeyed a strict family rule about not reading other people's mail.

Liisa read out the inscription. "'For Charity Liisa Halonen and Mercy Katariina Halonen in the event that Patrik Halonen dies before his parents die, and then only upon the deaths of both Toivo and Emma Halonen.'" She looked up, mystified.

Inky got ready to leave. "You two want to be alone."

Liisa and I said together, "No. Stay."

Inky moved the table lamp toward Liisa and sat down. Liisa opened the envelope, slid out several handwritten pages and read them to us. Beyond the first six words, which caused us all to exclaim, the only sound in the house was Liisa's voice.

Twenty

The Manila Envelope

F rom Patrik Halonen to his daughters, Charity Liisa and Mercy Katariina. January 7, 1940, Lake Worth, Florida.

My dear daughters,

Please know of my affection for you, my beautiful girls. Each day I come home from work eager to hold you. My future hopes for you are limitless. You have made life bountiful for your mother and me. We are blessed by your presence.

I want you to know certain facts that cannot be spoken of freely. Thus I write this letter and place it in safekeeping, in case I do not survive your grandparents Halonen. If I had lived, I would have told you this in person. My parents do not know of this letter. The following notes are in two parts.

I start the first part in frustration. I cannot speak to the characters in this dilemma. One is dead to himself. The other is dead to affection. They will not talk of the past, and I need to record the truth. I fear no one else will. The events I describe I either saw for myself or I heard from my mother, Emma Halonen, or from my brother, Esko Halonen.

242

My parents' marriage ended in Savonlinna, Finland. No, I must begin further back. When she was a young girl, Mother was in love with her first cousin. I do not recall his name. They were forbidden to marry. My father was, therefore, not her first choice as a husband, and that was the root of their problems. Father was a handsome man with a weakness for drink, but when Mother married him she hoped he had reformed. She told me these things when I was small. I believe she thought I would forget them, my being so young. But I remember them clearly.

In the early years, Father had a likable, boyish way about him, like a jester. That's what Mother said. But once they married, I believe she used his past trouble as a weapon. She held a power over him. She would let him get no closer to her than she wanted. She admitted as much to me. I do not condone what he did, but, maybe to make up for what he lacked at home, he found affection elsewhere. The woman had his baby. I heard Mother tell this to a neighbor lady in North Dakota when she thought I was sleeping. Brother Isaak was sleeping, but I was not. The neighbor lady died in childbirth soon thereafter, and it seemed no one else knew about the child born out of wedlock.

My father came to Minnesota alone in 1902 to work and save money to bring the family to the States. It is my opinion he emigrated to get as far away as he could from his past, and as fast as possible. Father never wished to talk about his life but his friend Reino Koskinen told me some. He said when he and Father worked in the Chisholm mine they stayed at a Finnish boarding house for single men, and men whose wives were in Finland. He said it was a good place to practice English, but mostly they liked the Finnish food and coffee and sauna, and the fact that they could talk Finnish there. It felt like home. I have often thought Father might have been happier as a single man.

After a time Father arranged for my mother and me to come to America. I grew up there on the farm. Of those childhood stories I shall tell at another time. Now I must tell something that has been buried in time. No one dares to say the name of my baby sister, Matilda. She was eighteen months old when she died at the hand of my father. I was not at home. I was grown and working on another farm that day. Brother Isaak was working east of here. Brother Esko told me this following. Father had been secretly drinking. He went to the woodshed, very drunk and angry, and started shouting at my brothers, scolding them and swinging a long-handled axe. It was the alcohol that made him this way. Matilda was playing behind a woodpile and he did not see her. He swung the long-handled axe, not at the boys but at the woodpile. He hit the baby. She died instantly.

He escaped going to prison due to a prosecutor's error. In order to go on living, a man who does wrong must forgive himself. When a man kills his baby girl, he must forgive himself much. Father could not.

There are only a few more things to say about this matter. Father was remorseful and turned to God. He stayed away from alcohol. But he could not forgive himself or accept forgiveness from anyone else, and Mother never let him forget his wrongs. The marriage was ruined. Father was at fault but so was Mother. She was a good woman but her sin was a hardness of heart. When Matilda died, Mother became less affectionate. Father became stern. I would have liked him better as the jester. As I entered adolescence, he and I had disagreements that turned into periods during which we did not speak to one another. I left home soon after Matilda died. There was too much hurt at home. Perhaps I was cowardly. If I hurt others by leaving home, I ask forgiveness.

Someday, when this record is found, I would ask you to view my parents as worthy people. They worked hard to provide for their children. I treasured them and wanted them to view me well. I was saddened to see them give up on life, the way they did. My dear daughters, perhaps this record will illumine the family's past and help you to not similarly give up on life, ever. Hard circumstances come to everyone, but if you trust God He will lead you through. I will probably have said this many times by the time you read this, but in any event I wanted to write it down.

In the second part of this letter, I wish to explain a decision your mother and I made before you were born. You may know that we went to Russia in 1933. I wish to tell you about that.

When I met your mother, it was love at first sight. We used to say we had one of the great romances. She was very pretty, fragile outside but iron inside, as she is today. We went around with Esko and Kaisa. Esko called Kaisa his cameo because of her strong face and the way she wore her hair, tied with a ribbon like George Washington. She and your mother worked for families in Minneapolis. Esko was a bookkeeper and I worked in roofing and construction. We felt fortunate to have jobs during the Great Depression. We enjoyed going together to Finn Hall. That was the beginning of our interest in Russia.

The Finn Hall speakers talked about American Finns going to Eastern Russia to help Karelians build a new life. True, Soviet Russia was a communist country, but at the time, with the Depression making misery, we were ready to listen to anyone who had answers. Esko was the one most drawn to the idea of going to Karelia. I happen to think it was the idea of distance that interested him most. He had always had a restless nature, and events on the farm only added to it. On the few trips he had taken to Dakota, he and Father argued. He was ready to go anywhere, as long as he would not have to see Father.

With the rest of us, it was not so simple. But the speakers said children needed schools in Karelia and families needed houses, and we could help build them. The more we listened, the more elevated the idea sounded. Once we decided, we got married in a civil ceremony and left as soon as we could.

Karelia was a disappointment. The government was slow and blind to people's needs. Buildings were falling apart from neglect. Materials were wasted. After working there for a time, your mother and I and Kaisa came back to the States. Esko would have come too, but he was falsely arrested and imprisoned.

He came home a broken man. He had been mistreated by the Soviets. He escaped after a year and was very glad to get back to the United States. All of us were glad to be home. Communism had as many injustices as they said capitalism had, and more. None of us viewed communism the same after that. All of us, in fact, denounced the atheism at the root of it and asked God to forgive us for following after false gods.

But we paid a price. My parents were shocked when they found out we had gone to Russia, to help the Russians. Russia was the enemy of Finland. We had gone over to the enemy. They felt that all the effort they had put forth to bring the family to the United States was to no avail. They never recovered. In the years since, I have made efforts to rebuild their trust. I have told them that, now that Soviet Russia is fighting Finland again, I would gladly go there and fight on the Finnish side were it not for my knee (I could not be accepted due to a hay hook accident from boyhood). But Father and Mother cannot forgive me. Brother Harald is the same. It is one trait they share. Once they make up their minds, they don't change. Of course, I wish they would.

This brings to a close what I wished to say. I hope that this is a helpful document. Again I express devotion to you, my daughters. Be well, and may God uphold you with His grace.

Your father, Patrik Halonen.

Twenty-One

Bequeathments

When Liisa finished, no one spoke. These were the words of *our father*, in his own handwriting. Love was reaching to us from our father in the letter, indirectly from our mother, but from the *past*. Too late. My chest felt sat on. I put a hand to my throat, trying to work out the knots. This kind of love hurt. I hardly knew what to do with it. I wanted to cry, but I couldn't. Liisa too looked all mixed-up. Had our parents lived, so much would be different. They would have held us and kept us safe. Our father would have told us in person what he had said in the letter. What had caused him to write this letter, just two weeks before he died?

"You'll want to see this," Inky said, sliding a white business-sized envelope toward Liisa. "The lawyer said it's a will."

In simple words written by her own hand, Mummo had divided the money in two bank accounts, one in Hibbing, the other in Savonlinna, among Aarnie, Liisa, and me. To Inky, she gave her sewing machine, yarns, fabrics. To Harald, the family Bible plus vital documents. To Marcie, her chiffonier. To Kaisa, table linens and silver plate. To Aarnie, Liisa, and me, any household goods left over ("Don't fight," Mummo wrote). To Harald and Isaak, she

247

left the Dakota farm, to Liisa and me, the apricot-painted house in Finland. She included upkeep funds for both properties for ten years.

* * *

The funeral was held in the same church where Grandpa's was held eight years earlier, where I got the giggles and Randall made one of his final appearances. No one had heard from Randall for years. In the months before he left, he became increasingly distant, so that when he left for good I hardly realized he was gone. Marcie took his leaving the way she took everything—in stride. Inky and Harald must have suffered deeply, but they did it in private. They searched for him, but they did not find him.

The service was like any other, with the addition of an open casket. Mummo, the true person, wasn't in the casket. The cosmetician had taken too much trouble gussying up an empty shell. Mummo had never been one for makeup, anyway, so the effect was garish. I was relieved when the pallbearers closed the casket. Mummo was crotchety, but she had believed in Jesus and she was with Him now. Not in that casket.

After the service, as people aimed for the basement, I spotted a new couple at the rear of the church. The man seemed familiar. I couldn't think why. I worked through the crowd toward the two, and when I got close I saw a small boy standing between them. He gave me the uncomplicated gaze of young children. I smiled, introduced myself. The woman was petite and sophisticated, a dark blonde with a face as symmetrical as a face can be. The man had brown eyes set in cavernous sockets under woolly-mammoth brows, and brown hair that rose in a cowlick before dropping toward his left eye. He held out his hand and jarred me, first with his rousing handshake, and then with his words.

He smiled widely and bounced up and down. "I am Esko! You are a Halonen? Very glad to meet you! This is my wife, Bridget, and this is Samson."

Numbly, I shook his hand, and his wife's. "Esko?"

"Yes! Here we are!" He laughed, "*Yuk-yuk*," and rocked on the toes of his brogues. "We have been looking and looking for you folks!"

I tried to get my thoughts in order. "But . . . ?"

"I am your *cousin*. Esko is my father!" He seemed ecstatic to give me this news. I squinted at him. What, exactly, was he saying? He was bouncy as men went, but I thought if he'd just stand still a minute I could figure this out.

With unadulterated good cheer, he asked me, "And whose daughter are you?"

"Patrik's. I'm Patrik's daughter." I found a canker sore in my mouth and bumped it with my tongue, keeping an eye on this new Esko.

"Ah!" he said. "Is he here?"

"No. He's dead."

"Sorry to hear it. My father is dead also. So I have learned. My mother died one year past."

"How . . . how did she meet your father?"

"She nursed him to health in Lahti."

Seeing my empty expression, he said, "You know. In Finland? In 1934, when he got away from the Soviets."

His eyes were like Uncle Esko's, the nose the same but not as big, the chin bigger. Both had cowlicks at the forehead and thistle brows and deep eyes. On the father, these features had added up to sadness. On the son they added up to mirth.

I said, "How do you know your father is dead?"

"I was calling Halonens everywhere! I learned it that way. Who among the brothers is left?"

"Harald. He's here. And Isaak. He's not here. . . . Did your mother tell you about the brothers?"

"Yes! She said I should find them." Esko smiled even more, enjoying all of this.

I needed to tell him something but I wasn't sure how to bring it up. "Um. Do you know about Kaisa?"

"No. Who is Kaisa?" He waited expectantly, willing to hear me out no matter what I told him.

"His wife. His widow."

"Ah, yes, his widow." He gave an overstated nod. Nothing seemed to faze him.

Rashly, I said, "Would you like to meet her?"

"Sure!" He swept his wife and son into an arc that aimed ahead, and I led them off to find Kaisa, to give her a surprise and a potential heart attack. What on earth would she do with *this* Esko?

What Kaisa did with him—after the first jolt—was to take him in and envelop him. She took the son of her husband's mistress and made him her own, scooping up his wife and child as added gain. Watching her accomplish this, I wondered how much she had known, or had guessed, about her husband's missing months in Finland.

*   *   *

Back at the Mahoning house, we groped our way along, acting out grief in different ways. Aarnie's was profound. He stayed occupied with work, appearing relieved in the mornings to go to the mine and staying busy in the garage after supper. For him, Mummo's death would take some getting used to. Liisa and I were snipping at each other. I knew it wouldn't take much to bring things into the open. What did it was a vase.

Sorting boxes in the garage, I found a gift that I'd given to Mummo the previous Christmas, a white tulip vase wide in one direction and slim in the other, a good example of spare Finnish design. I had bought it, at no small sacrifice, at the Sampo Store in Minneapolis. Now it sat in a box marked, "Give away."

Counseling myself to stay calm, I stormed into the house, shoved the vase under Liisa's nose and shouted at her. "You threw this away! I gave it to her! How could you *do* that?" So much for staying calm.

Liisa kept washing dishes. "She never used it."

I bristled. "But you didn't ask me! I would've *wanted* it. If I hadn't been digging in those boxes, it would've been *junked!*"

"She never cared for it, it wasn't her style."

"*So?*" Liisa infuriated me! Who was she to downplay my gift? I spouted, "What makes *you* the expert on what she liked or didn't like?"

"I was here," she said.

"And I wasn't?" Well. Of course I wasn't. *Liisa* stayed home. *Liisa* sacrificed her plans. But we'd already covered this! Did we have to keep going *over* it and *over* it?

"No, you weren't," Liisa said.

"Maybe I wasn't! But at least I wasn't stuck *here*, doing nothing with my life!" I didn't feel good about having said this, but I let it stand.

Liisa wiped her hands on a towel, turned around and leaned on the counter. "At least I was here," she said softly. "Mummo needed someone."

Here was a test. I could either grow up or keep fussing. I commanded my rebel self and brought it into line. "Sorry," I said. "I wish I'd been here more."

"It's been hard, ever since you went to college. When you were here, at least it kept the weight spread around. Not so much on just me."

I put down the vase and sat at the table. "Then Mummo dies and I'm gone again."

"I'm glad you got home when you did." She actually did look glad. She sat down across from me. "I was going to have a fall-apart," Liisa said, "if you didn't get here pretty soon."

"You? Have a fall-apart? I can't see it." I diddled with the pepper shaker, waddling it to and fro on Popeye's paddle feet.

Liisa said, "Want to know something? While you were gone, I took some bennies. You know what they are? Diet pills?"

"You don't need to diet!"

"That's not why I took them. Norma gave me some for energy. I tried one a couple of times and I got so keyed up I stayed awake all that night, right over to the next! I've never gotten so much done! . . . It *scared* me. Excited me, but scared me. I thought I could conquer the world."

This didn't sound like Liisa. The Liisa I knew had everything under control. She didn't need a pill to get her going. In the ensuing silence, there was a tacit admission from both of us that we didn't know much about conquering, not in the personal sense. A pill that made you feel you could conquer the *world* was tempting.

"Do you still take them?" I asked her.

"No! I could've gotten addicted, *easy*."

"Me too, if they made you feel that strong." Dangling that thought, I felt grateful for this limited salvation: Neither of us had any chemical addiction. I said, "In high school sometimes I felt heavy-hearted. If I'd known about those pills, I would have tried them. Anything to lift the spirits."

Liisa did something out of the ordinary; she touched my hand. She assumed I knew what she meant. I did. And I agreed. I agreed we should start acting more like sisters, stop competing with each other, and avoid addictions of all kinds.

Yet, that afternoon, we fell back into old patterns. We were upstairs going through Mummo's things, and I was emptying her purse. I had avoided doing it. Her purse was too personal, the heartbeat of her life. Still, the job had to be done. In addition to billfold, bankbook, nail file, handkerchief, plastic rain bonnet, pencil, calendar book, each of which caused a prick of sadness, I found an embroidery booklet. Inside the cover was a scrap of paper. On the scrap, Mummo had written an out-of-state phone number.

I went out to the hallway where Liisa stood on a stool, sorting items on the top shelf of the closet. I handed her the note. "Know whose number this is?"

She peered at it, gave it back. "No. Why?" But her eyes had quavered when she looked at it. She knew *some*thing.

"It was in this." I showed her the booklet.

"Probably nothing important."

"You're probably right," I said, pretty sure she wasn't. "Ready for coffee?"

"I'll be down in a minute."

Back in Mummo's room, I unzipped the interior pocket of my purse, slipped the note inside, zipped the pocket shut, and went downstairs to make the coffee.

Part 5

Labor Day

Twenty-Two

A Letting-out of Air

After Kaisa called Harald a phony, she picked up a plate and served herself a helping of Jell-O Fantasia, then turned in Harald's direction and waited. He stood at the far side of the table, flinching his brows and scrunching his eyes, not at her but at the near distance. He put down his plate, tried his hands in his rear pockets and in his front ones, and finally set his knuckles on his hips. Inky, who had stayed faithfully on her feet beside him, was doing her best to debunk Kaisa's words. She had her hands folded and her head cocked, lips pruney and disbelieving, like a teacher who had just been told a whopper.

Harald laid his hands on the table. Leaning over them, he roared, "Now *what* in tarnation is *that* s'posed to mean?"

The group took in air. *Harald had spoken to Kaisa.*

Kaisa stood taller and sallied forth. "Truth is, Harald, you pretend. You preach and carry on and pretend nothing's wrong. It's not right. You judge me too harshly."

The preacher in Harald stormed. "It was sin!" he boomed, shaking his wattles. "*Sin!* The whole blasted bunch of you, going over to the *Reds?*"

He blew a raspberry into the middle of the table.

Kaisa let his noises resound a bit, then she said, "We were wrong and we said so. But you've held it against me for thirty years, against Esko, too, when he was alive."

All eyes swung over to Esko, Jr., who put us at ease with a nod and a smile. Ever since the funeral, he, Bridget, and Samson had stayed here at the lodge, being fawned over by Kaisa and being inducted into the clan.

"We wanted to be in the family again," Kaisa said, "but you wouldn't have us."

Harald was scornful. "You had *Mother*, di'n't you? And Inky? Who *else* you want, anaway?"

"Well, *you*, Harald. You could have been a friend to me, especially when Esko died. I could have used a friend."

He piled his arms high on his chest, an act that thrust his belly out to a vulnerable extent. Evidently feeling foolish in that stance, he dropped into his chair and again crossed his arms. "Hmpff! You *would* have to do this now! . . . Naw! I don't like it."

Kaisa granted him that much. "No, I don't suppose you do. But we'd have to do this sometime. It might as well be now." She was holding her plate of Jell-O with both hands, like a peace offering.

"'*Have* to'!" Harald scoffed. "Don't *have* to do *nothin'*!"

"Oh, yes, we do. With Emma gone and all? . . . Harald, she took me in. *You* could have, too."

Harald's lower lip shot out. "Never could figure *that* one out, Mother doing that! Never *did* trust you guys!" Working up to his full accusation, he bellowed in Kaisa's direction. "Patrik was *fine* till you guys came along! You and Esko got him *all* mixed up!"

"That's not true," Kaisa said calmly. "Patrik had left home long before. Anyway, you didn't see him all those years. How could you possibly know anything about him? Or about Esko, for that matter?"

He threw a beseeching look at Inky. With a press of her lips, she urged him to keep going. He said, "I figured he might come back. But you guys got hold of him . . ."

Kaisa spoke rotely as though repeating common knowledge. "It was your father, you know it was. He drove Patrik away. And Esko. And Isaak."

Working his brows, Harald said, "Ya. Well." He glanced down the table and seemed to realize the rest of us were there. He looked startled.

"That's another thing," Kaisa said. "How could you stand by and let him do that? He broke off with every one of his sons except you."

Harald slipped farther down in his chair. "What could I do? Nothing I *could* do."

Kaisa was still holding her Jell-O, which I thought must be getting soupy. She said, "Why didn't you ever talk to me and get it over with? And why didn't you talk for *yourself*? . . . Why did you let Inky talk for you, all these years?"

Harald got to his feet and swung an arm in the air, the same way he caught flies on the wing. "You calling me *chicken*? Who's calling *who* chicken? Who snuck off to the Reds? You and that *bunch* o' yours!" He put on a sarcastic face and squawked, "Poor babies! Can't take the big scary Depression!" He rearranged his hair in quick slaps.

"Now, Harald," said Inky, who had stayed standing while he went up and down. "You hush now." We all hushed. Inky's hands grappled each other as she set her mouth in position. She addressed Kaisa. "I must say I was mad at you, myself. You, going over to the Commies and doing whatever godless thing, hey? Who knows *what*-all. Then you come back all sweet and light, and we're supposed to forgive and forget? *Voi, voi, voi!*"

Kaisa looked chastised. "Really, Inky? You really thought that?"

"I did." Inky snatched a breath in the Finnish way, two sharp gasps, and licked her lips with precision. "But I'm over it. I should've told Harald a long time ago. It's gone on too long! It's time to call a halt." She stood tall, all the way up to her Olympics speed-walker height, willing to end the feud single-handedly if necessary. She scolded Harald, "It's time this business stops, once and for all! After all these years? . . . Why, it's a crying shame."

"Thank you, Inky." Kaisa telegraphed fondness to her sister-in-law. It occurred to me that if we were a hugging family, a hug right then might have worked out well.

257

"So, Harald!" Inky said. "Do you admit you were wrong?"

Harald had crumpled by this time and was sobbing outright, folded forward in his chair. When he lifted his head, he was a bleary edition of Harald. I had seen him cry at church many times, but I'd never seen him disintegrate like this. His face seemed liquid, as though tears were coming from everywhere, his cheeks, eyelids, the folds of his chin.

Inky reminded him she had asked him a question. "Well? Do you?"

He slid a peek at Kaisa and wheezed, "Ya," looked at his lap and let the tears fall.

Inky said, "And Kaisa, can you forgive Harald and get on with it?"

Kaisa's eyes too were red and moist. She waited until Harald took another peek at her, and then she said, directly to him, "Yes. I can."

"Okay then," Inky said. "It's high time!" Boosted by her success, she gave one last order, a rehashing of orders she had already given. "Harald, you need to forget that other stuff. You need to start talking to Kaisa!"

"He did," Aarnie said.

The group laughed softly and shifted in place. Once again, Aarnie had picked the perfect time to say some of his several public words per year.

Twenty-Three

California Calling

My name is Siiri Matson," the woman said in a middle-aged, vibrant voice. "From Berkeley? My daughter said you had a question."

"Yes, thank you for calling." I was taking the call in Kaisa's room, for privacy. Who knew what this call might be about?

"I hear your grandmother died and left a telephone number, and it turned out to be mine!" She seemed thrilled to be involved in this intrigue.

"I was wondering why she might have your number," I said. "Her name was Emma Saari Halonen."

"Hmmm!" the woman sang. "No, dear, I'm sorry, I don't know the name. I can't imagine *why* she had my number! But let's *do* try to find out." She proceeded to tell me her personal history, beginning with her birth.

I had been standing by the night stand, but when she got to the part about a baby boy, after the part about a baby girl, I lowered myself, slowly, to the edge of the bed. What she had said was, "My sister Ritva was born in Finland. My parents adopted her before I was born, two years before. We grew up the closest sisters ever. You'd never know she was adopted! . . . Well, she married a Ray Tiskanen and she had one child, a boy. But she died young, poor thing."

Taking disciplined breaths, I said, "The baby . . . adopted in Finland. Was she adopted by people named Sakari?"

"Why, *yes*! . . . Sakari was our maiden name! How *ever* did you guess?" The woman chatted on, but I wasn't listening.

Adam was Grandpa's grandson.

Marcie was married to her cousin.

I thanked her and hung up, my mind doing loops and spins. Was it against the law to marry your cousin? I didn't know. Genetics? No problem, they weren't blood-related. Did Adam look like a Halonen? He had ash blond hair, same as lots of Finns. Sunken eyes and bushy brows. Did he look like Harald? The eyebrows, yes. Otherwise, no. Or like Grandpa as a young man? . . . Yes! Mummo's double take! Had she guessed? . . . Wait. Grandpa had a child out of wedlock, so did Esko. Does that run in families? Of course not! And Mummo fell in love with her cousin and so did Marcie! . . . Does cousin-love run in families? . . . Of course not. Besides, Marcie and Adam didn't *know* they were cousins when they fell in love.

Good grief. They still don't.

Marcie bundled into the room with her arms full of baby. I got to my feet, not knowing what to do or say. "Lunch time!" she said, piling pillows at the head of Kaisa's bed. She arranged herself and Michael against them and had undone her blouse and started nursing the baby before she noticed my face. "What?"

"Marcie . . . ?" My hands made useless motions.

"Spit it out."

Sitting at the foot of the bed, I said, "I found a note in Mummo's purse. It had a phone number on it. I called it. It was in California, the Bay Area. A lady named Siiri Matson." I checked for signs on Marcie's face. Distress, suspicion? Prior knowledge? Nothing. "Her daughter answered and said her mother wasn't home. I asked her if she, the daughter, might knew why Mummo had the number . . ."

I knew I was blathering. I resituated myself and sat on one foot.

Marcie said, "What's this *about*?"

"Hold your horses, I'll get to it. The daughter said no, that her mother was gone till Labor Day. I said I'd be here then and gave her this number."

"And . . . ?"

"It's about an adoption."

"Me?" Marcie said. "It's about me?"

"Not your adoption. Adam's *mother's* adoption. Adam is our cousin."

The baby suckled busily as Marcie watched me. Her face was a silent movie of responses: disbelief, doubt, hilarity.

"Marcie?" I was a little worried about her. She was too quiet. "It's okay. Really."

She smiled ferociously. "Go get Adam!"

"Don't you want to talk about it first?"

"No! Go get him. I want him here."

Childishly feeling ousted as the person she wanted to talk to, I went to find Adam. I delivered him to Kaisa's room. "You want to tell him?" I asked Marcie.

"No, *you*. . . . Adam, you better sit down." He stayed standing.

I told Adam what I knew. Then I left.

Harald had laid himself out like a contented corpse, his hands stacked on his belly and his weight sinking the center of the couch. A newspaper on his face whiffled as he snored. I had no idea where the others were. I climbed the steps to the guest room where Marcie and I at age twelve had joked about our Mystery Auntie Kaisa. Today, in the same house, the family was on the move. New people. Same people. Chaos and flux. I fell backwards on the bed and lay there, spread-eagled, as the ceiling went around and around. I had a feeling we were in for a long day.

* * *

Marcie came in and fell on the other bed, laughing so hard that she belched. In a natural progression with this kind of laughter, the laughing turned to tears. We said nothing intelligible until we had both stopped laughing and crying. She sat up and took a tissue from a box, brusquely dried her eyes, blew her nose. "At least my kids'll be related to you by blood. By accident, but by blood."

261

"Don't make dumb jokes. How's Adam doing?"

"He thinks it's funny. But he feels duped. He says someone should've told him. He's trying to call his dad."

"He's right. Someone *should've* told him. But who knew?"

"His mother would have, *if* she had lived, and if her adoptive parents knew the names of her biological parents, and if they told her the names. Those are some big ifs."

"But if Adam's mom knew the names, her sister would have too, and she didn't. By the way, did Adam know this Siiri lady?"

"Nope. He just knew she traveled for the U.N."

"What happened to his grandparents, the ones who adopted the baby in Finland?"

"They died when he was little."

"What about the hired granny?" I was bent on ferreting out facts that wouldn't change a thing. "Why didn't *she* know? All the Finns know all the other Finns . . . or those Berkeley people who used to come to services? They should've known."

"Remember, Adam was ten before he and his dad even *went* to church."

"Oh. Right. But you could call that Siiri lady and ask her questions."

"Nope."

Marcie timbered backwards on the bed, the same as I'd done earlier on the other bed. "What good would it do? It doesn't matter a hill of beans who knew or didn't!"

"But why did Mummo have that number?"

"I haven't got the faintest idea." She plonked her arms on the bed and gave them a bounce. Then she bounced them again and again, grinning to herself.

* * *

When Marcie left, I stayed upstairs to think about Jeff. My yearning for him was melancholy and dramatic. Melodramatic. I talked to him into the pillow. Where *are* you? Can you join this family? Are we all *nuts*? I had an idea Kaisa had planned this entire day, that she had meetings going on, all over her property, even now, and that everyone was supposed to talk to everyone else and get everything worked out . . .

Bridget appeared at the door, giving me a shudder of nerves. I bounded to my feet. What could she want of *me*, Bridget with her worldly grace? She had freed her hair from its French knot, and it fell to her shoulders, wavy and shiny-brown. Everything on her person—fawn gabardine, tawny silk, two-tone leather, old gold—complimented her hair. "May I?" she said, meaning, could she come in.

"Of course!" I brought her in and offered her the gingham chair. I sat on the foot locker, aware of the contrast in our clothes: her serene creams, my yappy yellow plaids. I asked her, "Are you getting acquainted?"

Her smile displayed good genes and good orthodontia. "Yes, I'm glad to get to know the family." Garnering her next words, she spaced them and distributed them with care. "There were some questions I wanted to ask."

That flimmer in my belly! Like being called to the principal's office. Bridget said, composing a pleat at the wrist of her blouse, "It has to do with your trip to Finland."

Ah! A fair wind blew. The *trip*. I said, "How about if we take a walk? Want to get some other shoes on?"

Bridget declined other shoes, and we ambled toward the lake on ground that was muddy in patches. I was worried about Bridget's pumps. When we got to the dock, we walked its length and jumped across a gap of water to the houseboat. I opened a storage bin and took out two deck chairs, un-crimped the X legs, locked the braces; we sat down. The sky was a precarious blue, holding out an option for gray. We could see miles of sandy beaches, cabins and docks, trees in clumps around the lake, one motorboat stopped in the middle of the lake. A fish jumped, making a blip of sound and a circle that enlarged upon itself indefinitely. Bridget's questions were softball questions. I figured she was making up excuses to talk to each member of the family. We talked about Halonens on both sides of the ocean.

"I had to go to Finland to learn all this," I said. "Mummo didn't talk about anything. Life, death, God, you name it."

263

Disquieted, I wished unnamed wishes having to do with Mummo. "I don't feel good talking about her like that," I said. "We just had her funeral." The motorboat raced ahead with a growl, then abruptly cut inward and made a tight spiral, waves bucking away from it. It stopped and rolled on the waves with the engine idling. "I was always mad at her. It never occurred to me to pray for her, the whole time I was growing up."

The boat took off again, straight ahead, and a skier rose from the lake like a phantom. "But finally, last year, I did." The skier fell. "And I saw her in a new way."

"Was that really an answer to prayer? Why not call it coincidence? Or fate, or maturity in you?"

"It could be all of those. It's just that when I asked God to work things out, things started getting worked out. And *I* got changed." I leaned back to face the sun, glad I could say the next part. "We made pretty good progress before she died."

My eyes weren't closed long; it didn't take long. I could see into the heavenlies! Mostly I saw Mummo. She came soaring across the lake in a garment of sun and clouds, whirling and dancing, asking me to join her, this time to slip the chains that had bound us. She was barefoot and powerful—left leg, right leg, both the same—and she had perfect grace. Pausing in midair, she looked down at her feet, moved them in patterns. Smiling, she spread her arms and flew off. Her dancing days had just begun.

Twenty-Four

It Was Not Your Fault

T he family regrouped, as families do on marathon holidays, this time for Kaisa's slide show, her own slides plus Marcie's and a few of Inky's. Marcie had owned a camera ever since junior high and had sometimes taken slides by mistake. Kaisa had taken hers on purpose. When she moved to Minnesota in 1950, she had started taking slides. This was her premier show.

Beside the fireplace, Kaisa and Samson set up a triangle of tall metal legs. Samson, proud to be an actor with us as his gallery, pulled the screen up by its ring as high as he could reach, and Kaisa took it from him and lifted it over its hook. A shaft of lightning split the sky and a growl of thunder answered, low on the horizon. Aarnie released a bamboo shade that said *Uf-uf-uf* on the way down. He went to every window and repeated the action. Adam turned out the lights. With the exception of the baby, who was sleeping in Kaisa's bedroom, the whole group was there, ten adults and one five-year-old on two long sofas, two stuffed chairs, a rocker, and a hearth rug.

Slide 1: Marcie, Randall, Liisa, myself on the steps at Rickety. Four wet kids in bathing suits. Two blonde heads (Liisa's and mine), one chestnut (Marcie's), one black-brown (Randall's). Marcie and I were twelve, Liisa and

265

Randall, fourteen. The smiles on the two oldest were restrained, as though smiling meant being a little kid. The younger ones were fooling around, pinching in private, probably. Marcie elbowed me. "Look at us. What goof-offs." It was the last time we would see Randall in a slide. The day the slide was taken was about the last time we saw him in person.

Slide 2: Aarnie in his '39 Chevy. Kaisa told us the only way she got Aarnie to pose was by making his car the star. There it was, with its sporty grill and low-down looks, the sinister slash windows. Mobster car, Harald called it. Before getting in behind the steering wheel, Aarnie had lifted the engine wings into two inverted V's and locked them in place. The effect was of a large bug taking offense or of Aarnie and his Chevy taking flight.

Slide 3: Mummo picking apples. She was wearing a lavender print dress and a cobbler's apron with Grandpa's church hat. She obviously didn't know she was being photographed, or she would have turned away. Seeing her crooked shoulders, I wondered belatedly, guiltily, if they had caused her much pain.

The storm came on with a crash and a bang, a regular Minnesota thunder-boomer, one of those sky-cracking, cannon-balling, tree-falling, piano-rolling, hot-rocks, pistol-shot, Tenpins-in-heaven, Good-golly-Molly, hide-be-hind-the-davenport, This-is-God-speaking monologues that showed us mortals just *Who* was *Who*. I took the afghan from the end of the couch and made a burnoose, and watched the show from underneath it.

Slide 4: Uncle Esko, two teen-aged girls, Pooka. Esko looked joyful, or as joyful as he ever looked, parked at a picnic table with identical blonde girls in a pool of too-bright sun. "Esko, Elise, Naomi," Kaisa said. "I hope you meet the girls someday." Sitting intently forward, the younger Esko studied the slide. His father. Dead. Two half-sisters. Alive. I compared the men, the son, tall, solidly built, the father slighter and somewhat stooped, shorter than his son, their faces similar. On the surface, the young Esko didn't much resemble his half-sisters. He had a craggy face and dark hair. The twins had yellow hair and delicate faces—like Liisa's. I glanced at Liisa. She smiled; she had seen the resemblance. She had inherited the daintier features from both sides of the family. I got the blunter ones.

Esko asked Kaisa, "Could I have a print of this?"

"Of course. Remind me later."

"Thanks." Esko leaned back, slipped his arm around Bridget. Samson, on the other side, laid a hand on his father's knee. Esko pulled him close.

Adam said, "Esko, you and I need to stick together. We're both kind of new here." In the hours since Siiri Matson's call, news of Adam's identity had spread through the crowd, behind the scenes, and now Adam himself was raising the topic, playing the host and welcoming Esko. Nice of him, I thought.

Esko said, "It's a deal."

Samson asked Kaisa, "Whose dog is that?" In the slide, Pooka looked aggrieved over some annoyance beyond the frame.

"Mine," Kaisa said. "Pooka. He was a Florida dog. He didn't take to Minnesota. It was too cold. He just shook and shook."

"What happened to him?" Samson asked.

"He died," she said shortly, and clicked to the next slide.

Slide 5: Mummo with her hand on the newer Chevy's door handle. I recognized the church yard. Our confirmation day. "I took that!" Inky said, exceedingly proudly.

Marcie seemed affronted. "Mom? You *hate* cameras. All those knobs?"

Inky puffed up her chest. "Sure, but someone had to do it. It was you girlses' confirmation, after all!" In the slide Mummo wore a gray dress and gloves. I didn't recall her *ever* wearing gloves.

Slide 6: Aarnie and Harald in front of Inky and Harald's house. "That's another one I took," Inky said. The men had posed for her, if not entirely willingly, standing side by side, eyes slit against the sun and heads tipped toward each other. Harald chuckled and called to Aarnie, "We look like a Wanted poster! Or like they already caught us, red-handed!" Aarnie grew red-faced in an effort to avoid notice.

Slide 7: Our confirmation class, posed by a tree. Mentally I filled in other scenes. The man doing sit-ups, the ice rink, Marcie and Adam in love at an early stage. "We had confirmation in Sweden, too," Esko said. "All the boys liked all the girls."

I said, "At our confirmation, Marcie met Adam. Talk about *liking.* Hubba hubba."

Marcie got up and sat on Adam's lap, and kissed him on the mouth, long and hard. Samson blushed and said, "*Eeee-uw!*"

Marcie laughed. "It's legal," she told him, falling back onto the couch.

Slide 8: Adam, looking rascally, perched on the Koskis' wooden fence. Kaisa said, "There he is, the man himself."

Marcie acted antsy, wiggling and grinning away. "*I* took that! The California stud!" Her words reverberated in a room filled with ex-farmers who knew the meaning of the word "stud." Adam wore the same expression that he wore in the slide: rascally.

Slide 9: Adam, leaning with a straight arm against an oak tree. Adam said, "Which one is holding the other one up?"

Slide 10: Adam, holding a rake wrong-side-up, gazing passionately at it. Harald swiped at his eyes, which had teared up. "Looks like Father clowning around."

The crowd reacted with an upward tilt, sort of a group *goose.* No one said a word, but there was celebration in the void. After the day's events, we had a new genetic sense, and Harald had just added to it: Adam was like Grandpa clowning around.

Adam told Harald, "Sometime I'd like to hear about your father."

"Ya, sure." Harald made his brows twitch and jump.

"And I'd like to hear about my father," I said.

Harald grumbled, "You coulda said so all along."

"I *did*! I asked you. Or maybe I didn't. Maybe it was Marcie who asked you." I revived my pique sufficiently to say, "But I asked *everyone.* I asked Mummo and she wouldn't say a thing . . . Well, I didn't actually *ask* her . . ." Tripping over my impertinence, I went on. "I asked Kaisa . . ." Ashamed, I turned to Kaisa. "You *did* tell me some things, thanks." I hung my head in Inky's direction. "You did too," I said, dribbling off to nothing.

Kaisa decided I'd whined enough. She clacked the projector to the next slide.

Slide 11: Liisa, age fourteen, in front of our house, holding up a quilt. Pinned to the quilt was a blue rosette, first prize ribbon at the Minnesota State Fair. Appliquéd to the quilt was a bull moose. I said, loudly and a little rudely, "Charity Liisa Halonen! Grand Prize Winner, two years in a row! Who else would think of doing a *moose*?"

"You always have to poke fun," Liisa said. "You push and push and make people feel bad."

Without saying it in so many words, I tried to tell her to *shush up*, to save it until we were alone, at least.

Liisa said, flinging resentment at me, "I don't care! I'm tired of it! Today we get to speak our minds, and here's mine. I'm tired of you bossing me around!" She gave me a cold-fish stare.

I said, "Bossing you around? Bossing you around? I don't know what you mean!"

"Oh, yes, you do. Don't go playing dumb. You always have to be the hero."

Again I repeated her words: "The *hero*?"

"Yes! You're always lording it over people. You think you're better than everyone else."

Flabbergasted, I said, "I don't think that!"

"Well, you act like you do. The rest of us have brains, too, you know."

Something picked at the back of my mind, a clue. *Brains.* I said, "You wish you were in college, don't you?"

This brought her up short. She flew a look at me, then focused on her hands and pushed her cuticles with a thumbnail, ignoring me and the others looking on.

"You can still go!" I enthused. "I'll help. We can check the . . ."

She sent me a loaded look.

"What? I'm being bossy?"

Her nod was nearly imperceptible. I sent a message to Jeff in Manitoba. You sure you want to hook up with me, such a bossy, nosy, gabble-gabble *busybody*?

Interrupting when an interruption was needed, Inky said, "Kaisa, could we take a break here? We need to talk about something."

"Sure." Kaisa turned off the projector and snapped on two table lamps. Inky asked Liisa and me if we'd tell the others about our father's letter. We said okay.

Liisa explained that our father left us a letter and in it told us stories he thought we should know. She said I'd heard the same stories in Finland. She asked me to tell them to the group.

I inhaled, exhaled, fighting nausea. This straight-talk made my head muzzy. I looked over at Harald. "One was about Grandpa . . . and Matilda."

The older generation darted looks at each other and hinched around in their seats. No one spoke.

Esko said, "I come from Sweden, and I don't know anything. So I can ask it. Who is Matilda?" He put his chin down and peered through brows as thick as thatch.

Inky told Harald, "*You* tell it."

Harald's face was a troubled surface as he made up his mind. He hauled in a scudding breath. "Matilda. . . . The one girl. She was just learning to run good." He sighed again and glanced at a few in the group. "Father got to drinking again, and Mother didn't want him to hurt us, so she sent us out to play in the woodshed. . . . She said to take Baby too. Baby liked to play Hide and Go Seek. She'd hide and think we couldn't find her, then when we found her she'd laugh and laugh. . . . She had a real purty laugh."

He raised his trunk, sucked in air, and slumped again. In a papery voice, he said, "She was hiding back of a wood pile. Father came in mad, hollering at *me* 'cause I left a wrench in the field. He picked up the long-handled axe and swung it. But he stumbled. He was going to hit the wood pile, but he hit Baby. He never saw her behind there. There was blood all over." Harald bent forward and caught a scream in his hands.

Inky knelt beside Harald, her great height allowing her to hide his head in her arms. A tortured keening came from Harald, from a long way back, an expulsion of pain so bitter it shook the room. Many of us cried with him.

After a time, Inky put her hands to his cheeks and tenderly raised his head. His face was a blur of grief. She lowered her face to his. "Harald. *It was not your fault.*"

Kaisa said, "That's right. It was *his* fault. It was the drink."

Harald took in a punishing breath. "Naw, it was me. I left the tools out."

270

"It *was not* your fault," Kaisa said firmly. "But Esko was like that, too. He felt guilty for things he didn't do. He thought it was his fault your father shut him out. He thought he'd let Toivo down once too often." She paused. "Esko never forgave himself."

"Toivo neither," said Aarnie.

Kaisa dipped her head at Aarnie and said to Harald, "Aarnie's right, isn't he, that your father never forgave himself? He closed down to himself and then to everyone else. Including you?"

Harald heaved a tremulous sigh. "Ya. It was pretty bad."

Inky offered him a hanky and returned to her chair. Harald blew his nose, put the hanky in his shirt pocket. Holding his knees, he said, "I was s'posed to be the one good son left. But I couldn't be that good."

Looking at Kaisa, he said, "Sorry then about Esko."

We all swayed on a wave of good will and Mummo came in on cue, like a fairy grandmother on an overdue call. (Didn't everyone see her?) She flitted around the room, *touching* us, of all things, giving to some and taking from others, everything according to our needs. She lifted us, released us, and improved our opinions for the long haul. When she faded, she left peace in her wake, and forbearance.

Kaisa said, "Tell you what. Let's save the other slides for next time." She gave Samson a head signal. "Samson, honey, let's take this down, shall we? Then we can go down to the cellar and get the watermelon. How does that sound?"

Beaming, Samson clambered up off the couch and met Kaisa at the projection screen. She laid her hand on his hair, drinking in the sight of him.

271

Twenty-Five

Sleuthing

W hen a member of the Finnish church died, the eulogy at the funeral was short, consisting mainly of the deceased person's birthplace, date of birth, children's names, a statement of faith. The personal stories got told afterwards over coffee in small, unplanned groups. But Mummo's funeral had been different. Esko had shown up with his family and, without meaning to, had drawn attention away from Mummo. I for one felt the angst of unfinished business. I worried that the stories might not get told. I shouldn't have worried. After Harald's big thaw, the talk naturally turned to the topic of Mummo.

Nobody had moved except for Kaisa and Samson, who pottered around taking down the screen, Kaisa clucking over Samson, Samson strutting with the importance of his job. Liisa said to no one in particular, "Would all this have happened if Mummo were alive?" I took her to mean: Would Kaisa have spoken to Harald, would he have answered, and apologized, would Matilda's story have come out, would we have experienced the meltdown and the mercy? (*Mercy.* My name as a good thing!) From the looks of him, Harald himself was hardly paying attention. He sat lumpily and complacently in an over-stuffed chair, half asleep.

"Your grandmother now, she didn't have it easy, you know," Inky said.

"Does everyone know about her cousin?" I asked the group.

Kaisa said, "Samson and I think we'll wait a while for the watermelon." Samson looked dubious about this, but he joined his father anyway on the couch. As Kaisa eased into the rocking chair, she grizzled her eyes at Samson.

I told the story of the cousins and their forbidden love. "Silvi thinks Mummo never got over Karl," I said at the end.

"She didn't," Inky said. "She was all tore up when he died." Inky narrowed in on Liisa and me. "Remember that first time she fell down? That was the time. She got a letter about Karl dying, and we talked about that and some other things, and pretty soon she fell on the floor and couldn't breathe."

I said, "But the mail comes in the morning. How come she fell at *night?*"

"It wasn't about Karl. She was mad at *me.*"

"I remember! You and Mummo were arguing." I was nervous about admitting I knew this, even at this late date, even on a day when we were admitting everything.

"Ya well," Inky said, "I'd been telling her she needed to rest, that she should retire. I wanted to take you girls, you know, raise all you kids together. I said it would be good for you girls. She got real upset and fell down."

"It was about us?" Liisa asked, as floored as I was. "*You* wanted to raise us?"

"Sure I did. *Voi, voi, voi!* I wanted to, all along, believe you me! But Emma wouldn't stand for it."

In a lowered voice, Kaisa said, "I wanted to, too. We lived in the same town, after all. But Esko . . . ?" She looked at Liisa and me, asking forgiveness. "He had all he could handle, with our two. I'm so sorry."

"It's okay," Liisa told her. "It never entered our minds."

"Never," I agreed. We smiled and nodded at her until she seemed mollified.

Inky said, "Emma was a bulldog when it came to you two. She was proud of you. Maybe she never said so, but she was." Liisa and I chewed on this bit of belated praise.

I said, "Inky, I've always wondered. Did Mummo ever say anything about her fainting, you know, about why she fainted?"

"No. What Emma didn't say spoke louder than what she did say."

"That's the way she was," Liisa said. The group hmmed and ummed: Yes, that's the way she was, Mummo, the keeper of the Silence.

"Another thing," I said. "That hard breathing she did when she fainted? I found out what it is. It's called hyperventilation. It's from anxiety. She wasn't faking."

"You thought she was faking?" Inky asked me.

"Well, I used to." I sat in my spot feeling mean-minded. Not only had I misjudged Mummo, but I'd hung onto the misjudgment long after I knew better. Changing the subject, I asked if anyone knew beforehand that Mummo had that phone number.

"I did," Liisa said.

Put out with her, I said, "But I showed it to you. You didn't say a thing!"

"You asked me if I knew whose number it was. I didn't. Besides, you didn't tell me you *called* the number."

She was right. I had placed the call when she wasn't home. "I was being a sleuth," I said. What I didn't say was: *I was jealous. You were with her at the end.* Despite our new openness, I couldn't say it.

"Mummo was being a sleuth, too," said Liisa. "She asked me how to call long distance but didn't say why. It was the day before she died."

I said, "But where did she get the phone number?"

"I think *I* know," Inky said. "Back in the spring, she got a letter from a Mrs. Virta, and she got all widgety. I'm just guessing, but, Adam, I think Emma knew about you! I think you look like Toivo did when they got married. I know she got excited-like whenever you were around."

Adam said sardonically, "She did a good job of hiding her excitement."

"I saw it once!" I told him. "At our confirmation. She did a double take when she met you! I think she *recognized* you." Marcie fluttered her eyes at Adam. He smiled down at her with a closed mouth.

Inky returned to her theory. "That Mrs. Virta lives in Wisconsin and goes to Finland every couple-three years. What if Emma had an idea who

Adam was, but she wanted to make sure, so she asked Mrs. Virta to look up records in Finland to see who adopted Toivo's child? What if Mrs. Virta did that and sent Emma the names and the phone number?" Inky blinked around at us. "What do you think, hey?"

Marcie clapped once. "That's *it*. Betcha anything."

"Sakari," I said to Adam. "George and Melba Sakari. The people who adopted your mother. Your grandparents." Adam showed no emotion whatsoever.

Harald rallied from his stupor to ask, "How in the *Sam Hill* do you know *that*?"

I told him Silvi gave me the names. He rubbed his face and mussed his hair. "I missed that. Musta been snoozin'."

Marcie wondered out loud, "Why didn't Mummo just ask her sister?"

"I think she was embarrassed," Inky said. "She wanted to do this on her own."

Esko scrambled up and offered his hand to Adam. "Now is my turn to welcome *you*. We are two lost boys come home again!"

Bemused, Adam got to his feet and shook hands with Esko, peering up through his eyebrows—a habit exactly like Harald's and Esko's. Was there a gene for that trait? Or for those hedgerow eyebrows?

Samson asked Kaisa, "Now-w-w can we have watermelon?"

275

Twenty-Six

Oo!

Mummo made us snowsuits out of men's wool suits," Liisa said. "She got them at rummage sales and cut out the good parts and pieced them. Black, gray, pinstripe . . ."

Only Liisa, Marcie, Bridget, and I were still in the front room. "Man oh man, they made us sweat," I said. "But it was the Depression, and she saved money however she could. Speaking of the Depression, I think *she* was depressed most of the time."

Liisa agreed, adding, "I thought I caused it, that I didn't do enough to help."

I said, "But you were the good girl! You did *everything*. You never got upset."

"Oh, yes, I did. It was always, 'Liisa will do it, Liisa will stay home and help.'"

"Ah, Liisa!" I was perturbed at her for staying home, and at myself for leaving, and at Mummo for letting us both feel we were wrong. "I wanted you to leave, you know I did. I kept saying, 'Go to college, move away, live on your own.'"

"It wasn't that easy. They needed my paycheck . . . with you in college."

I was exasperated. "We've been over this plenty-times. Can't you let it go?"

"What are you, the scorekeeper?"

I said, "*Oo!*" Then I blanched. I wanted to fight back, but all I could come up with was a baby word, "Oo." After years of silence, we were finally using words, but now I was tempted the other way. I wanted to use words that could disable or kill. I caught myself in time. "You're right. I can't tell you when it's over."

"It's not over," Liisa said.

She needed something from me, but what? I had a brilliant idea: *Ask her.* "What do you need from me?" I asked her.

"Appreciation."

"Haven't I appreciated you?"

"No! You come zooming in with your marvelous ideas, and there I am, still on duty, still at home, and you're off on your next screwball plan."

Shamefaced, I looked at Marcie and Bridget. I shrugged. "Oh, well, what the heck! We're all related." I faced Liisa. "I admit I've been a pain in the neck. I haven't carried my load. I haven't appreciated you . . . enough."

"That's better. Now ask my forgiveness."

"Boy, are you getting pushy! Will you forgive me?"

She laughed. "Sure."

* * *

I didn't know how the others felt, but I was tottering from all this talk. In theory I was all for it, but in practice it made my head hurt. Yet, at supper, so help us, we kept on talking. Kaisa had made three big casserole dishes of pasty (meat pastry), and we were eating it with vigor (and with ketchup, no insult to the cook) when Esko asked Adam how he was finding fatherhood. The baby in question lay on Marcie's left arm, awake and contented, while she wielded her fork with her right hand.

"It changes everything," Adam said. "I read up before he was born. Here's a theory. Starting at birth, or before, the baby starts trying to figure things out. He theorizes about cause and effect."

Liisa said, "Like what?"

"Like in the first hour of life. He hears Mom's voice, the same voice he heard in the womb. He hears her heartbeat and thinks, 'Yup, this is the one! I'm safe.' Then, when he cries, if he's picked up and fed and changed, he thinks the world's a great place. But if he cries and no one comes, he thinks he can't trust anyone. That's dangerous. He can't learn to empathize if he doesn't learn to trust."

Impressing her bosom on the table, Inky stage-whispered to Marcie, three chairs down on her side. "Is that why you feed him on demand?"

"I just nurse him when he's hungry." Marcie spoke at normal volume, which was okay, since we were in on it anyway.

Inky pulled herself upright. "Why, you'll spoil him rotten!" She flittered her cumbersome features, her lips, forehead, chin, and cheeks exercising separately in protest to modern thought. Marcie raised Michael into a seated pose facing her. His arms hung limply over her hands and his rompers rode up to show wedges of diaper and rubber pants. His fat legs flopped open like puffy parentheses. He didn't mind these indignities, but corkscrewed his hands and scrutinized Marcie's face, asking her the meaning of life. She nuzzled the fuzz on his head. He hiccupped a smile and wagged his body.

Adam said, "A baby can interpret harm when no one intends it. Say he's sick in the hospital, in pain. Mom or Dad should stay nights in his room. If they don't, he might take their absence as rejection. Even if they do stay, he might think they caused his pain."

"Even before he can *talk*?" Liisa asked.

"Especially then. One writer says a baby needs cuddling as much as he needs food. If he doesn't get enough, he grows up insecure. Starved for touch."

Those words! *Starved for touch.*

I threw a panicky look at Liisa, who was having the same epiphany I was having. Feeling pukey-sick, I started to get out of my chair. But my feet got tangled in the rungs. I plunked myself back down.

"No! I've been running away all my life. I was one of those babies. I grew up starved for touch."

Liisa squeezed her eyes shut and tears ran out. "Me too."

Inky clicked her tongue. "I knew it. I knew it. I just knew it."

"It was like a sickness," I said, "or a secret you were in charge of. Something was wrong at your house but you couldn't talk about it. The secret was: No one touched. If Mummo got too close to us, she backed away."

"You had it worse," Liisa told me. "You were just a baby."

Aarnie said, "Wish I could've took care of you."

Tears puddled in my eyelashes. Through a watery scrim I could see Aarnie across the table, ramrod-straight, concentrating on the air behind me. Dear Aarnie.

"I remember!" Liisa said. Her face recorded a process—a piece of the past rising to the surface. "Mummo made him leave you in the crib! He'd want to pick you up, but she wouldn't let him. But one time he *did* pick you up and he rocked you in the rocking chair and hummed a tune. You fell asleep and he got scared. He thought you were *dead.* When Mummo came downstairs, he said, very fast, 'I didn't mean it!'"

A shuffling amusement went through the group. Aarnie turned coral pink, but he was not displeased. I felt cleansed, relieved of something harsh.

"Emma was scared of you girls," Inky said. She adjusted her position to take in Harald, seated beside her. "Harald, I know it's hard for you if we talk about Matilda, but she was the miracle baby. When she died, your mother just iced over. She was scared to love *anyone.*"

Inky's homely face blazed and burned. She was beautiful. She turned to Liisa and me. "That's why I wanted to raise you." Her face contorted as she fought for control. Crying openly, she called out, "I shoulda hugged you all along! Even if she'd a got mad!"

My throat locked up; I tried to swallow past the pain. I thought if I could just stay in my chair, the pain would turn to plain grief, and I could cry it out and be done with it.

Kaisa said, "This calls for first aid. These girls need *hugs.* Inky, you take Kik."

279

We four got up out of the way of the chairs, and each aunt took a niece in her arms. Inky held me against her, protecting me with her body. The comfort was radiant. She felt like home. I buried my head and wept, for myself and Liisa, for everyone hurt by Mummo's silence, her children, even Grandpa. I cried for Mummo too, the same as I'd cried for her in Tim's group, except that now I knew more about *why*.

When we recovered, we mopped our faces with table napkins and went back to our chairs. Inky said, "Emma never could let go of hurts and worries. She worried about you girls. She didn't want her fainting spells to get passed on to you."

Another revelation! Liisa and I commiserated without words. I said, "Does anyone know, did my father ever get dizzy? I mean, does it run in the family?"

Harald sat up like someone who had been tapped on the shoulder and told it was his turn. "Patrik used to get so mad at Father, he'd about explode. I seen him hold his head, more 'n' once. He said it would kinda blow up inside there and he had to sit down with it. That's why he left home, 'cause he used to get so sick like that."

So it *did* run in the family. A word Harald used? . . . *Mad*. I said, "Listen to this. My father got mad and got a dizzy head. So did his mother. So did Liisa. So did I. We all had so much anger in us, it about blew our heads off!"

Harald said, "Say, I been listenin' here, ever'body talkin' about Mother. She was tough, but she did the best way she knew how. She di'n't know no way better." I creaked my neck, looking down the table at him. Why the fractured English?

Marcie couldn't sit still. "I hate to say it, Daddy, but she *should* have. What about the church? The catechism and all?"

Finding the right spot on his teaspoon, Harald balanced the spoon on one finger. He mused out loud, "Those days, no one talked about how believers should act. You know, every-day-like? Those preacher guys oughta do a better job of it."

We smiled as a unit and let him off the hook.

Liisa said, "Grandpa was another one who iced over. But everyone should read his diary. He was goodhearted, and funny. . . . Kik, bring it next time, okay? Some people haven't seen it."

I said I would.

Kaisa suggested the obvious next activity, the required ritual at this time or any other. "I'll go make coffee."

* * *

Saying no thanks to coffee, I went upstairs and took a nap. I dreamed I visited Mummo in the hospital. Three old women stood around her bed, nattering and bickering. One said to me, "Why, *you* should be in the hospital. You look awful." I took no offense but secretly smiled at Mummo. I said, "We should say *nice* things, 'Glad to see you, you make me happy, I remember the good times, would you like some water?'" Shrewdly, I winked at Mummo. She gave me an eye-sign: collusion. The old women left the room. I picked up Mummo, and we sat in a rocking chair. She was small and warm, as soft as a baby. She smelled of baby powder. I held her high in my arms with her cheek on mine, her arms around my neck, and we rocked and rocked. The rocking seemed *right*. Historic and satisfying, redeeming a lifetime of not-rocking.

I woke with tears on my face and the feel of Mummo still in my arms, both of us holding on for dear life.

Twenty-Seven

Esko's Story

W e sat in the flicker of an oil lamp, listening to Esko. The
world had funneled down to just this table, to faces and shoulders lit by a lamp,
white tablecloth, blue-and-white Finnish coffee cups, dessert plates, the crumbs of
Kaisa's pudding cake a lazy and late debris. "The Soviets were bombing Finland
in December of '39," Esko said. "The Finns saved their children by sending them
to Sweden. If they hadn't sent us away, I would not have met my Bridget." He
percolated joy in the direction of his wife, beside him. She aimed her dazzle at
him, and it rebounded in *zings* around the table.

"They put us in snowsuits and white hooded capes, and put name tags
on us, and shipped us like baggage! We tried to be brave, but of course we
cried. Our parents cried too. I was eight years old. We boarded the icebreaker, and I watched my mother from the railing. Our escorts held our hands, and
we waved good-bye. My mother waved until I couldn't see her. She was sorry
to send me, but she promised to come and get me when the war was over. I
tried to be cheerful. But I got seasick. That's what I remember of the trip! *Mal
de mer. Merisairaus. Sjösjuk.* The same in any language!"

He gave us a bilious grin.

282

"My reward for leaving Finland was my host family, the Jenssons. Mum and Dad Jensson were teachers. That's how I learned English. They had two sons near my age, Albin and Edvin. In Finland I had no brothers or sisters, so this was good. Albin became my best friend. The Winter War ended in spring 1940, but I stayed in Sweden. By then, my mother couldn't keep me. She had to live with her parents because she had M.S., multiple sclerosis. She had to live a slow life. She couldn't travel, so I went to Finland to see her on holiday. She tried many kinds of treatments, even one with bee stings! But she got pneumonia last year, a type that could not be cured, and she died. You might say she sent me to you, as she left me travel money. I had always wanted to come to the States. Bridget had, as well.

"I knew my father's name was the same as mine, but I didn't know which state was his. Mother said Michigan, but later she said Minnesota. We wanted a change in life, and Samson was at a good age to travel." He reached out and chucked his son under the chin. Samson had stayed close to the grownups all day. Like his father, he was curious; he didn't want to miss a thing. He dragged a finger through a sugar pile he had made on the tablecloth. His profile was like his mother's, precise and firm, his crop of hair like his father's.

Esko asked us, "Shall I tell how I found you? Or are you tired?"

"No, please, tell us," said Kaisa.

We multiplied her words, "Please, tell us."

Esko preened. "Okay then! It was based on chance and happenstance." He tapped his lips in a caricature of pondering. "First, I resigned my job—you know I taught violin at the conservatory?—and Bridget left the magazine. Of course you know she was editor-in-chief. We were ready to begin again." He surveyed us with a purpose.

I couldn't stand the suspense. "Are you staying? For good?"

"*Yes!*" He expanded with the size of his news. "In Minneapolis!"

We cheered in our various ways. Marcie yodeled, Aarnie blushed, Inky wrapped her lips around her teeth in strong approval. Samson looked at Kaisa to see what *she* thought. Patting her chest, she smiled at him and nodded. She was heartened by the news, but she had the aura of a person who had known the news ahead of time.

"We came to America altogether on a fancy!" Esko said. "We knew it was one of the M states, Minnesota or Michigan."

Samson angled his head to catch his father's eye. "'Member I *said* it was Minnesota?"

"That's right, son, you *did.*" Esko gazed at him with unfettered amazement. "He's a good boy," he confided in us. Bridget bent to Samson's ear. He said yes with his body, slid off the chair and hustled down the hall.

Esko said, "We came to New York and stayed in a hotel two days. I told the concierge of my search. He brought phone books, and we looked up everything Finnish in New York! . . . There were two Halonens in Manhattan, no relation. I called them. That's how I know. I called the Brooklyn Society for Finnish-American Friendship. A woman there told me Halonen is a common name in Minnesota and Michigan. But she was happy to help. She called back and said Minnesota was the place! She had found an Esko Halonen in Minneapolis, a Toivo in St. Paul, another Toivo in Hibbing. I called the Esko in Minneapolis. No answer. Now I know it was Kaisa, listed under my father's name."

He asked Kaisa, "Is that for protection?"

"Yes," she whimpered, "one never knows. Burglars? A helpless little old lady living alone?" She patted her hair, enjoying her joke. Kaisa was anything but old and helpless. When Samson returned, he wiggled his ears at her. She rabbited her nose at him.

"So I called the St. Paul number," Esko said, "and talked to a woman who didn't know any Esko Halonen. I called the Hibbing number and got an old woman with a Finnish accent. Now we know it was Emma. It was Sunday. I said I was Esko Halonen. Before I could say more, she said I *couldn't* be, that Esko died ten years ago. Then the line cut off. I tried again and got a peep-peep signal."

I said, "Can a person die of shock? What if Mummo heard the name Esko and died of shock? The phone was off the hook . . ."

I stopped, horrified. I had just blamed Esko for Mummo's death. "Esko, I'm sorry, I didn't mean . . ."

"Of course you didn't," Kaisa said.

Esko waved away my apology. "I didn't expect to find him alive. My mother said he was sickly even as a young man. I was happy just to hear Emma say my father's name! I knew I had found my family." He smiled broadly at us.

Liisa said, "Mummo helped us find *both* you and Adam! She answered the phone when you called, which she hardly ever did, and she was tracking Adam down, again *by phone*. She outdid herself there at the end."

We concurred. She really *had* outdone herself there at the end.

Esko said, "We got to Minneapolis on Monday. I tried Kaisa's number again. Kaisa, you were here by then?" She nodded. "I called all the Finnish organizations in Minneapolis, looking for anyone who knew the name Esko Halonen. I found an old man who was nearly deaf. He remembered my father from the socialist days."

We sucked in air and gave him unblinking blank looks. Socialism was *taboo*. Didn't he know?

Esko smiled easily. "Don't worry. Kaisa told me everything. The old man had seen in the newspaper that a Halonen had died. He left the phone for a minute and was gone so long I thought *he* had died too! But he came back and said that he saw in the obits (Is that what you say, the 'obits'?) that Emma Halonen, formerly Saari, wife of the late Toivo Halonen, had died. He read it to me. We came to the funeral and here we are!"

As proud as a boy with the biggest fish, he asked us, "Is that a good story?"

"Yes, Esko." Kaisa spoke the name with awe, getting used to it all over again. "It's a very good story."

* * *

The group broke up, and thirty minutes later we met again. The house looked its best at night, I thought. No lamps, just candles and a fire. One log was burning from the inside out. It glowed orange through holes in its side like a cottage in the dark, giving out cheer even though its own death was imminent. Flames lapped under it, around it, out both ends, singing and snapping, ripping at the shell, making a long "Sssssss" when they hit a wet spot. Finally the log imploded with a pop and shot embers at the screen.

"I'm pooped!" I said. I was slumped on a sofa next to Marcie. Everyone was back in the front room including Michael, held by Adam on Marcie's other side. Samson and Aarnie were playing checkers on the rug. Aarnie sat in a curl with one knee raised and tucked in, taking up the smallest possible space, being the least bother, and Samson lay sprawled on his stomach. Kaisa added wood to the fire and came to sit in the rocker.

Marcie said, "What are the odds of marrying into your own family?"

"A million to one," Liisa said.

"A gazillion to one!" This from Samson. Marcie reached over and gave his head a knuckle-rub. He yanked away, grinning and resembling his father.

Adam took on a fake pomposity. "Synchronicity. Carl Jung. It's when events converge like that, a sort of extra-coincidence. It has a mathematical base." He was poking fun at himself. "That's *my* theory, anyway," he grinned.

Marcie crooned, "Oh, Adam." She swung her leg over his and cuddled toward him. "You *thrill* me with your numbers." He melted her with an intimate look. He melted *me* with the spill-over and left me missing Jeff.

"Now it is my turn," Bridget said. She got to her feet, being careful not to step on the checkerboard or on Aarnie or Samson, and went to stand by the fire. The action of the flames made her appear mobile even as she stayed still. "I have been watching all day, and I must say you are stubborn people. You think your own ideas are best, and you go the long way to prove it. Maybe it is *sisu*. *Sisu* is good, but so much stubbornness is not good. Your secrets and your angers? You kept them too many years."

Bridget spoke with authority. Like an editor-in-chief.

"I will live in America. I am happy to live here. But I must say this. You don't realize what you have. Minnesota, and this family. You don't know how lovely the place is or how lovely you are! Please don't take time—I mean to say, don't waste time—being angry. Not any more."

She was finished. We sat there, silent again. We had just been preached at by our newest cousin. She was cautioning us: *Do not repeat the harm.*

Esko sprang up and took his place beside her. He hung an elbow around her neck and said, "My Bridget."

As she went to sit down, Esko chortled and scanned the group. "This is what I was looking for, people with my same name, so we can argue and be friends!" He swept one arm at us, two wide strokes, as if painting us the color Halonen. From a shirt pocket he took out a fold of paper and crackled it and studied it, grinning at us, elongating our wait. He held the paper in one hand and tucked his sweater into his slacks with the other.

Turning solemn, he said, "I wrote this." He read to us from the paper:

"'On this date, 5 September 1960, at Swan Lake, Minnesota, in the United States of America, we, the descendants of Toivo and Emma Halonen, acknowledge the history we have inherited from them. We forgive them any wrongs they brought upon us. We honor the thrift, hard work, honesty, and faith that marked their lives. In their memory, we promise to pass on these virtues to our children. In addition, we forgive each other any wrongs we have brought upon ourselves. We promise, from this day forward, to be forthright and kind to each other in all circumstances.'"

He refolded the note, put it away. Gravely he said, "Okay?"

"Okay," we said, equally gravely.

With his document, Esko had punctuated the past. Period, paragraph, end of chapter. And he'd started us on a new chapter. We had reconfigured ourselves, and as a group we had something now that we lacked a few hours ago: a new sense of order.

We had Mummo and Grandpa resting in peace, as well as my mother, my father, Uncle Esko, and Baby Matilda.

We had three new members, the latest immigrants, Esko, Bridget, Samson.

We had Adam in an added role that brought him, Marcie, and Michael into the family twice over.

We had Harald as a free man.

We had Inky as a mediator.

We had Kaisa as the Convening Hostess.

We had Liisa and me as a sister team, finally.

That left Aarnie as the new hub, satisfied as always by simply being present, and, without meaning to, showing the rest of us how to be.

Epilogue

Not long after that Labor Day, the Mahoning big shots gave us notice that ten months later our house would be moved to make way for the steam shovels. But by then we were gone anyway. Before the mine ate up the street, we had one final event at the house, a joint wedding in April, during one of those early springs we sometimes had.

Liisa and Bill honeymooned at Niagara Falls and moved into a duplex in a new part of Hibbing. Bill went back to his fifth-graders, who called him Mrs. Renfro to his face, and Liisa went back to junior college, preparing to become a social worker. From my perspective, anyone who asked for such a thankless job as social worker had better want it very much. Liisa did.

Jeff and I flew to Florida to see where I was born. We found blazing yellow days and a bath water beach, powdered sand on the sidewalks, and palm trees that clacked like old men's false teeth. We loved rolling in the surf and in the marriage bed, and we went back home tanned and happy. In Minneapolis, we took an apartment not far from Kaisa's house, classes at the U of M, and two part-time jobs each.

The third couple married that day, Aarnie and Kaisa, skipped any honeymoon and instead emptied the Mahoning house. They filled a trailer with furniture that Liisa and I didn't need and pulled it to Minneapolis. After Mummo died, Aarnie and Kaisa had started keeping company behind our backs. Their futures simply blended, she told us later, just ran together naturally like streams becoming a river. In March, when Liisa and I had our double wedding planned, Kaisa came to us and asked us (shyly, as if picking up Aarnie's habits) if they could join the ceremony. We took the span of a gasp to say, "Yes! Of course!" So, on a warm Saturday afternoon, we six stood before Harald and our friends and whatever relatives weren't standing up front, and we said our vows. Aarnie and Kaisa took up bowling and eventually joined three leagues, his, hers, and theirs. They enjoyed having company in their big Minneapolis house. Aarnie still peeked from the kitchen before greeting guests, but he had come up with a shorter ritual—peek, step in, say hello—to replace the lengthy one he had engaged in, in Mahoning.

Every other month the fourteen of us got together, in Hibbing one time, in Minneapolis the next. In August the summer after Mummo died, we met in Hibbing for Abe Pesonen's funeral plus the St. Louis County Fair. Abe Pesonen had been a longtime name among the Finns. He had provided well for his wife and thirteen children, worked his farm for fifty-some years, and stayed true to his branch of Believers.

A closed casket occupied the center front of the auditorium. To one side, on straight chairs, sat two ministers in black suits and white shirts, no ties. Latecomers made a clatter folding down the connected wooden seats. We sang the first hymn in English, both branches having switched to English by then. It had been a year since I had attended either branch of the Finnish church, and the a cappella chords moved me. They found a remote spot inside me and sounded a sense of home, giving comfort where I hadn't known I needed it. The ministers read from the Bible and declaimed the faith of the deceased. Men and women wept. Kids punched each other, smothered laughs, kicked the chairs in front of them. Babies climbed their mothers' laps.

Two men opened the casket. Abe's family and friends passed by. When it was our turn, we got up and passed by. What we saw was a pale wax image, not the real Abe.

After the funeral, three hundred people tramped down to the basement for coffee and food. Noises ricocheted off the concrete surfaces and made a generalized screech. Metal chairs scraped the floor, men shouted and laughed and pounded each other on the back, women who hadn't seen each other since the last funeral or wedding called Hello. Kids freed from the forced sit-down upstairs ran pell-mell, screaming and chasing each other, crashing into women bringing more food to tables already loaded with fried chicken, corn on the cob, sandwiches, macaroni salad, potato salad, Jell-O salad, cakes, pies, cookies. "Talk about a wild funeral!" I said to Marcie.

I checked to see how Michael was handling this. He was being a regular little man, holding Marcie's hand and watching other kids act silly. He had shadowed eyes like Adam's and Grandpa's, and the start of a chestnut mane like Marcie's.

She said, "Ya, but they're happy. That's better than scared to death of death."

A woman called my name. I didn't recognize her at first. It was Starr Pesonen. I had heard she moved to the East Coast and cut her hair. And here she was, wearing a beige gabardine suit and high-heels, earrings, even lipstick. Her hair was curled and short. A little shocked, I hugged her, said I was sorry about her father.

She stepped back and smiled. Her smile had tears in it. "He's at peace." When I focused on just her eyes and bone structure, she was the same as ever. She still had the wide, genial face that was the family trademark, the same confidence in being a Pesonen.

I said, "You remember Marcie?" The two women said hello. "And this is Michael, her boy. Are you home for long?"

Marcie hoisted Michael into her arms and reached for an egg salad sandwich, broke off a piece and pointed it into his mouth. He chewed thoughtfully, showing the dimple he had inherited from her. "I'll be back," she said, and disappeared with her son.

"Two weeks," Starr answered. "I came home because Mom wasn't doing well."

Before the funeral, Inky had told us that Miriam Pesonen suffered from arthritis, high blood pressure, leg and stomach ailments, and that if anyone had been expected to die, it had been Miriam, not her husband.

I asked Starr how her mother was doing. "Better," she said. "We got to go visiting before Dad died. I got over to Duluth and saw my friends from confirmation school."

I wondered what her friends thought of her new look. Feeling nosy, trying to find out *why* she had a new look, I asked, "Are you involved in church back East?"

"They don't have our church where I live, but I go to church when I'm home." She said this lightly, without any reference to short hair or lipstick.

Two young women shouted from behind us. "So, Kik! You finally came to see us? What took you so long?" They were Pesonens, I knew that much, but I had to think for a minute to know which ones: Susannah and Sylvia. They looked alike. They both had long blonde hair pulled back into buns, no makeup, longish dresses. How old were they now? Thinking back to sauna night when I was twelve, I figured Susannah must be nineteen, Sylvia, twenty-two. They already had that ageless look of women in both branches of the Finnish church, defined by the group, comfortable in their skins. Four toddlers clutched at their mothers' skirts.

"It's good to see you," I said, receiving one embrace and another. I smiled at the children. "Which ones are whose?"

"These are Sylvia's." Susannah made a little circle with an index finger. "Maylon, Mary, Maureen." She palmed the head of the child at her knee. "And this is my Carol." Susannah was in the late weeks of pregnancy. I tried to guess the name of her new baby. Curtis, Carrie, Cory, Caleb?

"Do you still live around here?" I asked, trying to adjust to the changes. I told myself that people *do* change. Julianna had become a nun, for instance, the last thing I had expected. I made a mental note to write to her.

Sylvia picked up her youngest, who I guessed was Maylon as he was the only boy, a pokerfaced contrast to his sisters who were tittering and signaling to each other, in cahoots, still locked to their mother's legs. "My Dennis has a body shop not far from here," Sylvia said. "Susannah's Gary works the farm. The folks get to take it easy." Her tone intimated that her folks were the best folks around.

Susannah laughed her imp's laugh, which hadn't changed since childhood. "Ya! They don't do much these days except watch TV!" (*Their church allowed TV?*)

Wading among the children, Starr reached around her sisters' shoulders and gave them a prolonged squeeze. The way she was stretching, her lapels made triangles forward and her blouse came nearly unbuttoned, but she kept her arms around her sisters.

"Look at them!" she exulted. "Aren't they *great*?"

* * *

It was twilight when we got to the fair, just as lights started to show. Tiny bulbs made squiggles on the Mad Hatter's Tea Party and a rainbow sprayed *out, out, out* on the Ferris Wheel. The man on the chairs had barely enough daylight for his final show.

The stack of chairs was three stories high. The man on the top chair wore a business suit and tie, as if he'd been whisked from his office to this pile in the sky. Slowly, the stack began to sway, forward over the midway, backward toward the horse barn, forward again, and so on, and all the while the man frantically rolled his hands in a muff-circle, backward, and forward, as if correcting the sway with his rolling. The stack bent farther each time, and each time it seemed the man would surely slide off. But he just rolled his hands faster and called, "I don't *ca-a-a-are* . . . if I fall *do-o-o-o-own!*"

Every time the stack swayed, I hid my eyes. Jeff laughed. I blocked Samson's eyes with my hands. "Don't look," I told him. As I'd expected, he shook me off and gave me a down-turned smile. "I'm not scared," he bragged. He had become an American boy in one short year. Adam had been touting Fendway for Samson, and after looking at other schools Esko and Bridget had agreed. Samson would be a Fendway day student in the fall. His hair still fell in his face, but his new haircut gave him a knowing look. "It's a trick," he said. "They make it so he can't fall."

"How'd you get to be so smart?" Marcie asked him. Samson had a smile that started behind his cheeks, a clenching of muscles that kept his mouth shut. Michael was keeping a close watch on him, apparently ready to be his shadowing younger cousin.

"Who wants cotton candy?" Adam asked us, knowing we would groan. We had eaten too much at the funeral. We came to the Tilt-A-Whirl, which was having trouble attracting business. Empty cars bumped around the hilly track, lurching and spinning, no riders getting sick or screaming. No riders, period. The teen-ager in charge didn't bother to call us over or watch for interest on our part. Curving a hand over his cigarette, he watched only for closing time.

Marcie said, "Anyone up for the Tilt-A-Whirl?"

Jeff said. "Not me. I'd throw up."

No one wanted to go on it. As we walked by, the tune from the Tilt-A-Whirl tinkled on, gradually fading into the organ grinder mix on the midway. Something glommed itself to the sole of my loafer and made kissy noises as I walked. I lifted my foot: a caramel splat. A Big Daddy, or what was left of it. Jeff found a stick; I did a quick operation; I washed up in a fountain and we walked on. Jeff had his hands in his pockets, and I couldn't resist. I eased my hand into his near pocket, and we held hands flat. It was warm in there, and sensual. I could feel his thigh muscles walking. He gave me a private Jeff-look, an invitation to the depths of him. I reveled in my pure good fortune.

At the front gate we had spun off into three groups. Jeff and I and the couples with children came to the midway. Inky, Harald, Aarnie and Kaisa went to the horse barn. Bill and Liisa went to the crafts center. Liisa had entered two items in competition, a baby comforter for Marcie, who was pregnant again, and Elberta peach preserves. It was the first time since Sandy's death that Liisa had competed. As we now headed for the crafts center, I told Bridget, "She's a pro. I'll bet she gets two blues." Less outgoing than Esko, Bridget had nevertheless met countless people and braved a full day, a stranger's funeral and the county fair, becoming a Minnesota Halonen by increments.

We found Liisa satisfied with one blue ribbon. For the comforter. She had won a red for the preserves. "A lot of people brought in peach!" she told us with that elevated, elated look of competition. "It's hard to get Elbertas right. I was lucky to get a red." Bill stood at her side, eclipsed by her and cheerful about it.

The show would begin in twenty minutes. The main attraction was a Hibbing High School graduate, a singer and guitar player named Robert Allen Zimmerman, now called Bob Dylan and living in New York. He had come back to St. Louis County to reshape his old band, the Rock Boppers, for a special show on his home turf.

As we sat in the bleachers watching people file in, I noticed a contrast in faces. Stepping into the tent were women who had put on makeup and summer clothes and come to the fair to have fun. But instead they looked *forlorn*. They scouted for seats with a kind of desperation, as if they just *knew* the best ones were already taken. They climbed the risers with their husbands and kids, searching the stands, waiting impatiently for people-snags to untangle, and, when they spotted empty seats, they sprinted for them, bumped into peoples' knees, fell into peoples' laps, and finally dropped with their families into spaces too small for them. They didn't smile during any of this (which was pretty funny from a distance). They just got grouchier, poor dears. Their makeup wasn't helping them at all.

That same day Sylvia, Susannah, and Starr buried their father. They had reason to be forlorn. But instead they were *luminous*, their faces open and fresh, washed by grief and forgiveness and tears well spent. Their beauty had nothing to do with makeup.

I made up a contest right on the spot, a fresh-face contest, and the Mourners beat the Merrymakers, hands-down! I looked down our rows to see our group, judging faces, one by one. Every last face was open and fresh.

There was a commotion up front—the band was coming to life. In flew Mummo like a senior citizen Wendy, in bloomers filled with air and a gown that skimmed behind her as she sailed, arms out, for center stage, sweeping upward just in time to miss Bob Dylan as he stepped to the mike. She stayed there in midair, doing the air-equivalent of treading water, a small twittering of hands and feet, while he adjusted his harmonica rack and guitar strap. He gave the count and out came the song, "Don't Think Twice, It's All Right," and from the first beat forward, Mummo kept pace.

In company with this newfangled talker of tunes, this rule-bending harbinger of things to come, this unknown-becoming-an-icon (she knew these things before they happened, she was privy already to the timeless view), Mummo bent some rules of her own. She practiced her routine in the August night: Minuet, polka, Lindy Hop, bebop! Charleston, jitterbug, waltz! A tap-dance to take her to Finland and back (it was that fast and victorious)! Some shimmies and a shag and a slow rock 'n' roll! And, against her principles, she

294

was *showing off*! There was silence around her, as always, but this was a *gilded* silence, her new realm higher than earthsound and tuned to its own music. The biggest change? She was laughing. At her mistakes, of all things!

She paused and motioned to somebody offstage, a come-on-over-here wave, and a toddler in pajamas giggled and bounced through the air and landed in her arms. The baby hid her own eyes, peered out, chuckling, put her hands on her mother's eyes, popped them off; the two laughed. They had the same laugh, or versions of it, the toddler version and a grownup version.

Holding Matilda, Mummo curtsied to an old man who had appeared at stage left. No flying around for *him*. He stood with his hands behind him and his shoes planted hard, doing folks a favor by anchoring the stage. His beard was long and white, his suit black and formfitting. Eyebrows stiff as brushes! Everything the same. What was different was the hope. It showed in his face like a light turned on.

Three others stepped from the wings. I recognized Uncle Esko, the cramped posture and shaggy head, the apologetic clothes. But he was different: *purged*. Then, the other man! He still parted his hair in the center and wore pleated slacks and a pirate shirt, like a 1940s film star. His smile was a closed-mouthed affair, suitable for a mystic. My mother put her hands to her heart and smiled. She nodded to me, and to Liisa. Her dress was flowery and knee-length and flipped up at the hem. Her high-heels had the toes cut out. Her hair was long again, pinned loosely above her temples so that it fell behind her ears in tumbled brown curls. She was even prettier than I had imagined.

Keeping a strong hold on her daughter, Mummo started up again, the minuet, the polka, and so on. She was bungling steps but having a fine time, dancing to beat the band.

With her posing and her ease, she was telling us, No worry! No hurry! I've got *plenty*-time. I've got all the time in the world.

THE END